SECRETS
AND
SILENCE

BOOK YOUR PLACE ON OUR WEBSITE AND MAKE THE ARABESQUE ROMANCE CONNECTION!

We've created a customized website just for our very special Arabesque readers, where you can get the inside scoop on everything that's going on with Arabesque romance novels.

When you come online, you'll have the exciting opportunity to:

- View covers of upcoming books

- Learn about our future publishing schedule (listed by publication month and author)

- Find out when your favorite authors will be visiting a city near you

- Search for and order backlist books

- Check out author bios and background information

- Send e-mail to your favorite authors

- Join us in weekly chats with authors, readers and other guests

- Get writing guidelines

- AND MUCH MORE!

Visit our website at
http://www.arabesquebooks.com

SECRETS
AND
SILENCE

*Linda
Hudson-Smith*

BET Publications, LLC
http://www.bet.com
http://www.arabesquebooks.com

ARABESQUE BOOKS are published by

BET Publications, LLC
c/o BET BOOKS
One BET Plaza
1900 W Place NE
Washington, DC 20018-1211

All Kensington Titles, Imprints, and Distributed Lines are available at special quantity discounts for bulk purchases for sales promotions, premiums, fund-raising, and educational or institutional use. Special book excerpts or customized printings can also be created to fit specific needs. For details, write or phone the office of the Kensington special sales manager: Kensington Publishing Corp., 850 Third Avenue, New York, NY 10022, attn: Special Sales Department, Phone: 1-800-221-2647.

First Printing: January 2006
10 9 8 7 6 5 4 3 2 1

Printed in the United States of America

CHAPTER ONE

The sound of the conference room door opening made sign language instructor Scotland Kennedy turn her hazel eyes to the back of the room. As the man entering the door lifted his head and looked directly at her, Scotland's breath caught instantly. Her heart began to beat erratically, scaring her silly. Breathing normally had suddenly become difficult for her, but she didn't need to be a genius to figure out why. The strikingly handsome man coming toward her had simply taken her breath away. She'd never before laid eyes on the gorgeous man making his way toward the front, yet she silently declared him her future husband.

Scotland believed wholeheartedly that her soul mate had finally arrived.

She couldn't help wondering if he was a new student or if he was just there on an official visit of some sort. She'd find out quickly enough, since he was now standing right in front of her. Scotland did her best to compose herself, but it wasn't an easy task. This guy had unnerved her in a way that was totally foreign to her. She had been wildly attracted to many men in her twenty-six years, but this one was something special. She felt him down deep in her soul.

Nodding politely, Jordan La Cour handed Scotland his neatly filled-out registration form. He then stood back a slight distance from her.

Glad for the space Jordan had put between them, since his closeness had made her even more nervous, Scotland perused the information before her. He had printed the entire form rather than using cursive handwriting, which made everything very easy to read. His home address was certainly a familiar one. Waterfall Lane was located in the same Southern California housing division she lived in. Windmill Court, the street she lived on, and Waterfall Lane were only a couple of blocks apart. *Very interesting,* she thought. Although she'd never think of calling him without his permission, her photographic memory easily memorized his phone number.

Jordan La Cour, she mused, *strong name for a powerfully built guy.* His date of birth showed that he was two years and seven months older than her, which meant he was almost twenty-nine. He was no Michael Jordan in height, but he was quite tall, especially compared to her petite, five-foot-four frame. His body, hard and muscular, looked as if he indulged in routine workouts. Scotland hadn't seen too many guys with amber eyes, but his were more of a dark gold rather than a yellowish brown, complementing his wavy, neatly cut, light brown hair and pecan brown complexion. With his looks, he passed her hunk litmus test with flying colors.

Scotland fully checked out all of Jordan's physical attributes—and she definitely liked what she saw. But a man had to possess more than good looks and a great body to hold her attention. Scotland was more interested in Jordan's spiritual makeup. Hunky, gorgeous-looking men were a dime a dozen in Los Angeles. A day rarely went by that she didn't run into at least five or six dangerously handsome males. It was the God-loving men that were so hard to find. And it wasn't as if she wasn't looking in all the right places. Since she didn't hang out in nightclubs and other popular social venues, she couldn't be accused of looking for Mr. Right in all the wrong places. Scotland preferred to meet eligible bachelors at a variety of church functions, especially those held exclusively for Christian singles. Besides the special occasions she shared with her family, the majority of her social outings were in some way church related.

Scotland looked up from the papers she held and smiled brightly at Jordan. "Welcome, Mr. La Cour. It's certainly a pleasure to have you as a new student in my class. Please take a seat so we can get things under way."

Jordan didn't make any attempt to verbally communicate with Scotland. He simply nodded in response and then turned around and headed for the only empty seat in the front row, which he considered a lucky find. His deep interest in this particular class had him completely revved up. Sitting in the front of the class would allow him to be right at the center of the action.

Staring after Jordan, Scotland had to wonder about him. It seemed to her that he could hear, but was he able to speak? Or perhaps he was a deaf-mute and could read lips. He hadn't responded verbally to anything she'd said to him. She glanced at his registration papers again to see if he'd ever taken a sign language class before. The "no" box was checked to that particular question. She also saw that he hadn't filled in the box where it asked students to give their reason for taking the class. His reticence heightened her Curious George–like nature.

Pushing aside for now her intense curiosity about one Jordan La Cour, Scotland quickly wrote down a few notes on the blackboard. She then turned to face her students, smiling sweetly. She told her class a little about her personal and educational background, including how she had come to learn and then teach sign language.

As if there hadn't been enough tragedy in the Kennedy family, at the age of fourteen, Brianna Kennedy, Scotland's first cousin, had gone deaf after suffering an extremely high fever. So that she could continue to communicate with Brianna, Scotland had taken a course in American Sign Language, often referred to as ASL. It didn't take Scotland long to decide that she wanted to be a signer/interpreter when she grew up. Her passion for signing had flared immediately.

Although Brianna's speech had already been fully developed by the time she'd gone totally deaf, she had no choice but to learn new ways to communicate. Both Scotland and Brianna used a combination of signing, which included finger spelling, speaking, and mouthing words, as well as facial gestures and body movements, to convey their messages.

Scotland and Brianna had been practically raised as sisters by their fathers, who were also brothers. Scott and Brian Kennedy had both lost their wives in the same fiery car crash. The two women, Victoria and Solange Kennedy, had been Christmas shopping for their families the entire day. During their evening drive home on a Los Angeles freeway, the driver of a semi had lost complete control of his big rig and had slammed into Victoria's car, killing her and her sister-in-law instantly. Despite all the years that had passed since the accident, Scott, Scotland's father, still had a hard time with Victoria's death. Scotland and Brianna, who had been given versions of their fathers' names, were only six years old at the time of their mothers' tragic demise.

After asking her students to open their American Signing Language textbooks to the first chapter, Scotland read to her class the parts of the book she'd highlighted in her teaching manual. She then closed the large volume and placed it on the podium. "In my beginners' class, I first go through the alphabet with my students. Does anyone already know how to sign the alphabet?"

Jordan stared straight ahead when Scotland made eye contact with him. No communication of any kind seemed forthcoming from him, Scotland mused.

Still not knowing if he could hear or not, Scotland sighed hard, wishing she knew everything there was to know about him. He certainly had her more than a little intrigued. She then spotted the one female hand that had been raised. "Now that I'm aware that you know the alphabet, I may need to use you as a backup teacher one day," Scotland joked as she gazed at the woman who had raised her hand.

Everyone but Jordan laughed at Scotland's comment. She hated to see that he seemed like such a solemn cuss. She was almost certain that he'd be completely irresistible if he just forced a bright a smile with his soft-looking, kissable lips. Scotland silently scolded herself for what she was thinking of. The thought of kissing him senseless made her shudder. "Okay, class, watch closely as I sign from A to Z. A lot of the letters look just like the alphabet; we'll use those in learning finger spelling during the course." Working her hands slowly, so that her class could catch every single letter, Scotland went through the alphabet with professional ease, making signing look totally effortless.

As Scotland moved back and forth along the front row of metal desks, she made it a point to make direct eye contact with each of her students, following it up with a bright smile; it was her way of putting the class at ease. "I'm going to go through the letters one more time, and then we'll go through them together. Don't worry if you don't catch on right away. Signing can be difficult to learn for some. But it's also such a beautiful way for us to express ourselves."

Scotland's nostrils flared slightly as she stopped in front of Jordan's seat. The manly scent of his cologne teased her senses, causing her curiosity about him to blossom further. Finding it hard to concentrate in such close proximity to him, she quickly moved away.

For the next thirty minutes Scotland lectured her class on the art of American Sign Language. She was very articulate, and it was easy for everyone to discern that she definitely knew her stuff. Confidence flowed from within her . . . and no questions were thrown at her that she wasn't able to answer. Her students hung on to her every word, fascinated by her graceful hand movements, as she followed up all her comments by signing them. Her body language was every bit as fascinating as her flashing hand gestures.

Although Jordan had done his best to remain completely aloof, he finally had to admit to himself how extremely impressed he was with Scotland Kennedy. As pretty and shapely as she was, with her expressive hazel eyes, smooth caramel complexion, and shoulder-length sandy brown hair, he was more interested in her intellect and had taken special note of her compassionate spirit. Her reason for becoming a signer had awed him the most.

Jordan thought that Scotland's story about her family was a downright sorrowful one. Yet she appeared to take everything in stride. He didn't see any visible signs that she might be struggling with her emotions. It seemed to him that she had turned her emotional scars into a badge of courage. The only person he'd ever met who could sign as effortlessly as Scotland was a juvenile offender who just happened to be deaf. The troubled young man was the only reason Jordan had registered for the class since he was the boy's probation officer.

"Before I bring our first class session to a close, I'd like each of you to introduce yourself, and then let us know your reasons for taking this course. I know the question was asked on the registration form and that you probably filled it in, but I'd like the class to know. My request is not a mandatory one, so you don't have to participate unless you want to."

"My name is Connie England. I'm a member of the First Horizon Christian Center." She made a sweeping hand gesture toward three other students, two middle-aged women and a young man. "We're all members of the church choir. Jody, Leann, Wylie, and I are taking the class to interpret for the deaf during song service and the preaching of the sermon," Connie said.

Since Connie had already given their reason for being in the class, Jody Banks, Leann Townsend, and Wylie Cooper only stood up to introduce themselves to the other students.

"Welcome to each of you," Scotland enthused. "I know what you're referring to since I'm a member of our church's praise dance group. For those of you who are not familiar with this sort of deaf ministry, the praise group performs in front of the congregation while signing the words to church hymns. The program was designed around the needs of the hearing impaired."

Martin Jones, a young black man, got to his feet. "My mother recently lost her hearing. She's taking classes at an accredited school for the hearing impaired, so I'm taking this course so that I can continue to communicate with her. Otherwise, I'd be lost. We are very close."

Scotland turned her attention to the next student in the front row, Jordan La Cour. When he signed his name only with the alphabet, which he'd learned from his young client, she was almost convinced that he could hear. With his eyes fastened so intently on her lips, she once again reassessed her evaluation of him. If he were a deaf-mute, he would probably be quite adept at reading lips. If that were the case, it was puzzling that he'd chosen to take a course from her instead of attending a specialty school.

Scotland waited for Jordan to sign his reason for taking the class, but he didn't offer any information other than his name. Careful not to infringe on his privacy, Scotland quickly moved on to the next person.

Scotland continued to listen with keen interest to the detailed explanations from the dozen or so students. None of them was taking the class for reasons she hadn't already heard before: to communicate with a loved one or friend who had gone deaf, to assist the hearing impaired in their church, to sign gospel songs in the praise choir group, or to land gainful employment as signers. One student was an emergency room nurse and recognized the need to learn how to communicate with hearing-impaired patients, who often came into the ER all alone. Another student, an employee with the Social Security Administration, wanted to be able to communicate with hearing-impaired clients who came to sign up for disability or retirement benefits.

Although Jordan was the only student who hadn't given a reason as to why he was there, Scotland was confident that he'd eventually do so. Once he began to trust her, she knew that he'd definitely want to talk about the class and why he had decided to learn signing. All of her students opened up to her sooner or later. Her honesty, compassion, and fun-loving personality were her greatest assets. Scotland had a special way with people, a blessed gift from God.

After giving her students a reading assignment for

next week's class, Scotland handed out her business cards to everyone. Her contact phone numbers were on the cards, which gave her students easy access to her. She then bade each person a good evening. Once the classroom was cleared, Scotland quickly gathered up her belongings and headed out of the conference room, careful to lock up behind her. Setting the building's alarm system came next.

The trek to the community center parking lot was a short one, but Scotland felt completely worn-out by the time she reached her late-model SUV, a Toyota 4Runner. It had been one long day for her. As an independent signer contracted by the courts, Scotland was always on call for trials during normal working hours, but her on-call duties didn't end there. If she was needed in an emergency situation in the middle of the night, she was always available. Because she taught sign language classes three evenings a week and also worked as a part-time youth counselor at her church, Scotland found very little time for herself.

The whirlpool tub in her modest but tastefully decorated three-bedroom home beckoned Scotland the moment she walked in the front door—and she couldn't wait to heed the call. In the next half hour or so, she planned to be up to her neck in steaming hot, swirling water. A light dinner, a half hour or so of Bible study, and then a little television, followed by a few minutes of deep meditation, would finish out her day. Falling fast asleep was the one thing Scotland never had a problem with. She found complete peace in sleep.

The garden salad, broiled chicken breast, and fresh asparagus spears completely satisfied Scotland's ravenous hunger. For dessert she had one half of twin cherry and blueberry Popsicle. She wished she'd eaten dinner before lounging in the tub, since she was now feeling much too full and very sleepy. Her nightly routine wasn't over, which meant she'd have to fight hard to stay awake a little longer.

Dressed in warm pajamas, since the fall nights in Los Angeles had suddenly turned very chilly, Scotland closed the Bible, placed it on her nightstand, and turned off the bedside lamp. Several burning votive and tea-light candles kept the beautiful mahogany-furnished master bedroom from complete darkness, bathing the entire room in a soft glow. All of the luxurious linen, window treatments, and complementing accents were in shades of soft blue and stark white. Scotland had chosen a décor that created a serene, heavenlike place for her to rest peacefully.

After moving to the center of her queen-size bed and crossing her legs Indian style in preparation for a few moments of meditation, Scotland began to take deep breaths, exhaling slowly to help heighten her senses. Within the next several moments, once she allowed her mind to go totally blank, she became completely relaxed. Immediately after her serenity session and her uplifting talk with God were over, Scotland turned on the television, only to fall into a deep sleep immediately afterward.

Jordan wasn't having an easy time of falling asleep. Lying upon his king-size bed inside his custom-built four-bedroom home, he replayed in his mind the troubling events that had occurred during the past sixty-hour workweek. Overtime was not an exception for him; it was the norm. He couldn't remember the last time he'd had an eight-hour workday.

Vacation time during the past couple of years had been just a dream that never seemed to come true for him. He now had more vacation time stored up on the books than he knew what to do with. The last time he'd taken a few extra days off, to go on a five-day cruise to the Caribbean approximately six months ago, the entire trip had turned out to be disastrous, so he wasn't too keen about being off from work, anyway. His job kept his mind occupied and helped him to avoid getting involved in any more serious troubles with women.

Jordan's forty-five minute session that day with his hearing-impaired offender, twelve-year-old Gregory Robinson, had left him pretty shaken. The boy reminded Jordan so much of himself that it had been easy for him to quickly develop a fondness for the young man whose parents had deserted him for the roaring call of the mean streets. Although very intelligent and streetwise, the adolescent lacked the kind of love and guidance that only grounded parents could provide for him. Jordan's deep desire to try and make a difference in the young boy's life was what had made him decide to take the course in sign language. Communication was everything.

Gregory hated his foster parents, the Turners, and he had expressed his disdain earlier with such vehemence in his agitated body language and scowling facial expressions. Gregory's state of mind had Jordan gravely concerned about the safety of the Turners and it also had him worried about the well-being of his young charge. He didn't know if Gregory was being totally honest with him about how badly the Turners treated him. But as an officer of the court, it was his duty and obligation to have the allegations investigated immediately by child protective services. Jordan's written request for an in-depth investigation of the Turner home had already been sent in.

Getting social services involved in his cases was a nightmare most of the time. There was so much red

tape to wade through. By the time the official investigation was completed, more often than not, the situation
had gotten completely out of control. Being a juvenile
probation officer was a tough, thankless job, yet Jordan
couldn't imagine himself as anything else. He loved his
work but detested the tasteless office politics that came
along with it.

Beyond tired now, Jordan wished for sleep to come
and whisk him away, but he knew it probably wasn't
going to happen any time soon. He had too much on
his mind to rest.

As Jordan's thoughts turned to the last time he'd
taken off work for pleasure, he fought hard to tamp
down the urge to revisit those horrendous days at sea
and the events at the very last port of call. No matter
how hard he tried not to rekindle the past, his mind was
already taking him there.

Cynthia Raymond, a woman with whom Jordan had
been involved in a casual relationship, had disappeared
a few months back, while they were on vacation in the
Caribbean. She'd vanished without a trace and hadn't
been seen or heard from since. Her family had blamed
him for her disappearance and had forbidden him
from having anything to do with the investigation into
it. Cynthia's family had once been very kind and warm
to him, but now they felt nothing but contempt for
Jordan.

That nightmarish situation still plagued Jordan both
day and night, and there seemed to be no end to his
torment anywhere in sight. Not knowing what had happened to Cynthia made him crazier than crazy. How
someone could disappear without leaving behind some
sort of clue puzzled him to no end. The police were of
the mind that no foul play was involved in Cynthia's disappearance, but they hadn't been able to sell that piti-
ful theory to Jordan. How could there be no foul play

involved when a woman went missing in a foreign land she'd never visited before?

Jordan felt awful that he hadn't been able to provide adequate protection for Cynthia. His ego was crushed. Guilt overwhelmed him because he'd known before they'd gone on the trip that she definitely wasn't the one he wanted to spend the rest of his life with. Even though they'd often dated other people, Jordan and Cynthia had hung out with each other more than with anyone else. He had completely ended the casual fling with Cynthia over dinner one evening. But she had later won a trip for two to the Caribbean and had asked Jordan to join her for old times' sake. Besides wanting the companionship of someone familiar to her, Cynthia had also planned to celebrate her thirtieth birthday on the high seas and wanted to share the milestone with a friend.

The lively birthday party had gone off better than Jordan or Cynthia had expected, especially since they hadn't known anyone else aboard the cruise ship. Cynthia, not one to meet strangers, had made quite a few acquaintances in the days before the celebration, all of whom she'd invited to join her in the ship's Sea Breeze lounge to help her celebrate.

Jordan had recently started going through a metamorphosis that he didn't quite understand. As he began to look forward to solitude and quiet time, partying and clubbing soon lost importance. Jordan had never been a loner as a child, and always being in a crowd of people had kept him from feeling so lonely. Since he lived with so many inner demons, spending time alone was indeed a scary thing for him.

Then Jordan found himself craving something different in his intimate relationships, something other than the meaningless, casual flings he had a knack for getting himself involved in. He had begun to tap into his spiritual side and now desired to have a spiritual woman to share all these strange, new feelings with. He had talked in depth to Cynthia about what he thought might be happening to him, but she had completely dismissed his feelings as ludicrous. She was a party girl who wasn't ready to deal with anything that had to do with religion or spirituality. In all reality, they just didn't have what it took to make a lifetime of it. Jordan had previously sworn to himself that until he was sure that his soul mate had come along, he'd never involve himself in any relationship. He was sure he was destined to a life of loneliness.

It didn't matter that he wasn't in love with Cynthia, or she with him. They had truly cared for each other and had become very close friends. The decision to discontinue their romantic involvement was Jordan's and had been amicably agreed upon by both parties, though Cynthia really hadn't believed he could give up the physical part of their relationship. Her disappearance had left him terribly fearful about the future. There was no way he could move forward in his life without achieving closure regarding Cynthia's fate. Until he found out what had happened to her, Jordan didn't think he could ever be truly happy in life or in love.

Thinking about relationships and spiritual love brought Scotland Kennedy to Jordan's mind, another person he really didn't want to ponder. Admitting that he was impressed with her was one thing, but he wasn't up to entertaining how wildly attracted he was to her.

His attraction to Scotland wasn't all about the physical aspects, either, which was very surprising to him. The condition of a woman's anatomy was the first thing he normally checked out when he was attracted to someone. His response to Scotland had been so different. He liked how much spirit she seemed to have, which caused him to wonder about her spiritual nature. It was his best guess that she was rather pure at heart, which suggested a pure spirit. Her deep compassion for her cousin had indicated that much. Her deep intellect also blew him away.

Feeling that he could probably fall asleep now, Jordan turned off the bedside lamp and thrust his body beneath the white down comforter. Although he had no plans to pursue any sort of relationship with Scotland, he found himself eager to attend the next signing class session.

As Jordan envisioned Scotland's bright smile and sunny disposition, the days until the next class suddenly seemed like an eternity to him. Troubled by these thoughts, he closed his eyes, hoping for the sandman to claim him right away.

"Two eggs over medium, a slice of wheat toast, and a large orange juice will do it for me," Scotland told the waiter whose table she always sat at at Breakfast at Belle's Café.

The small restaurant was a very popular spot with local residents, especially senior citizens. It was a busy little place where many of the housing area residents loved to convene and chat over some of the best breakfast food in the area. Belle's was open from 6 a.m. until noon every single day.

The waiter frowned slightly. "No meat?"

"Not this morning, Roy. I ate too much chicken last night. But thanks for asking."

"Good enough. We'll have your breakfast out in a jiffy, Scotland. Is there anything else I can get for you before I turn in your order?"

Scotland shook her head in the negative. "I'm just fine, thank you."

As Roy turned to leave, Scotland reached across the

table and picked up a copy of the *Los Angeles Times*. After reading a few of the story captions, she scowled. The front-page headlines often disturbed her. Murders and mayhem were happening all over the city, and the hour of the day or night didn't seem to matter. People had become so brazen in their crimes these days. She could see that Satan's followers had been as busy as beavers during the past twenty-four hours. Very few positive events graced the front page.

Scotland laid the paper aside just in time to see Jordan take a seat in the back of the restaurant. As many times as she'd eaten breakfast at Belle's, she'd never seen Jordan there. He could've just moved into the area, she surmised, especially since it was still being developed. New houses were going up in her development every day. As soon as one phase was completed, the builder began working on another one. The homes in Landing Lakes ranged from twenty-five hundred to five thousand square feet. Scotland owned one of the smaller houses in her subdivision.

Unable to stop herself, Scotland fastened her eyes on Jordan. However, he didn't seem aware of anything around him. He actually appeared lost in thought. Then he suddenly opened up his briefcase and removed a notepad. Scotland began to watch him intently now, wondering if he was ever going to notice her seated across the room. Wishing he'd look her way seemed futile. It would be nice to have him to sit with over breakfast, but she wasn't very optimistic about that happening.

The arrival of her breakfast order pulled Scotland's attention away from the most enigmatic man she'd ever encountered. Jordan didn't seem like an easy person to get to know, so getting him to the altar may prove to be one big challenge for her. But since Scotland was so sure that Jordan was her future husband, she would get to know him.

Doing her best to keep her eyes from straying back to Jordan, Scotland began to eat her delicious-smelling food. Seconds later she became lost in her own grand musings. As ludicrous as she knew it would probably seem to her family and friends, she happily entertained the idea of spring or summer nuptials for Mr. La Cour and her. Scotland even imagined what type of wedding dress she'd wear on her special day, laughing inwardly as she saw herself walking down the aisle on the arm of her father. As sure as she was breathing, Scotland was positive that her soul mate occupied a table only a few yards from hers.

Jordan had spotted Scotland the very moment he'd entered the restaurant. He had wanted to acknowledge her presence or even sit at her table, but he wasn't sure if it was appropriate or not. He certainly didn't want her to think he might be coming on to her. He had to wonder if she lived in the neighborhood, since Belle's was off the beaten track for anyone other than local residents. The restaurant had a great reputation for the best breakfast food around, so she didn't necessarily have to live in the same development as he did.

Because he didn't want to get caught staring openly at the beautiful woman across the room, Jordan pulled out his notepad to keep his mind otherwise occupied. He quickly abandoned the idea of at least signing hello to her. She might get the wrong impression of him. This was so silly of him, he thought, scolding himself in silence for acting like a smitten teenager. *Acknowledge the woman. What could it hurt?*

Lifting his head up from the notepad, Jordan looked

over at Scotland, hoping to get her attention. With her head lowered, he thought he might have to flail his arms about to get her to notice him. He wasn't about to make a spectacle of himself by doing something as idiotic as that. Instead of making a complete fool of himself in public, Jordan got up from his seat and walked the short distance to Scotland's table.

Scotland didn't look up for several seconds, not until she realized someone was standing over her. Seeing Jordan right there before her eyes made her want to shout out a dozen or so hallelujahs, but she knew that coming unglued in front of him wasn't at all in her best interest. This situation called for her to remain cool, calm, and collected. "Oh, good morning," she said, immediately hating how breathless she sounded. "Nice to see you again, Mr. La Cour."

Jordan was surprised but flattered that Scotland had remembered his name. "Same here," he signed, using finger spelling as his way of communicating. He pointed at his table. "I'm sitting right over there. I saw you and just wanted to say hello."

Scotland had noticed right away that Jordan was very slow with his finger spelling, as he continuously fumbled over signing the alphabet to convey his thoughts. But it also showed her that he had a lot of spunk and determination. Patience was a must in learning sign language. If he was patient in his desire to learn one of the hardest ways of communicating, she guessed that he was more than likely a patient man by nature. Learning ASL was hardly a walk in the park for the impatient people of the world.

"That was so nice of you, Mr. La Cour. I'm glad you came over to say hello." Forgetting that she wasn't communicating with someone fluent in signing, Scotland let her fingers fly in her response to Jordan.

Jordan suddenly felt nervous and unsure of himself. Scotland's beautiful smile, soft and captivating, had knocked him for a loop. Her enchanting hazel eyes also had him mesmerized. He had to get far away from her. Seeing her in any other way than as his signing instructor was dangerous. A romantic entanglement was the last thing he needed in his life right now. Had he just stayed put in his seat, he wouldn't be feeling so darn awkward, Jordan told himself. His wild attraction to Scotland couldn't be acted upon, no way, no how. Since his life was full of complications, he didn't want to create another obstacle for himself.

A weak and lopsided smile slowly appeared on Jordan's face. He felt as if he were sweating bullets and wished he could disappear into thin air. "I'll see you next week," he signed, backing away. Before Scotland had a chance to respond, Jordan was back at his table.

Although Scotland thought Jordan's behavior was rather strange, she chuckled inwardly. He was probably shy, she thought. *A shy man! How unique and refreshing is that?*

Many of the guys Scotland ran into were so brash and far too sure of themselves for her liking. There were a lot of fellows who'd run a tired line by her even before asking her name. On the other hand, she'd also met a lot of very decent, respectful men around the various halls of justice, many of them lawyers. A lack of spiritual chemistry kept her acquaintances with them from developing into anything other than good-natured friendships.

Jordan could run, but he couldn't hide, she mused. They were destined—and he'd better just get used to the idea of them as a couple. Scotland had never before pursued a man in any form or fashion . . . and she didn't think she'd have to resort to being hot on his trail. But if all Jordan needed was a little prompting and a bit of encouragement from her, Scotland wasn't above doling that out to him without feeling any shame whatsoever.

Scotland paid her check and promptly left the restaurant. Looking back at Jordan was a no-no. She'd have to wait until next week to see him. Seeing Jordan again would make her ecstatic, so Scotland silently prayed for the hours until then to fly by with the speed of light.

CHAPTER TWO

Seated at the computer in her home office, Scotland smiled when she saw that Brianna was already online for their nightly gabfest. She quickly typed in her message and then hit the SEND key on the instant message screen. "How are you, Bri?"

"Just fine. How about you, Scotty?" Brianna wrote back.

"Super! How was your day?"

"Busy, as usual. I've barely had time to breathe. How are you feeling?"

"Pretty good, Bri. No aches and pains to complain about. I'm blessed. How's Nathan?"

"Mr. Connors is just fine. He's taking me out to dinner tomorrow night. We're going to the Seafood House at the Oceanside Marina. Want to join us?"

"Three's a crowd, Bri. But thanks, anyway."

"We don't see it like that. . . . and you know it. I'm just dying to hook you up with Mr. Right, the same way you did for me. What if I have Nathan invite one of his friends along?"

Remembering the night she'd introduced Brianna

to Nathan caused Scotland to smile brightly. Nathan was also an independent signer/interpreter contracted by the judicial system. He and Scotland had become fast friends during the first legal case they'd ever worked on together as interpreters. They'd been very helpful to each other and had worked extremely well as a team.

The stars in Nathan's and Brianna's eyes had collided one night nearly two years ago. Brianna had met Nathan when she'd accompanied Scotland to a yearly Christmas party sponsored by one of the numerous large organizations supporting the hearing impaired. One date had led to another, and another. A year later the couple had gotten happily engaged. Brianna truly felt that she owed all her and Nathan's happiness to her beloved cousin Scotland.

Brianna was a remarkable young woman in Scotland's estimation. Scotland loved her cousin dearly and had cried as many happy tears as Brianna had when she had first learned the news of Brianna and Nathan's upcoming nuptials. Scotland saw them as the perfect couple.

Nathan was a great guy. His spiritual makeup reminded Scotland of her father and uncle. He once said that before he'd become an interpreter, he never imagined himself falling in love with someone that couldn't hear. It didn't take him long to come to understand that Brianna was no different from anyone else. As a woman, Brianna was unique, a one of a kind. Loving her was his greatest joy. Brianna was just as smitten with Nathan. She had always said that she'd one day marry a special man just like her father. Nathan was that man.

Scott Kennedy and Brian Kennedy had raised their daughters like sisters—had raised them under the very same roof after the untimely deaths of their mothers. The two men hadn't moved into separate residences until after the girls had graduated from college.

"I've met Mr. Right, Bri! I'm ready to start planning a

spring or summer wedding. Want to help me with all the arrangements?"

Scotland waited and waited for Brianna to respond to her message, wondering what was taking her so long, although she had a pretty good idea. Brianna was probably in a state of shock over her wedding announcement. Scotland snickered, imagining the look on her cousin's face.

In response to Scotland's last message, the words *when, where,* and *how,* typed in bold print, finally came over the screen. "I can't believe you're telling me something this exciting over the Internet. What's up with that? You've got me screaming all over the place."

"Unfortunately, our engagement is not official. The man I'm going to marry doesn't even know it yet. But he will, all in due time. I just met him. He's one of my sign language students."

"That's it!!! I'm having Uncle Scott make you an appointment to see a psychiatrist. Your mind is off the chain, girl. But tell me more. LOL. I want to know everything you know. Start by telling me what he looks like."

"The brother is come-alive gorgeous, too fine to fit any single description. Let's just say he's tall, milk chocolaty, and handsome. There's not very much else to tell you at this point. His name is Jordan La Cour, and he lives in the same subdivision that I do, over on Waterfall Lane. You know, the street adjacent to the main lake. He's a couple of years and a few months older than me. I haven't heard him utter a single sound. . . . and I really don't even know if he can speak at all. Nor do I care one way or the other. I'm in love!"

"What you are *is* insane! Maybe I should come over there and spend the night with you, Scotty. I think you need to be under a 24/7 suicide watch. LOL."

"Girlfriend, you need to keep your cute little behind right at home. You're hardly a match for the tough, unpredictable streets of L.A. in the daylight, let alone after dark. You also need to mark my words when I say Jordan *is* the man. When he and I do get engaged, I'm serving you up a nice big plate of crow. Rare, medium, or well done? You can let me know how you want your crow cooked on my special announcement day."

"I'm feeling you, cuz! Back to the subject of dinner. Nathan and I'd love to have you join us. You know he loves it when the three of us get together. Please say yes."

"Rain check, Bri? I promised Dad I'd have dinner with him tomorrow evening."

"Uncle Scott can come, too. I'll invite both our dads along. The more the merrier."

"You don't ever give up, do you? E-mail me all the details, the place, time, etcetera." Scotland conceded to Brianna's whims more often than not because she loved her so much and had a hard time denying her anything. At first, it was because she felt so sorry about Brianna losing her hearing, but now giving in to Brianna was solely from the heart.

"Will do, Scotty. Dad will probably want to bring Carolina along, too. They've gotten really close. I wonder if he's thinking of asking her to marry him."

"You think it's that serious, huh? If so, how do you really feel about Uncle Brian getting married again, especially after having him to yourself all these years?"

"It's serious enough, Scotty. I'd be very happy for my dad if they did get married. I don't ever want him to go back to being as lonely as he used to be. Both of our dads stayed so sad for a very long time. I love all the hearty laughter I've seen coming from Dad lately. Ms. Carolina Johnston is really good for him. She keeps his spirits uplifted."

"I'm glad to hear you say that, Bri. We both know that Uncle Brian's not going to marry anyone you're opposed to. I hope my dad finds the same kind of happiness as Uncle Brian has. Maybe Carolina has a close relative or a good friend she can introduce Dad to. LOL. Since he's so special, Dad needs a very special lady in his life."

"I agree, Scotty. If we decide to play matchmaker, we need to use discretion. Uncle Scott won't like it if he thinks we're purposely trying to hook him up."

"Wow, do I know that! Dad would freak out over us doing something like that. He's dating more now, so that's a good sign. We probably should just stay out of it and let nature take its course. Dad will know when just the right sister for him comes along."

"I think so, too. It was just a thought, Scotty. When our dads are happy, so are we."

"You can say that again. Look, I'd better get off this computer. I have several things to do before I go to bed. I'll see you tomorrow evening at dinner. Love you, Bri."

"Love you, too, Scotty. Until tomorrow. Sleep tight."

Scotland turned off her computer and then picked up her teaching manual. Needing to feel more relaxed, she rose from the chair at her desk and walked over to her bed. She stripped off her bathrobe and draped it across the top of the cedar chest stationed at the foot of the four-poster. After propping up two pillows against the headboard, she climbed into bed, squirming about on the mattress until she'd made herself totally comfortable.

Although Scotland knew her subject matter frontward and backward, she read a few chapters of the teaching manual as a refresher course. She then began to outline her lesson plans for the next three class sessions. She liked to be well ahead of the game just in case something unexpectedly came up, which might find her pressed for time. Being prepared for the expected and unexpected was important to Scotland. There was always someone counting on her for one thing or another, and she didn't like to let anyone down.

ASL wasn't the only method of sign language used in the United States, but it was the most popular in deaf communities. Scotland preferred ASL over other ways of signing, but she was well trained in alternative methods. In her first couple of classes, she normally concentrated on teaching her students the alphabet, as well as the number signs.

Learning to finger spell was a very important element of the class. When someone couldn't remember a particular sign, finger spelling could be used as an alternative. The basics of making hand shapes and using facial expressions and body language to communicate were also covered in the earlier classes. Combining all the different elements of communication was crucial to becoming proficient in the art of signing.

Scotland would tell the students that hand shapes were hand formations used to sign each letter of the alphabet and that the hand used for writing was known as the dominant hand, or active hand, while the other hand was considered the base hand, or passive hand. Even though most illustrations given in sign language manuals were geared to right-handed users, Scotland would explain, the majority of left-handed users were able to make the transition with very little difficulty.

After going through the basic steps of finger spelling and signing, Scotland would then teach her students about the natural signs, or iconic signs, signs that looked just like what they meant. Putting up your dukes was the iconic sign for boxing. Pretending to steer a car specified driving, and the motion of putting something in the mouth indicated eating.

Happy that she'd accomplished what she'd set out to do, Scotland closed the teaching manual and laid it aside. She then went through her nightly rituals of Bible reading, prayer, and meditation. Once she'd turned out the light and had made herself comfortable in bed, it didn't take long for her thoughts to settle on Jordan. Certain that pleasant thoughts of him would relax her and help her fall asleep in record time, Scotland laid her head on the pillow and closed her eyes. God only knew how tired her body was.

The cool morning air felt good on Scotland's face as she took her daily two-mile walk. The sun had just come up, and it hadn't had a chance to heat the air. The plumes of mist rising from the lake shrouded the landscape in an aura of mystery. Mornings were the best part of her days. She loved waking up and getting out of the house to explore the great outdoors. A chorus of sweetly singing birds always accompanied Scotland on her trek around the neighborhood.

Since Jordan's address had been rolling around inside her head from the day she'd seen it on his registration forms, it didn't surprise Scotland all that much when she ended up on his street. She'd been dying to see which model home he'd chosen to build, thinking it might give her a little insight into his personal taste. Although she felt a little uncomfortable in her quest to learn more about Jordan, she still headed toward his house, needing desperately to satisfy her shameless curiosity.

When she found what she was looking for, Scotland's eyes widened with wonder, and her mouth fell open in awe. On one of the lakefront properties, Jordan's house was huge, with one of the largest floor plans the builder offered in this particular subdivision. Scotland thought that the size of the house might mean that he required a lot of space in which to function. Then it suddenly dawned on her that he could be married and might have already fathered several children. That she hadn't thought of his marital status before now was rather upsetting to her.

A flood of terribly uneasy feelings slowly crept over Scotland, making her realize she was acting like a deranged stalker. Even though she immediately turned around and began retracing her steps, she kept looking back at Jordan's residence, continuing to wonder about the handsome stranger who lived inside.

Once Scotland arrived on the other side of the lake and was certain that she was far enough away from Jordan's house to avoid detection, she sat down on one of the wooden benches to think about what she'd just done. Something as insane as casing a man's house was so out of character for Scotland—and her irresponsible actions had her worried. There was no reason in the world for her to take her curiosity this far. She realized that she had to talk to someone about her feelings before she drove herself completely over the edge. That she was already teetering on the brink of psychosis was evident to her by her weird behavior.

Less than an hour in Jordan's presence shouldn't have her feeling as though she was ready to go through the fiery furnace for him, Scotland mused. Declaring him as her future husband was one thing, but casing his house wasn't a very intelligent move on her part. No one but Brianna, her cousin, best friend, and confidant, could even begin to understand what was happening to her. Scotland had to admit to herself that she wasn't able to grasp the full meaning of her own absurd thoughts and odd behavior. So how could she ever expect anyone else to understand them?

It always thrilled Scotland to see Brianna so animated. Her cousin's mouth and hands had been moving nonstop since they'd arrived at the restaurant over thirty minutes ago. Nathan looked on in open admiration of his fiancée, his love for her apparent in his eyes. Although Scotland didn't envy the couple in the least bit, she certainly wanted to find what they had.

As was planned, Scotland's father, Scott, and her Uncle Brian were also present, but Brian hadn't brought along his girlfriend, Carolina, as both Scotland and Brianna had anticipated. All the meal orders had already been taken by the waitress. While everyone waited for the food to be served, they took the opportunity to catch up on things.

"How are things going with you and your future husband, Scotty?" Brianna signed to Scotland, giggling like a silly teenager. The inquiry had come completely out of the blue.

Brianna's statement caused all stunned eyes to fall on Scotland, who looked downright distressed. It was obvious that she hadn't expected her madness to be exposed in this manner. "Why did you have to go there, Bri? What were you hoping to accomplish?" Scotland signed, feeling slightly betrayed and also a tad angry with her cousin for embarrassing her like that.

Brianna immediately felt and saw Scotland's displeasure with her. Realizing what she'd done and how badly Scotland had taken it, she felt awful. Never in a million years would Brianna set out to intentionally hurt her cousin. "I'm sorry, Scotty. I just wasn't thinking."

Silently fuming inside, Scotland totally ignored Brianna's humble apology. For the first time ever, Scotland felt that her cousin had breached their very special bond. The two women shared everything and kept so many secrets and precious memories between them. Scotland had once jokingly told Brianna that she'd always keep her as her best friend because she knew way too much about her.

With a puzzled expression pasted on his face, Scott looked over at his daughter. "Future husband? What's that all about, Scotland? Are you keeping secrets from me?"

Scotland shook her head from side to side. "No, Dad, not at all." She went on to explain what she already knew would make no sense whatsoever to him or anyone else at the table. That she had to clarify it at all made her anger toward Brianna intensify.

Looking as though he was about to cry, Scott drew his daughter into his warm embrace. "I don't think you're the least bit crazy, Scotland. I guess you've forgotten that I felt the same way about your mother from the very first moment I laid eyes on her. Before we exchanged a single hello, I knew without a shadow of doubt that Victoria Clemens was the woman I'd marry. Is there anything I can do to help with Jordan? All you need to do is ask."

Scotland couldn't help crying. She hadn't forgotten her parents' magical love story, but she hadn't thought of it, either, when her mind had been so busy claiming Jordan as a life partner.

Scott Kennedy had met the vivacious Victoria Clemens in a Laundromat, of all places. Although they had both attended the same college, which was located only a couple of blocks from the laundry facility, he'd never laid eyes on her before that day. Instantaneously, he fell head over heels in love with the beautiful brown-skinned brunette. It had taken him a couple of weeks to approach her, but by resorting to some of Scotland's same tactics, Scott had found out right away as much as he could about the woman who had captured his heart in an instant.

Brian was the next to tell Scotland that there was nothing for her to be ashamed of. The heart had a mind of its own, he told his niece, and she should go with her instincts. "Nothing ventured, nothing gained, sweetheart," Brian said softly.

"Scotland," Nathan signed for Brianna's benefit, "there's nothing stupid about your feelings. Just look at Brianna and me. Our hearts united at the same moment you introduced us to each other. Go for it, Scotty. You won't find out what might come of your attraction if you deny yourself the opportunity to explore the possibilities."

Scotland dabbed at her moist eyes with a paper napkin. "Thanks, guys. It's nice to hear that you all don't think I'm loony. I promise to tell each of you if anything develops between Jordan and me. With that settled, mind if we chat about something else?"

The others nodded in agreement.

For a brief moment Scotland looked over at Brianna. Her intention had been to smile to ease the tension between them, but she found it hard to send a message that all was well when it wasn't. She'd later tell Brianna how she really felt about what she'd done, and then she'd move on. The hurtful remark wouldn't cost them their close friendship. Scotland was sure of that.

Scotland felt relieved when the waiter arrived at the next moment with several plates. It gave everyone a chance to put aside what had occurred. Once everyone received their entrées, the animated chitchat, mostly achieved through sign language, died down.

Wishing that her secret hadn't been exposed wasn't going to change the fact that it had been, Scotland pondered. As she looked around at those seated at the large table, she suddenly felt warm and fuzzy inside. So much palpable love was present in this one place. The hearts of her father and uncle always overflowed with love. The two men were tall, medium complexioned, single, and very handsome. Both were electrical engineers and business partners in Kennedy & Kennedy Engineering, Incorporated.

Raising two little girls without the assistance of their wives had been one heck of a challenge for the Kennedy brothers. Scott and Brian had given their daughters the very best of themselves, each totally devoted in their duties as single fathers.

Moving in together under the same roof so that they could help each other out had been a wise decision. One parent had worked dayshifts and the other had worked nights so that an adult would be home at all times. Until the girls were old enough to look after themselves, Scott and Brian made sure they were always there for Scotland and Brianna. The girls' maternal grandparents had offered to take them, but their fathers had wanted to raise them in the same city. Both sets of maternal grandparents lived in different states from where their children resided. It had been a miracle for two men to work together in such perfect harmony. Scotland silently thanked God for the blessed gifts of her wonderful father and uncle.

Too full to enjoy even a small dessert, Scotland pushed her chair back from the table. She then looked down at her watch. It was much later than she'd thought. With an early morning court date scheduled, she knew she'd better get on home. Scotland quickly made her way around the table, hugging everyone and wishing them a good night.

The moment Scotland had gotten to her feet to excuse herself, Brianna had stood up, too. Brianna linked arms with Scotland when she finally came up to her. "I'll walk you out to your car, Scotty," Brianna signed, her tense body language revealing how distressed she felt.

Scotland gently covered Brianna's hand with her own. "You don't have to. I'll be okay."

"Then I'll just walk you up to the front entry," Brianna signed in response, her eyes begging Scotland not to reject her again.

The miserable look in Brianna's eyes caused Scotland to wince. Knowing that her cousin wasn't going to take "no" for an answer, Scotland nodded her approval. As the two women walked toward the front entrance, Brianna tearfully signed her deepest regret for ruining Scotland's evening and asked for forgiveness.

Her compassion rising to the top of her heart, Scotland accepted Brianna's genuine apology without hesitation. Warm hugs were exchanged between the two cousins before Scotland stepped out into the cool night air.

Lying in a fetal position in her bed, Scotland felt miserable. That she was no closer to getting to know Jordan had her feeling somewhat disillusioned. He was still such an enigma. Not knowing very much about him was driving her bonkers. He'd been in her class for three weeks running but was still a perfect stranger to her. How could she continue believing he was her soul mate when he refused to communicate with her about anything other than the signing course? He had yet to utter a word in class, but she was still waffling back and forth on whether he could speak or not. Deep down inside she somehow felt that Jordan was able to talk. The reason he refused to do so, if he could, was every bit as puzzling as everything else about him.

Although Scotland was tempted to throw in the towel, she wasn't ready for that just yet. Jordan was in her life for a reason, for more than any teacher-student relationship. Their lives were meant to be entwined, for forever and a day. But how could she embrace him when his arms were folded tightly across his chest, blocking direct access to his heart? It was as if Jordan were purposely locking her out.

"Well," she sighed, "I've had just about enough of this, Jordan La Cour. The next time I see you, I'm putting you on notice of my intent to win your heart. Our destiny is not up to just you, Mister. This imminent union of ours is an ordainment from God. Convincing you of that may be a huge undertaking on my part, but I'm more than up to the challenge. Look out, Jordan, Scotland Yard is on the case. Scotland Victoria Kennedy was indeed on the case.

Remembering all the times her father had referred to her as Scotland Yard, because of her highly inquisitive nature, made Scotland smile. Her dad always worried that her almost desperate need to know everything about a person or thing she was interested in might one day get her into big trouble. Scotland, on the other hand, believed that you could never know too much. Knowledge was power in her estimation. Not knowing everything you should about someone or something was where a body could get into real trouble, which was why Scotland made it her business to be as informed as possible in all things.

Thinking that she should try to get some sleep, which would hopefully give her mind a break from confusing thoughts of Jordan, Scotland turned off the bedside lamp. Nestled down under the warm comforter, she sighed heavily, hoping for a brighter tomorrow.

The musical ringing coming from her cell phone caused Scotland to bolt upright in bed. Upon glancing over at the lighted clock radio stationed on her night-stand, she saw that it was nearly 1:30 A.M. Although she received emergency calls at the oddest hours numerous times a month, her first concern was always for the safety of her family. As Scotland prayed that no harm had come to any of her loved ones, she picked up the receiver. "Hello," she rasped, pausing to clear the sleepy frog from her throat.

"Miss Kennedy?"

"Yes, who's this?"

"Jordan La Cour, one of your students."

Jordan La Cour, she mentally reiterated. Scotland was dumbfounded. Hearing him speak was astounding. Learning that he wasn't deaf, mute, or both confirmed her suspicions. He had a strong bass voice, possessing the kind of timbre that made a woman want to swoon at the scrumptious sound of it. She was now more curious about the handsome hunk than ever before.

Miracles, miracles, miracles, she happily ruminated. *No one could ever foil destiny.*

"Sorry to call you so late, Miss Kennedy, but it's urgent, and I need your help if at all possible."

Scotland rested her back against the headboard. "In what way, Mr. La Cour?"

"I'm a juvenile probation officer, and I have a twelve-year-old deaf boy assigned to me. His name is Gregory Robinson. I just got a call that he's run away from home again. I think I know where he might be, but I need an interpreter if I find him. Can you help me out?"

It began to dawn on Scotland that Jordan hadn't gone through the system to contact her; the operators were the ones who always put the calls through to her cell or home. He must've dialed the number on her business card. She saw that as very optimistic, since as an officer of the court, he could've gone through the emergency system instead of making direct contact with her. Had he not been one of her students, he wouldn't have had direct access to her.

"Sure, I can help you, Mr. La Cour. What do you have in mind?"

"Go with me to where I think he might be hiding out. I can communicate with him through finger spelling, but I can't sign nearly as effectively as is warranted in this particular situation. I'm sure you've noticed in class how slow I am at getting my point across. It takes me forever."

"Don't worry about your performance in my class. You've only just begun." Scotland rubbed the sleep from her eyes. "I'd be happy to interpret for you. Where do I meet you?"

"If you don't mind, I'd like to pick you up. It's terribly late. If Gregory is where I think he is, it's a rough neighborhood. I'd really feel horrible if something happened to you out there."

Although Jordan lived right there in her own neighborhood, Scotland had to think hard about giving out her home address. That he was an officer of the court carried some weight in his favor. After a couple more seconds of deliberation, she decided to go for it. How could destiny be fulfilled if she balked at the process?

"Do you have a pencil handy, Mr. La Cour?"

"I'm ready to copy, Miss Kennedy. Thank you for doing this for me."

"You're welcome. But we're both doing this for Gregory."

Scotland and Jordan found Gregory under the bleachers at the junior high school football stadium, exactly where Jordan thought he'd be. Jordan had explained to Scotland that Gregory desperately loved football, but his inability to hear had kept him off the team. Every chance Gregory got to slip away from what he claimed was an abusive situation, he went to the stadium to watch the players practice. It had become a refuge to him.

The glint of unshed tears in Jordan's eyes was not missed by Scotland. His compassion for the young boy was also apparent in his anxious expression. When Jordan discreetly wiped the tears from his eyes, Scotland's heart went out to him.

Jordan looked Scotland right in the eye. "There's no time for me to fumble through this thing with finger spelling. Please ask Gregory to come out so we can take care of him."

Scotland nodded, happy that Jordan had included her in his statement about taking care of Gregory. She liked the sound of "we." It seemed very personal, somewhat encompassing. Kneeling down at the end of a tier of bleachers, she expertly signed Jordan's request to Gregory. The young man shook his head in the negative, cowering further back under the stands.

Jordan realized he was too tall to go in after Gregory unless he got down on his hands and knees and crawled in. Mindful of the lateness of the hour and the chilly night air, Jordan wasted no time in dropping down on his knees and making his way under the bleachers, hoping Gregory wouldn't scramble away and run from him.

After bumping his head a time or two and scraping his elbows and knees, Jordan finally reached Gregory, pulling him into his arms, hugging him tightly. Scotland nearly lost her composure at the beautiful sight before her. If she hadn't known better, she would've believed that Gregory was Jordan's son. The tender way in which he embraced the boy brought tears to her eyes. Male bonding was something very special. Finding out that Jordan was a caring and gentle man made her heart rejoice.

As Jordan continued to hold Gregory, mumbling incoherently, he gently massaged the back of the boy's head. Watching the two of them attempting to crawl out from under the cramped space caused Scotland to laugh inwardly. As he led the way, holding on to Gregory's hand, Jordan looked so ridiculously silly down on his hands and knees, but that didn't stop Scotland's heart from swelling to near bursting. This was definitely a Kodak moment.

Standing at the stove inside his large kitchen, Jordan filled three mugs with hot chocolate and then placed them on a lacquer tray, alongside a plate full of cinnamon toast, which he himself had fixed. He had baked chocolate chip cookies earlier that morning, but he thought they might have too much sugar for Gregory, especially in the wee hours of the morning. He then carried the tray over to the kitchen table, where Scotland and Gregory waited. Jordan joined his guests after placing a mug of hot chocolate in front of each of them.

Jordan's admiration and respect for Scotland had grown tenfold after seeing how kindly she'd treated Gregory. She had embraced the young man as though she'd known him all her life, as if he were related to her by blood. Her hands had moved so fast in her communications with Gregory that Jordan hadn't been able to decipher all of what she'd said to him. But how she'd so effectively communicated with his young client wasn't what had amazed Jordan the most.

Scotland had managed to get the young boy to do something Jordan hadn't ever seen him do. She had actually made the saddest little boy Jordan had ever encountered laugh out loud. That no one had loved or valued this kid had been obvious the first day Jordan had met Gregory. Seeing him relaxed and happy made Jordan feel optimistic about the boy's future.

The huge smiles on Gregory's almond brown face and his occasional laughter also gave Jordan some insight into how infectious Scotland's great sense of humor was. He not only admired how Scotland and Gregory communicated with such ease, he thoroughly enjoyed the camaraderie that had been so easily established between them. Jordan was glad that he'd called Scotland for assistance; he could tell that this woman was something very special.

With Jordan's permission, Scotland looked around Jordan's house while he tucked Gregory into bed. They'd made the decision to let him sleep for a couple of hours before returning him to his foster family. Jordan wasn't too keen on returning Gregory to the very place he hated living in, but he had no choice in the matter.

The Turners had sounded concerned about the boy over the phone when Jordan had talked with them right after Gregory's disappearance, but the love of money had a way of making people give the best performances of their lives. If Gregory was removed from the Turner home, they'd lose the income that came along with him. Money alone was enough motivation for the many foster families who took in children for all the wrong reasons. Jordan had been around this business long enough to know that things weren't always as they seemed.

This was a highly unusual situation for Scotland to find herself involved in, but she'd relished every moment she'd spent with young Gregory, not to mention being in Jordan's company. Although she didn't know all of the boy's issues, she was sure there were many serious ones. He had the look of a child who'd been lost to the world. At times—as if believing no one even wanted to find him—Gregory appeared scared to death.

Scotland had never before seen such palpable sadness in the eyes of one so young. That she couldn't replace the sorrow in his large brown eyes with unending joy made her heart ache. But if she knew Jordan—though she really didn't know him at all—he wouldn't allow Gregory to just fall through the cracks. She'd seen and had felt in spades his deep compassion for Gregory Robinson. Jordan's genuine concern for his client's well-being had been clearly demonstrated through his actions.

CHAPTER THREE

Upon returning to the kitchen, Jordan gently put his hand under Scotland's elbow, guiding her over to the table, where he pulled out her chair before seating himself. Seeing that she got back home safe and sound was on his mind. He felt guilty about depriving her of any more sleep, even though she'd agreed to stay on until Gregory awakened.

"Can I get you a refill on the chocolate, Miss Kennedy?"

"No thanks. I've had enough." She smiled softly. "Do you have a problem calling me by my first name? I really don't mind, you know."

Jordan hunched his shoulders. "I didn't know if it was appropriate or not. And I hope you'll just call me Jordan. I happen to like my first name. Now that you've given me the okay to use it, I'll refer to you by your first name, except for when we're in class."

Scotland chuckled. "There's no reason for you to revert back to my surname. My students are all free to call me Scotland. I normally make that very clear on the first day of class, but I guess I forgot to announce it this time around. Sorry about that."

Pausing for a moment, Scotland wondered if she should ask the question that had just popped into her mind. She quickly decided that asking Jordan if he was married was totally inappropriate, but she didn't get a sense from the manly décor that a woman resided on the premises. His digs resembled a bachelor pad more than a family abode. The skimpily clad bikini models featured in the girlie calendar posted on the kitchen wall were one stark indication that he might be single. Yet there were a lot of strong women with open minds, she reminded herself.

But was he available? She'd just have to wonder about that for now.

"I know why you began signing in the first place, but what made you decide to work for the judicial system, Scotland?" He had purposely tried out her name to hear how it sounded coming from his lips. He liked how he'd pronounced it, so softly, yet distinctly.

Scotland gave his question a minute of thought. "I guess you could say the judicial system decided on me."

"How's that?"

"A lawyer friend of my dad's told me about the job opening after I'd helped him out with one of his cases involving a hearing-impaired client. I didn't apply for the position then, but I did much later, after several other judicial employees mentioned how badly the courts needed good signers/interpreters. The rest is history."

"Now I see what you mean by the courts deciding on you. Are you happy with your job?"

"Very much so. It didn't take long for me to realize I was providing a great service to all concerned. Although many of the court cases sadden me, I really love what I do. How about you, Jordan? What made you get into your line of work?"

"Plain and simple, I became a juvenile probation officer to help kids out, those who were just like me, lost and all alone in the world. Like Gregory, I've been hurt, miserably disappointed in, and totally disillusioned by, so-called adults. Some of the kids today are a new breed of animal, born from unending pain. We've moved from Generation X to Y. Gregory is scared in his new foster home, and he's also lonely and unhappy there."

"Were you ever a foster kid, Jordan?" Scotland reluctantly inquired.

Fighting off a wave of unexpected emotions, Jordan briefly lowered his head. "Not on a regular basis. My placements were more a state of emergency. I spent a night or two in several different foster homes. I think the longest stay was close to a week. My parents' verbal fights often turned into physical altercations. When the police had to be called in, I was hauled off to a more protective environment, which wasn't always safer. I had some mean emergency foster parents, but I also stayed with a few very kind and loving families."

Jordan began telling Scotland about how gung ho he'd been when he'd landed his first job as a probation officer with the Los Angeles County courts. His loftiest goal was to save all the youth whose cases had the good fortune to cross his desk. However, Jordan's jubilant outlook was rather short-lived.

The cases that had been assigned to him were unbelievably bloodcurdling ones. Kids were no longer indulging in minor offenses. No longer were they just throwing rocks and breaking the neighbors' windows. Today's youths were firing off rounds from handguns and other deadly assault weapons. Harmless messages from prank phone callers had become a thing of the past; the new messages being left were downright terrifying.

It appeared to Jordan that slashing up folks with box cutters and other sharp objects had actually become a strange teenage fad of some sort. He could go on and on about the young drug dealers and their predatory approach toward unsuspecting kids.

Female gang members were as hard-core as the males, and in some instances, they were even worse. Killed or be killed was a sentiment shared by both genders. The worst case Jordan had been assigned to to date involved two newly recruited gang members who'd kill their father because they had tired of adhering to the curfew they thought he'd imposed on them unfairly.

Young boys were sexually assaulting their female counterparts and then proudly boasting to their peers about their horrific crimes. On the other hand, young girls were purposely trying to get pregnant, citing their desire to give an abundance of love and to have love and affection given to them in return. It had become an epidemic.

Astounded by the number of teen pregnancies in this country alone, Jordan had begun to take a hard look at how he handled his own intimate dealings. He'd never been a love-them-and-leave-them kind of guy, but he hadn't always been as responsible as he should've been. Having unprotected sex was about as irresponsible as anyone could get. Abstinence was the advice he gave, when asked, but the majority of his juvenile offenders were already sexually active.

Jordan often wondered how he was supposed to save the world's youth when they were really their own worst enemies. Despite the statistics, he'd never give up on America's kids.

Scotland was shocked that Jordan had opened up to

her, and so easily. She was very pleased that he'd trusted her enough to discuss the details of his life with her. She had received even more insight into the seemingly wonderful man she hoped to learn everything about.

"What about your parents? Where are they now, Jordan?"

Jordan shrugged. "They live right here in L.A. Supposed to be born-again Christians, according to them."

Scotland raised an eyebrow. "You don't sound convinced of that."

"'Cause I'm not. Do devils ever really change?"

Putting a finger to her right temple, Scotland smiled sympathetically. "As a matter of fact, they do. Bad spirits can turn into good ones—and often do. Nothing in this world is perfect, Jordan. No flesh and blood being will ever achieve perfection, not in this lifetime."

Jordan laughed heartily. "I know a couple of people who'd passionately argue with you on that point. Mr. and Mrs. Perfect live right next door to me, Scotland, but you may not want to meet them. Being in their company is not a very pleasant experience, if you know what I mean."

Both Scotland and Jordan had a good laugh over that.

No one had to tell Scotland about the so-called perfect people of the world. She came into contact with faultless folks on a daily basis. Although they could be extremely annoying at times, Scotland reveled in the opportunity to acquaint herself with the people she held in high esteem. She found them very interesting to watch and to learn from. It was always quite an experience to meet the people she never wanted to become like.

"Are you friends with your neighbors, Jordan?"

Jordan nervously fiddled with the handle of the empty mug in front of him. *Friends,* he mused. It both-

ered him that he didn't even know the real meaning of
the word. He made a mental note to look up the defini-
tion in the dictionary. "Let's just say we're cordial.
Getting into a couple of conversations with them has
been enough for me. Every word they utter is about
themselves and how perfect their lives are. Hello, how
you doing, and good-bye are about it for us. As for
friends, I don't have any real ones to speak of. I've always been a loner. People don't seem to take to me too
well."

Scotland folded her hands and placed them on the
table. Jordan's remarks worried her. She felt sorry
about his quandary, and she needed to understand why
his life was so lonely. It seemed to her as if the absence
of friendship was by choice. Perhaps she was confusing
loner with loneliness, she thought, even though they
seemed to be one and the same to her. "It's been my experience that you have to be a friend to gain one.
People can't reach out to you if you somehow put them
off. By your own admission, you're a loner. Why's that?"

Jordan took a minute to think about what Scotland
had said. It made sense to him that people couldn't get
close to him if he didn't let them in. Shutting folks out
was a learned behavior. It surprised him that he'd
opened up to her as much as he had. She was easy to
talk to, which wasn't always the case with others. But it
was when a person let someone in that they got hurt the
most. Everyone he'd ever trusted had let him down in
one way or another. Betrayal by those he'd once believed in was the story of his life. Trust came hard for
him.

"What are you thinking, Jordan?"

"What you said about being a friend. I guess I just
don't know how to be one. As a child and as an adult,
I've never really tried to get close to anyone. Keeping to
myself is much easier."

Scotland frowned. "Isn't there anyone that you're close to?"

"Not really. I used to be very close to my mother. That is, until he ensnared her."

"Who's he?"

"James, my father. There was a time when my mother, Regina, used to protect me from his alcoholic rages. She'd keep him off me even if it meant getting herself hurt. Then one day she decided to join him."

"What do you mean by that? Join him how?"

Looking distressed, Jordan closed his eyes and put his head down on the table. This wasn't a subject he really wanted to get into, but he felt that he needed to. He might never have this kind of opportunity to open up again. Jordan realized he had closed himself off from the world for far too long. Scotland seemed so caring, but was it fair to unload his baggage on her?

Only a couple of days ago Jordan had vowed not to get involved with Scotland despite his wild attraction to her. He wasn't looking for a love affair with anyone, but he did need a friend—and the most compassionate woman he'd ever met was seated across the table from him. What more could he ask for?

Jordan lifted his head and made direct eye contact with Scotland. He then bit down on his lower lip. "I used to hear him asking her to have a drink with him, telling her how good it'd make her feel. She turned him down, countless times. . . ." Jordan released a frustrated sigh.

Thinking back on those unpredictable and very volatile times in his life was hard for him. It was as though his father had been in competition with him for his mother's affection. James couldn't stand to see them enjoying each other's company. Whenever James had come home from work, he made sure he separated the two of them, often sending Jordan off to his room under the guise of needing to discuss something important with Regina. Jordan's happiest memories were of the quality times he'd once spent alone with his mother.

"Do you drink, Jordan?"

The expression on his face said that Scotland's question had caught him totally off guard.

"Are you okay, Jordan? You suddenly seem so far away."

"I was back in the turmoil of the past. I don't like going there, but sometimes it's necessary. Like now. To answer your question, I used to drink, excessively. Listen to this crazy incident. It'll completely blow your mind."

Jordan went on to tell Scotland how he was so drunk one evening at a nightclub that he could barely find the ignition to insert his car key. Before leaving the nightclub, he'd known he was too intoxicated to get behind the wheel, but he'd done so anyway. His last coherent thought was that he shouldn't drive, that he should just stay put and sleep it off. He had ignored his inner voice.

Then Jordan told Scotland how he'd come to this bridge after weaving and bobbing all over the road. On the other side of the bridge was the street he had to turn down to get home. He had convinced himself that he could make it across the bridge even though he had a hard time keeping his eyes open. Just as he'd reached the other side, he lost complete control of the car, which then plunged straight down into the frigid waters below. Jordan nearly recoiled as he recalled how he'd frantically kicked at the windows when he couldn't get the driver's door open. The water had begun to pour into the car. He'd never known such deep fear as he thought of drowning.

"The water was coming up over my head. I just knew I was going to die. Then I woke up on the couch and realized I'd been having the worst nightmare of my life.

Somehow I had made it home and had passed out in the living room. I haven't had a drink since, nor have I ever been able to make any sense of that horrific nightmare, Scotland. It has scared me sober. What do you think it all meant?"

Scotland raised an eyebrow. "I'm no Daniel or Joseph. I can't interpret dreams. But it's my guess that the nightmare meant you'd just hit your rock bottom."

Jordan ran a nervous hand through his hair. He had no clue who Daniel or Joseph was, but he somehow got the feeling from Scotland that he should. Instead of asking her about it and risking coming off stupid, he decided to let her remark slide by without comment. "I'm sorry for dumping so much garbage on you, Scotland. I hope you don't mind me heaping all this dead weight on your shoulders."

Scotland had an overwhelming urge to take Jordan's hand and squeeze it. The expression on his face was one of a little boy who just needed someone to love him and approve of him. She somehow got the sense that Jordan was still stuck in his unhappy childhood. "You mentioned not having friends, Jordan, but I'd like for you to consider having me as one. Friends listen when their friends need to talk. That's just one of the things friends do for each other."

"I know I need a friend, Scotland, but I'm not sure I can ever be one. I may not be able to give back to you in the same way I believe you're capable of giving. I'm not sure I'd even know how. Please understand that I don't want a girlfriend. Only a friend. Please don't take it personal, but I just can't involve myself in any other kind of relationship. Is that okay with you?"

Feeling as though Jordan had just stuck a dagger right into her heart, Scotland winced in agony. Although she was hurting inside, she smiled, anyway. She then scolded herself for being downright silly. Jordan hadn't meant to hurt her. Of course, he hadn't. So there was no reason for her to take his position personally. He had no idea she thought of him as her future husband. In any relationship, you had to crawl before you could walk. Becoming Jordan's friend was the first step toward fulfilling destiny. He desperately needed to trust someone. He'd soon come to learn that he could trust her with his life. Scotland had every intention of seeing to that.

As hard as it was to do, Scotland resisted the urge to cover Jordan's hand with hers, just as a gesture of understanding. "Friendship, first and foremost. I'm definitely okay with that, Jordan. Do you mind telling me more about your parents? But only if you want to. No pressure."

Jordan rocked back and forth in his chair for several seconds before bringing it back level with the floor. *Pressure. What a word,* he mused. No one would ever know how much pressure he was living under. His cool exterior belied the pent-up anxiety he often felt inside. It wouldn't take much for him to blow up like a malfunctioning pressure cooker, but he wasn't going to allow that to happen, not if he could help it.

Accepting his parents' repeated pleas for forgiveness was Jordan's greatest challenge. Then there was the unsolved mystery of Cynthia Raymond. Together these predicaments created more pressure than any one person should ever have to endure.

"Dad finally convinced Mom to have that one drink with him," Jordan finally responded, "then another and another. What came next was just that single hit on a joint. Then one day I lost my mother to all my father's evil vices. He led Mom to places she'd never been. He had her hanging out with him in the worst areas of the city. They've recently come back into my life, wanting me to forgive and forget. Tell me, how's that possible?"

Scotland fought back her tears. "With God, all things are possible, Jordan."

Jordan totally rejected the idea of seeking out God. Where was God when he'd needed him the most? No, he didn't want to hear about some redeemer. Jordan had never really sought out God, because he could only imagine that He'd let him down, too, just like everyone else had. However, Jordan had to admit to being very curious about the Supreme Being, before whom innumerable folks constantly bowed down in prayer. Jordan had never been taught to pray by his parents. . . . and he'd never tried to learn from any other source, despite his curiosity.

If only he had the nerve to reach over and touch Scotland's beautiful sandy brown hair, lose his nose in its fullness, and then smooth it back from her face, Jordan thought. It looked so soft, causing him to imagine what it might feel like against the pads of his fingers. Silken threads instantly came to his mind. Jordan closed his eyes and envisioned his fingers entwined in her hair.

Although he couldn't be one hundred percent sure, Jordan couldn't help thinking that Scotland was the very woman he'd dreamed of having as a lifetime partner. That kind of relationship wasn't possible for him right now. He wasn't sure marriage would ever be possible in his future. Jordan felt so messed up, so mentally unhinged, and emotionally scarred.

Why had Scotland come into his life during so much turmoil, especially when he was so fearful of everything around him? He'd heard that guardian angels always showed up when a person needed them the most. Jordan had never met an angel before now. Finding himself face-to-face with an angelic host was downright surreal. Her brilliant light was steadily luring him, nearly blinding him to the darker side of the world. Could he truly lose himself in her brilliance?

Sensing the presence of another, Jordan turned his gaze toward the doorway. Rubbing his eyes with the heels of his hands and looking somewhat confused was Gregory. It appeared as if the boy had no idea where he was or how he'd gotten there. Jordan's home was just one of many strange places that Gregory had found himself in during his short tenure on earth. According to his records, he'd already lived in seven different foster homes. . . . and he was only twelve.

Gregory had re-dressed himself in his own well-worn clothing. Jordan had given him a clean pair of sweatpants and a white T-shirt to sleep in. Although both articles of clothing were way too big for him, he hadn't seemed to mind. He had surprised Jordan by inhaling the scent of the clothes before putting them on. Gregory had later finger signed to Jordan that the clothes smelled so nice and fresh.

Momentarily, Jordan was at a loss for words. The sight of the boy had caused a flash flood of sorrowful scenes to replay in his brain. How many times had he looked into the mirror and seen that same confused expression on his own face? *Too many times to recall,* Jordan unhappily mused. At one time his clothes had also been un-ironed and tatty.

"We have company, Scotland. Please tell Gregory in sign language to come in and have a seat. I'm sure he's hungry so I'm going to fix him some breakfast. Would you like me to take you home first, or can you stay a little longer? I can fix you something to eat, too."

"I need to go, Jordan. You don't have to drive me home. A long walk around the neighborhood is a part of my morning routine. I prefer walking. Great exercise."

Scotland fulfilled Jordan's request as she got to her feet. She then opened her arms wide to Gregory. Without the slightest bit of hesitation, the young man fell into her warm embrace. Scotland kissed his forehead ever so tenderly. "Good morning, Gregory. Did you sleep well?"

"Best sleep I've ever had. The bed was off the hook," he signed to Scotland.

As much as Jordan tried to keep up with the quickly moving hands of his two guests, he just couldn't do it. His fascination with the art of sign language was growing by leaps and bounds. He couldn't imagine himself ever being that proficient in signing, but he was going to give it the old college try. Until he'd gotten involved with Gregory—and then Scotland—Jordan hadn't realized there were so many reasons for a person to become a signer/interpreter. Now the list seemed endless.

Even though Jordan felt obligated to make sure Scotland got home safely, he quickly decided not to object to her desire to walk. She had come across as adamant when voicing her decision. Jordan had Scotland tell Gregory that he was going to see her to the front door and come right back. After bidding farewell to Gregory, she let him know what Jordan had asked her to say. Gregory nodded to her his understanding before plopping down in a chair at the table.

Just as the two reached the front door, Jordan started laughing. The trilling sound of his laughter excited her more than she wanted to admit. Seeing him blush like crazy caused her breath to catch. He was so handsome, yet he seemed not to know it. He also had no idea of the profound effect he had on her. Allowing himself to be loved by her wasn't going to be easy for him, but that wasn't going to stop her from loving him, anyway. One day he'd come to realize that he wanted and needed her every bit as much as she did him.

"What's so funny, Jordan?"

"Just imagining what the neighbors will think if they see you leaving my house at this time of the morning. You can bet your last dollar that their thoughts will be negative ones."

"Do you care what they think, Jordan?"

"Yeah, I do. For your sake, not mine. Protecting your reputation is important to me."

Scotland was quite pleased that he wanted to protect her. His remarks made her feel good all over. She wrinkled her nose. "I wouldn't worry about that if I were you. I know exactly who I am. . . . and we both know why I was here. People are going to think what they want to, no matter the truth. Since we can't do anything about that, we shouldn't worry about it. See you later."

Jordan extended his hand to Scotland, warding off his strong desire to pull her into his arms and hug her tightly. If only he could tell her what a difference she'd already made in his life. He hadn't laughed like that in ages. He couldn't ever remember his heart being this light and carefree. It was a darn good feeling, one that he wanted to experience again.

Scotland told Jordan good-bye and then turned to walk away. She'd only gone a couple of steps when she turned around and made her way back to him. "We've done a lot of talking, you know, but you haven't told me why Gregory is on probation. Is that something you're free to share with me?"

"I probably shouldn't, but you've been kind enough to help me out. Since I might need your services again, I think it's okay for me to tell you. The charges are stealing and receiving stolen property. Breaking into and burglarizing cars is also one of his major crimes. He's committed these same offenses numerous times in the last couple of years. Finally, they landed him on probation. It's my best guess that an older guy has been using him as a fence, but he's not giving up any names. These young kids don't realize that adults, who'd go straight to prison for the same crimes, are using them to do their dirty work. It happens all too often."

Scotland looked alarmed. "I hate to think like this, but aren't you concerned about having Gregory stay in your home? Not to mention letting him know where you live. Sounds like a recipe for disaster to me. What if he decides to rip you off?"

"His immediate needs are greater than my fears of being ripped off. I'm really not worried about it. I have to trust him if I ever hope to gain his trust. Recently, someone very wise told me that you first have to be a friend to gain one. That piece of good advice has really sunk in."

Scotland smiled broadly. "Okay, this sagacious kid can't argue with that. Have a good one, Jordan." Aware that her feet wouldn't touch the ground for the remainder of the day, Scotland floated away from Jordan's house.

"Brianna, you're not going to believe what happened last night!" Scotland rapidly typed on the computer, smiling all the while.

"Probably not, but I bet you won't let me sign off until you tell me about it. LOL." Relieved that Scotland hadn't stopped trusting in her, Brianna smiled brightly.

"You're right about that, Bri! So here goes. My future husband called me up last night."

Brianna sent an alarmed face from her special graphics program. "Shocking! What prompted the call?"

Scotland typed in most of the details from the previous evening spent with Jordan.

"So, after all that, did Jordan propose, Scotty?"

"Tsk, tsk, tsk. Be nice now, Bri. Ugliness doesn't become you. Just give him more time. He'll be on bended knee before you know it. In fact, he *was* down on his knees last night."

"Doing what? Please don't make me wonder. You know I have a naughty imagination."

Scotland explained to Brianna how Jordan had crawled under the bleachers to rescue Gregory both physically and emotionally. Just the thought of those tender moments made her feel warm and happy inside. Scotland had witnessed humanity in one of its finest hours.

"Jordan sounds amazing. I'm already dying to meet him. The scary part about this whole thing is that you always get what you want. So I have to believe you'll land Jordan, too. I can't wait to see how this all unfolds."

"Remember our dinner date, Bri. Cooked crow coming up very soon now."

"Ugh. How could I forget it? You're still crazy as ever, but I love you, anyway. How was your workday?"

"I had two grand jury indictments to interpret. Both were pretty bad, the kidnapping of a child and then a woman who'd been severely battered by her spouse. After years of emotional and physical abuse, she finally got up the nerve to press charges against him. The battered woman is deaf, and so is the mother of the kidnapped child. By the way, the child was recovered unharmed. The proceedings were very emotional. I'm thinking of taking a course in closed-captioned court reporting. It seems very interesting, but I'll need to do a lot more research on it."

"Hmm. I don't think you'd enjoy it as much as what you're already doing, Scotty. You'd have to sit for long periods of time. You know how fidgety you are."

"You got a valid point there, Bri."

"Have you told Uncle Scott about seeing Jordan last night?"

"Not yet. I plan to call him after I finish chatting with you. Our dads are so supportive of us. They're all for whatever makes us happy."

"Do you and Jordan have plans to see each other again, outside of class, that is?"

"No plans for that. But we did decide to become friends. He made it clear that he doesn't want a girl-friend. If he knew what I have in mind for him, he'd probably never agree to see me again. He's scared of getting involved in a personal relationship. What I'd like to know is why."

"He's told you a lot about himself already, so I'm sure he'll enlighten you about it one day. Seems to me that you might need to take things real slow with him. He'd probably freak out if he knew you were already planning to marry him."

Scotland cracked up. "Tell me about it. Got to run now. Still lots to do before bedtime. My stomach is also growling up a storm. Love you, Bri."

"Later, Scotty. I love you, too."

Once again Jordan was having a hard time falling asleep. Thoughts of how he could keep Gregory from becoming another wretched victim of the judicial system had bombarded his entire day and evening. There were far too many black youth locked up in county and state detention centers. He didn't want to see Gregory end up in the same horrible predicament as many of his young clients had. Jordan had had to save himself from all the numerous enticements of the streets, in the absence of his parents, so he believed he might be able to save Gregory, too.

Taking Gregory back to his foster home had been a miserable time for both of them, especially when the boy pleaded with Jordan not to make him go. Jordan could've had the police pick him up and take him home, but he knew firsthand how traumatic that would've been. Besides that, Jordan had wanted some time to observe Gregory with the Turners inside the home. He needed to see how they reacted to each other.

The interaction between Gregory and his foster family hadn't been at all good. No one had been able to put up a façade during the strained homecoming. It was obvious that they were very upset with Gregory for running away again. Jordan was terribly worried about what Gregory was up against in the Turner home, since Mr. Turner had exhibited intense anger, yelling and cursing at the top of his lungs. Knowing that he'd already put in a request for social services to investigate Gregory's living situation helped Jordan breathe a little easier.

As though it was the most natural thing in the world for him to do, Jordan picked up the phone and dialed Scotland's number upon returning home from the Turners. On the second ring he hung up. Seated on the side of the bed, he stared at the receiver, his hands itching to pick it up again. Believing he couldn't phone her without a good excuse for doing so had caused him to end the call. He didn't understand why he wanted so desperately to talk to a woman he barely knew.

Oddly enough, Jordan felt that he did know Scotland, that he'd known her all his life. Scotland was the woman he'd been impatiently waiting for, the one who would help him begin his life anew. He had been waiting for her to make an appearance for years. She was here now, but he had no clue as to what he was supposed to do with her.

Then Jordan thought about the upcoming youth camping trip he wanted to get Gregory involved in. There were many questions he needed to answer before he could approach the trip sponsors with his idea. Scotland might be able to answer at least one or two of his queries. That brilliant thought gave him the perfect excuse for phoning her. He only wished he'd thought of the camping trip earlier, which might've helped out during his time of indecision about calling her. Hoping that she was at home, Jordan redialed Scotland's phone number, his heart beating faster than normal.

CHAPTER FOUR

Seated at the desk in her bedroom, Scotland carefully looked over her appointment calendar for the rest of the month. Unable to believe how many things she had scheduled, she groaned loudly. There were hardly any openings left for social events, since her business appointments also occupied much of her evening time. She had two signing classes to teach at a couple of different churches, and she was glad they were in close proximity to each other. That would cut down on driving time.

A speaking engagement at the Los Angeles Senior Center on Wednesday caught Scotland by surprise. She had completely forgotten about it, but mingling with the seniors was always a delightful and interesting venture for her. Teaching sign language wasn't why she visited the senior centers. Scotland scheduled monthly health seminars with the elderly to give them information on all the new audio devices and advanced technology available to those whose hearing was no longer as good as it once was.

After delivering her speech, she loved to sit, chat,

and sip tea with the older folks. They had so many wonderful stories to share with her about their youth. Spending time with the wise women often caused her to pine for the relationship she'd missed out on with her mother. Many of the ladies referred to her as their adopted daughter, which made her feel really special. Scotland had quickly established quite a rapport with the older generation.

Scotland had started the health seminars as a way to earn extra money; she later purchased stock in one of the hearing device companies that employed her to do the presentations. When she realized how interested folks were in the products, she understood that the seminars were really helpful to the seniors. She was all for helping to enhance people's lives.

Scotland smiled when she saw the date for a special party penned in on her calendar. Her Uncle Brian was throwing a surprise birthday bash for Brianna at a posh hotel restaurant in Beverly Hills. Scotland couldn't wait to see the look on her cousin's pretty face when she realized what was going on. Brianna was going to positively freak out.

As it stood now, Brianna thought that the family was just getting together for a special birthday dinner. She had no idea about all the special plans her father had made to make her birthday the most memorable one to date. Scotland knew that Brianna was going to be so surprised. Her hearing impairment didn't stop her from being a party girl. She didn't have to hear the music to dance. She had learned to listen to the songs in her heart. Brianna simply loved life and lived every day to the fullest. It had been depressing for her when she first lost her hearing, but her enthusiasm for living had rapidly kicked the doldrums clean to the curb.

A brief sadness made Scotland's hazel eyes glisten. She sighed hard, wishing her mother were still alive.

The double tragedy had hit the Kennedy family hard. Holiday and birthday celebrations always caused the family to reflect on how everything might've been more wonderful if Victoria and Solange had lived. The two girls had been taught by their fathers to play the hand dealt to them, so they refused to dwell on the past.

It fleetingly crossed Scotland's mind that she should invite Jordan to the party after this evening's class was over, but her emotions became mixed when she thought of what had happened the previous night. The phone had rung several times, but the caller had hung up each time. Her caller ID had revealed to her that Jordan had been the one phoning, much to her surprise and delight. She was sure her heart had stopped a few times during those moments.

Scotland didn't understand why Jordan had picked up the phone to call her home, only to hang up. Had it been anyone else calling her, she would've dialed the number right back. It was her guess that Jordan probably didn't even know about caller ID and that he'd gotten cold feet before she could answer. She didn't think he would've hung up as many times as he had if he'd been aware that she'd know who'd phoned. Scotland had to admit that he was a strange one, but it didn't dampen her desire for him, not one iota.

Scotland closed her shoulder-style briefcase and gripped the strap tightly. That she'd had another successful signing session pleased her. Her students were coming along nicely. Jordan was the last one to leave the classroom, and she hurried through the security routine, hoping to catch up to him before he pulled out of the parking lot.

Scotland reached Jordan before he got into his car.

"Before we go home, what about stopping off and having a cup of coffee with me, Jordan?"

Jordan appeared totally put off by the offer. "I don't think that's a good idea. I've already told you I'm not interested in a relationship. That's just how it is."

Scotland cracked up, making Jordan feel downright silly and immature. "I can see that you think quite a lot of yourself. Coffee-mate, Jordan, not a committed relationship, was all I was asking for. You should learn to lighten up a bit. See you next week, Jordan. That is, if you're not too scared of me to come back to class."

Scotland wasn't laughing one bit on the inside. Her feelings were terribly hurt by Jordan's cold rejection of her, but only because her intentions had been good. She'd thought he'd accepted her offer of friendship, but it looked as if she had been sorely mistaken. She was fiercely attracted to him all right, but she wasn't an aggressive pursuer of men by any stretch of the imagination. If he expected her to chase him down, he'd better think again.

Despite all her spouting off a few evenings ago about putting Jordan on notice of her intent toward him, Scotland made the quick decision that she certainly wasn't going to make known to him her interest in him, especially since he still showed no signs of any romantic interest in her. Given how standoffish he was, she knew that that would be a huge mistake. She still felt confident that he was her soul mate, but until he also realized it, she'd have to sit back and wait him out.

As Scotland opened her car door, she heard Jordan calling out her name. She turned around and saw him running toward her. Her heartbeat quickened. To calm her twanging nerves, she put her belongings in the backseat and then leaned against the door on the driver's side, inhaling and exhaling slowly to stabilize her heart rate.

Jordan stopped right in front of Scotland, looking a tad sheepish. He glanced down at the ground and then up at her. "Can I change my mind about the coffee invite?"

Acting as if it didn't matter to her one way or the other, Scotland hunched her shoulders. "That's up to you. If you decide to show up, I'll be at the Starbucks right around the corner." With that, Scotland got in her car.

Jordan nodded, motioning for her to roll down her window. "I'll see you there, Scotland."

Glad that she hadn't sent Jordan packing out of spite over his blatant rejection of her, Scotland stirred hazelnut cream into her coffee with a slender wooden stick. She then lifted the cup and pointed it toward her companion in a toastlike gesture. "Here's to friends enjoying a good cup of java."

Jordan chuckled lightly, tipping his cup toward her. "Ditto."

For a couple of minutes Scotland and Jordan sipped coffee in total silence, each lost in their own thoughts. She was already mentally planning her activities for the next day, and Jordan was busy thinking of ways he could help make life better for Gregory.

Breaking the silence, Jordan said Scotland's name, and she looked over at him. "Uh, there's this camping trip coming up with one of the local community centers. I'd like Gregory to go on it. What do you think of the idea?"

Scotland shrugged. "I don't see a problem with it. It's really a good idea."

"Even if Gregory can't hear what's going on? He won't be able to communicate, either. Won't the other boys treat him differently? I worry about him being teased and taunted."

"I understand your concerns, Jordan, but hearing is only a part of living. He can feel, see, and read. His speech isn't perfectly developed, but he can be understood. His senses are more heightened than yours or mine. A smile can be seen but not heard. Facial expressions communicate so many things. Laughter can also be discerned by body language."

Jordan raised his eyebrows. "I hadn't thought about any of that. You never know how many ways there are to communicate until you run into a situation like this. How difficult was it for you to communicate with your cousin when she first lost her hearing?"

"Brianna can talk, remember. I started out by writing everything down since she couldn't hear me. Even though we lived in the same house, we used our individual computers to send each other messages. We still do. I took my first sign language class shortly after she started hers, so we pretty much learned signing at the same time. Practicing with each other was fun. We were already extremely close, but we grew even closer through signing. Both of our fathers can sign, too. I guess you can say signing is a family affair in our brood."

"How did you feel about what happened to your cousin?"

"I was really sad about it. When she started attending a special school, I felt lost. We'd been together every single day, all of our lives. That's when I decided to take the class, too. It was the best decision I've ever made. All of it has been a life-changing experience."

"In what way, Scotland?"

"Brianna and I had entered into a whole new world; we had to learn an entirely new way of communicating. In some ways it was freeing. It was like being bilingual.

I've studied several foreign languages. None of them has ever excited me the way signing does. All the ups and downs aside, this journey has been one beautiful, liberating experience."

Jordan felt Scotland's passion right down to the core of his being. He wondered if she knew how beautiful she looked with her stunning expression of wide-eyed wonder. Her eyes were all aglow with something he couldn't put a name to. It couldn't be the look of love, yet that's exactly what it appeared as to him. Since she loved her cousin like a sister, it wasn't so unusual that love would show up in her eyes when she talked about Brianna. *Love*, he mused, wondering how it would feel to fall completely in love with someone. Not just anyone, though. He imagined that falling hopelessly in love with Scotland would be an awesome experience.

Not at all happy with where his thoughts had taken him, Jordan turned his full attention back to Scotland. "I think I know what you mean. Being able to communicate with Gregory, despite the difficulty, has been a wonderful experience for me, too. It has also been a real challenge, one that I have taken on eagerly and willingly, despite all my concerns."

"You should be proud of yourself, Jordan. I know I am. Involving yourself in Gregory's life this way is something very special. He must be thrilled that you care so much about him."

Jordan swiped an open palm across his forehead. "I wish I knew that for sure. You can never tell with him. He's really an angry kid, justifiably so. I get the impression that he wants to believe I'm his friend, but his issues of trust keep him from getting too close to me."

Exactly the same way you are with me, Jordan, afraid of getting too close.

It was easy for Scotland to see that Gregory and Jordan had the very same trust issues. In many ways, the two were mirror images of each other. Jordan was actually reaching out to himself, and he didn't even know it. He *was* Gregory, as a despondent little boy. Those lost years couldn't be retrieved, but Jordan didn't seem to know that, either, since he still lived in them.

Scotland knew it had to be hard on Jordan to reach back for something repeatedly only to find out that it was no longer there. She knew all about that. How many times had she tried to reach back for the loving memory of her mother? Scotland was so young when her mother died that many of the memories she did have were blurred. It exasperated her that she couldn't remember all the details of the painfully short time she'd spent with her mother, Victoria.

Various pictures of Victoria with her and her dad were all that Scotland had left of her mother. The recent family portraits would always be incomplete without Victoria in them. Although her dad had given her Victoria's wedding rings, they didn't bring Scotland much comfort, either. If Jordan didn't eventually come around to her way of thinking, Scotland wasn't sure she'd ever get to wear her late mother's rings. She didn't know how she was so sure that there wasn't a man other than Jordan out there for her, yet she was.

The one huge difference between Scotland and Jordan was that his parents were still alive. She felt that she had to somehow get him to embrace that fact so that the La Cour family could finally make amends and become whole. Conflicts or not, there was nothing in the world like family. Jordan needed to have his parents back in his life more than he realized.

Scotland had to force her mind to focus on the conversation she'd been having with Jordan before she'd stepped into outer space. She recalled that he'd been chatting about Gregory's anger and issues of trust. "That's understandable, Jordan. From what you've told me, adults have constantly disappointed Gregory. You're an adult. My advice to you is to keep being there for him. Consistency is what he needs most in his life. No matter how hard things get, Gregory needs to know you won't abandon him. He's watching your every move, expecting you to fail him, positive that you're going to. He's had no successes with adults so far."

Jordan sighed hard. "I know that for a fact. I hope I can help turn things around for him."

"Do you plan to go on the camping trip with Gregory?"

"I think that's the only way to make it happen. He'll need someone to look after him."

"Then you shouldn't be worried about him. You can help interpret for him."

Jordan turned up his nose at that idea. "I don't know. I'm slow as molasses in finger spelling. Signing is really hard for me to learn. I don't want to make Gregory's life any worse than it already is. I feel so sorry for this kid."

"You're doing just fine with the class, Jordan. I've told you that several times already."

Scotland paused a moment to collect her thoughts. She was about to broach a delicate subject, and she didn't want to offend Jordan in any way. He was far more sensitive than most of the men she'd encountered. Choosing her words carefully was necessary.

"Listen, Jordan, please don't make the mistake of pitying Gregory. He doesn't need that from anyone, especially you. He's going to love the fact that you want him to have this great outdoor experience. And please don't look at his hearing impairment as a disability. If you harbor pity for him, he'll see it in your eyes. Focus on his strengths, not his weaknesses."

"I try not to see his weaknesses, but it's difficult at best. I don't want to hurt him, Scotland."

"I know. Try to treat him as normally as you possibly

can. Those with special challenges often see themselves as different because that's how some people make them feel. I've heard it said over and over again that people may forget what's been said or done to them, but they'll always remember how someone made them feel. Help him feel good about himself."

Jordan snapped his fingers. "I have a great idea. Gregory seems to really like you, so why don't you come camping with us? I could really use your support."

Scotland's mouth fell open. She was astonished. Less than an hour ago Jordan was outright rejecting her. Now he was inviting her to go on a camping trip with him. Talk about mixed messages. Jordan sure knew how to send those to her. Well, she mused, he wasn't exactly asking her out on a date. With that in mind, she didn't allow herself to get too excited.

"There'll be other female volunteers going along, Scotland. You won't be the only girl."

Girl. How nice and innocent that sounded. She hadn't been a girl for a very long time, but there were times when she felt girlishly giddy, just like she had in her youth. Scotland and Brianna loved to laugh and cut up. They still even had "girls' night out" pajamas parties . . . and they loved to gossip, but not maliciously.

The Hollywood stars were often the favorite topic of gossipy conversation between Scotland and Brianna. Brianna was mad crazy over Will Smith, and Scotland panted over Michael Ealy, the handsome, blue-eyed hunk from *BarberShop* and *BarberShop* 2. But no one could ever top Denzel Washington, not as far as they were concerned.

The two women loved to watch award shows using a closed-captioned television device, each signing their opinions about the stunning or horrid fashions worn by celebrities. They each made their own best and worst dressed list to discuss after the shows. The best dressed list was always longer than the worst. Each of them loved to eat popcorn and Popsicles and watch reruns of all the African-American sitcoms. *The Steve Harvey Show* was their favorite.

Yes, Scotland mused, there were still times when she was very much a little girl at heart.

Scotland looked up at Jordan and smiled. "Camping, huh? I admit to being a nature girl, but I'm definitely not into roughing it. My idea of enjoying the great outdoors is a walk in the park, jogging alongside a lake, or a leisurely stroll on the beach. Cooking steak or boneless chicken on my George Foreman grill out on the patio is the closest I ever come to outdoor grilling. I have no clue how to start a campfire or even how to roast a marshmallow. As much as I'd like to help you out on this, I think I'd be more of a liability than anything. Thanks for the offer, but I think I'd better pass. Besides, I'm terrified of big, ugly bugs."

Laughing, Jordan shook his head from side to side. "You're really funny, you know."

How could one tiny woman be so genuinely endearing? He was sure she had no idea how adorable she was. His knuckles ached to brush themselves across her full lips. Her eyes seemed to expose everything she felt inside, and he once again wished he could lose himself in their reflecting pools of dazzling light. She constantly amazed him. Jordan wondered whether she would change her mind if he told her how disappointed he was in her answer about the trip.

Did he dare put that kind of pressure on her? Would Scotland misinterpret his disappointment in her answer as more than it really was? Probably so, because his camping invitation entailed so much more than he wanted to own up to. It was true enough that he wanted her along to help him communicate with Gregory, but he also wanted her to go because she was such great company. Jordan enjoyed being with Scotland. She kept him from feeling hopeless and lonely. Turning down her offer of coffee had been utterly ridiculous. Look at what an engaging evening he would've missed out on had he not changed his mind, he mused. Maybe she'd change hers as well. He'd certainly altered his thinking about wanting something special with her. Whether it was possible or not, he didn't know.

Scotland's smile was devilishly charming. It was as though she harbored a naughty secret of some sort. She had clearly seen in his eyes his disappointment over her refusal to go camping. The last thing she wanted to do was disillusion him. Her presence on the camping trip seemed important to him. That was encouraging. "Can I change my mind about the camping trip invite?"

Recognizing that they both had refused each other's invitations only to change their minds, he threw his head back and laughed. "I can't think of anything that'd make me happier."

Scotland's breathing stopped momentarily. That unbelievable smile of his had done it to her again. If only she could tell him how beautiful it was and how it utterly took her breath away. His laughter sent chills up and down her spine, just as it had before. She had accused him earlier of thinking too highly of himself, but if he did, he had every right to. Inside Jordan's chest beat a precious heart of gold; Scotland was willing to bet the farm on it. Jordan seemed to want to keep that heart hidden, but she was going to expose it. It was her suspicion that his heart was buried beneath layers and layers of gut-wrenching pain. Scotland vowed to do everything in her power to help Jordan unearth it so the healing process could begin. He had much more to offer than he might even realize. Someone had hurt him badly, and he had yet to recover from the devastation to his spirit. He deserved to find eternal happiness, even if it wasn't with her.

"The camping trip, exactly when is it supposed to take place, Jordan?"

"Next weekend, departing early Friday evening."

"Ugh," Scotland moaned. "I'm supposed to help my Uncle Brian fine-tune the plans for Brianna's surprise birthday party. We had set aside next Saturday to discuss everything and get all the issues resolved. It looks like I'll have to pass, anyway. Family duty calls. I'm sorry."

Jordan looked upset. "That's too bad. We would've had a great time." He grew quiet for a moment. "Is there any way you can reschedule with your uncle for Sunday? We can come back real early that morning."

"I don't think so. Uncle Brian spends practically all of Sunday in church. He's a stickler for keeping that day holy. Our entire family attends church regularly. However, I can ask him if we can meet earlier in the week. He may be open to that. But if he can't do it any other day than Saturday, I won't be able to go camping. My word has always been my bond, Jordan. I made a promise to help my uncle out, and I feel obligated to keep it."

"That's highly commendable, Scotland. There are times when all we really have is our word. That's why it's so important for me to keep any promises I make to Gregory."

"It's imperative, Jordan. That's the best way to win over his little heart."

Jordan suddenly got a funny look on his face. The mention of the holy day had caused an age-old question to rise from deep within him. "Do you believe God's real, Scotland? If so, how do you know for a fact that He really exists?"

That Jordan's question had caught Scotland completely by surprise was obvious by the stunned expression on her face. Since his question had come right out of the blue, she couldn't help wondering what had made him ask it in the first place. Regardless of his reason for asking, she was going to answer him—and relish doing so. God was one of her favorite topics of conversation. "I know He's real, Jordan, by all the things He's done in my life. Besides that, there's evidence of His existence all around us."

"Like what?"

Scotland looked perplexed. That Jordan might not know the answer to his question concerned and saddened her. Maybe he did know and was just testing her belief in God. At any rate, he'd knocked on the right door. Sharing her love for God with others was one of her greatest purposes in life.

Scotland folded her hands and put them on the table. She looked up at the clock on the wall to see how much time was left before the coffeehouse closed. She didn't want to delve too deeply if there wasn't enough time to really explore the question of God's existence. An hour remained until closing, which gave her time to scratch below the surface.

"That is one question that always astounds me. How can anyone look up at the sky, hear the birds singing, gaze at the majestic mountains, stroll along the ocean's shore, and still ask that question? Man's hands shaped none of those amazing miracles I just mentioned. God *is* real, Jordan, and He's certainly real to me. Nothing exists without Him, including you and me. God resides inside of us so that we may live and breathe through Him."

A single tear fell from the corner of Jordan's right eye. Then a few more drops cascaded from both of his eyes. "I'd like to believe all of that, Scotland, but I haven't been able to find Him for many years now. How am I supposed to locate Him when I don't even know where to begin looking? How do I converse with something or someone I can't even see?"

The revelation of exactly why Jordan had come into her life hit Scotland like a ton of bricks. God *had* ordained their meeting, just as she'd suspected. His asking about God out of the blue had revealed that much to her. Had God sent Jordan to her for some sort of guidance and direction? If so, God would direct her path in this, too. Her optimism arose from the ashes.

Scotland was all choked up inside. Swallowing the lump in her throat seemed darn near impossible. Fighting back her tears was just as difficult. "He's only a whisper away, within a prayer's reach, Jordan," she finally managed. "Call on Him. He'll hear you, and then He'll answer, but only in His time. You don't have to see Him because you'll feel Him. He'll let you know He's present."

Scotland went on to tell Jordan that those may not be the answers he wanted to hear, but that God would only do what He thought was best for his life. Although she was thrilled that Jordan wanted to talk with her about God, she wasn't sure he was fully prepared to receive the answers. That he was in a search mode was apparent, but she wondered how deeply he really wanted to go in his spiritual investigation. Whatever Jordan's spiritual needs were, she vowed to do her best to help him meet them. "Would you like to go to church with me one day, Jordan?"

Jordan thought hard about her question, upset with himself that he'd gotten into this particular conversation. Scotland had a way of extracting all sorts of troubling things from deep within him. He wished it wasn't so easy for him to let himself go with her. Getting too involved with her could spell another emotional disaster for him, yet he couldn't seem to prevent himself from surrendering to her intoxicating magnetism. Even though he was highly curious about the Creator, he was also embarrassed by his lack of knowledge of Him. "Is attending church the only way I can seek God?"

Shaking her head in the negative, Scotland smiled gently. "There are people all over the world who've never seen the inside of a church, Jordan, and there are those who've never had access to a Bible, yet they know Him and worship Him from wherever they stand. In turn, He meets them right where they are. As I said before, God resides in the hearts of his creations. He's always as close to us as our own breath. We should congregate and fellowship with each other, but that's not always possible." Ecclesiastes 4:9-12 was the first passage of scripture to come to Scotland's mind as she thought about fellowship. I John 1:3, 7 came next. Scotland then recited Matthew 18:20. "For where two or three are gathered together in my name, there I am in the midst of them."

Suddenly feeling completely out of his element, Jordan began to experience jagged pangs of discomfort. Talking about a subject he knew very little about was disconcerting for him. He didn't want to appear totally ignorant in front of Scotland. He'd heard that ignorance was bliss, but he wasn't feeling the least bit blissful over his lack of God and Bible knowledge. In fact, he felt downright intimidated. It was then that Jordan silently vowed to finally begin reading the world's best-selling book. The Bible he'd purchased a couple of months ago had been collecting dust on his nightstand.

Jordan glanced down at his wristwatch. He didn't want to end this conversation, but he'd gotten in way over his head and was terribly fearful of getting in any deeper. "I'd better run, Scotland. I have a lot to do before this night ends."

Scotland looked Jordan right in the eye. "Running

away isn't the answer, Jordan. I get the sense that you're somewhat ashamed of yourself. You don't have to feel embarrassed over what you don't know about God. No one knows everything about Him. I won't ever make you feel inadequate when we're talking about God or the Bible, or any other subject for that matter. Okay?"

Jordan smiled sheepishly. "Are you free for the next couple of hours?"

Scotland looked puzzled. "Free for what?"

"I think I want to continue our discussion."

Scotland lifted an eyebrow. "Think?"

Jordan grinned. "I know for sure I do. We can go to my place. So, are we on?"

Scotland stifled a giggle. "Absolutely."

Having difficulty falling asleep was becoming all too commonplace for Jordan. He'd begun suffering insomnia after meeting the incomparable Scotland Kennedy. Much to his dismay, he had to admit that she had him going around in circles. One minute he wanted to be with her in every way, and then, in the very next instant, he thought he should distance himself from her altogether. All these mixed emotions had him feeling a little insane. A grown man should be very clear about the direction in which he wanted to take his personal life, but he hadn't the slightest clue as to where his was going.

At Scotland's suggestion, Jordan had begun reading Genesis, the first book of the Bible, after she left his house that night, but he hadn't been able to make heads or tails of most of what he'd perused. After reading the first chapter, he was no closer to understanding it than he was when he'd first laid eyes on it years before. The second chapter, which dealt with the Creation, had made a little more sense to him.

Jordan had phoned Scotland a couple of times to ask

her a few questions, but he'd had second thoughts each time because of the late hour. She hadn't left his home until nearly midnight, and now it was after two o'clock in the morning. He didn't think she'd take too kindly to being awakened at such a bewitching hour. Just because he couldn't sleep didn't mean he should deprive Scotland of a good night's rest.

Jordan allowed his thoughts to zero in on his parents, something he rarely did. It was hard for him to think of his mother in particular. Once she had been so beautiful, inside and out, but Regina had completely let herself go. Drug and alcohol abuse had taken their toll on her good looks and gentle nature. During the times when she was strung out on one thing or another, her clothes never looked clean and pressed, and her hair was always in disarray.

The last time Jordan had seen Regina, she looked pretty much like her old self. It seemed to him that she had once again started to care about her overall appearance. Her clothes were fashionable, and they fit her slender figure very nicely. Her hair also appeared salon fresh.

It had blown Jordan away to learn that Regina and James had started going to church. Regina had tried to talk to him about God that day, but he'd completely rejected the idea of them as born-again Christians. They might be able to talk the talk, but he didn't know for sure if they were actually walking the walk. He had only seen his mother two or three times in the last couple of months, but he'd yet to see or talk with his father. Regina had asked Jordan if he'd have lunch with her and his dad, but he'd turned her down. He might've jumped at the opportunity had she asked him to have lunch with just her.

Breaking bread with a straight-up demon was a no-no for Jordan.

Jordan was very uncomfortable around his father. He thought it would be much easier for him to forgive his mother than his father. But he wasn't in the mood to forgive either one at the moment. He blamed James for all that had gone wrong in his life and for all the things that his mother had gone through. James had introduced his mother to a world that no man should ever introduce anyone to, especially his own wife. Jordan felt that he had been robbed of a happy, stable home because of the irresponsible actions of both parents.

Jordan's father hadn't led or taught by example. Had Jordan patterned himself after his dad, he knew he would've become a lost cause. Although he'd found himself on that same destructive path for a minute or two, he had turned things around before it was too late. Jordan had long ago vowed never to take another taste of alcohol as long as he lived. The vivid nightmare he'd had about drowning in his car had taken away his desire for all harmful vices.

Jordan's deep desire to tap into his spiritual side was overwhelming. He had felt this restlessness in his soul for some time now. He knew next to nothing about God, but in recent months he'd grown very curious about this supernatural being that people touted as the Creator. Growing up as a street kid, with parents who'd paid him very little attention, Jordan knew more about surviving the mean streets of L.A. than he'd ever know about religion.

Then beautiful Scotland had popped into his life, or he into hers. However he wanted to look at it, they'd come together at the same place and at the same time, causing his lack of spirituality to stick out like a sore thumb. She'd seemed very angelic to him from the beginning, but their recent conversations had confirmed for him how deeply her spirituality ran.

Was there a specific purpose for their meeting? Why

had Scotland really come into his life? He had to wonder.

Jordan looked over at his Bible for the umpteenth time, something he'd done every single day since purchasing it. He'd heard that the Bible was the number one best seller in the world, but it was still the book least read. He didn't know what had kept him from opening it until now, but he was glad that he'd finally begun reading it.

Although he desperately wanted to know God, Jordan's fears were greater than his desire. God had been used as a weapon of mass destruction in his home. The only time his parents ever mentioned God was in the context of punishment. When he'd done something wrong, he was told about all the horrible things God would do to him if he didn't behave himself. For a child, the notion of burning in hell for all eternity was a scary thing. Who'd want to know a God who'd intentionally burn you at the stake? Where was the love in that act of utter cruelty?

Jordan suddenly realized he feared God's punishment more than he relished His love.

CHAPTER FIVE

Listening to Nathan talking about Brianna and how much he loved her made Scotland want to cry happy tears. Her father and uncle also looked ready to let loose with a tear or two. She only hoped that her cousin knew how blessed she was to have a man who cared so much about her. Scotland would give anything to have someone like Brianna's Nathan.

Scotland Kennedy, you do have someone very much like him, she reminded herself. Jordan more than likely possessed all the same wonderful qualities as Nathan, but his numerous fears made him keep everything pent up inside. Sure that it would happen one day soon, Scotland couldn't wait to see Jordan open up to the world like a flower to sunlight. He'd been in the dark too long.

Scotland laughed heartily, looking down at her wrist-watch. "Okay, Nate, I think we all get the picture—and we all know for a fact that you love Brianna like crazy. Now can we please get back to the plans for the party? I have a weekend trip to prepare for."

Nathan laughed, too. "Sorry, everyone. You know how it is when I start talking about my sweetie. I can go on and on and on. Getting back to the business at hand, I've hired someone to organize a karaoke session. The guests can enjoy the music, and Brianna will be able to see the words to the songs on a video screen. Even though she dances to her own inner tunes, I didn't want to hire a band for the party."

"The karaoke session is definitely more appropriate," Brian said to Nathan. "There'll be other guests attending that are also hearing impaired. I think it's a great idea."

"Me, too," Scotland chimed in. "What about you, Dad? Do you like the idea?"

Scott nodded, smiling at his beautiful daughter. "Love it. Knowing our Brianna as we do, she'll be up there with the mike in her hand, singing her heart out. She'll enjoy the karaoke idea more than a band. Have you found out if the hotel can accommodate a karaoke session, Nate?"

"Yeah, I checked that out with the catering sales rep before I started looking for someone to hire. Shannon assured me that it's not a problem."

"Okay, so we have the music taken care of," Scotland said, checking it off her list. "I also need to check with Shannon to see if we can bring in a cake from an outside bakery. Brianna loves the cakes from the Crème Crop Bakery. I can't imagine her party without her favorite cake. The hotel catering office may let us bring our own cake if we order a birthday cake from them as well."

"I checked that out, too," Nate said. "We can do it, but they'll charge us a cutting fee. She started out with a dollar per slice, but I got her down to fifty cents. As if we can't cut the cake ourselves. But that's the hotel's way of making money. It's the same as wine corking fees. That won't be a problem since we aren't having wine."

Brian stoked his chin. "I'm not concerned at all with the expenses. This is the first adult birthday bash I've ever thrown for Brianna. Let's not make money a factor in planning the very best party she's ever had. It'll be her special night, and I want her to enjoy it to the fullest."

As the group finalized their plans for the birthday bash, Scotland saw that they had nothing much to worry about, since Nathan had covered all the bases. He had been very thorough in checking out all the services they'd need for that night. Once the plans were all confirmed, Brian led the small group in a moment of prayer.

After bidding her Uncle Brian and Nathan a good evening, Scotland left arm in arm with her father, who was seeing her safely to her car. She could tell that he had something on his mind. The nervous twitching of his eyes was a dead giveaway. Wanting to get a possible lecture over with, she leaned against the passenger door of her car. "What's up, Dad? You have that uneasy look."

Tousling her hair playfully, Scott grinned. "You know me too well, don't you?" His expression then sobered. "It's this camping trip I'm concerned about. You don't know this fellow well enough to be going off into the woods with him. What if he turns out to be a big, bad bear?"

Scotland cracked up. "Dad, I already told you that Jordan and I won't be alone. A whole group of folks will be with us, many of them teenagers. Most of the adults are associated with the judicial system in some capacity, and some are members of area churches. It's a camping trip for underprivileged kids. Everything will be just fine."

Scott brought Scotland into his loving embrace. "I guess I'd better be okay with this trip, since I know I can't get you to change your mind. Make sure your cell phone stays charged. If you feel the slightest bit of discomfort in your surroundings, call me and I'll come get you."

Scotland couldn't help laughing. Her dad would always fuss over her like she was a two-year-old. There was nothing she could do to change that—and she really didn't want to. Knowing she was so loved was one of the things that had helped her become the woman she was today. Her confidence and self-assuredness were born out of all the love she'd been showered with as a child. Scott had sheltered Scotland to a certain degree, but he'd also given her plenty of freedom. A good parent, her dad had constantly given Scotland plenty of guidance, but he'd also allowed her to choose her own path. In allowing her to make her own choices, he knew he was permitting her to make her own mistakes. He had loads of confidence in Scotland. Over the years his daughter had proved herself to be responsible and quite reliable. Scott was extremely proud of the way he'd raised his and Victoria's precious daughter.

Scotland hugged her father tightly. "This little girl of yours has been all grown up for some time now. She'll be okay. I promise to call if I get into difficulty. I'll call you either way. I understand how you feel about me going off with someone I don't know. But I do know him, Dad, though I can't explain how. You've experienced this with Mom, so I know you know. You and Mom fell in love before knowing each other's name. If it happened like that for you two, it can happen for me, too. For whatever reason, no matter how crazy it seems, I feel that Jordan's the man for me. Trust me to know my own heart."

Scott smiled gently, giving his daughter another warm hug. "I do trust you, Scotty, and I know *you* know that. You haven't failed yourself yet."

* * *

Seated in front of a crackling fire, with Jordan right next to her, was the last place Scotland would've imagined herself being this soon, especially after the way he'd been doing all he could to keep her at bay. There were twelve other people present, but to her it felt like only the three of them existed. Gregory sat to Jordan's left, and Scotland thought the boy looked happier than she'd ever seen him. His face was aglow with the huge grin he kept pasted on his lips. The constant attention Jordan showered on Gregory had helped him to blossom. There was no mistaking the excitement and contentment brimming in the preteen's eyes. In fact, it seemed to Scotland that both Gregory and Jordan enjoyed a certain degree of satisfaction. Although Gregory was preoccupied with his Game Boy, she felt that he was happy as a lark to be hanging out with Jordan far away from his foster home.

It was too dark out to see much of anything but the white caps sloshing against the sandy shore. The sea breeze was both chilling and electrifying to Scotland, but there were plenty of blankets around to keep warm. Seeing so many stars lighting up the sky was unusual in the city, but not in many of the coastal areas. Scotland thought there was something wonderful about the smell of skewered hot dogs and marshmallows roasting over a fire in a large metal pit. The silver moon provided a romantic ambiance.

The tranquil atmosphere surrounding her brought back to Scotland the summer weiner roasts the Kennedy men had often staged in the backyard for their two daughters and their neighbor friends. Marshmallows weren't on the menu back then, but it hadn't mattered. Any time their family and friends got together, it was always loads of fun.

Jordan started to take a bite of his hot dog, but then

he suddenly presented it to Scotland. "I'll let you be the first to test my outdoor cooking skills."

As Scotland nibbled on one end of the slightly charred hot dog which Jordan held for her, their eyes locked in a heart-melting stare. Then her tongue accidentally brushed his fingers. Upon hearing his sharp intake of breath, a wave of smoldering heat slithered right through her. Seeing that he wasn't as immune to her as he'd have her think had her smiling inwardly. She affected him, too.

It took Jordan several seconds to recover from the tingling sensation of Scotland's tongue on his skin. Although the sensuous contact had been innocent enough, it had blown his mind. He had to drag his eyes away from her beautiful face. "How was it?"

Scotland picked up a paper napkin and wiped a spot of ketchup from the corner of her mouth. "Very good. Almost as delicious as your cinnamon toast."

After taking a bite of the hot dog, Jordan closed his eyes. "Mm, it is good. Take another bite of mine, Scotland. I can always get another one. There are plenty more."

That Jordan wanted to share his food with her made Scotland feel special. He could've easily suggested that she get her own hot dog, but she was so glad that he hadn't. She loved the warm feelings his kind and rather intimate gesture had stirred up inside of her. There was something to be said about a man who was willing to share his meal with someone when he didn't have to. There were more than enough hot dogs, snacks, and desserts to feed everyone a few times over. The group actually had an overflowing abundance of goodies.

Upon hearing the soft strumming of guitar strings, Scotland looked over to where the music was coming from. One of the camping guides, Trevor Jackson, was playing the guitar. Scotland could play it, too, but she wasn't about to reveal her talent. Her dad had begun teaching her to play both the guitar and the piano when she was ten. Since her mother had served as the musical director at their church, Scott had known without a doubt that Victoria would've wanted her daughter to study music. Scotland regretted that Gregory couldn't hear the music, but if he was anything like Brianna, he'd surely feel it.

Jordan found the music sweet and scintillating. In a playful manner, he lightly touched Scotland's shoulder, smiling brilliantly at her. He loved all the heady sensations that had been coursing wildly through him since he'd first picked her up at her home. Each time he touched her or their eyes met, he felt something new and wonderful. He wasn't sure if that was a good thing or not, especially given the current predicaments in his life. Yet he vowed to enjoy it all.

Butterflies in his stomach weren't something Jordan was used to. Of course, he mused, Scotland's proximity to him probably had a lot to do with his nervousness. He wondered if she noticed the unusual quaking in his stomach. He sure hoped not. That would be downright embarrassing.

"Can anyone else play the guitar?" Trevor asked, his eyes scanning the lively group.

Unable to stop herself, and yet reluctant, Scotland raised her hand. How could she deny something she loved so much? She couldn't, no more than she could deny her dizzying feelings for Jordan La Cour. At the moment they both made her heart feel like singing.

In awe of her newly revealed talent, Jordan gazed softly at Scotland's face, wondering why he wasn't terribly surprised. *Angels played golden harps, so why not guitars,* he concluded. As far as he was concerned, Scotland was definitely an angel. He was sure that quite a number of other people saw her in the same angelic light. Jordan couldn't help wondering if God forbade mortal man to fall in love with His glorious angels.

"Will you play a song or two for us, Scotland?" Trevor inquired, smiling in admiration.

When Gregory gave Scotland a puzzled look, she explained to him what was going on. He then jumped up and down, clapping his hands in excitement, surprising everyone. His desire for her to play the guitar, though he wouldn't hear it, touched Scotland deeply.

Wiring him a dazzling smile, Scotland winked her left eye at Gregory. She then looked back at Trevor. "After that animated show of support from my little buddy, I get the feeling I'd be in big trouble if I don't play. Any requests?" She signed her question for Gregory out of respect for him. The last thing she wanted was for him to feel left out.

"'Amazing Grace,'" Trevor shouted. "One of my favorites."

"Thank God I know that one," Scotland said with a deep sigh. "I'll play it if everyone who knows the words agrees to sing along. Okay?"

Several nods and loud sounds of approval instantly came her way.

Upon strumming the first notes, Scotland also began singing the words to the song. Then her eyes closed as she lost herself in the sweet chords of music. Her slender fingers caressed the strings as if they were stroking a newborn babe. She felt a surge of peace wash right through her, the kind of serenity that washed burdens away. Scotland then felt God's presence in this place.

Although He always resided in her heart, was always close by, she strongly felt Him there in their midst. Perhaps He had dropped in to enjoy the concert being held on one of His finest beaches. Handing out amazing grace was one of His specialties. The title of the song she performed was a fitting tribute to His goodness and unyielding love. Knowing God was there beside her, Scotland relaxed completely, and her voice took on a richness that hadn't been there before.

Jordan gasped within, feeling the music reaching down deep into his soul. He already knew that Scotland had the disposition of an angel; now he could hear that she had the voice of one. He closed his eyes, too, imagining her strumming his heart in the same gentle way she stroked the stringed instrument. As she had already touched him a time or two, he knew that her hands were warm and tender, soothing and healing.

Well aware that he was losing his battle against his desire to know her in every way possible, Jordan sighed deeply. Should he just concede to his strong feelings for her or continue to fight a war he didn't think he had a chance of winning?

Suddenly realizing that she was the only one singing—though, unbeknownst to her, she'd been solo for a while—Scotland opened her eyes and saw all the orbs fastened on her. "You all promised to sing along," she shrieked, laughing softly. "Looks like everyone reneged on their promise."

Looking totally mesmerized by Scotland, Trevor smiled warmly at her. "Sorry. Your voice completely took us over, and we were all compelled to just sit back and listen. You've got a great set of pipes, Scotland. I could listen to you sing all night long. Maybe you could come down to the community center where I work part time and play for the kids there. I know everyone would love to have you as a guest performer. I'll give you my business card before the trip is over. I hope you'll at least visit the center."

Scotland smiled back at Trevor. "That would be nice, Trevor. Thanks for asking."

Trevor was eyeing Scotland with such intensity that Jordan took instant notice. The look unnerved Jordan.

As he tried to assess Scotland's response to Trevor, he felt streaks of jealousy racing up and down his spine, causing him quite a bit of discomfort.

Yet another foreign emotion had Jordan going nuts. He hadn't ever been jealous of another man, except for his father. James La Cour had been king in their house. His word had been gospel. The relationship between his parents had been a very unhealthy one, but Regina adored James. Jordan often wished his mother had not chosen the ill will of his father over him. He felt that James had done everything in his power to separate him from his mother's love. When excluded by Regina, Jordan had always felt jealous of his father.

Jordan then recalled Trevor asking him earlier if he and Scotland were an item. His quick response to the question had Jordan mentally kicking himself. "No, she's nothing more than my sign language instructor and a friend," roared loudly in his ears. *What a stupid answer,* he mused. Although he really didn't know how he should've responded to Trevor, he certainly shouldn't have given the impression that Scotland didn't mean anything to him.

Nothing was further from the honest-to-goodness truth.

Although it would make a liar out of him in Trevor's eyes, Jordan knew that he had to restate his position. He somehow had to show Trevor that Scotland was very important to him, that he wanted their relationship to go beyond instructor and friend. Jordan felt that it was time to make some kind of telltale romantic move on her, that is, if he was to keep from losing her to someone else, someone like the seemingly already smitten Trevor. Actions always spoke louder than words. Jordan was amazed at how another man's interest in the very same woman could cause a brother to quickly reevaluate his former position.

Admitting to himself that Scotland meant quite a lot

to him was hard for Jordan, but he figured it was easier for him to accept it than it was to continue denying it. Denial was one of Jordan's strongest adversaries. He'd lived most of his adult life in a state of contradiction, but he could clearly see that it was time for him to make a few serious changes.

To reclaim her attention from Trevor, Jordan nudged Scotland with his shoulder. "Why didn't you tell me you could play and sing? Any other hidden talents I should know about?"

Scotland looked right into Jordan's eyes. "You never asked. But it's not that big of a deal, except for when I sing in the church choir. I love singing God's praises. Since you've asked, I also play the piano. As for all my other talents, you'll just have to stick around to see."

Wanting desperately to stick around Scotland, Jordan liked the sound of that. Discovering her other hidden talents would give him something to look forward to. He could only imagine the intriguing things about Scotland yet to be revealed. "I see that you give God praise in so many different ways. I guess you're what's called a witness, huh?"

Scotland thought Jordan's statement was very interesting. That he saw her as a witness for Christ was quite a compliment. "Well, yeah, I guess you could say that. I do love talking about the Father above. To really understand why I feel the way I do, you'd have to know about all the miracles He has performed in the lives of my family . . . and in mine." Scotland turned to face Gregory. "Are you enjoying yourself, sweetie?"

Gregory laid down his Game Boy so his hands would be free to respond. "This is the best time I've ever had. These people don't seem to notice I can't hear. Can we do this again sometime? Maybe next weekend?" Gregory's eyes had lit up to match his enthusiasm.

Jordan chuckled. "Whoa, little fellow, maybe we

should slow down a bit so we can enjoy this camping trip. But I'm sure we'll find time to do this again, as well as other fun activities."

Proud of the way he had signed his response to Gregory, Jordan smiled, patting himself on the back. He hadn't resorted to finger spelling. He had Scotland to thank for his progress, since she constantly shored up his confidence by always reassuring him that he was doing just fine in her class. She also kept reminding him that he had to use his skills often if he wanted to become proficient. Because he'd known that was true, he had only signed in the class from the very beginning. His desire from the onset had been to communicate effectively with young Gregory.

"Yeah," Gregory's animated fingers enthused. "I can't wait to tell everyone I know."

Scotland reached over and mussed Gregory's hair. "I'm thrilled to see you so happy."

Recalling all the red tape he'd had to go through to get this trip scheduled made Jordan bristle inwardly. Had it not been for the efforts of those at the community center, Gregory might not have been permitted to come along. There were certain policies in place that forbade juvenile probation officers from getting directly involved in their clients' personal lives, but Jordan had found a way around that by getting the counselors at the center to intervene on Gregory's behalf.

In order for Gregory to participate in the special outing, he had to travel in the community center van along with the rest of the group, but separate from Jordan, who followed closely behind in his own vehicle. He would also return home with the group. The ride to the beach was such a short one that Jordan wasn't concerned with communication issues. Also, there was one counselor in the group who was taking a course in sign language. Jordan was no longer worried about getting

Gregory involved in other activities, since he now knew how to make it happen.

After Scotland had returned the guitar to Trevor, he led the group in singing several more songs. He had a great voice, too, which made Jordan realize that music was something special that Scotland and Trevor had in common. He couldn't sing a lick, nor could he play any instrument, so he knew he couldn't compete there.

After Jordan thought more about Trevor's possible interest in Scotland, he decided that he would not engage in a competition for her with Trevor. If nothing else, she had come there with him—and she'd be leaving with him. That alone gave him the upper hand, Jordan mused. Seeing her in class every week and living in the very same housing development improved his odds.

Jordan leaped to his feet and reached his hand out for Scotland to take. "I think it would be downright sinful for us to waste all this beautiful moonlight. Up to taking a stroll with me?"

Before Scotland could voice her thoughts, Jordan walked over and helped Gregory to his feet. She had to wonder if he'd read her mind. She hadn't wanted to go off and leave the young boy behind, especially since this trip was supposed to be all about him. Her smile showed how happy she was that Jordan hadn't intended to exclude Gregory from their trek down the beach.

As though this was his very own family, Jordan positioned himself in between Scotland and Gregory, tossing an arm around each of their shoulders. Why it felt so darn good to embrace them, Jordan didn't know, but that didn't stop him from savoring every single moment. All they had was right now. For all he knew, tomorrow might never come.

Walking only inches from the water, the threesome could be heard laughing. Jordan sensed that Gregory had a yearning to feel the water beneath his feet, so he encouraged him to take his shoes off and kick up the surf. It had saddened Jordan when he'd learned earlier that Gregory had never been to the coast. Because he'd run across many children in Los Angeles who'd never been to the beach, the news hadn't surprised Jordan.

Jordan and Scotland weren't able to resist the temptation of the water, either. Skipping around in the surf with Gregory was a delightful experience for both of them. The risk of catching a cold didn't matter to the adults, but Jordan was concerned for Gregory, so he called a halt to the frolicking in the water only minutes later.

Scotland believed that this was a special night for each of them to remember. She couldn't have hoped for a better outing. She felt that she and Jordan had made a lot of headway with each other. He seemed so comfortable with her now. She didn't know what tomorrow might hold, but she was now more optimistic about their future. Things had finally started to look up for them. Scotland believed that romance was waiting for them just around the next corner.

For whatever reason, Jordan had relaxed and had finally let down his guard. He wasn't shutting her out like before, and Scotland no longer felt that his arms were blocking the entry to his heart. Jordan had made a few intimate gestures toward her, which had thrilled her. She couldn't have asked for more in that area either. Time would eventually tell all. Scotland had to believe that time was now on their side.

Scotland was also very pleased with her and Jordan's loving interaction with Gregory. A special bond had formed between the three of them. There was no doubt in her mind that the young boy was having the time of his life. Although she was rather concerned about Gregory's future and hoped his criminal activities were a thing of the past, she was sure Jordan would see to it that he had a bright one. He seemed truly committed to Gregory. Glad that she'd decided to come along on the overnight camping trip, Scotland sighed with contentment.

The feel of Scotland's small hand entwined with his positively electrified Jordan. Her skin was so soft and velvety, it felt like he was holding a handful of rose petals. The tantalizing scent of her perfume had not faded despite the hours they'd spent outdoors. She smelled like she'd just recently stepped out of a scented bath.

Jordan stopped dead in his tracks and then brought Scotland into his arms, happy that he'd already sent Gregory back to the campsite to put on dry clothes. He looked as surprised as she did when he pulled her so close. He'd embraced her without giving it a moment's thought. Holding her felt so natural to him, but it also scared him. He'd shown quite a bit of intimacy toward her throughout the evening, but how she really felt about being in his arms had him worried, though she didn't look as if she minded.

Holding her slightly away from him, he looked deeply into her eyes. "Comfortable?"

Scotland brought her forehead within a fraction of his. "Very. What about you?"

Jordan fought the urge to kiss her forehead and then take possession of her mouth. "In every way. I find comfort in just being with you. Does that scare you as much as it does me?"

Scotland gently placed her hand over his heart. "I've learned not to fear what I have no control over. In time, you'll learn that, too."

Jordan looked over at Scotland and smiled. Seeing her nestled cozily in the sleeping bag had his heart doing flip-flops. With her hair spilled out over her pillow, she was already fast asleep. Awake or asleep, he thought she was beautiful. She looked so comfortable and totally at peace. He smiled broadly as he recalled the last thing she'd said to him before falling off to sleep. Scotland had made him an offer that he hadn't been able to turn down, one that he was actually looking forward to.

"You've cooked cinnamon toast, and you've roasted hot dogs for me, so now it's my turn to show off my culinary skills. Dinner at my place tomorrow night?"

Gregory was knocked out, too, Jordan noticed, his heart growing full at the sight of the sleeping boy. Gregory's day had been a very active one. He had expended quite a bit of energy. That Gregory was completely exhausted didn't surprise Jordan one bit. Since both of his companions had deserted him for the sweet peace of sleep, Jordan suddenly felt alone again. A few of the other campers were still milling about, but the two people he could relate to the most had checked out on him for the night.

Beginning to feel sleepy, Jordan settled down into his sleeping bag and closed his eyes. Slumbering right next to a beautiful woman, yet so far away from her, was a new experience for him. Although his physical desire for Scotland was strong, he had yet to have the intense cravings he'd often felt in the presence of other women. Getting to really know her, inside and out, was far more important to Jordan than satisfying the wild, urgent needs of his masculinity.

Fleetingly, Jordan allowed his mind to entertain thoughts of Cynthia. Finding out what had happened to her would make all the difference in the world to his future. Knowing all the details of her disappearance would make it so much easier for him to lose himself to love. He could definitely fall in love with Scotland, if he hadn't already done so. He'd never been in love before, but that was really the only name he could put to what he felt for Miss Kennedy. Every experience he'd had thus far with her felt new and wonderful.

The mysterious disappearance of Cynthia might never be solved, Jordan mused, but loving Scotland could turn out to be a sure thing, a wonderful mystery yet to unfold.

Turning on his side, Jordan groaned at the sudden burst of pain in his hip. The hard ground was a far cry from his comfortable mattress at home, but Jordan tried to imagine that he was resting on a fluffy cloud. With his guardian angel right there to keep an eye on him, he suddenly felt blessed. He'd never felt this way before, yet he was sure that he had received a blessing from God in the form of Scotland.

Even though Jordan recognized Scotland as a keeper, he knew he wasn't spiritually good enough for her. He didn't have to be a genius to know that she needed a godly man in her life, a man that knew her God in every sense of the word. His deficiencies in that particular area were of monumental proportions. Was he capable of bringing about a spiritual change in himself?

Very pleased with how the camping trip had turned out, Jordan walked Scotland to her door, wishing their togetherness didn't have to end. He couldn't recall the last time he'd enjoyed himself so much. After following the van back to the community center, where they'd waited until Mr. Turner had picked up Gregory, he had stopped at the grocery store for a case of bottled water. Jordan had then talked Scotland into stopping by his office so he could retrieve his laptop, which he'd accidentally left behind on his last workday. Figuring he'd prolonged their parting long enough, he gave her a warm hug, bade her a good day, and then turned to walk away.

Hating for their time together to end, too, Scotland called out to Jordan, smiling when he turned back to face her. Even though he was coming for dinner later in the evening, she still wanted more in his company. "I make a sinful batch of silver dollar pancakes. I also plan to cook up a few turkey sausage links. Care to join me for a late Sunday breakfast, Mr. La Cour?"

Jordan knew he was grinning like a Cheshire cat, but he didn't care one iota about how silly he probably looked. "I'd love to have breakfast with you, but only if the offer doesn't cancel out our dinner date for tonight."

Scotland sighed a breath of relief. "Looks like we're on, then. Come on inside."

Jordan couldn't seem to concentrate on the probation cases he'd decided to look over before going to work on Monday morning. Over the last hour all he'd accomplished was a bunch of doodling on a piece of white bond paper, on which he'd also written down Scotland's name a couple dozen times. He hadn't been able to get her off his mind. Everything about this sweet woman held him captive. Jordan just couldn't wait to see her later in the evening.

Over breakfast Scotland had had him hanging on her every word. She was so knowledgeable on a variety of topics, but the one thing that had surprised him most was her passion for politics. Her views about the last presidential election had been most intriguing. It was her belief that it didn't matter who had won the presidency, not when God was in control of the entire world. She felt that everyone on the planet who be-

lieved wholeheartedly in the Almighty and dared to
stand on His promises was going to be just fine.

Scotland didn't feel that survival was solely depen-
dent on what the government did or didn't do for the
people. Her outlook on many of the issues that most
Americans were gravely concerned about had astounded
him. She wasn't that worried about the economy, but
she was very compassionate about the war and those
who'd died in it. Her prayers were constant for those in
the military and their loved ones. She also believed that
every war ever fought was a part of prophecy being fulfilled, citing the wars and rumors of wars found in
Matthew 24:6. She told Jordan that he'd begin to understand what she was talking about regarding prophecy
after he read some of the correlating stories in the
Bible. With God at her beck and call, Scotland felt fearless.

That Scotland relied solely on God for her every
want and need was inconceivable to Jordan. Not only
did she rely on God, she trusted Him to deliver. She'd
told him that in order to achieve anything she desired,
she knew she had to believe in Him. That kind of faith
in God was foreign to him. Jordan was eager to learn
more about God, and he had some very significant
questions to pose to one Scotland Kennedy.

Seven o'clock couldn't come soon enough for
Jordan.

Forcing himself to get back to his work, Jordan
picked up a manila folder and opened it. After carefully
perusing its contents, he laid it back down, shaking his
head in dismay.

Another sad case, he mused. A preteen committing
armed robbery and aggravated assault was all too
commonplace these days. The young boy hadn't fired
the gun, but he'd held it on the store owner while the
older guy had emptied out the cash register. Once he'd

gotten what he'd come for, the kid had hit the owner with the gun several times, knocking him unconscious. The entire act had been caught on the hidden security camera's tape.

Mandatory sentences were imposed on defendants when a weapon was involved in a crime in the state of California. The prosecutor had wanted to charge the young man as an adult, but a compassionate judge had rejected the idea. Jordan agreed with the judge's decision. Putting another kid behind bars wouldn't solve the state's monumental problem of youth delinquency. There had to be a way to get through to the youths who were committing serious crimes, but so far a solution had eluded Jordan. Counseling didn't always work, but it was better than throwing kids behind bars and tossing away the key.

Oftentimes children committing serious offenses were a desperate cry for help.

Jordan looked over at the telephone when it rang, then reached over and picked it up. Upon hearing his mother's soft voice, he grew tense. Talking to her on the phone always left him drained by conversation's end. She always ended up demanding things of him that he couldn't possibly give. He didn't think this call would be an exception. Jordan hoped that their exchange wouldn't end up ruining the rest of his day, especially since he had a dinner date with Scotland.

"Hello, Mom."

CHAPTER SIX

Jordan admired Scotland's collection of beautiful, highly polished seashells, which were on display throughout her home. He hadn't noticed the vast array of shells earlier because his visit had been mainly confined to the kitchen. When she'd given him a short tour of her lovely home, he'd wondered if there was a story behind each shell. It seemed to him that the seashells weren't just insignificant décor. There were far too many of them for that.

The warmth of Scotland's family room gave Jordan a slight rush. The room was large yet cozy. She had the log lit in the gas fireplace, though it wasn't the least bit cold outside. All sorts of scented candles were burning, too. The sofas and chairs were done in fine leather. A variety of stunning African-American artwork graced the off-white walls.

When Scotland came back into the room, Jordan jumped up from the sofa. He then rushed over to help her with the glass appetizer tray she carried. Once he took it from her hands, he placed it on the coffee table. After she seated herself on the sofa, he reclaimed his seat.

As Scotland placed pieces of fried zucchini and squash, mozzarella cheese sticks, and onion straws on small plates, Jordan watched her every movement. He couldn't help noticing how delicate her hands were. He already knew they felt as soft as rose petals. He thought that she had gifted hands and that she used them for the good of others. Scotland communicated with her hands as well as she did with her beautiful mouth. Rose petal soft was how he imagined her kiss.

Unnerved by his thoughts, Jordan instantly turned them off. "All the seashells, Scotland. Is there a history behind them?"

Noticing how keenly interested Jordan seemed in her shell collection, Scotland smiled softly. "Each and every one has a story behind it. I love the sea and seashells. All of these represent the different coastal areas I've visited throughout the states and in foreign countries. Some of the seashells come from as far away as the Caribbean, Australia, Asia, and Europe. However, there are many foreign countries that don't allow tourists to remove the shells from their beaches. Parts of the Caribbean adhere to that rule."

Mention of the Caribbean caused Jordan to become momentarily distracted. That was one area he never planned to travel to again, despite its beauty. The unpleasant memories of his last visit there were a constant thorn in his side. Police officials there hadn't treated him too kindly. The entire trip had been and was still a total nightmare for Jordan.

Jordan stroked his chin. "World traveler, huh?"

Looking thoughtful, Scotland nodded. "I guess you could say that. I love to travel for pleasure, but I also attend a lot of educational symposiums throughout the world, mainly sign language conferences."

Jordan was impressed with her world travels. "Sounds

interesting. Mind telling me a few of the stories behind your shell collection?"

"Not at all." Scotland pointed at the large, polished conch shell on one corner of the coffee table. "That one came from Hawaii. Maui to be exact. I discovered it while snorkeling."

Scotland went on to point out a number of different shells on display in her family room, naming them for Jordan and telling him how they'd come into her possession. "Do you collect anything, Jordan?"

Jordan laughed. "A lot of dust around my house. No, just kidding. As a matter of fact, I collect sports pennants, specifically baseball. I also have quite a collection of autographed baseballs. Those I keep locked away in my closet." With his stomach growling, Jordan picked up a cheese stick and popped it into his mouth.

Follwing Jordan's lead, Scotland reached for a piece of the fried zucchini. "That explains why I didn't see them when I was at your house, but I think it's a shame to lock them away. Baseball, huh? I used to think it was the most boring sport in the world."

"Used to? What changed your mind?"

"Attending a game. It was way more exciting to be there versus watching it on television. I love seeing the unbelievable reactions of the fans. My dad is a baseball fanatic, so we all go with him to a couple of games a year. We're a Dodger blue family all the way."

Jordan clapped his hands. "A family after my own heart." *Family,* he mused.

Although Jordan never felt like he had ever belonged to a family, he liked the sound of the word, which connoted the bonds of kinfolks. Bonding had yet to happen with him and his parents, but they were still trying. His earlier conversation with his mother had him in a state of limbo. She wanted him to visit them in their home, and he wasn't so sure it was such a great idea. Seeing his father face-to-face was still a big problem for him.

Since Jordan didn't know how he could keep turning the invitations down, and because Regina had sounded more than a little odd to him, he had promised to call her no later than tomorrow with an answer. He still had no clue what his answer might be.

Scotland looked perplexed. "Jordan, are you okay? You're so quiet all of a sudden."

"I'm fine. I was distracted by something that occurred earlier. Nothing to worry about. Getting back to the Dodgers, I share season tickets with a couple of guys at work." A shiny pink seashell suddenly caught Jordan's eye, causing his mind to wander again. "What about this shell? It's so different from the others."

"Atlantic City. The beaches on the East Coast seem to yield much larger shells than those on the West Coast."

"Why did you start collecting shells in the first place?"

"They're beautiful and mysterious; many of them come from the very depths of the ocean. They make me real curious about life in the deep. I'm simply fascinated by seashells and their history."

Scotland got up from the sofa and walked across the room, where she removed a large album from the bookshelf. Once she was reseated on the sofa, she opened up the large volume. Inside the album were a variety of seashells mounted in deeply inset pages. The name of the seashell and where it was collected was printed below each one. Her love for the sea was apparent in her sparkling hazel eyes.

Jordan grinned. "Nature girl, that's what you are. For someone who'd never gone camping, I'd say you adapted to your surroundings pretty darn well. But then again, we were down by the ocean, a place you obviously love."

"I can't deny that." Scotland continued to talk about the seashells and other beautiful gifts of nature. "God created all these things of beauty, you know."

Shaking his head in the negative, Jordan raised an eyebrow. "No, I don't know. So why don't you enlighten me?"

Scotland didn't know if Jordan was being facetious or not. His expression revealed nothing more than his bland tone of voice had. She eyed him closely, hoping he'd say something else to let her know where he was coming from. When he remained quiet, looking like he was at odds with the world, she got to her feet. "I'm going to put dinner on the table. You can go sit in the dining room if you'd like."

Scotland knew men well enough to step back and let them work their dark moods out for themselves. She wasn't about to start babying Jordan and blaming herself for how he might or might not be feeling. Without giving him a chance to respond, Scotland left the room. Jordan had unnerved her, but she'd never let him know it. She hoped she hadn't offended him by talking about God. But if that was the case, they had a really big problem.

Singing His praises was what kept her hope alive. Scotland wouldn't stifle her love for God for anyone or anything. She had come too far in her faith to lose it now, especially over some man. In her opinion, love wasn't that blind, not blind enough to make her lose sight of what was most important in life. Hers had been a hard-fought battle. She still had to engage in a war against evil every single day. The closer she got to God, the harder Satan tried to win her for himself. Warding off the enemy wasn't always easy for her, but the second she remembered to put on the full armor of God, Scotland became tireless in battle.

Maybe Jordan needed to hear more about her struggles, see that he wasn't alone in facing adversity and dealing with tragic circumstances, which might help him understand his own conflicts. With that in mind, on her way into the kitchen, she turned on the CD player, which was stacked with nothing but spiritual music. She hoped the inspirational songs would be as uplifting to him as they always were to her. The sweet sounds and lyrics of gospel music were a powerful ministry, and they had a way of bringing about a mighty restoration of the soul. It was her best guess that Jordan needed spiritual healing, a complete divine makeover.

After slowly making his way into the dining room, Jordan took a seat at the head of the beautifully set table. His dad had always sat at the head, though it had been rare for them to take meals all at the same time. Jordan ate alone more often than not. For as long as he could remember, he had had to fend for himself at mealtime.

Cereal, milk, and canned soups had been Jordan's mainstay. He had found a few microwavable food items from time to time, but rarely had the pantry and refrigerator been abundantly stocked. He had taken a cooking course all four years of high school just so he'd know how to prepare solid meals for himself when he was grown and out on his own. At the age of sixteen, money from his part-time job had allowed him to purchase a piece of meat every now and then. Jordan had been a latchkey kid, a very sad, lonely one.

Scotland walked into the dining room and simply nodded at Jordan. When he gave her a broad smile, she felt relieved. It appeared to her that his dark mood had passed. After placing two large bowls of salad at each place setting, she retrieved from the kitchen a wild rice and mushroom casserole, steamed asparagus, and the fresh vegetable and fruit platters she'd prepared.

Condiments and a pitcher of white cranberry and

white grape juice mixed together were the last things Scotland placed on the table. Before seating herself, she turned off the light and lit the centerpiece candle-holder. Scotland loved to dine by candlelight, even when dining alone. With such a hectic pace at work, surrounded by constant evils, a serene atmosphere at home was important to her. She saw Jordan's eyebrows go up when she lit the candles, but she decided to ig-nore it. This was her space, and he had to learn to be comfortable in it if they were going to spend time to-gether.

Jordan bowed his head upon Scotland's gentle com-mand, listening intently to her humble prayer of thanksgiving. He'd already picked up his fork when she'd begun to pray. He felt embarrassed that he'd never been taught to pray before eating. That was an ac-ceptable excuse when he was a child, but he was an adult. Surely, by now he could've taught himself to at least give a few words of thanks. Jordan saw that he had a lot to learn about God; a long journey lay ahead of him if he was ever to know Him like Scotland did.

"Amen," Scotland said softly. "We can dig in now."

With an amused expression on his face, Jordan looked around at all the dishes. He then laughed heartily. "I can appreciate that nothing had to die for this meal, but, girl, I'm a meat-eater. Where's the beef!"

Scotland cracked up. Jordan's amber eyes, dancing with pure mischief, fascinated her. The expression on his face was so bratty yet so darn sweet. "I'm sorry. I guess I wasn't thinking about your dietary needs, but I should've been. I only eat meat once a day. The turkey sausages at breakfast satisfied my limit. Other than my family, I don't often have guests for dinner."

Wishing he hadn't confronted Scotland about her food choices, Jordan's eyes softened. He felt so sorry that he'd been rude to his hostess. "No need to apologize. Don't worry about it. We have a Popeye's right around the corner. I'll just stop by there before I go home. There may be something to eating healthy, but I'm a junk food junkie. I get plenty of exercise, though."

Scotland felt terribly embarrassed by her meatless blunder, but she wasn't going to come down too hard on herself. She'd only done what came naturally for her. There was no one else in her household to consider. And she was not used to cooking for men. She hoped Jordan didn't think she was selfish. It had simply been an honest oversight on her part.

Scotland laughed inwardly. If the only way to a man's heart was truly through his stomach, Scotland figured she'd blown it big time with Jordan. "I hope you won't hold my oversight against me, Jordan. I'm truly sorry about the meat."

Jordan reached over and briefly covered her hand with his. "Please don't give it another thought, Scotland. It was rude of me to even mention it. I had a hearty breakfast, wonderfully prepared by you, and I ate an even bigger lunch. I'm cool. I'm really just happy for this opportunity to have dinner with you." He dug in to show her how much he appreciated it.

The song playing in the background immediately snatched Jordan's attention away from the food. He loved the sound of the music, but he was interested in listening to the lyrics, especially since he'd heard mention of an angel. As he absorbed the wonderful lyrical content, the song grew and grew on him. Jordan remained silent until it was over.

Jordan turned his attention to Scotland. "Do you listen only to Christian music?"

Scotland shook her head, swallowing the food in her mouth. "I listen to all kinds of music, but I admit to being very choosy. When I need to be inspired, I turn to gospel. I don't listen to anything that denigrates women.

As for love ballads, the kind that uplift, I'm there. What about you, Jordan?"

Jordan shrugged. "I can't say I've ever really listened to gospel, at least not by choice. Of course, I've heard plenty of it. I'm a vocal jazz buff, but I'm also into easy listening music. Who sings the last song we just heard?"

"Ruben Studdard."

Jordan looked surprised. "The American Idol winner?"

Scotland giggled. "One and the same."

"I thought he was R & B."

"He sings both, but his roots are in gospel. The CD playing is his first gospel album. The last song we heard was "I Need An Angel," the CD's title track."

"That was a nice song. I loved it after hearing it only once." As Jordan continued to eat his meal, he kept his ear tuned to the music.

Jordan loved the first song because it reminded him of how much he needed an angel. Perhaps there was a God somewhere, and he had been praying to Him unconsciously. Was that the reason Scotland Kennedy had come into his life? Had he subconsciously prayed her into being? There was one thing he knew for sure. No mere mortal could've created the woman seated to his left. Lots of love and compassion were the basis of her creation.

Jordan looked over at Scotland, momentarily admiring her angelic beauty. He then cast her his brightest smile. "I'm sorry if I upset you earlier. I didn't mean to. Didn't know I had done something wrong until you walked out on me without saying a word."

Stunned by Jordan's assessment of what had happened earlier, Scotland tilted her head to the side. "Funny you should say that, since I thought I had offended you. I left the room to give you time to come to grips with whatever had annoyed you. I know I talk a lot about God, but I can't apologize for that. I normally say what I feel. My faith is what sustains me and makes my life worth living. I'd be completely lost without God."

The conviction in Scotland's eyes made Jordan's spine tingle. She was mentoring him in more ways than just sign language. She made him crave what she had. Peace seemed to surround her. Her inner glow was highly visible, so much so that the light from her dazzling halo darn near blinded him.

"You're perfect, aren't you, Scotland?"

"Of course, I am! I'm a portrait of absolute perfection." She harrumphed. "Get real, will you? I'm as far away from perfect as I can be. There is no such animal called *perfect*, not even your next-door neighbors."

Jordan laughed at that. "You're a good listener with a great memory. I forgot I'd even told you about my perfect neighbors. I have to agree with you, though. Perfection is not of this world, but that's how you seem to me."

Scotland laughed. "That's because you're just getting to know me. You've not heard my loud roar yet, nor have you felt the razor sharpness of my tongue, especially when I'm dissatisfied with something or someone. You don't know my dark, murderous thoughts when I hear in court some of the horrific things being done to children by their own parents. You couldn't possibly know how intolerant I am of ignorance. I can also be very judgmental. I'm a real sore loser and a boastful winner. All of the things I've mentioned are what make me human and tremendously sinful."

Scotland went on to tell Jordan that people, including her, had a way of justifying certain sins. A particular sin was okay for whatever reason, but that other sin was too far over the top to be forgiven. A sin was a transgression of God's law, she explained to him. No matter how big or small, a sin was a sin. Scotland then told Jordan that putting someone or something first before God was also a sin.

Jordan listened intently to everything Scotland had to say. He understood more about sin than he liked to admit, even to himself. No one had to tell him he was a sinner. He had a real hard time digesting Scotland's flawed evaluation of herself. No matter how hard he might try, he wasn't sure he'd ever be able to see her as anything but an angel. He couldn't help wondering if he was viewing her through the eyes of love. But Jordan was sure Scotland knew who she was and that she wasn't better than anyone else. Her honesty was impressive. She wasn't afraid of saying exactly what she thought.

Since Jordan had nothing to compare his feelings to, he couldn't know for sure what he felt for Scotland. Then he thought about his feelings for his mother. He had no doubt that he loved her with all his heart and soul. His feelings for the two women were totally different, yet there were some similarities.

"Are you afraid of dying, Scotland?"

The quizzical look on Scotland's face betrayed her utter astonishment. "That's such an odd question to pose right out of the blue. Why are you asking me that?"

Jordan hunched his shoulders. "I guess it's 'cause I want to know."

Not needing to give any thought to Jordan's question, Scotland pursed her lips, looking at him in a most curious way. "I try to concentrate on living, Jordan, not dying. I think I've said this to you before, but if I haven't, I'll say it again. I've learned not to fear what I don't have any control over. So my answer would have to be no, I don't fear death."

Jordan looked thoughtful. Scotland's answer had been so provocative that he wanted her to expound on it. "If what you say is true, why do you think you don't have any control over dying, Scotland?"

Scotland looked slightly annoyed. "Does anyone? We

plain folks down here on earth don't decide on life or death. God has a lock on that gig."

"God, huh? Why do you think that?"

Unable to believe her ears, Scotland jerked her head back. "What is going on with you? Your questions are downright weird. God is the Creator, Jordan. He's the only One that gives life, the only One to take it away."

Jordan smoothed down his hair with the palm of his hand. "I don't mean to be weird, but I'm searching for answers as to why I'm so fearful of death. I often wonder if I fear it because I haven't surrendered all, not that I'd even know how to give up my will. I can't help wondering whether if I died tomorrow, I would go to heaven or hell. I think about that a lot, which is probably why I have so many nightmares about it, like the car accident I told you about."

Scotland felt so sorry for Jordan. He seemed so sad and confused. Conflicted? Yes, she'd have to say that he was, terribly so. The fact that he was searching for answers about life and death was a good sign. People questioned mortality all the time. She herself had done so enough times, though she'd never discussed it with others. Although he may not know it yet, Scotland felt that Jordan was, in fact, seeking the face of God. "Jordan, do you know that you can choose between hell and eternal life?"

"How's it my choice? You just said God was the only one who can make that decision."

"That was about life and death, Jordan. We just can't choose the time or the place for it. I believe that God has the final say even in suicide attempts. Jesus made the ultimate sacrifice so that you and I can have eternal life. But we're the only ones who can make the choice between eternal damnation and eternal life. How we choose to live our lives is the deciding factor. Jesus won't make us accept those things that He died for. He wants us to come to Him willingly."

"Legacy, Scotland. What legacy would you leave behind if you died tomorrow?"

Scotland pulled a face. "God, please forbid such a sorrowful event!"

Although Scotland was concerned about Jordan's line of questioning, she was more curious as to where he was trying to go with it. That he was searching for something that had somehow eluded him was obvious. Exactly what he was looking for—and what he'd do with it if he found it—was the mystery of it all.

"That's a good question, Jordan, one that I haven't given any thought to. I haven't done anything spectacular in my lifetime, but I'd say that helping others would have to be it. The work I've done in my career has always been geared toward lifting people up. I've tried to give folks, especially the hearing impaired, that extra boost to help them get on with their lives. If I'm not in a person's life to enhance it, I shouldn't be there. What would you leave behind?"

Jordan's laughter rang with undisguised cynicism. "Nothing. I can assure you of that." Jordan scratched his head. "I'm afraid I don't have a legacy to leave behind. If I checked out of life's hotel today, I'd be just another anonymous dead man. I don't even know who'd attend my funeral besides my parents."

Upon hearing his shocking statement, Scotland turned down the corners of her mouth. "Hmm. I find that hard to believe, Jordan. I know that I'd attend, and I'm sure many of your coworkers would pay their last respects." She didn't like this morbid conversation one bit, but she didn't know how to tell him that.

"Legacy, Jordan, is not a complicated word, yet it's often wrongly defined. I think you really need to take a hard look at your life and then begin to identify the positive contributions you've made to society and to others. No matter how small your good deeds might seem to you, they do count."

Jordan shrugged. "I can take a look, but I already know I won't find much there."

"As a probation officer, I'm sure you've done a lot of good, Jordan. Think back on some of your cases that seemed insurmountable . . . and then look at the end results. I'm sure there were things you were able to work out despite all the odds against you."

Gregory came to Jordan's mind instantaneously. The red tape for the camping trip had been one complicated matter, yet he'd surmounted it. "That should be easy enough to do, but I know I've also mishandled a lot of cases. Often frustrated with the mountains of red tape, I'm sure that I didn't give my all to some cases. I'm not proud of that, either."

Scotland closely studied the different expressions that crossed Jordan's handsome face. Her guess about him being conflicted was so right on. It seemed to her that he was having a major wrestling match with the devil. Scotland could easily recall the time when she was also deeply conflicted.

Although Scotland had been raised in the church and had been brought up in admiration of the Lord, there had been times when she'd openly courted rebellion. She had asked many questions, too; most of them had been directed at her father. Having her father to talk to about God had been her saving grace.

As a child, Scotland had trouble understanding why so many people were living in misery if God was so kind and loving. The deaths of her mother and aunt in the same fiery car crash had caused Scotland to further question God's tender mercies, but only after she'd gotten much older. For the longest time she hadn't been able to fathom how the loving God she'd been taught so much about had taken her mother away in a blink of an eye. Unlike Jordan, Scotland had had a concerned father to guide her path and help her understand God's way.

"So, are you telling me you don't question God about His love and goodness anymore?"

Hoping she wasn't confusing Jordan any more than he already was, Scotland shook her head from side to side. "I'm not saying that at all. I think as long as we have breath in us, we'll try to get answers from God on the things that happen in our lives, especially the really bad stuff. I was terribly upset with God when my cousin lost her hearing. Until Brianna made me see her situation differently, I was beside myself with anger. I questioned Him something fierce."

Scotland then shared with Jordan how Brianna had eventually taken it upon herself to help her cousin come to terms with the loss of her hearing. Brianna had made Scotland see how grateful she was that she'd gotten a chance to hear the birds sing and to listen to the loud crashing of thunder. Brianna also remembered how the splash of water sounded and how different animals made themselves heard. The pitter-patter of raindrops on the roof had been one of her favorite melodies. And the sound of waves crashing against the shoreline had excited her as a small child.

The sound of music now came from within Brianna's soul, Scotland told Jordan. She loved to dance to the rhythm of her heartbeat, and she still hummed the tunes of the songs she'd loved before her hearing had totally failed her.

It bothered Scotland to no end to see Jordan looking so lost and in deep pain. Many of the things he'd revealed had helped her to understand why he was so enigmatic. Scotland could clearly see that Jordan was very uncomfortable with his past and that he wasn't at all optimistic about his future. "Your parents, have you talked with them recently?"

Jordan got a faraway look in his eyes. "I talked with my mother earlier. Nothing much to report there."

"How's your relationship with her, Jordan?"

"Practically nonexistent. She says she wants to have a good relationship with me, but I don't trust anything to do with my parents. I'm afraid of establishing any sort of relationship with either of them. They've continuously let me down . . . and in so many ways. What's to stop them from doing it over and over if I get involved in their lives again?"

"The only certainty in this life, Jordan, is God. If we live long enough, we learn how to take risk after risk. Stepping outside our doors every day is a big risk we all take. Sometimes we have to step out on a limb, even when it looks fragile. It's not always the easiest thing to do, Jordan, but taking risks is also known as stepping out on faith."

Wondering if he should ask his next question, since it was a rather sensitive one, Jordan cleared his throat. Scotland had talked a lot about God, faith, and Brianna's situation, but she hadn't said too much about her own childhood. It didn't take him long to decide to take the plunge. "I know you lost your mother at an early age, but how was your childhood otherwise?"

Tears immediately sprang to Scotland's eyes. "If I had to sum it up in a word, I'd say fantastic. I guess life can be hard when you grow up without a parent, but it was all I knew. I was too young to really understand it. My dad played the role of both parents, remarkably so. If I was missing out on something, I didn't know what it was. That is, not until much later."

"What did you miss out on later, Scotland?"

"Just girl stuff. The mom and daughter things I heard my friends talking about made me long for my mother from time to time. Dad and Uncle Brian never let Brianna and me want for a thing. I'm sure that on my wedding day I'll miss the benefits of having my mother around, but I don't think I'll have any less of a perfect day. Brianna and I are so blessed that our dads are unbelievably supportive of us. We were raised really well by them."

Jordan squirmed in his chair. "You mentioned that God is the only certainty in this life. What did you mean by that?"

"Just that. God is one hundred percent reliable. He's never too busy to listen to His children, and He never leaves them alone. He's always there for us, there to take care of our every need and desire. Like I've already said, He's the only certainty in this life."

"You seem so sure about that. Why?" Jordan was fearful of annoying Scotland by bombarding her with so many questions, but she was the only one he felt comfortable talking about God with.

Surprised by Jordan's question, especially after all she'd just shared with him, Scotland laughed lightly. "Do you have all night, Jordan? Actually, it would take me a lot longer than that to explain why I feel the way I do. But I think I can convince you that He's the real deal in less time than that. Still want to know the whys and wherefores, Jordan?"

Jordan nodded his head in the affirmative. "A cup of coffee will help me stay alert. All night is a long time. But there's this one thing I want to ask you before we delve any deeper into this subject. Will you hear me out?"

Scotland raised an eyebrow. "Of course. What is it?"

"Will you go to my parents with me one day next week? My mom wants to fix dinner for me. I'm really nervous about seeing them alone. I could use your support."

Scotland saw the opportunity to resort to a little blackmail and to fulfill one of her deepest desires in the process. "I'll agree to go with you, but only if you'll agree to attend Brianna's surprise birthday party with me this coming weekend."

Although her question had caught him off guard, Jordan was pleased by the invitation. "I'd love to go to the party with you. Going to my parents' place won't be anything akin to a party. It'll probably be a very tense visit. Knowing that, do you still agree to go with me?"

"If your parents don't have a problem with me tagging along with you, I'd love to go."

"They won't have a choice in the matter, Scotland. This visit has to be on my terms, or it won't happen. So, do we have two dates lined up?"

"Two dates, Jordan. Before we get further into our discussion, would you mind helping me clear the table?"

Jordan smiled sweetly. "You got it, babe. By the way, the food was great. Thanks."

First term of endearment from him to me, Scotland mused, liking what she'd just heard. It pleased her to check another score on her card. Perhaps she was going to win him over after all.

CHAPTER SEVEN

Nervous couldn't begin to define how Jordan felt about being around both his parents. It was the first time he'd been in the company of his mom and dad for quite a while. He had seen his mother periodically, always in a neutral setting, but his dad hadn't been present at any of their meetings. Jordan had preferred it that way. James was not Jordan's favorite person.

Both surprised and happy to see that their new home was neat and clean, which had rarely been the case when he was growing up, Jordan felt relieved. He would've felt embarrassed in front of Scotland had their house been in a state of disarray. Regina had once been a very good housekeeper and an excellent wife and mother, but that was before alcohol and drugs had come into play.

Jordan thought his mother looked real well. Her gray pinstriped pantsuit was simple but classy, and she smelled of sweet jasmine, her favorite scent. He noticed that her hair was once again salon fresh. It pleased him to know that she hadn't backslid and that she was still taking good care of herself. James was much thinner than he remembered. Something about his dad's over-all appearance alarmed Jordan, but he couldn't pin-point what exactly was wrong.

As though she could feel Jordan's deep apprehen-sion, Scotland closed her hand tenderly over his. His warm smile showed her his appreciation. Her soothing touch was instantly calming. The introductions had gone off without a hitch, but James La Cour, a rather tall, solidly built man, hadn't said a word, only nodding his head now and then, reminding Scotland of her first encounter with Jordan. Not a single smile had ap-peared on James's face.

Regina La Cour was a slight woman, a little over five feet in height, with beautiful cinnamon brown skin. Her amber eyes, nearly the same color as Jordan's, twin-kled when she smiled. Her hands had been tender and warm when they'd briefly taken hold of Scotland's. Regina seemed to be a very loving, caring person, which was surprising to Scotland after all the disturbing things she'd heard about her from Jordan. But Scot-land was not there to judge her.

Seated on the love seat with her husband, across from where Scotland and Jordan sat on the matching sofa, Regina smiled at Jordan, looking so happy to see him. "We're so glad you could come see us, Jordan. It's been a long time. We weren't sure you'd make it," Regina uttered rather timidly. "It's such a pleasant sur-prise for us to meet your girlfriend. Scotland, we're glad you're here with Jordan."

Even though Jordan had introduced Scotland as only his friend, he didn't so much as flinch at his mother's intimate reference. He hoped Scotland didn't mind being called his girlfriend, but he figured that she considered it an honest mistake. When a man brought a woman home to meet his parents, he was usually in love. He believed there was a special bond between them, but he knew that neither he nor Scotland was ready to take things to the next level. If they weren't falling in love with each other, he didn't know what was going on between them. Whatever it was, it felt good and right.

"Jordan and Scotland, can we get you anything? We have plenty of soft drinks, fruit juices, and snack items. What can we get for you?"

Jordan resented that his mother spoke for both herself and his father. She kept saying "we," while his dad sat by totally still. Since it had always been like that, Jordan didn't know why he continued to let it get to him. James never had to communicate with his son because Regina had always done it for him. He didn't have a voice, unless he was full of liquor. He had a voice then, a loud, roaring one.

Scotland smiled sweetly. "No, thank you. I'm just fine. Jordan and I had lunch just before we came here."

Too much information, Jordan thought. His parents didn't need to know any of his personal business. It wasn't as if they really cared. If they had cared about him, this god-awful awkwardness wouldn't be wedged tightly between them.

The light dimming in Regina's eyes made Scotland feel really bad. The woman looked as if she felt slighted by the refusal. Thinking that she was being downright rude, Scotland decided to accept the hospitality simply because it had been offered. "On second thought, Mrs. La Cour, I think I'll have some juice. My throat is a little dry. Any flavor is fine with me."

Regina smiled brilliantly at Scotland. "What about you, Jordan? I know that white grape juice is your favorite. I have a large bottle chilling just for you."

"That'll be fine, Mom. I'm thirsty, too."

The last thing Scotland wanted was to slight Jordan's parents, her future in-laws. She was pleased to learn that white grape juice was Jordan's favorite, since she had already served it to him time and time again without knowing he relished it.

After the iced drinks were served, for the next forty-five minutes or so, Jordan, Scotland, and Regina made light conversation. James only nodded every now and then, making not so much as a slight grunt.

James's behavior both puzzled and troubled Scotland. If he wanted to rebuild his relationship with his son, he surely wasn't acting like it. He seemed completely detached from the family circle. Wanting desperately to know if the man had a tongue, Scotland tried to engage him in conversation. "Mr. La Cour, Jordan tells me that your church has a new pastor. What's his name?"

"Reverend Lance McCray," Regina responded for James. "He came to us a couple of months ago from a church in Detroit, Michigan. We're enjoying him so much. He's a very young man, yet he's an old-school preacher, full of fire and brimstone."

That test sure flopped, Scotland mused. James had use of a tongue all right, his wife's.

It annoyed Jordan something terrible that Regina kept speaking for his father. It was as if she was afraid that James might embarrass her if he spoke. "Dad," Jordan said, looking his father directly in the eyes, "how do you like your new job?"

Jordan was determined to make his father say something. If his mother was the only one pushing the idea of rebuilding their relationship, he needed to know that. As it appeared now, Jordan didn't think James was all that keen on having his family back together.

"He already loves it," Regina said, looking as though she were fighting back tears.

"Mom, can you please let Dad speak for himself. I want to hear from him."

James blinked hard. Then sweat appeared on his

forehead and his upper lip. He looked very uncomfortable. James glanced over at his wife, helplessly, slightly shrugging his broad shoulders. "I . . . like . . . it just . . . fine," he slurred badly.

Believing that his father was drunk, Jordan could barely contain his anger. How could he get drunk when his son was coming to visit, Jordan thought. The very thought of his father doing something so vile cut him to the quick.

His mother's talk about them being born-again Christians had been nothing more than a truckload of crap. Jordan felt deceived. If James hadn't stopped drinking heavily, then that meant he was still in and of the world. Jordan felt horribly sick on the inside to learn that nothing had really changed, except his mother, perhaps. Now he wasn't even sure about her. She was still covering up for James, still sheltering him from the consequences of his dire mistakes. It seemed to Jordan that his father would never stand up and be a real man. James had disappointed his only son over and over again.

Jordan got to his feet and then reached back for Scotland's hand. "I think we should go now. In my opinion, we've already stayed too long. This isn't what I'd bargained for."

"Jordan," Regina cried out, "please stay. I thought things were going pretty well for us. Please don't run out like this. You've only been here a short while."

Burning tears filled Jordan's eyes. "Then why does it seem like forever to me, Mom? We really have to go now. It's for the best."

Scotland didn't know what to make of the situation, since she really wasn't sure what had sparked Jordan's anger. Everything had happened so suddenly. Regina was frantic. . . . and they were leaving so abruptly. She figured she'd just have to wait until later to find out what was going on from Jordan. Now wasn't the time to ask questions. Tensions were running too high.

It never dawned on Scotland that James was drunk.

Looking tired and defeated, James staggered to his feet. "Son, we'd . . . really . . . like you . . . to stay." James's speech was just as slurred as before, if not more so. "I know . . . what you're . . . thinking, and it's not . . . that—"

"Then what is it, if not that, Dad? It seems like the same old same old to me."

Scotland had finally gotten the drift of things. That James was slurring his words was obvious to her now. She felt horrible for all of them. It appeared as if their family reunion hadn't turned out like any of them might've expected. Disappointment was written all over Jordan's face, and Regina was now sobbing.

What's to stop them from doing it again? She clearly remembered Jordan asking her that question in reference to his parents wanting another chance to rebuild their relationship with him. Scotland's heart ached for everyone in the room, but her heart was breaking for Jordan. If he needed her, she'd be there to help him work through his pain.

James tottered from side to side before he was able to lower himself back down to the love seat. His skin had paled considerably. He then took a minute to catch his breath, which was now coming in short spurts. "Son, I've . . . had . . . a stroke."

Jordan could've been knocked over by a whisper. His gasp was loud enough for everyone to hear. He dropped back down onto the sofa, looking stunned. Jordan gazed over at his mother. "A stroke! Why didn't you let me know, Mom? Why?"

Regina blinked back fresh tears. "I tried to let you know. I left you several messages to call me after it first happened. You never returned my calls, son. When I did get a hold of you, you were very hard to communicate with, so I thought it best not to mention it. To be perfectly honest with you, I didn't think you'd care, Jordan. I'm sorry, but that's how it seemed to me."

Jordan had never felt closer to breaking down and crying his eyes out than he did at that very moment. That his mother hadn't been able to count on him, much the same way he hadn't been able to rely on them, had Jordan feeling terribly crushed. Of course, his mother didn't think he cared about what happened to them, because he didn't. At least he hadn't thought he did.

All his ill feelings toward Regina and James evaporated at that moment. He suddenly felt responsible for their well-being. He was the only child the couple had. In his quest for revenge on the people who'd brought him into the world, he'd somehow forgotten how to be human. No one had to teach him compassion. He was a very caring, sensitive person, but he just hadn't exercised those qualities around his parents. Jordan knew that he had to make a change.

Everything had suddenly backfired. Sure, Jordan had wanted them to hurt like he'd hurt all those years when they had acted as if he didn't exist. Just as they'd failed him as parents, he now believed he'd failed them as a son. He was every bit as guilty of being uncaring as they were. Hard-heartedness was only one of the ugly lessons he'd learned from them. Unfortunately, it wasn't a lesson he could ever be proud of. "Why didn't you just say what was wrong on the answering machine, Mom? I would've come to be with you."

Regina wiped her eyes with the hem of her suit jacket. "That's not the kind of message anyone should ever leave on an answering machine, Jordan. I thought you should hear it directly from me, but it didn't happen that way."

Angry with himself, Jordan threw his hands up in frustration. "I'm sorry. I didn't know you needed me. How are you doing now, Dad?" Genuine concern was apparent in Jordan's tone. The shakiness of his voice revealed his fear. All he really wanted to do was throw his arms around his father and beg for his forgiveness, but uncertainty about how James would receive him kept him rooted to his spot on the sofa. Though he'd had a miraculous softening of his heart, Jordan hadn't lost his fear of rejection. His phobias were still unrelenting.

"Much . . . better, son. Thank you." Every word spoken seemed burdensome to James, but it didn't stop him from trying his best to let his son know that he'd like for him to stay. His staggering to his feet had given credence to Jordan's theory about him being drunk, but that hadn't been the case at all.

Discreetly, Scotland wiped the tears from her eyes. This was such an emotionally charged time for the La Cour family. She didn't think she should even be there. She felt as though she were an intruder, yet she was glad she was there for Jordan. He was going to need her to talk to when this trying visit was over. Her shoulders would be available to him for as long as he needed them. No doubt about it. The reasons for Jordan's issues of trust were becoming clearer and clearer to Scotland every single day they were together. Although she believed he had come to trust her a great deal, she knew he had a long way to go in completely trusting anyone.

Sensing Scotland's concern, Jordan reached over and took her hand, squeezing it tightly. He didn't know what he'd do without her, and he hoped he didn't ever have to find out. She had already seen the worst of him before she'd ever gotten a chance to see the best in him. "Sorry you had to witness this. I guess you have a totally different opinion of me now. I hope you won't judge me too harshly, Scotland. This isn't all there is to me."

Scotland removed her hand from Jordan's grasp and placed it lovingly on the side of his face. "Please don't concentrate on what I think, Jordan. This isn't about me. I'm not going to judge you, period. You guys need each other. I hope you can see that now. They've already extended the olive branch, now all you have to do is take hold of it. It's all up to you."

Wanting to give the La Cour family a few moments of privacy, Scotland excused herself and headed for the guest powder room, located a short trek down the hallway.

After Scotland disappeared down the hall, Jordan walked over to where his parents were seated and knelt down in front of them. He then took each of their hands in his. "I apologize again, but I know it'll never be enough to heal the hurt I've caused you both. It's time for me to grow up and get over the past and get on with living in the present. If it's not too late, I'd like to accept the olive branch you've graciously extended. I want us to try and be a real family. Mom and Dad, do you think you can give me another chance at trying to get this right?"

Regina's tears fell. "We're more than ready for a new beginning, Jordan."

Regina and James leaned forward at the same time, each reaching out to bring Jordan into their embrace. These were the four arms that should've held him tightly all along, he thought, but he was so happy to have them holding him now. It was such a strange feeling to have James touching him. Jordan couldn't remember his father ever hugging him or showing him any kind of affection. There had been no romping on the floor or bed, no trips to the playground, nor had they ever tossed baseballs, shot a game of hoops, or thrown each other any football passes. Hanging out and playing or watching sports with his father was what every boy lived for.

Had it really been that bad between him and his father, or was that the way he chose to remember it? Jordan wasn't sure, but he decided not to rehash the past ever again. He promised himself to never drudge up again all that incredible hurt and pain. If the La Cour family was to have a fresh start, Jordan realized he'd have to be completely finished with reliving all the old stuff. Thoughts of his father dying had him badly shaken.

Scotland carried into her family room a pot of hot tea, two mugs, and slices of pound cake on Styrofoam dessert plates. She then sat down on the sofa and began fixing her tea to her liking. Although she'd brought in a slice of cake for herself, she really wasn't hungry for dessert. She hadn't eaten anything since lunch, but it was too late at night for a big meal. Scotland always tried to eat her last substantial meal before seven o'clock in the evening.

As she waited for Jordan to return from the bathroom, she thought back on what had happened earlier at the La Cours'. So much had happened in such a short time. When she'd come out of the powder room, the three family members were holding each other and crying their eyes out. It had been such a touching scene. She had stayed out in the hallway, looking at the pictures on the wall, just to give them more time alone.

It had struck Scotland that there wasn't one photograph on the wall of Jordan in any stage of his life. Every single picture was of James and Regina. She thought that was rather odd, but it was just another clue into Jordan's psyche. He had told her he was a loner, and now she was beginning to really understand why he was that way. Unfortunately, being alone was all that Jordan had known.

It saddened her that Jordan had had to spend so much time alone while growing up, that he'd felt so unloved and unwanted as a child. She couldn't begin to imagine how that kind of loneliness might've felt. She and Brianna had never been left alone, had never felt lonely.

However, before Scotland and Jordan had left the La Cour home, the family had promised to have dinner together within the next few days or so. They would set a time soon. With James's rehabilitation appointments at the local hospital, not to mention his poor health, their schedule was rather hard to arrange. Jordan had told Scotland that for the first time ever, he felt confident that his parents would make every effort to keep their word to him.

"Hey," Jordan said, taking a seat next to Scotland, "what's all this?"

Scotland turned her palms up and shrugged. "Thought you might like a little snack before you head home. I baked the cake myself."

Jordan laughed lightly. "Thanks, but my stomach is geared up for a little more than tea and cake. Our appetites are so totally different. You seem to exist on practically nothing, girl. Do you realize we haven't eaten a thing since lunch?"

Smiling sheepishly, Scotland nodded. "Yeah, I do. But it's kind of late for me to be eating a whole lot. Again, I apologize. It looks like I was only thinking of myself. I can warm you up some leftover spaghetti and meatballs. Would something like that satisfy your appetite?"

"Sounds good, but it depends on how old the leftovers are."

Scotland shot him a look of intolerance. "Do you really think I'd serve you something that might give you food poisoning? Not a chance. The spaghetti was cooked yesterday. Normally I don't have leftovers, but I cooked too much this time."

Jordan chuckled, winking at Scotland. "Sounds like you *were* thinking of me," he joked. "It seems to me you're getting used to cooking for two. At any rate, I definitely accept your offer of real food."

Scotland wasn't going to respond to Jordan's provocative statement about cooking for two. He was way behind her on that idyllic thought. All she'd ever thought about from day one was how wonderful life was going to be for the two of them.

As Scotland rose to her feet, Jordan stayed her with a gentle hand to her arm. He had something he needed to say to her, something that couldn't be put off any longer. Why this woman made him so nervous, confused, and comfortable all at the same time was no longer a mystery to him. His deep feelings for her had taken him over completely.

Jordan was sure he'd fallen head over heels in love with Scotland Kennedy.

Denying what he felt for her was impossible. He could only hope Scotland felt the same as he did. If not, he was about to jump off a bridge without a life jacket. God forbid that he should end up drowning, making his watery nightmare a reality.

Jordan cleared the nonexistent frog in his throat. He then wiped his sweaty palms on his jeans, hoping she wouldn't notice the beads of sweat on his brow. "We've had one crazy beginning to our friendship, Scotland. I've gone from totally ignoring you, to running away from my attraction to you, to soliciting your help with Gregory, and then to wanting to be with you as much as possible."

Fearful of moving forward with his speech, lest Scotland should reject him, Jordan put his head in his hands, sucking in a few calming gusts of air. Confessions weren't easy for him.

Hoping Jordan was going where she thought he was, Scotland held her breath in eager anticipation. When he stopped abruptly, she wasn't sure what to expect.

Seconds later Jordan sought eye contact with Scotland, apologizing for leaving her hanging. "So much emotional stuff has gone on this day. But because I really believe I can now move out of the past and into the present, I feel confident that I'm prepared to take our friendship to the next level. That is, if we're on the same page. Are you interested in having a personal relationship with me, one that might blossom into something very special for us?"

Scotland eyed him with open curiosity. Jordan had said exactly what she'd wanted to hear, but she wasn't as thrilled as she thought she'd be. His voice had betrayed some uncertainty, which had put her on uneasy street. "Are you sure about this, Jordan?"

Jordan momentarily closed his eyes. His heart was off to the races, and he was desperately trying to catch up with it. "I had hoped you wouldn't ask me that, Scotland. But to respond to you with your own response to me a few days ago, God is the only certainty in this life. I want so much to believe that. All I can ask is that you try and believe in me. I want you to continue to be patient with me. I also need you to trust me. I want to be everything you need me to be."

Without giving Scotland a chance to respond, Jordan took her in his arms, holding her slightly away from him. Looking deeply into her eyes, he kissed first her forehead, then each of her eyelids. His mouth slowly moved down to her quivering lips, caressing them ever so gently with his own. As he deepened the kiss, his arms went around her, holding her as tenderly as he was capable of. With fireworks going off inside his head, Jordan knew without a shadow of a doubt that his heart had at long last found a permanent home.

Unable to stop reliving every single romantic moment she and Jordan had shared earlier, Scotland smiled with knowing. Shivering with delight, she sat up in bed and wrapped her arms around herself. For a day that had started out rather troublesome, it had certainly turned out to be magnificent. The last thing she would've expected was for Jordan to tell her that he wanted to take their relationship to the next level. She wasn't even aware that she'd made it to first base with him. He was so good at keeping her in the dark about everything. But he'd certainly made his intentions perfectly clear by the end of the evening. Crystal clear.

As Scotland thought about Jordan's remark that he wanted to be all that she needed him to be, she recalled his astonishment at her passionate response. When she had told him that he first needed to be all he could be to himself before he could be anything to anyone else, he had looked at her in amazement. He had then asked her to explain what she meant.

Trying hard not to offend Jordan, Scotland had talked to him about self-love. Then, when he'd asked what she needed from a man in an intimate relationship, she'd told him without reservation exactly what she looked for in a partner. In order for Jordan to meet her expectations, and the requirements of his current and future family, Scotland had helped him see that he had to first meet his own needs.

It had been Jordan's turn to astound Scotland by informing her that he believed that no one other than a Godly man would ever live up to her expectations. He then assured her that he desired to be that kind of man, not just for her but for himself as well. He also let her know in no uncertain terms that he was ready to learn all he could about what God expected of him—and to prepare himself to lead a Christian life. He once again asked Scotland to be patient with him during his journey toward spiritual fulfillment. He wanted to walk slowly.

Jordan had told Scotland that he knew he was a sinner, but that now he was a hopeful one.

That Jordan was so eager to be in tune with her every want and need made Scotland feel as if they had every chance to make a go of things. Their future looked rosier than ever. She now expected life to get really interesting for them. Things had already gotten more romantic and cozier. His kiss was unforgettable. They also had a solid friendship and lots of honesty going for them, which were important elements in a successful relationship.

The edge of dawn found Jordan waking up after only a couple of hours sleep. Lying in bed, the Bible right next to him, he'd practically had an all-night reading session. He was grateful for the Bible study lesson guide Scotland had let him borrow, which had helped him figure out what he should focus on. The more he'd read, the more he'd found himself wanting to go on a little farther. He had eventually fallen asleep with the Bible on his chest, right after he'd entertained the idea of being baptized. Jordan's last conscious thought had been about Scotland's detailed explanation of what baptism really meant.

Reading hadn't been the only thing that had kept Jordan awake. The innocent intimacy he'd shared with Scotland had been hard for him to get out of his mind.

It had been so different from what he was used to. If a woman wasn't offering, he hadn't been above a little prompting in that direction. Of course, he had always respected that no meant no. Such thoughts hadn't even crossed his mind with Scotland. What they'd shared was nothing short of sweet and harmless. Not once had either of them conducted themselves in what some folks might consider an improper manner.

Although Jordan didn't regret any of the things he'd revealed to Scotland, since he'd meant every single word, he was worried about attending Brianna's birthday party. Showing up at the special event with Scotland meant that he'd have to meet her dad and her other family members and close friends.

Was he really ready for that?

Whether he was ready for it or not, being a man of his word, Jordan didn't see how he could renege on his promise. Scotland had already fulfilled her end of the deal by visiting his parents' home with him. She had only agreed to the visit if he agreed to attend the party.

Jordan was doing everything he could to keep his feelings of unworthiness at bay. He had no doubt that he wanted to be with Scotland, just as he'd expressed to her last evening, but some roadblock always seemed to pop up out of nowhere. Meeting her family was the latest one.

If he kept thinking he might be unworthy of her, Jordan was sure it would get in the way of progress. He knew that what Scotland's father thought of anyone she got involved with was very important to her. She had admitted to wanting her father's approval on her choice in a mate. Were these obstacles of his making? Was he creating problems that didn't exist other than in his mind? Jordan couldn't help but wonder.

Scotland was a church girl, while Jordan wasn't a member of any religious organization. Did that make them unevenly yoked? He knew that such a possibility existed only because he'd read something about it in the Bible study guide. Did he dare think he could be the kind of man this angel of his needed? Could he give her all that she sought in an intimate relationship?

Last night Jordan had surely believed that anything was possible for them.

Regardless of his fears, Jordan still felt that he owed it to himself to give it his best shot. Scotland was very special to him, and he couldn't imagine a day in his life without her.

Jordan got out of bed and immediately fell down on his knees, looking as if he didn't know what he was supposed to do next. Should he close his eyes or keep them open? Should he speak aloud or only talk to God in his thoughts? Feeling completely out of sorts, Jordan started to sob lightly. He desperately wanted to communicate with Scotland's God, to tell all to the Creator, with whom he hoped to establish a new, meaningful relationship. He wanted Scotland's God to become his Savior, too. Jordan also wanted his natural father to become a real father to him.

Now that he was down on his knees, Jordan wondered how he should begin? In what way should he address Him? *Father, God, Master, or Savior?*

Any one will do. He's waiting on you to make the first move. Don't delay. Time is short.

Jordan was frightened now. Had he really heard a voice whispering in his ear? The voice had been so real. He couldn't deny that he'd heard it loud and clear, yet there was no one else in the room. The uttering had ceased, but his sobbing had grown louder. There, on his knees, Jordan began to tearfully pour out his burdens and lay them at the feet of the Savior.

For the first time in his life, Jordan was bowing down before God. He asked God for deliverance of his soul and for restoration of his spirit, which were some of the things he'd heard Scotland talk about. In praying about his relationship with his parents, he had to humble himself completely, because he wanted and needed them back in his life. When he learned of his father's stroke, he realized how wrong he'd been to deny them his support, no matter what they'd done to him. Jordan knew that he should've been bigger than that.

Jordan then asked for divine guidance in his relationship with Scotland, praying to God to bless their union if it was His holy will. He didn't know where all the words were coming from, he just felt grateful to have them pour out of his mouth so easily. He needed to rid himself of all the bad feelings and diseased thoughts he'd been carrying around inside for years. Jordan then prayed fervently for a total cleansing of his mind, body, and spirit.

Thirty minutes later, as Jordan got to his feet, he somehow felt lighter. He didn't know how that was possible, but he truly felt as if the weight of the world had been lifted from his bone-weary shoulders. The thought of being baptized suddenly overwhelmed him, yet it also freed him even more from his inner shackles. Jordan knew that baptism entailed more than just submerging oneself in water. Scotland had told him a baptism ceremony was something he had to prepare himself for spiritually. She had described being baptized as a ritual that represented an outward showing of an individual's acceptance of Christ as their Lord and Savior.

As Jordan thought of how happy his pending decision to get baptized would make Scotland, his sobs came again. More importantly, he was very much aware that a complete spiritual makeover would make him the happiest of all. Jordan was sure his decision would make God happy, too. Preparing himself spiritually still had to come first, and he realized it could take quite a bit of time. It was not something he could rush through. Jordan expected his rebirth to be nothing less than the biggest challenge of his lifetime.

Needing to hear Scotland's sweet voice, hoping she had already made it in from work, Jordan sat down on a leather bar stool at the built-in bar in his large upstairs game room. Since he hadn't decided on how to furnish the massive space, bar stools and a chrome and slate, fully equipped, state-of-the-art entertainment center were the only pieces of furniture in the room. Oversized pillows were scattered all over the carpeted floor.

As Jordan thought of how harried his day had been, and how much he would benefit from getting in a bit of relaxation, he reached for the telephone and dialed Scotland's home number. He laughed when he realized he knew her number by heart.

Jordan smiled broadly the second he heard Scotland's voice. "Hey, girl. It's Jordan. I'm getting ready to take a walk around the lake. Please join me. I could sure use the company of a pretty, smiling face." It felt good to be openly flirtatious with her.

Grinning from ear to ear, Scotland closed her eyes, savoring yet another delicious moment. "I'd love to. Since it's not quite sunset, maybe we can catch the sun before it goes down. Meet you down by the park bench nearest the lake?"

Jordan grunted his disapproval. "You already know I prefer to come to your door. Can you let this gentleman be a gentleman? Is that okay with you?"

Scotland giggled. "Fine with me. I sort of like that you're an old-fashioned kind of guy. Can I interest you in a hot drink at my place after our walk?"

"I'd like this evening to be on me. We haven't convened over here in a while, at least not for a meal. What about a pizza delivery? We can also watch a DVD if you'd like."

Scotland didn't have the heart to tell Jordan she wasn't all that crazy about pizza. Besides that, she'd had spaghetti recently. *The things you do for love*, she mused, laughing inwardly. "I can live with that, Jordan."

"Good, because I'm not letting you turn me into a prissy, tea-drinking male. You don't sound too excited about the pizza idea. I keep forgetting you like to eat healthy for the most part. What if we pick up a couple of sandwiches at Subway? I'll even spring for a salad for you."

"How gracious of you, Mr. La Cour. Subway *is* more to my taste. As for the prissy male bit, I'm not going to try and change you, period. I like you just the way you are. Any changes in you will be your own doing. Let's be clear on that."

"I really appreciate that, Scotland. I'll be at your place in a few minutes."

"I'll be waiting with bated breath, Jordan," she sang out, jumping up and down like a small kid. Scotland could not believe her good fortune, which was more a blessing than anything.

CHAPTER EIGHT

Scotland's head became filled with thoughts of Jordan as she laced up her black Nikes. She loved how he was suddenly taking the bull by the horns where their personal relationship was concerned. It had certainly taken him long enough to get on board. She had wondered a time or two if the ship might have to sail without him. But it now appeared that once he'd made up his mind about something, he got right down to business. His study of the Bible was a perfect example. His desire to take the initiative to lead the way in their personal affairs had her pleased as punch. Scotland was happy that she'd no longer have to nudge Jordan in the right direction.

Now that Jordan had finally accepted the idea of them as a couple, Scotland could breathe a lot easier. She was downright thrilled by all the special attention he had begun to pay her. Although she knew the potential for things to become so much better for them, she was still content to let Jordan set the pace. The ball rested in his court, where she hoped it would stay.

Upon lacing up her tennis shoes and donning a

jacket, Scotland went into the master bathroom, where she dusted her face with corn silk and dabbed a bit of blush on her cheeks. She applied clear lip gloss to her generous mouth, then ran a quick brush through her hair.

As Scotland and Jordan walked along the lake, hand in hand, his arms ached to be filled with her. He wanted them to come so close together, closer than close. Her smooth skin was warm, and his hands itched to caress its softness. He loved that her hair was shiny, squeaky clean, and that it always smelled like fresh flower blossoms. Jordan often wondered if she gave her tresses hundreds of strokes with the brush nightly, because it appeared that she did.

Abruptly halting just before they reached the bench from where they'd planned to watch the sunset, Jordan reached for Scotland and brought her into his arms, hugging her fiercely. He then captured her hazel eyes with his bewildered gaze. As he brushed his knuckles down the side of her face and across her lips, an unexpected electrical jolt of pure desire went right through him, the first uncontrollable rush of physical wantonness he'd experienced.

Denying his needs in that area came easy to Jordan, since he was looking for so much more with Scotland. The intertwining of their spirits was what made their union perfect. As long he kept their relationship on a spiritual plane, he knew he'd win her heart completely. He silently promised himself to never lose sight of all that was important in building a solid future with her. What he felt for her was so real.

That Jordan had begun to think about forever with Scotland had surprised him the first time it had occurred. Although "forever" was a long way off, he still had niggling doubts about whether Scotland would even consider him as a lifelong partner. An angel marrying a mere mortal somehow didn't seem feasible. He'd have to get real busy earning his own set of wings to make sure their union was a sacred one, should it become a reality.

Jordan guided Scotland over to the lakeside bench, where they both took a seat. He then turned to her and kissed the tip of her nose. "It's gotten a little chilly out here. Are you warm enough, Scotland?"

On fire from him, Scotland couldn't help blushing. He had the ability to set her ablaze with a mere look from his mesmerizing eyes. "My jacket's doing its job. Are you cold, Mr. Man?"

Jordan laughed at her name for him. "Just my face, angel."

Babe, now angel, Scotland mused, relishing both terms of endearment. Jordan was certainly coming on like gangbusters with his sweet talk. He had practically wooed her right off the planet during their phone conversation the night before. His engaging sense of humor had kept her in stitches. She had hung on every sugary word he'd uttered.

Scotland moved closer to Jordan and placed her hands on his face. She then delivered butterfly kisses all over his face and lips. After giving him one last kiss on the lips, a much deeper one, she looked up into his eyes. "Did that help warm you any?"

Jordan had repeatedly gasped inwardly, continuously reminding himself that he was only human, as Scotland had explored his face with her fiery, gentle mouth. Warming him up was an understatement. A cold shower wouldn't douse the fire raging inside of him. He told himself that the physical feelings he had were quite natural. He knew he was powerless over the sensations coursing through him, but it was up to him to maintain control over how he acted upon them.

Gazing over the lake, Jordan saw that the sun was about to set. Pulling Scotland back into his arms, he guided her head onto his shoulder. "The light show is about to begin, girl. I'm so glad you're here to enjoy the sunset with me."

"I'm glad you called and invited me." She pressed her cheek against Jordan's. "Oh, look, Jordan, the sun is going down much faster now."

Sunrises and sunsets were a mystery to a lot of people, but not to Scotland. She knew exactly how the sun, moon, and stars had come into being. She had been taught the story of Creation week as a small child, and she continued to study the details to this day. As they watched the sun disappear, Scotland told Jordan the story about the formation of the sun, moon, and stars, quoting Genesis 1:14-17. "And God said, Let there be lights in the firmament of the heaven to divide the day from the night; and let them be for signs, and for seasons, and for days and years. And let them be for lights in the firmament of the heaven to give light upon the earth: and it was so. And God made two great lights, the greater light to rule the day, and the lesser light to rule the night: he made the stars also. And God set them in the firmament of the heaven to give light upon the earth."

Jordan's brilliant idea of dining and watching a movie up in the game room hadn't gone over too well with Scotland. She'd gotten a glimpse of the plush, off-white wall-to-wall carpet and was worried because she knew how sloppy she could be. It made her downright nervous to think of accidentally spilling reddish orange

French dressing on his white carpet, which was a real possibility.

Scotland tapped Jordan on the arm. "Uh, do you have a place mat I can use? The thought of ruining your carpet is destroying my appetite. Do you have any Italian dressing? At least it won't stain."

"You don't need to worry about the carpet, Scotland. It can be cleaned."

"Jordan, I'm already past worried about it. You have no clue how sloppy I can be. Please, for my sake, and for the protection of this beautiful white carpet, find me a place mat. In fact, I'd probably do a lot better with two."

Chuckling at the comical expression on Scotland's face, Jordan left the room to search for place mats. He never used them, but he knew he owned several different kinds, which had been given to him as gifts for his new home. It was just a matter of locating them. He had Italian dressing in the refrigerator, so Scotland's request for that would be easy enough to fulfill.

As Scotland waited for Jordan to return, she walked over to the large window that looked out on the back of the property. The sight of a humongous, deep hole in the backyard took her by surprise. In fact, the entire backyard looked as if had been completely dug up. There were little bright orange and blue markers stuck in the ground all over the place.

"A pool," he said, wrapping his arms around her waist from behind. "I love to swim."

Even though Jordan's sudden embrace had startled her, since she hadn't heard him reenter the room, Scotland immediately laid her head back against his chest. Tilting her head at a slight angle, she looked up at him. "That's a pretty big hole back there. Your pool's going to be huge. Jacuzzi, too?"

As he deeply inhaled the scent of her hair, Jordan let

his lips wander in its thickness for a couple of seconds. "Most definitely. There's nothing like going straight from the pool to the Jacuzzi. Since I'm expected to make payments on this place for the next umpteen years, I figured I may as well have my home just like I want it. My backyard will be my haven of peace."

Scotland moved away from Jordan and sat back down on the floor. "What's up with no furniture in this mammoth-size room?" she asked as she reached for the bottle of dressing Jordan had set on one of the three place mats he'd spread on the floor. Scotland couldn't imagine how all that activity had gone on in the room without her hearing it. She then figured out that she'd been too busy being nosy about what was going on in his backyard.

"I haven't decided what kind of furnishings I want in here yet." Jordan dropped down on the floor, too. Just to appease Scotland's fear of his carpet getting ruined, he had brought a place mat for himself as well. He unwrapped his smoked turkey and cheese Subway sandwich and then placed it on the mat. Jordan then popped the tops on two cans of soda.

Scotland opened her container of salad and drizzled Italian dressing over it. "I thought most men went for leather furnishings in a big way. Leather is easy enough to care for, especially the darker colors—though I opted for taupe. I love my leather sofas, matching chairs, and ottoman. Are you interested in a pool table? This room is certainly big enough to hold one."

Jordan shook his head in the negative. "Not that much into pool. I know how to shoot really well, but it's not a real big turn on for me. I'm leaning more toward turning all this space into a media room. What do you think of the idea of putting several leather recliners in here, or perhaps theater-style seating of some sort? I already have the big screen."

Since Jordan had confessed to being a loner, Scotland wondered why he'd need that kind of seating. Then she laughed inwardly, imagining her entire family gathering in his media room to watch a movie. Her family combined with his would fill all the seats. "I think it's a brilliant idea. I've seen several model homes that have media rooms in them. Not all of the rooms were arranged the same, either. Maybe you should go look at a few of the models to get some ideas."

"That sounds like a great idea. Would you mind taking me around to some of them? That is, if the subdivisions they're located in haven't already been completely sold out. I'll do all the driving."

"The first phase hasn't been sold out yet in the developments I'm referring to. I'd love to go with you. Do you have a particular day in mind?"

"What about Saturday?"

Scotland gave Jordan a strange look. "Don't tell me you've forgotten about Bri's party?"

Jordan waved his right hand, shaking his head at the same time. "No way. But I'm talking about during the day. Who looks at models at night, anyway?"

"You'd be surprised. I love to ride by at night and see them all lit up. I did that when I was first considering buying a home here in our subdivision. It gives you a sense of what it might be like after dark. As for Saturday, that won't work for me. I'm the one who'll have to keep Miss Bri busy during all the last-minute party preparations. She thinks we're just having a family dinner for her special day. I can't wait to see her reaction."

Speaking of reactions, Jordan saw this moment as the perfect opportunity to ask Scotland about how she thought her father, uncle, and cousin might receive him. It might make the first meeting go better if he had an idea of what to expect. Scotland had spoken highly of her dad, but only from a father and daughter stand-point. Men could be very protective of their daughters.

Outside of the normal jitters a man had when meeting a woman's family, Jordan was also terribly worried that they might not like him. It just wasn't his method of operation to get all involved with the family of someone he was dating. He'd only been around Cynthia's family half a dozen or so times—and that had only come about at her insistence.

Jordan smiled nervously. "I'm a little worried about meeting your family, Scotland. I'd really like to make a good first impression. Is there anything significant that you think I should know about them beforehand? Are there any dos and don'ts that I should be aware of?"

"The only advice I can offer you is to be yourself, Jordan. If you try to be anyone but who you are, my folks will pick up on it. If you're hiding something, they'll sense it. The important things you should know about them I've already shared with you. They're good Christian people. I have a very loving family."

Hiding something, Jordan mused. He didn't know if Scotland would consider his failure to mention Cynthia as hiding something. He wanted to tell her what had happened, but he just hadn't been able to bring himself to do so. The timing had never seemed right. How much longer he should keep it to himself was troubling for Jordan, especially since he'd told Scotland that he needed her to trust and believe in him.

Scotland knew that no matter how much she tried to convince Jordan that everything would be just fine, he'd be a nervous wreck until he finally met everyone. Her dad had been concerned about her going off on a camping trip with a stranger, and rightly so, but he hadn't tried to discourage her from getting more involved with Jordan. Scott trusted his daughter's judgment, especially where men were concerned. He was aware of how determined Scotland was to select the right kind of man for herself.

"How does your dad feel about you dating a non-Christian man?"

"First of all, it's not up to my dad who I date. I believe you're a good man, Jordan, and that'll be good enough for Dad. I have felt that way about you from the moment I first met you. Non-Christians aren't always bad people, Jordan. Everyone doesn't come to God at the same time. Some never will. It's really all about what's in a person's heart, which is where God resides."

Jordan was well aware that Scotland was her own person. He liked the fact that she didn't allow others to influence her decisions. It seemed to him that she was the only one to make the call on anything to do with her life. He also got the sense that she willingly accepted the consequences of all her actions. Jordan saw Scotland as a very grounded, mature woman.

Through with her salad, Scotland cleaned up, stashing the trash back in the bag the food had come in. When she noticed that Jordan was finished with his meal, she gathered up his trash, too. He told her he'd dispose of everything when they went back downstairs.

"What movie are you interested in watching, Scotland?"

Yawning, Scotland stretched her arms high above her head. "I'll let you make the decision, Jordan." Scotland had a feeling that the movie was going to be watching her before it was all over. She felt like she could fall asleep at the drop of a hat.

As Jordan rifled through his extensive DVD collection, he ran across one that he'd never opened. He had, in fact, forgotten he bought it. He tenderly fingered the face on the cover, wondering if he'd been drawn to the title by divine intervention. Deciding that it would be a good movie for them to watch together, especially because of the content, he took it over to Scotland for her to see what he'd chosen.

Scotland's initial reaction was one of surprise. That Jordan owned *The Passion of The Christ* proved to her that she was right about him seeking the face of God. Otherwise, why would he choose to purchase this particular movie? Even slight curiousity about God was more than enough to send one on a search for truth.

Scotland glanced at her watch. "I have to tell you, Jordan, this is a very long movie."

Jordan looked disappointed. He had hoped Scotland hadn't seen the movie, though it had already been out for quite some time. "Does that mean you've already seen it?"

Noticing that Jordan was a bit disheartened that she might have already seen the movie, she replied, "I saw it when it first came out, but I don't mind watching it with you, Jordan. I always get more out of a movie when watching it again. I'm amazed at how much more I pick up the second time around."

"How long is it?"

"About three hours or so. It's nearly nine o'clock now. That means it'll be after midnight before it's over. I'm not sure I can stay awake that long, Jordan."

The disappointed look on Jordan's face deepened. He wanted to see the movie, but only with Scotland. He believed it was an appropriate film for them to watch together since he was seeking to discover more about God. Jordan was sure Scotland would be able to explain some of the things in it that he might not understand.

Scotland couldn't stand to see Jordan looking so disappointed. "I've got an idea. Let's watch an hour tonight, an hour another time, and we can later decide on when to watch the final hour. It'll surely give you something to think about by doing it that way. You might even get more out of it by dividing up the viewing time."

"I like the idea. But I suggest that we save the first hour for another time. You're already looking pretty sleepy. Would you mind if we just chilled out and listened to some jazz?"

Looking relieved, Scotland smiled. "That'll work for me." Her expression quickly sobered as she looked up at Jordan. "Hey, guy, I need to say something to you." She patted the space on the floor next to her. "Mind coming down here for a minute or two?"

A tad worried about what she might say, Jordan dropped down next to Scotland. "What's on your mind, angel?"

"You, only you. I just want you to know that you don't have to rush your spiritual journey, Jordan. Let it come naturally. Your curiosity about God is already there, which is a good thing. If you just open up your heart to God, He'll come right on in, without the slightest hesitation. He already knows your every thought. All He needs is an invite."

Scotland went on to tell Jordan that contrary to popular belief, all Christians weren't uptight, straightlaced, poker-faced people. For the most part, they are very happy people, she told him. She explained to him that the love of God was what gave Christians the freedom to live life to the fullest. When trusting in Him, there was no room for worry or doubt.

Scotland brushed her fingers over Jordan's face. "I find complete happiness and peace in believing in Him and the promises He's made. There are so many fringe benefits in being a child of God, Jordan. So just try to take your journey at a moderate pace. Enjoy it, but try not to fear it, though you probably will. Rome wasn't built in a day, my friend. Your faith and belief in God will not necessarily evolve quickly." She shrugged. "That's all I wanted to say."

Jordan wrapped Scotland up in his arms. "You are a godsend, whether you know it or not. Having you around is going to make this journey so much sweeter. I don't want to become fanatical, because I've seen people who are like that . . . and it's a big turnoff. Thank you for your guidance. Ready for that jazz now?"

Nodding her approval, Scotland grabbed one of the large overstuffed pillows on the floor. After stretching out on the carpet, she laid her head back on the pillow. The second the sounds of Najee rent the air, Scotland knew that staying awake was going to be next to impossible. Not wanting to be rude to her host, she vowed to do her best to stay awake. Propping herself up on her elbows to help her stay alert was a possibility, but she was already too comfortable to change positions now. *Stop worrying,* she told herself, *just let everything come naturally. Follow the same advice you've given so freely to Jordan.*

Sliding up beside Scotland, Jordan threw his arm loosely across her stomach, resting his head on her pillow. "Does it get any better than this, Scotland?"

Scotland laid her hand on Jordan's. "Possibly. I want to enjoy what we have right here and now. Let's not rush a thing. We can't afford not to take our time." With that, Scotland closed her eyes. All she wanted to hear was his breathing and the sweet sounds of the magical music. Being with Jordan like this made her feel safe and serene.

"Hey," Jordan whispered softly, gently nudging Scotland's shoulder, "wake up, angel. It's 2 a.m. Man, where did the time go?"

Scotland buried her head deeper into the pillow, groaning. Her fear of going out like a light had come true. The hour didn't concern her as much as the thought of having to get up and go home. Then she'd have to find the strength to drag herself into the house and off to bed. She had been sleeping so peacefully. From all indications, Jordan had fallen asleep, too. Scotland was sure he would've awakened her long before now if that weren't the case.

Slowly, Scotland sat up, looking around the room through the haze of sleep. Getting to her feet too quickly could prove disastrous, so she decided to just sit there until she got her bearings. The thought of Jordan having to take her home this late made her feel bad, but there was no other alternative.

Jordan put his arm around Scotland's shoulders, resting his head against hers. "You look really out of it. Why don't you just go back to sleep in one of the guest rooms? You'll be safe. I'll wake you up and take you home at the break of dawn. I'm sorry I let this happen."

The alternative Jordan had offered was very appealing to Scotland, but she thought perhaps she should be concerned with appearances, especially since they both lived in the same neighborhood. "Thanks, Jordan, but we don't want the neighbors to get the wrong impression of us. I'd walk home if it weren't this late."

Jordan bumped her with his shoulder. "I recall someone telling me that people are going to think what they want . . . and that we can't change that. Do you remember saying that?"

Scotland rolled her eyes. "I do. Show me the guest room. I'm too tired to worry about what anyone thinks at this point. Can I borrow one of your shirts or a pair of pajamas?"

Jordan chuckled. "Is that your way of trying to find out if I sleep in the buff or not?"

Scotland blushed deeply, disappointed in herself for

doing so. "If I wanted to know that, I'd just ask." She looked him dead in the eye. "Do you?"

"Do I what?" he asked, trying to string her along for fun.

"Stop playing, Jordan. At any rate, I couldn't care less what you sleep in. I just need something to cover me up. Guest room please!"

Laughing, Jordan helped Scotland to her feet. "Since we're on the subject, *do* church girls require their men to sleep in pajamas?"

Mildly resenting that Jordan had refered to her as a church girl, Scotland rolled her eyes at him. "When you find a church girl, I suggest you ask her. Let me know when you find out."

Jordan cracked up. "I can see that I need to let you get back to sleep. Your halo is starting to dim a little, girl. I don't want you to fool around and let the light go out completely."

Scotland sucked her teeth. "Nice to know you got jokes this early in the morning."

Jordan took her by the hand and led her down the hallway. Upon reaching the first guest room, he opened the door and escorted her inside, wasting no time in turning back the white eyelet comforter. "I'll run and get you something to sleep in. Don't fall asleep."

"I won't, but please hurry, Jordan." Fearful of not being able to fall back to sleep, Scotland wanted to get back to bed as soon as possible.

Scotland stretched out on the mattress, pulling the comforter halfway up. She'd have to wait until Jordan got back before taking her clothes off, she thought, ogling the room as she waited for him to return. Blue and white, she mused, the same colors as her own bedroom. She liked everything about the spacious sleeping quarters, but she had to wonder if he was the one who kept his place so neat and clean. There didn't seem to be a thing out of place. And there was no dust anywhere, despite a remark he'd once made to the contrary. Jordan seemed to have it going on in the housekeeping department. She was pleased that he took great pride in his beautiful home.

As her eyes drooped shut, Scotland found that she had no power to keep them open. She thought for sure that Jordan would've come back by now. Sleeping in her clothes wasn't her favorite thing to do, but she'd have to deal with it for tonight. She couldn't stay awake another second.

Jordan skidded into the room moments later. Finding Scotland fast asleep didn't come as a big shock, but he had hoped he'd get back to her before she drifted off. Finding something for her to wear hadn't been as easy as he'd thought. He had no idea what was or wasn't appropriate for her to put on. By the time he'd remembered that she'd simply asked for one his shirts, he had already wasted several minutes trying to decide on a decent sweatshirt and a pair of sweatpants.

Seeing Scotland asleep in one his beds gave Jordan a warm rush. He couldn't help wondering if she'd ever share the master suite with him. They had a long way to go before that happened but having her stay over at his house seemed so natural. She looked as if she belonged there. Perhaps she did. *As his wife, of course,* he pondered thoughtfully. Knowing Scotland as he did, Jordan knew she wouldn't settle for anything less. He respected that.

Careful not to wake Scotland, Jordan pulled the comforter up over her. He turned to walk away, only to turn back after taking a couple of steps. He stared at her sleeping figure for several seconds, silently thanking God for bringing her into his life. Bending over the bed, he lightly kissed her hair. "Goodnight, angel," he whispered softly.

Jordan was smiling as he made his way around his kitchen. He had had a decent night's rest, the first sound sleep he'd had in quite some time. He attributed his peaceful night to Scotland's presence in his home, since many of his sleepless nights were the result of staying awake thinking of her. His mood was extremely upbeat. Jordan actually felt like singing.

At the sound of the alarm on his clock radio, Jordan had instantly jumped out of bed and had run into the bathroom to freshen up. Then he'd gone downstairs to the kitchen to fix a light breakfast for Scotland. He didn't want her to get home and have to do anything but shower and get dressed for work. Jordan was aware that she'd be pressed for time.

Jordan had prepared a halved and sectioned grapefruit, two hard-boiled eggs, and a slice of whole-wheat toast for Scotland. After setting a pitcher of white grape juice on the table, he rushed up the back staircase leading to the upstairs bedrooms.

Just as Jordan reached for the knob, the door to the guest bedroom opened. Without any thought whatsoever, he pulled Scotland into his arms. "Good morning, angel. How'd you sleep?"

Scotland would've kissed Jordan on the mouth, but she was mindful of morning breath. She hugged him instead. "Like a log. The bed was very comfortable. You know I've got to be going, don't you? I have just enough time to get ready for work and eat something quick."

"I already have breakfast covered for you. There's a washcloth and towel in the bathroom adjoining this room. Come on down to the kitchen when you're through."

"That's so sweet of you." Scotland smiled broadly. "I'm way ahead of you, since I've already washed my face and hands. But I couldn't find a toothbrush. That means I rifled through your medicine cabinet. So, with that confession, I'll just come downstairs with you now."

"Sorry about that. I'll get you a new toothbrush out of the downstairs linen closet." Jordan held out his arm for her to take. "May I escort you down to the kitchen, Miss Kennedy?"

Giggling like a teenager, Scotland crooked her arm through Jordan's. "I wouldn't mind one bit, Mr. La Cour."

As Scotland took a seat at the kitchen table, she looked pleased with Jordan's breakfast choices, pretty much the same kind of selections she'd make for herself. She sincerely thanked him for taking the time to prepare the food for her, telling him that his gesture was very thoughtful. After bowing her head and saying a blessing, Scotland made quick work of her meal. She had to get her day started in a hurry.

Scotland had taken the quickest shower in the history of her lifetime. It had been difficult leaving Jordan's house right after breakfast, but eat and run she did. He'd understood perfectly, as he'd also had to prepare himself for work. They'd spoken of seeing each other in class that evening and then had exchanged a few passionate kisses. The memory of such sweet carrying on made Scotland smile.

Used to having her clothes and shoes all laid out for the next workday, Scotland had to decide on and then locate her outfit for work in an instant. She preferred being prepared over rushing through things this way. In her opinion, haste normally made waste.

Remembering the day she'd gone to work wearing shoes of different colors made Scotland howl. Fashioned in completely different styles, one shoe had been black and the other dark blue. That fiasco had been the result of haste. Her coworkrs hadn't allowed her to live down that comical blunder for a long while.

After slipping on a great-looking dark blue double-breasted pantsuit, complemented by a simple white T-shirt-style silk jersey, Scotland looked over at her computer, realizing immediately that she'd made a big mistake. "Ugh," she moaned, "Brianna is probably fit to be tied by now." Scotland knew that Brianna was probably still going crazy over the fact that she hadn't shown up online for their nightly chat. What a mess she'd unwittingly made!

As she imagined the FBI out combing the countryside for the Kennedy family's missing person, Scotland laughed out loud. She realized she had to call her family right away, but she'd have to do it from the car. She had no doubt that Brianna had sounded the alarm when she hadn't been able to touch base online. Scotland could only imagine the scene that followed.

Being so darn predictable wasn't always a good thing, Scotland mused on her way out to the garage. Her family always knew her every move, which was something she'd have to take total responsibility for. She called them about everything and anything to do with her life. Any change of plans warranted a call to her dad or uncle. But then again, they were all the same way with her. Everybody in the Kennedy clan knew what everybody else was doing and where everyone was throughout the day and night.

Although Scotland had once thought it was necessary for everyone to be informed of each other's whereabouts, now it suddenly seemed downright ridiculous to her. She made a mental note to inform everyone in her family to just assume that she was with Jordan if they couldn't make contact with her right away. She had to laugh at that thought, since no one even knew that her relationship with Jordan had risen to another level.

That juicy tidbit of information would certainly open up a can of worms, Scotland thought. Although her dad was no prude, and she thought he'd understand under the circumstances, she wasn't thrilled about telling him she'd spent the night at Jordan's.

Wasn't a girl entitled to keep a few precious secrets?

Seated at the desk in his office, Jordan frowned as he read the report regarding the outcome of the investigation into the existing conditions in the Turner home, where Gregory unhappily resided. No wrongdoing whatsoever on the part of the foster parents had been uncovered. The Turners had received a favorable grade on every page of the report.

Jordan was very much aware of the stellar reputation of the caseworker in charge of Gregory, so he had no reason to doubt her word or believe that she hadn't conducted a thorough investigation into the matter. Janice Simpson would never allow a child to remain in a home where dangerous conditions or any kind of abuse existed.

Deciding to reassess what he'd witnessed the day he'd brought Gregory back to the Turner home after he'd run away, Jordan pulled out the pad he'd written his notes on from that particular incident. He had witnessed a very loud Mr. Turner, a man who was clearly upset, allow his anger to give way to cursing and yelling.

Was it possible that Mr. Turner had just been upset over the child running away again? Had his anger been an expression of relief that the boy was safe?

It was Jordan's experience that natural parents had a tendency to react the same way as Mr. Turner had when a runaway child was returned to them. Some parents cried and hugged their children, while others screamed

A Message From The Arabesque General Manager

Dear Arabesque Reader,

I invite you to join the club! The Arabesque book club delivers four novels each month right to your front door! It's easy, and you will never miss a romance by one of our award-winning authors!

With upcoming novels featuring strong, sexy women, and African-American heroes that are charming, loving and true… you won't want to miss a single release! Our authors fill each page with exceptional dialogue, exciting plot twists, and enough sizzling romance to keep you riveted until the satisfying end! To receive novels by bestselling authors such as Gwynne Forster, Janice Sims, Angela Winters and others, I encourage you to join now!

Read about the men we love… in the pages of Arabesque!

Linda Gill
GENERAL MANAGER, ARABESQUE ROMANCE NOVELS

SPECIAL OFFER! 4 BOOKS FREE!

A SPECIAL "THANK YOU" FROM ARABESQUE JUST FOR YOU!

Send this card back and you'll receive 4 FREE Arabesque Novels—a $25.96 value—absolutely FREE!

The introductory 4 Arabesque Romance books are yours FREE (plus $1.99 shipping & handling). If you wish to continue to receive 4 books every month, do nothing. Each month, we will send you 4 New Arabesque Romance Novels for your free examination. If you wish to keep them, pay just $18* (plus, $1.99 shipping & handling). If you decide not to continue, you owe nothing!

- Send no money now.
- Never an obligation.
- Books delivered to your door!

We hope that after receiving your FREE books you'll want to remain an Arabesque subscriber, but the choice is yours! So why not take advantage of this Arabesque offer, with no risk of any kind. You'll be glad you did!

In fact, we're so sure you will love your Arabesque novels, that we will send you an Arabesque Tote Bag FREE with your first paid shipment.

* PRICES SUBJECT TO CHANGE.

YOU'LL GET 4 SELECT ROMANCES PLUS THIS FABULOUS TOTE BAG!

ARABESQUE

THE "THANK YOU" GIFT INCLUDES:

- 4 books absolutely FREE (plus $1.99 for shipping and handling).
- A FREE newsletter, *Arabesque Romance News*, filled with author interviews, book previews, special offers, and more!
- No risks or obligations. You're free to cancel whenever you wish with no questions asked.

INTRODUCTORY OFFER CERTIFICATE

Yes! Please send me 4 FREE Arabesque novels (plus $1.99 for shipping & handling). I understand I am under no obligation to purchase any books, as explained on the back of this card. Send my free tote bag after my first regular paid shipment.

NAME _____

ADDRESS _____ APT. ____

CITY _____ STATE _____ ZIP _____

TELEPHONE (___) _____

E-MAIL _____

SIGNATURE _____

Offer limited to one per household and not valid to current subscribers. All orders subject to approval. Terms, offer, & price subject to change. Tote bags available while supplies last.

Thank You!

AN016A

ARABESQUE

Accepting the four introductory books for FREE (plus $1.99 to offset the cost of shipping & handling) places you under no obligation to buy anything. You may keep the books and return the shipping statement marked "cancelled". If you do not cancel, about a month later we will send 4 additional Arabesque novels, and you will be billed the preferred subscriber's price of just $4.50 per title. That's $18.00* for all 4 books for a savings of almost 30% off the cover price (Plus $1.99 for shipping and handling). You may cancel at any time, but if you choose to continue, every month we'll send you 4 more books, which you may either purchase at the preferred discount price... or return to us and cancel your subscription.

* PRICES SUBJECT TO CHANGE

and yelled at them soon after the initial euphoria of their safe return had dissipated. Jordan couldn't rule out that possibility in the Turner case.

Gregory was good at lying to everyone, which meant he could be lying about how he was being treated by the Turners. His pattern of lying was well documented. He was an extremely unhappy child who'd been dissatisfied in every home he'd ever resided in. He also knew the system very well, so Jordan was sure Gregory knew exactly how to play the sides against the middle.

Jordan was left to wonder whether Gregory had played him. He'd find out soon enough. Although he was satisfied with the outcome of the report, he planned on keeping a close eye on Gregory and the Turner household. Jordan also decided to sponsor Gregory for membership in the Boys and Girls Club of America.

It was really hard for Jordan to devise fun and educational activities for the young man because of his impairment, but hearing wasn't a requirement for hitting a Ping-Pong ball across the table or playing board games. Jordan even thought of hiring an interpreter to assist Gregory in participating in club activities. Keeping Gregory's mind occupied in a positive way was his main objective. Jordan planned to become an anonymous benefactor to Gregory, but he'd continue to foster their relationship.

The moment Jordan thought of Scotland, he picked up the phone to call her, wanting to make sure she made it to work okay. Her cell wasn't on when she was working a case, so he planned to leave her an inspiring message if she was unavailable. The thought of seeing her in class later in the evening made him smile. Jordan realized he'd done a complete one-eighty in their relationship, but it was the best turnaround he'd ever made. If he could make the same drastic alterations with his parents, his life would be much rosier.

CHAPTER NINE

Scotland hadn't felt this bad in a long time. Her throat was hurting something awful, and her stomach had been upset all day. Although she hadn't taken her temperature since she'd had to return home from work early, over five hours ago, she knew she had an abnormally high one. Her body felt like it was on fire. Sweats and chills had pervaded her entire being.

Just before leaving work Scotland had called on Nathan to take over her evening signing class as a substitute. She hoped everyone would take kindly to him. He was a great instructor, but a no-nonsense one. Nathan wasn't known for coddling his students. He believed that a strict approach would help them meet their goals more readily. There was no way Scotland could make it in to the community center. Just lying there in her bed took more energy than she had to expend, so she'd just have to rely on Nathan to take care of everything.

Thinking about how she often coddled Jordan in the class made Scotland wince. Nathan more than likely would've thrown him out of his class by now. Jordan needed special attention because he didn't believe wholeheartedly that he could really accomplish his goal in signing. But she had to admit that she'd seen a lot of growth in him. He was more confident now.

Jordan had come a long way from when he'd first started the class. He'd come full circle in more ways than one. She was thrilled by all the changes in him, yet she realized his fears weren't very far away. He could easily go back to allowing fear to control him if he reverted to living in the past. Deep down she knew that he wanted to live a Christian life, but she still wasn't convinced that Jordan believed he deserved everything his heart desired, including her. Scotland vowed to never stop praying for Jordan's deliverance from all the fears afflicting him.

Lifting her throbbing head from the pillow made it hurt even worse, but Scotland needed a drink from the large bottle of water she'd placed on the bedside table. As she twisted the cap off the plastic container, she noticed the red message button flashing on her cell phone. Since she'd cleared up her previous night's absence with her family—without saying where she'd been all night—she didn't think the message was from any one of them.

Scotland hoped it wasn't an emergency call. Although she had left the courthouse early, she'd forgotten to contact the emergency registry to let them know she'd be unavailable for the next day or so. Before checking her messages, she decided she should call the registry first.

Hearing Jordan's message on her voice mail lifted Scotland's spirits. His voice did all sorts of crazy things to her, never failing to excite her. She thought it was so sweet of him to call and see if she'd made it to work okay. It suddenly dawned on her that he didn't know that she wasn't going to be in class. Although he probably wouldn't ask Nathan why she wasn't there, that is, if Nathan didn't tell the class first, Scotland was sure that

Jordan would worry about her. It was too late to reach him on his cell since the class had already started.

Yeah, she had made it to work okay, Scotland mused, but not long after her arrival, the real problems had begun. She'd had to take care of her first court case of the day because it would've taken too long to get someone to cover for her, which more than likely would've resulted in the postponement of the case.

This court case had turned out to be much like something on one of those court television shows. It was sad and disheartening to everyone involved. A hearing-impaired father had asked for a paternity test twenty years after his son's birth. He no longer believed the young man was his son, stating that he'd always been suspicious that he wasn't the father. The DNA test results were to be read by the judge.

The plaintiff had indicated to the court through Scotland's interpretation that he had a strong desire to rid himself of his wife, the mother of the young man. It was his belief that his wife had duped him into marrying her, knowing all along that he wasn't the father. He had even called her a churchgoing heathen, making repeated references to her being seated in the front pew at church every week. Things had gotten pretty heated between the couple from that point on.

All three family members were present, and it broke Scotland's heart to see how much it hurt the son to be openly rejected by the only man he'd known as his father. Scotland had watched the son experience total devastation during the proceedings. What had made no sense whatsoever to Scotland was the fact that it was far too late for child support to be the bone of contention, since the son was now nearly twenty years old.

Scotland later learned that this case had to do with inheritance issues. The plaintiff wanted solid proof of paternity before executing his last will and testament. If the young man turned out not to be his biological child, the plaintiff planned to remove him from his will.

Unfortunately, the DNA tests had proved that the plaintiff wasn't the biological father. Scotland's silent condemnation of the plaintiff and his irredeemable actions belied her Christian values. She couldn't understand how a man could live with a child for twenty years and not bond with him in some way.

Then Scotland had thought of Jordan and James, a perfect example of a serious lack of father and son bonding. After recovering from her bout of condemnatory thinking, Scotland had fervently prayed for God to have mercy on both misguided families. Every man who treated his son with open contempt was to be pitied, not censored. She had also prayed for forgiveness for her repulsive thoughts.

Reliving the court case brought tears to Scotland's eyes. She now felt even worse. She was now an emotional mess as well as a physical one.

As Jordan raced his silver BMW SUV toward his house, he was beside himself with worry over Scotland's absence in class. The news that a substitute was standing in for her had come as quite a shock. He'd wanted desperately to ask the instructor why she hadn't shown up, but he hadn't wanted to draw attention to himself by showing a personal interest in her whereabouts. He had kept hoping that someone else would ask, but no one had. Since he'd been a little late to class, he didn't know if the instructor had explained Scotland's absence before he'd arrived.

It had dawned on Jordan only after the class had ended that the substitute instructor was Brianna's fiancé. As he thought back on some of the things Nathan had said about how well his fiancée functioned with her hearing impairment, Jordan wondered why he hadn't figured out who he was sooner. Would his knowing have made a difference in whether he asked about Scotland? Jordan wasn't sure.

On the other hand, if Nathan had known anything about Jordan, he hadn't said a word to him. That made Jordan believe that Scotland hadn't mentioned him to anyone in her family. He figured that if Brianna knew about him, then Nathan would also know something.

Jordan could honestly say that he hadn't heard much of what had been said in the class, nor had he learned anything more about signing. His mind had stayed stuck on Scotland. It disturbed him that she hadn't called him to let him know she'd be absent. Keeping his old insecurities under wraps was difficult for him.

The same stinging questions had popped into Jordan's mind over a dozen times already. Did Scotland's unexplained absence have something to do with the sudden change in their relationship? Was she regretting spending the night in his home? Had she experienced a sudden change of heart? Had she decided that he wasn't good enough for her after all—and was she now avoiding him because of it?

No sooner had Jordan picked up his cell phone to call Scotland when it rang. He let out a huge sigh of relief when he saw her number on the viewing screen. "Are you okay, Scotland! Where are you?"

Scotland was concerned hearing the anxiety lacing Jordan's voice, yet she smiled weakly. "I'm at home, Jordan, sick as I've ever been in my life. Just wanted to call and let you know why I wasn't in class, in case Nathan didn't mention it."

Jordan's anxiousness instantly turned to concern. "Sick. Sorry to hear that. What's wrong with you, angel?"

Scotland moaned. "Stomach flu of some sort, I'm assuming. My throat hurts too. In fact, I ache all over. Nausea and fever are kicking my butt."

"Do you need me to come over there and see about you? I'd really like to."

"I'm too weak to get up to answer the door, Jordan. I've been no farther from my bedroom than my bathroom since I first got home. I'll probably be okay in a day or so."

Scotland had been thinking earlier about how happy she was that she'd had the good sense to purchase a one-story home. Getting up and down stairs in her condition would've taken some serious maneuvering. Jordan had two sets of staircases in his home, a back one and front one, and she wouldn't want to tackle either feeling as bad as she did now.

"Don't you keep an emergency spare key somewhere outside the house?"

"As a matter of fact, I do." Scotland told Jordan where she kept the key, glad that she hadn't turned the house alarm on yet. However, she could've always given Jordan the pass code and then changed it later if the need arose.

"I'm just entering our development. I'll be there in a jiffy. Dr. Feel-good is on the way."

Scotland managed to laugh lightly. "Aretha will be awaiting your healing touch, honey," she joked, wincing at the burning in her throat. Keeping her mouth shut might be a good idea, she mused, since her throat burned every time she spoke.

It felt kind of strange to Jordan to let himself into Scotland's house, but he knew it was for a very good reason. She'd sounded horrible, and he needed to check on her condition for his own peace of mind. He'd never get to sleep knowing she was all alone at home and ill, with no one to look after her. He had to chuckle at that. Scotland had an entire family at her beck and call, a family who loved her dearly.

As Jordan headed toward the back rooms of the house, not sure where the master bedroom was, he stuck out his chest in a proud manner. Although Scotland probably would've called on her family sooner or later, she'd phoned him . . . and then had allowed him to come over when she could've easily turned down his request to see her. Her desire to have him there with her at a time like this made him feel really special. Jordan dared to think he was the man.

"Scotland, it's Jordan," he yelled, "give me a shout so I'll know where to find you." After he called out to her several times with no response, a bout of fear snatched at his calm. Had she gotten worse in such a short time, he wondered. Jordan hoped not.

Finally locating what he thought might be Scotland's bedroom, figuring the double entryway was a good indication of such, Jordan opened the door and stepped inside. Stretched out on the bed, fast asleep, and bathed in perspiration was the woman he hadn't been able to stop thinking about. Thoughts of Scotland consumed him night and day. Seeing her looking so fragile and helpless made his heart ache.

Not sure if he should wake her up or not, Jordan walked over to the bed and looked down at her. Her skin was too pale, but her cheeks were as red as fire. *High fever*, he mused, knowing that getting her temperature back down to normal was the first order of business. He knew exactly how to achieve it, but he was sure that Scotland wasn't going to let him put her in a tub of cold water naked. He'd have to run the cold water for her and then let her do the rest herself. This wasn't the role he'd had in mind for Dr. Feel-good, but someone had to play the part.

Jordan sat down on the side of the bed and woke Scotland by nudging her gently. The second she opened her eyes, he carefully lifted her head and took her in his arms, kissing her forehead. "Thanks for letting me come see about you. I hate seeing you feeling like this."

Scotland felt better just having Jordan there with her. Her dad would've come running had she called him, but she was happy that Jordan had offered to come "Thanks for wanting to come," she rasped, her throat raw and scratchy.

Jordan looked at Scotland with grave concern, laying her head back down on the pillow. "You know we have to get this fever down, don't you? Getting you into a tub of cold water is the only way I can think of to do it. Are you ready for that?"

To show her displeasure at his suggestion, Scotland made a shivering gesture, chattering her teeth. Fever or not, there was no way she was baring her body in front of Jordan. If she had to get into cold water, he wouldn't be in the bathroom with her. Just imagining that scene caused her utter embarrassment. "Don't be so cruel, Jordan. Icing myself down is a very chilly thought. Let me try a couple of Tylenol first since I haven't taken any kind of medication yet. You'll find a bottle in my bathroom on the lower shelf of the medicine cabinet." Scotland didn't know why she kept on talking when it hurt so much.

Jordan frowned heavily. "We can try that, but I think you're beyond the Tylenol stage. You may as well get your mind and body geared up for taking an icy dip in the tub. Taking you to the emergency room is another alternative."

Scotland quickly shook her head at that suggestion. Hospitals weren't her favorite places to visit, let alone to be a patient in.

Jordan walked the short distance to the master bathroom and then disappeared inside, returning seconds later with a large red-and-white bottle in hand. He repositioned himself on the side of the bed. After opening the container of Tylenol, he removed two tablets and handed them to her. He then uncapped her bottle of water so that she could swallow the tablets. "Do you have a plastic basin of some sort around here?"

Just to see if Jordan would understand what she was going to tell him, and to hopefully give her throat a bit of rest, Scotland signed her response. The instant Jordan stood and headed back to the bathroom, she knew he'd understood. That made her smile. Her teaching was paying off.

With a basin in hand, Jordan came right back into the room. "Where do you keep your nightclothes?"

Scotland looked puzzled. She then asked him "why," using sign language again.

"The things you have on are soaked with perspiration," he signed, proud of how proficiently he'd done so.

Pointing at the chest of drawers, Scotland couldn't help smiling. Jordan was definitely a take-charge kind of man, and she loved his method of taking over. Her clothes were wet, and she did need to change them, so he'd get no argument there. But he'd have to leave the room for her to change. Jordan wasn't her husband yet.

Jordan retrieved from Scotland's dresser drawer what he thought was appropriate sleepwear for a sick woman: a pair of warm but lightweight pajamas. Her temperature was high, and her skin needed to breathe. After tossing the pajamas on the bottom of the bed, Jordan went back into the bathroom to fill the basin with water for her to wash up with.

* * *

Awakening from a fitful sleep, Jordan sat up straight in the comfortable overstuffed bedside chair and removed his feet from the hassock. According to the clock radio, it wasn't even midnight yet, but he would've guessed it to be much later than that. It had been after nine in the evening when he'd first arrived at Scotland's place. Time had a way of flying when one was having a good time, but in times of misery the minutes ticked by very sluggishly. It seemed to Jordan as if he'd been asleep in the chair for hours.

Looking over at Scotland, Jordan saw that she was still knocked out cold. Although she'd fought him tooth and nail, he had insisted on the cold bath when her fever wouldn't come down with just the Tylenol. Once he'd won the war, Jordan had handed her a bathrobe before he'd gone into the bathroom to fill the tub. The look Scotland had given him as he'd helped her out of bed had Jordan worried that her halo was about to slip off the top of her head.

The devil couldn't have appeared any more hateful than Scotland had at that very moment. She hadn't cursed at Jordan, but as far as he was concerned, she may as well have. The scowling expressions on her face and her angry mumblings had been nothing less than substitutes for real expletives. The funny thing was that she'd also signed her cutting remarks while voicing them. Hands with a really bad attitude weren't something new to Jordan. Gregory also had quite a way with expressive hand gestures.

Jordan had chalked up Scotland's ugly behavior to her illness, but he'd really itched to tell her she wasn't acting very Christian-like. His angel acting out like an advocate of the devil hadn't sat very well with him. Scotland needed to go back to practicing what she'd been preaching to him, but he had to admit she'd warned him of how she could be at times. Getting a glimpse of her in the throes of sin hadn't changed his mind about her, though.

In fact, if he were to be completely honest about it, Jordan had also found her bad behavior somewhat amusing, but that didn't excuse it. Scotland had looked utterly ridiculous to him throughout her naughty performances. Flawed or not, she was still Jordan's angel.

Not wanting to awaken Scotland, Jordan eased out of the chair and tiptoed down the hall to use the guest bathroom. He also needed a shower, but that would have to wait until he got home.

Jordan had already planned to call in and take a vacation day so he could continue to care for Scotland. But if her bad temperament persisted, he wasn't going to waste any time in telling her exactly what he thought of it. Their first argument wasn't something he looked forward to, but Jordan wasn't going to back away from it, either.

He had decided that people could treat him only the way he allowed them to.

After setting up the television tray next to Scotland's bed, Jordan retrieved the hot chicken broth, oyster crackers, and white grape juice he'd placed on her nightstand. Without uttering a single word, Scotland had eyed Jordan's every move with suspicion. Her expression indicated to him her displeasure. Poised to do battle, should Scotland refuse to try and eat something, he helped her sit up in bed. She had already washed her face and hands with the toiletry items he'd brought her. That she hadn't resisted his help thus far was a good sign to Jordan.

Scotland shook her head from side to side. "Jordan, I

don't know . . . about this. I still may not be able to keep anything down."

Jordan held up his hand in a halting gesture. "You won't know if you don't at least try. You have to keep your strength up, Scotland."

Looking as if she were about to object, Scotland thrust out her chin in defiance. Then her shoulders sagged. She realized she should save her energy for getting well, not use what little oomph she had to fight with Jordan, the guardian angel who'd watched over her throughout the night. Before picking up the soup-spoon, Scotland smiled at Jordan. "I think I should accept that Dr. Feel-good knows what's best for me. You haven't been wrong yet."

Grateful that Scotland had a least acknowledged his good treatment of her in some small way, Jordan smiled back at her. He would've preferred it if an apology had come from her sweet lips, but since it hadn't, he'd leave it at that. He didn't want an apology if she wasn't truly sorry.

"I'm sorry for how bad I acted last night, Jordan," Scotland said with deep regret, as if she'd somehow read his mind. "I realize I wasn't very nice to you. I hope you'll forgive me."

Jordan's yet to be named feelings for Scotland filled him up to the brim. Her apology had been sincere and immediately his disillusionment with her faded. He was much happier with the old Scotland and hoped the one who'd shown up last night wouldn't ever make another appearance. Jordan hated conflicts. "Forgive you? But of course! How's your stomach reacting to the broth?"

Scotland nodded. "So far so good. Thanks for taking such good care of me." She glanced over at the clock. "If you don't get going, you'll be late for work. I'm much better now."

Jordan looked down at the floor then back up at her. "I decided not to go into work today. I thought you could use me around here. But if you'd rather be alone, I can go on home. I'll stick around my place just in case you need me to do something for you. We need to get you well so you won't miss your cousin's surprise birthday party. It's only a few days away."

Touched by Jordan's willingness to miss a day of work just for her, Scotland had to choke back her tears. All his kindness and goodness had thrived in the wake of her tantrums. She couldn't feel any worse than she did over her mistreatment of him. "I'd really like for you to stay here with me, Jordan. It would mean so much to me. As for missing Brianna's party, I won't. If I have to arrive at the hotel by ambulance, I'll be there."

Scotland had to laugh at her own hilarious remark, right along with Jordan.

Jordan was relieved that he wasn't going to suffer another major disappointment at the hands of Scotland. Knowing she was only human allowed him to remove her feet from the fire he'd been holding them to. "At least your sense of humor has returned. I'm happy you want me around. Would you mind if I run home to shower and change clothes? I promise to come back as soon as possible. Then you can do anything you want with me for the rest of the day."

Scotland raised a suggestive eyebrow, smiling flirtatiously. "Anything, Jordan? You might need to define that one. My imagination is off and running."

"So am I. I'm going to leave that one alone, Miss Kennedy."

Happy to see that she'd finished both her broth and juice, Jordan walked over to the bed, where he cleared the tray and then removed it from the bedside. He stored the crackers on the nightstand in case she wanted to eat them later. Jordan then sat down on the very edge of the mattress. Taking Scotland in his arms, he gave her a warm hug. "Will you be okay until I get back? I promise not to take too long."

Scotland pressed her forehead against Jordan's. "I'm going to hold you to that promise. At the same time, I'll be counting the seconds till you return."

"We've got a date," Jordan said, rising from the bed. Since Scotland had already made it perfectly clear that she didn't want him to catch whatever she suffered from, he bent over and kissed her forehead. Jordan had told her that just being in the same room with her made him susceptible to her airborne germs. "See you in a few."

"Hey, Jordan," Scotland called out, "this might be a good time for us to watch *The Passion of The Christ*. If you're okay with that, you can bring the DVD back with you."

Jordan smiled. "Sounds like a plan. I'll put the key where it was until I get back."

Stretched out at the bottom of Scotland's bed, Jordan could hardly believe what he'd witnessed during the first hour of the film. The unspeakable violence had left him uncertain as to whether he wanted to see the rest of it. Scotland had sobbed off and on during the entire first part of the movie. She had been visibly shaken by the content of the movie . . . and she'd seen it before. After several failed attempts to console her, he'd decided to allow her to let her emotions run their course. Watching the film hadn't been a good idea, especially when Scotland was feeling so ill. Spiritually uplifting, it wasn't.

The Son of God was more real to Jordan now than ever before. He'd heard a few Bible stories about Jesus' walk on earth, but he'd never checked out all the details for himself. Although he was now studying the Bible, he hadn't read about any of what he'd seen thus far. Jordan hated to admit it, even to himself, but he was scared to view the last two hours of the film, which depicted among other things Jesus' crucifixion. Jordan couldn't even begin to imagine the bloodshed yet to come.

Scotland reached over and put her hand on the small of Jordan's back. "Hard to watch, huh? I guess I should've told you what to expect. I'm sorry."

Jordan shrugged. "No need to be. It's as broad as it is long. I could've asked. I was surprised that the dialogue is in Aramaic and Latin. I guess they couldn't have shown it in English-speaking countries without the subtitles."

Scotland looked thoughtful. "I was surprised by the Aramaic and Latin, too. How do you feel about the film so far?"

Jordan pondered Scotland's question. The film had put a human face on Jesus for Jordan. It had also allowed him to get more than just a glimpse of Jesus as a mere mortal man. He had always thought of the Almighty as hard-hearted, with the strength of a brute, a super being that had the power to take on the world and destroy it if necessary. Jordan had been taught that God would take him out in a heartbeat if he didn't behave himself.

"That's a hard question for me to answer right now. Things are still sinking it. The violent content is bam, right in your face." He became quiet and pensive.

Scotland got the impression that Jordan really didn't want to talk about the film, but she could understand that. Its subject matter was hard to digest. Jordan seemed so disturbed by what he'd seen. Something about him had suddenly changed. For the better or worse? She wasn't sure.

"We can always talk about it later, Jordan. I know what you're feeling right now."

It had been mind-boggling for Jordan to learn that, just like every other human being, Jesus had experienced gut-wrenching pain. He'd felt what other human beings feel. The violence perpetrated against Him had begun almost immediately after the soldiers had discovered Him in the Garden of Gethsemane. If the punching, slapping, kicking, and spitting had caused him unmitigated anguish just by watching it on a screen, Jordan couldn't imagine how Jesus had withstood it.

Jordan thought that every gang member and every person who had committed spousal abuse should be forced to see *The Passion of The Christ* when they came before the courts. Perhaps it would help them change their violent ways. It hurt like the dickens to get punched and kicked. Verbal jabs hurt just as much.

Jordan most identified with the betrayal of Jesus by His own disciples. He knew firsthand how painful it was when someone very close to you betrayed you. Most surprising to Jordan was when Jesus showed anger toward His Father.

Jordan turned over on his back and looked up at the ceiling. "I was surprised when Jesus exhibited anger toward His Father, then humbly prayed for the hour of death to pass Him by. In the next breath, He asked for His Father's will to be done, not His."

Scotland turned her mouth down at the corners, shaking her head. "I don't think He was angry, Jordan. Passionate and emotional is how I perceive His conversation with God. Jesus knew He was about to die, that the prophecy of His death was soon to be fulfilled. I know we all perceive things differently, so I'm not trying to change your mind. Can you imagine how He must've felt knowing the time for His death was at hand? I can't."

Stroking his chin thoughtfully, Jordan looked Scotland dead in the eyes. "Were you just passionate and emotional last night when you were giving me all that attitude? I perceived it as anger toward me, when all I was trying to do was help you out. Am I wrong, Scotland?"

Thoroughly ashamed of herself, Scotland closed her eyes for a moment. She could now see that she had deeply wounded Jordan. Being sick was no excuse for how she'd made him feel. She had felt that he was forcing her to do something against her will. That had angered her. That must've been how Jesus had seen His imminent demise. He hadn't wanted to die anymore than anyone else, yet He had to. He was on earth to die for the sins of all mankind. Maybe it *was* anger that He'd displayed toward the Father.

"I can't take back any of what I said or did last night, but I can try hard not to let it happen again. Jordan, if you're looking for perfection in me, you won't find it. I'm not perfect, just as I told you before. I'm not using that as an excuse, either. But, Jordan, sin is a condition of the human spirit. It's what makes us human. Please don't entertain any unrealistic expectations of me. I do enough of that myself."

The tension Jordan felt was visible in his rigid jawbone. "Then treat me the same way you expect me to treat you. Aren't you same person who told me that people might forget what you do and say to them, but never how you made them feel? I won't sit idly by and have you disrespect me like you did yesterday."

Scotland looked startled. This side of Jordan came as a complete shocker to her. She had offended him more than she'd initially thought. The fact that he hadn't been able to move past the incident, even after her apology, indicated that he'd been stewing in his own juices all night long. Jordan had trusted her with his history of emotional and psychological abuse. Look at what she'd done with it. She had turned around and had inflicted the same kind of pain on him that he'd accused his parents of. Her regret was soul-deep.

Jordan sat straight up. "Since you always speak of the human spirit, you should already know that as humans, our feelings are easily hurt." He opened one hand and slid his other hand down it in a zooming gesture. "Disrespect me again . . . and I'm out. Since you like everything so crystal clear, let's be clear on that, Scotland."

Scotland blinked back tears, biting back the sharp retort on the tip of her tongue. "You've made yourself very clear, Jordan." Thinking it was best to stop right there, Scotland remained quiet. Her acrid tongue had already gotten her in enough trouble. It was quite apparent that Jordan didn't want to hear her voice another weak apology. He obviously hadn't accepted the first one she'd offered. But she refused to admit that she deserved his wrath.

"Through it all, Satan had been right there to tempt Jesus to follow after him."

It took Scotland a minute to realize Jordan had gone back to talking about the film. How he was able to change directions so quickly amazed her. He was the type of person who said exactly what they had to say and then moved right on. Talking about temptation, Scotland was glad that she hadn't given in to retaliation against Jordan.

Jordan couldn't even remember all the temptations he'd resisted over the years. Then there were those numerous enticements that he hadn't been able to resist. Jordan recalled every one of them. As Scotland's bad behavior again came to Jordan's mind, he knew he had to soften his heart toward her and accept the fact that she *was* only human.

Jesus had displayed human emotions of every kind. He had laughed and had cried, and had experienced both joy and sorrow. He had also eaten, drunk, and slept like any other flesh and blood person. It was clear to Jordan that Jesus' heart was vulnerable to human suffering and irreparable breakage.

Unsure if Scotland would allow him to touch her, Jordan nonetheless reached for her hand. He was over what had happened, and he hoped she was also, but he wasn't going to apologize for something he'd meant to say. "Are you hungry?"

Scotland's first thought was to roll her eyes at Jordan and then turn her back and completely ignore his presence. Human nature worked in all sorts of ways, but rarely could it override the pureness of the heart. Scotland also believed that Jordan would make good on his threat and bid her farewell; she really didn't want that. If she was going to be a role model for Christianity, she had to be ever mindful that she could only lead by example. Scotland got the feeling that she was going to learn every bit as much from Jordan as he might glean from her.

Scotland smiled softly. "I'm starving, but maybe I should stick to the liquid diet another day, just in case this is more than a twenty-four-hour bug. Would you mind fixing more soup?"

Jordan felt relieved but did not show it. "A bowl of soup coming right up."

As Jordan prepared for bed, he smiled to himself, pleased with how well the rest of the day and evening had gone for Scotland and him. Although she was feeling much better, he had offered to stay with her another night. Scotland had declined his offer, stating that she'd be fine. There hadn't been any further mention of their minor blowup, for which he was grateful.

Jordan laughed out loud when he thought about

how they had played the board game Yahtzee Deluxe
Poker. Scotland's game-room closet held every board
game imaginable. For a Christian girl, she sure knew a
heck of a lot about poker. He'd ended up winning as
many times as she had, but she was the one who'd taught
him the game. It had been a lot of fun.

However much fun he'd had, the games were just
something else to remind Jordan of all that he'd missed
out on due to his father's lack of interest in him. James
had never played a single board game with Jordan, but
Regina had engaged him in a game of checkers a few
times. When Scotland had proposed reading a story to
him from one of her inspirational novels, Jordan had
felt like a small child inside, eagerly nodding his approval.

No woman Jordan had been romantically interested
in had ever offered to read to him. After Scotland had
read the first two chapters, Jordan had wanted to hear
more. Scotland had promised him that she'd periodically read a chapter until they'd reached the end. He
wasn't sure why sharing a book appealed so much to
him, but he was looking forward to the next reading
session. The whole idea of it was rather titillating.

Being with Scotland was an entirely different experience for Jordan. It was amazing how much fun they had
doing nothing at all. That he wasn't consumed by the
possibility of a physical relationship with her was a nice
change. He didn't feel pressured to pursue that.

Although spending money on Scotland wasn't a
problem for Jordan, she had described all the fun times
they could have without it costing them a thing. He had
learned a lot of things about her just from being in her
surroundings. Scotland was a bubble bath and candlelight kind of girl, and she liked a variety of perfume
scents. Her master bathroom was stocked with all sorts
of bath and body products. Her sleepwear drawer was

filled with quite a selection of nightwear, including silks, satins, and flannels. Scotland had told him that she loved jewelry, simple pieces, but very expressive ones, like the diamond cross pendant she wore often. She had also showed him a stunning diamond star pendant and a diamond butterfly, both of which were gifts from her father. Dainty gold necklaces and earrings were also among her favorites.

From books to jewels, Jordan now knew many of Scotland's personal preferences.

Ready to pray to the Master before he climbed into bed, Jordan fell down on his knees. For him, it was no longer about measuring up to the ideas of man. Jordan had always wanted to be a much better man than James, to show his father that he'd become a man despite the way James had withheld his love from him. It felt good to Jordan to know that he didn't have to prove a thing to any human. Man could not save his soul.

Even though Jordan knew there was no way in the world that he'd ever measure up to Jesus, that it was impossible to do so, he had the desire to come as close as he could. All the years he'd thought he was unworthy of love had been disapproved by a mere sixty minutes of film. Jesus had suffered the unthinkable to save each and every one of His children. Jordan knew that he could never repay such unfathomable mercy, but he could give Jesus his heart in return.

"Please come into my heart, Lord Jesus. Save me, change me, then make me whole."

CHAPTER TEN

The Esquire Hotel's ballroom was very festively decorated. Silver and blue helium-filled balloons shaped like stars and half-moons and silver streamers hung from the ceiling. Lighted candles, also shaped like stars and moons, served as decorative centerpieces on the tables. The celestial theme of the party reflected Brianna's fascination and love for astrology.

The moment the Kennedy clan walked into the ballroom, the entire place fell into a state of animation. The bright lights came up at the same time everyone yelled "surprise." Brian then led everyone in singing "Happy Birthday To You" to his daughter, who appeared to be in a state of shock.

Scotland saw that getting Brianna to calm down was an impossible task at the moment. The animated birthday girl had already run from one end of the ballroom to the other no less than three times. With tears flowing down her face, Brianna was laughing and crying at the same time. Seeing all of her family, friends, and associates in one room had her emotional beyond words.

There was no doubt in the minds of the Kennedy

family that they'd successfully pulled off the surprise party of the century. Each of the family members had received big hugs and dozens of kisses from Brianna. That their loved one hadn't had a clue about the party made everything even more special for the Kennedy clan. Almost as inquisitive as Scotland, Brianna had her own special way of finding out what she wanted to know, but this time she hadn't suspected a thing. Everyone had Nathan to thank for that. He had done most of the legwork in planning the party, which enabled them to keep Brianna totally in the dark.

Brianna couldn't have been more pleased. Seeing his daughter so happy, Brian knew he'd accomplished his mission. Nathan was ecstatic, too. He'd also been a recipient of Brianna's love and affection. It appeared as though she couldn't show her appreciation enough.

Smiling sweetly, Scotland took hold of Jordan's hand. "We did it! We actually pulled it off. Brianna is one very happy lady." Scotland's eyes softened. "Thanks for being here to help us celebrate. I'm glad you were here to witness Bri's reaction. My cousin is on cloud nine."

Jordan kissed Scotland's cheek. "Thanks for inviting me, babe. I bet you thought I was going to change my mind after that little heart-to-heart we had about your family, huh?"

Scotland chuckled. "You'd win the bet hands down. I half expected you at some point to bow out gracefully. I know we had a deal, but you've been really nervous about this."

Jordan squeezed her hand. "It worked out for both of us. Once I get to officially meet your family, I'll be able to relax more, hopefully. I guess I should consider myself lucky to be sitting at the head table with you?"

"No luck here. It's a blessing to sit with the Kennedy clan. You're a part of us tonight."

"Just for tonight?" Jordan joked, raising a questioning eyebrow.

"For as long as you want to be a part of us, Jordan. Everyone will love having you around as much as I do. Let's get to the table so we can get this first meeting out the way. You look too good in that fabulous tuxedo to get yourself all sweaty from a case of nerves. This may be Brianna's party, but I'll be the envy of every single woman here. You got it going on, Jordan."

Jordan drew her to him for a warm hug. "That makes two of us. You're a ten plus in that little black number. I love the sheer sleeves and neckline. Are church girls allowed to look this sexy, Scotland? Shouldn't you be wearing something akin to a habit?"

"Flattery will get you everywhere. It'll also allow you to get away with that last remark. But I wouldn't push the envelope any further if I were you," Scotland warned Jordan in a teasing manner. "That reference to me being a church girl is going to get you into hot water yet."

"Promise?"

Rolling her eyes at Jordan in a dramatic fashion, Scotland sucked her teeth. "Oh, you're just too incorrigible for words this evening, Mr. La Cour. The fine way you look tonight must be going straight to your head."

"Being here with you is the only thing that's going straight to my head. I'm sure lots of envy will come my way as well. You're so beautiful, Scotland."

"Thank you." Gripping Jordan's hand tightly, Scotland led him around the perimeter of the dance floor to the head table. With his hand literally shaking in hers, she knew that Jordan was still very nervous about meeting her family. Scotland wanted to get the formal introductions over as soon as possible so that Jordan could relax and have a good time. She hoped it wouldn't take him long to see that everyone in her family was A-OK.

Scotland first introduced Jordan to her father, Scott, then stood back to allow the two men to shake hands. Scott was very amicable toward his daughter's date, welcoming Jordan to share in the family birthday celebration. The rest of the Kennedy family was just as friendly toward Jordan, telling him they were glad he could make it to the party. Brianna really surprised Jordan by hugging him as if she'd known him all her life. She then signed her joy in finally getting to meet him, mouthing her warm sentiment at the same time.

Jordan was awestruck by the touchy-feely Kennedy clan. He was surprised by how relaxed he felt after only a short period of time. The way Scotland's father looked so adoringly at her touched Jordan deeply. He also saw how special the relationship between Brianna and her father was. Everyone at the head table seemed so genuine to him. He soon realized the Kennedys were a real down-to-earth American family.

Even though Jordan was aware that most people were on their best behavior during a public outing such as this one, he didn't believe for one second that the Kennedy family's feelings for one another were insincere. From all indications, they all had healthy relationships, though no one ever really knew what went on behind closed doors. But Jordan both felt and saw the love flowing between them. He couldn't help envying them.

Even though he had had Nathan as an instructor for only one signing class, Jordan could tell that Nathan was a good person. His attentiveness toward Brianna showed how much he loved her. They couldn't seem to keep their hands off each other. Jordan couldn't help imagining a relationship with Scotland that mirrored what Nathan and Brianna had.

Scotland leaned into Jordan with her shoulder,

breaking his train of thought. "Feeling better about things now?"

Jordan cast Scotland a dazzling smile. "It's all good. I'm very comfortable. This is really a great celebration you've all put together. I've never had a birthday party."

The sadness in Jordan's eyes pierced Scotland's heart. He appeared so childlike when his pain showed. The longing in his eyes cut her to the quick. Never to have had a birthday party was unimaginable for her, because she and Brianna had had one every single year of their childhood. Their eighteenth birthday had been the only huge bash that she could remember. All the birthdays after that one were celebrated with quiet family dinners at home or in a special restaurant. Once they were married, Jordan would have a birthday celebration, too, she vowed.

Soft music floated in the air, signaling the beginning of the karaoke session. Scotland was glad for the musical interlude, because she was at a loss for words. She didn't know how to comfort Jordan without seeming like she was smothering him. It was good for him to face his demons, but she knew that it was also very painful for him. He hadn't spoken of his parents since the day they'd visited them. Scotland was dying to know if they were staying in touch as promised, but she wasn't going to pry. Jordan would let her know when and whatever he wanted her to know.

Scotland squeezed Jordan's hand in a reassuring manner just before turning her attention to Brianna, who was making her way to center stage. Since it was her party, she felt that she should perform first, which would hopefully loosen up everyone else who had a desire to sing. Feeling very patriotic, Brianna chose "God Bless America" for her solo performance. So many horrific things had happened during the last couple of years in the lives of the American people, yet America still stood tall and proud.

As Brianna mouthed the beautiful song and signed the lyrics, wearing her heart on her sleeve, Scotland's eyes wandered over to Nathan, who was every bit as emotional as Brianna. His deep, abiding love for his fiancée made his eyes shine brightly.

As a United States Air Force reservist, he had once been assigned to Baghdad for three months, which had seemed like an eternity to Brianna. He and Brianna had missed each other terribly, communicating by e-mail and snail mail on a daily basis. He'd been one of the blessed ones, returning to his homeland unharmed, while many of his comrades had been brought home on stretchers or in flag-draped coffins. That Nathan may have to return to the war was still a big possibility since he was still active in the reserves.

Scotland encouraged Jordan to go next, laughing at the weird look on his face, but he wasn't having any of it. Since she couldn't get Jordan to perform, she decided to take a turn. Scotland had an idea in mind that she thought Jordan might love. At least she hoped so.

Once on stage Scotland made direct eye contact with Jordan. She began to sing Ruben Studdard's "I Need An Angel," which had become Jordan's favorite song, just as the video to the song came on. As she poured her heart and soul into singing the lyrics, Scotland's eyes never once left Jordan's face. She was his angel, the one that God had sent to him, and she could only pray that he recognized it. Jordan was her angel, too. Scotland had no doubt about it.

Jordan felt a wild thumping inside his chest. Knowing Scotland was singing to him filled his heart to near bursting. Her angelic voice was sweet music to his ears, and the song she'd chosen to sing had him on the verge of tears. How could he feel so much for her so darn soon? She'd walked into his life and had turned him completely around in a matter of seconds. Jordan saw no way of turning back now, nor was it his desire to do so.

Cheering and shouting filled the ballroom as Scotland finished her performance. Her family and friends were cheering the loudest, while Jordan seemed to be in a total daze. He just couldn't believe how incredibly lucky he was to have met Scotland. The one woman he'd run away from at every chance had turned out to be the only woman in the world for him.

Jordan watched in awe as Scotland made her way back to her seat. He could see her wings flapping and her halo glowing. As she neared the table, he stood up and then drew her into his arms. He would've kissed her passionately had her family not been looking on, especially her father. "I get the feeling you sang that song just for me. Am I right?"

Scotland's soft kiss on Jordan's lips responded for her. "Only you, Jordan. Only you."

While many of the guests danced during the musical performances, Scotland and Jordan were content to just sit and chat with each other. When her family members joined in the conversation, Jordan's nervousness reappeared, but soon he began to relax. He'd suddenly realized that no one was going to cut his head off and hand it to him. The Kennedy family members were easy enough to converse with.

Cynthia's family's violent reactions toward Jordan were more than likely a product of their grief. He didn't ever want to have a bad experience with Scotland's family. If only the issues with Cynthia were resolved, Jordan knew that he could make a life with Scotland. He wasn't so sure that he should even dream the biggest dream of his life with Cynthia's fate still unknown, but there were times when he just couldn't help himself.

Scotland was surprised to learn that Jordan couldn't dance. His excuse was that he'd never been interested in learning. He reassured her that he'd try anything once if it would make her happy. Scotland didn't want him to embarrass himself out on the dance floor, but when he insisted on giving it a try, she saw how serious Jordan was about wanting to please her. That in itself was a change from the male attitudes she was used to.

However eager Jordan was to please her, Scotland didn't want him to lose himself while trying to do so. His own needs and desires should always come first with him. Not wanting to hurt his feelings by refusing to dance with him, she decided to wait for a slow song to come on. That way Jordan could follow her lead.

Jordan chuckled. "I guess you're surprised at a brother not being able to dance, huh?"

"Not really, Jordan. I'm sure there are plenty of brothers and sisters who can't dance. Your willingness to try is admirable. I thank you for at least wanting to give it a shot."

"Then why aren't we already out there on the dance floor?"

Scotland looked slightly abashed. "I thought we'd wait for a slow song."

"Don't want me to embarrass you, huh? After sitting here watching for a few minutes, I'm sure I can learn a couple of moves. What folks are doing out there on the dance floor doesn't look all that hard to me. Some of them look as if they're hardly moving."

Scotland laughed heartily, loving Jordan's spirit. "Then let's get out there and give it a whirl," Scotland said, getting to her feet, reaching her hand out to Jordan. Arm in arm, smiling at each other, Scotland and Jordan made their way to the dance floor.

It didn't take Jordan long to fall right into step with Scotland. He made a few missteps in the beginning, but they weren't that noticeable to anyone other than Scotland. Then a slow song came on, and they both smiled knowingly.

Eager to take Scotland in his arms, Jordan rubbed his hands together before allowing them to span her slender waist. "Now this is what I'm talking about," he whispered near her ear. "Holding you like this feels so good. If I step on your toes, just slug me, but lightly."

Scotland pushed herself slightly back from Jordan and looked into his eyes. "Stepping on my toes is perfectly acceptable, but please don't ever step on my heart, Jordan. It's breakable."

Jordan gently pressed his lips against Scotland's forehead. "The last thing I'd ever want to do is break your heart, Scotland. Please keep in mind that my heart is fragile, too. Knowing we're on the same page about this should keep that from ever happening. Now let's just close our eyes and let the music seep into our souls. This is a night for lovers to discover paradise."

Scotland loved the sound of discovering paradise. Laying her head on Jordan's chest, she allowed the music to take her away. Being in his arms was the only place she wanted to be. They were a real couple now, a very happy one. Despite the few snags they'd encountered along the way, things were coming together so nicely for them. Even though he hadn't gotten into any deep conversations with her family thus far, she felt that a comradeship would develop between them all very soon. It was just a matter of time before Jordan felt like he was one of the Kennedys.

Once Scotland and Jordan returned to their table, Scotland excused herself to go to the ladies' room. Brianna went along with her, the two of them holding hands, so they could have a chat about the party.

* * *

Standing at the bathroom sink, Scotland filled her hands with liquid soap, gently wringing them together. After Scotland dried her hands, Brianna came up to her and hugged her warmly, signing her feelings about how wonderful she thought the party was, thanking her cousin for helping to make it happen. "You and Jordan look so cozy together, Scotty. You two seem so happy."

Scotland got a warm feeling inside. "We *are* happy. I hope he's not too nervous out there all by himself. He was really worried about meeting you all."

"Why in heaven's name would he be nervous about meeting us? We're so easy to get along with. He doesn't seem so anxious to me. I hope he's feeling better about us now."

Scotland shrugged. "How would Jordan know what to expect from our family? He and I were perfect strangers only a couple of months ago. He's a lot less nervous now that's he's been introduced. But until he gets into a real conversation with you guys and gets to know everyone a lot better, he'll probably continue to feel a little uneasy. That's pretty normal, though."

"You're right there. Have you been around his family since the initial meeting, Scotty?"

Scotland rolled her eyes to the ceiling. "Let's save that conversation for another time, but, no, I haven't seen them, Brianna. I'm not sure Jordan has seen them since that day, either. Let's get back to the table just in case Jordan's feeling kind of out of place."

"Come on, Scotty. I know you don't want Jordan to feel alone, though I doubt that's the case. I'm sure Dad and Uncle Scott aren't allowing him to feel left out."

Scotland looped her arm through Brianna's, smiling sweetly. "I'm sure you're right, Bri. If anyone touches on Dodger blue, Jordan will probably begin to feel as if he's one of the guys."

Scotland smiled to herself as she neared the table,

silently thanking God for performing another of His miracles. Seeing that her father, her uncle, and Nathan had Jordan all sewed up made her heart swoon. Jordan was laughing his head off and nodding at the same time. A sense of peace suddenly came over her at the sight of the four men, their heads bent low together, chatting up a storm. Jordan had cleared what he'd thought was the highest hurdle he faced. He never really knew that the barrier he'd imageind was nonexistent. Other than some day becoming Jordan's wife, Scotland couldn't be happier than she was at the moment.

When it was time for Brianna to open her numerous presents, Scotland stood by her cousin's side while she ripped into the wrapping paper like a kid on Christmas morning.

The gaily decorated packages contained everything from perfume to loungewear. Brianna giggled and gushed over every single gift she received, holding up the items for all her guests to get a good glimpse of. She couldn't have asked for more out of this day. The surprise birthday party had, indeed, come as a surprise to her—and she'd loved every moment of it.

Nathan had brought along a huge plastic bag to put all the gift wrappings in. Brianna collected wrapping paper and ribbons to use for various art projects. She was very creative with her hands. As she carefully tore open each of the packages, Nathan tossed the wrapping in the bag. Not long after all the presents were unwrapped, the party came to a close.

As far as Jordan was concerned, the party had ended all too soon. He had had more fun with the Kennedys than he'd ever had in his life. Once he'd gotten into several in-depth conversations with the men in Scotland's family, he'd begun to really feel good about everyone. No one had gone to the extreme to try and make him feel comfortable, nor had they done anything to make him uncomfortable. Jordan appreciated their genuineness.

Standing outside of Scotland's front door, Jordan kissed her on the forehead. "I know it's late, but I'm having a hard time ending this spectacular night. You think a brother can get a cup of brew? It'll sure help me stay awake on the drive home."

Scotland swatted Jordan playfully on the shoulder. "Brother, you live right around the corner. You can walk home if you're that sleepy," she joked. "But I'd love to share a cup of coffee with you. Since neither of us has to work tomorrow, we can sit for a while and rehash the festivities. However, I do have to get up and go to church tomorrow. I already missed last week."

As Jordan looked down at his watch, he began to feel guilty. It *was* after midnight. Perhaps he should go on home. He knew that he was being rather selfish, and had been so on more than one occasion, but that still didn't stop him from wanting to spend a little more time with Scotland. This woman had rejuvenated him, and he wanted one or two more shots of the dynamic energy she always delivered to him. "I promise not to keep you up too long, angel. Okay?"

Scotland laughed, handing her key to Jordan for him to open the door. "I already said it was okay. You're the only one burning up time."

In less than twenty minutes Scotland and Jordan were seated at her kitchen table, drinking coffee and nibbling on some of the birthday cake she had brought home from the party. The cake, with its buttercream icing, was delicious. The cake had consisted of three large tiers, each of a different flavor: yellow, white, and chocolate.

Scotland set her coffee cup down and then looked over at Jordan. Sometimes it was so hard for her to believe how far they'd come with their relationship. Even though she'd known from the start that he was her soul mate, she had thought it was going to take him a lot longer to come to that realization. Jordan had closed his heart off to everyone and everything, it had seemed to her, but now it was wide open to receive and give love.

Scotland smiled gently, reaching over to cover Jordan's hand with hers. "Had this not been an adult event, we could've brought Gregory along. He would've enjoyed himself a lot. He certainly would've had a lot of folks to communicate with, including all my family."

Jordan scooted his chair closer to Scotland's and then kissed her tenderly on the mouth. The same fiery sensations he always felt from her lips nearly took him over, making him admit to himself how much he desperately needed to make physical contact with her. As he wrapped his arms around her tightly, he kissed her again, only with more passion this time. His hands stroked her arms, fanning the wild flames of his passionate heat.

Minutes later, feeling as though he was losing control of himself, Jordan decided he needed to cool his heels. He wanted Scotland in the worst way, but he wasn't going to blow what they had by coming on too strong. She had pretty much made it clear that she wasn't looking for a frivolous affair, though that wasn't at all how he saw what they had.

Scotland was the kind of girl a man married. Consummating the wedding vows came afterward. Jordan didn't doubt that for a measly second. Scotland Kennedy was definitely the marrying kind. But was he really the right man for her? Better yet, was he suited for marriage?

Jordan scooted his chair back to its original spot, feeling that he should put a slight distance between them. Touching her so intimately already had him half-crazy. His body felt like he'd stepped into the middle of a forest fire; his loins were about to burst from the all-consuming heat. Scotland wasn't in much better shape than Jordan. She was a little frightened by how easily she could've given in to his physical desires. She wanted him every bit as much as he wanted her, but she was a holdout for the whole nine yards. In her early twenties, Scotland had nearly made a few serious mistakes with a guy, but she was much stronger now.

After quickly composing himself—though his desire for Scotland was as strong as ever—Jordan nervously cleared his throat. "Gregory probably would've enjoyed himself, but this was our evening to spend with Brianna and your family. We'll have plenty of other good times to share with Gregory, Scotland. You can rest assured of that. In fact, I'm going to spend time with him at the local Boys and Girls Club next week."

Scotland was pleased by Jordan's news. "That sounds like fun." Her expression grew sober. "Where do you want your relationship with Gregory to go? I have to wonder if you've thought this all through. At least to the point where you understand what it'll do to Gregory if you one day up and disappear from his life."

As Jordan gave deep thought to Scotland's question, he appeared a bit stunned. "Do you think I'm making a big mistake by getting so involved with him?"

"That's a question you should answer for yourself, Jordan. I just think you should know what end result you're looking for. Gregory has already been so disappointed by others. He trusts you now. . . . and I believe you should know how far you want this to go."

Jordan scratched his head. "I know I want him happy and in a stable environment, but beyond that, I'm not prepared to say. Do you think I'm hurting him by spending too much time with him if I don't have any long-term plans in mind? I just want to help this young kid get on the right path, Scotty."

Scotland couldn't help laughing when Jordan called her by her nickname. He had said it so endearingly. No one other than her family had ever called her by her nickname. "It seems like an evening with my family has taught you a new thing or two. Scotty, indeed!"

Despite Scotland's laughter, Jordan looked a little troubled. "Does it bother you when I call you that?"

Scotland shook her head in the negative. "I actually like the way you say it, Jordan. It sounds so sweet coming from your lips. I have no objections to you calling me by my nickname. None whatsoever."

Nodding his head, Jordan grinned. "I'll try not to make a habit of it. Getting back to Gregory, I promise to think all of this through to the very end." He got a puzzled expression on his face. "Are you by any chance talking about the possibility of me adopting Gregory?"

"No, I wasn't, but now that the idea has been laid on the table, where do you stand on that issue?"

Jordan shrugged. "I don't know, since I haven't given it any thought. However, I can't see myself as anyone's father right now. I've had to be my own parent for so long that I can't imagine taking on that monster of a responsibility again, at least not any time soon."

Jordan continued to look perplexed. "If you and I . . . were, you know . . . ever to get . . ." He just couldn't bring himself to say the word "married." The very idea of it scared him to death, but he wasn't ruling it out, either, not by a long shot. "You know what I'm trying to say, don't you?"

Even though Scotland knew exactly what Jordan wanted to say, she feigned total ignorance. If he couldn't even say the word, how would he ever accomplish it? No, she thought, he'd have to figure this one out, too, all on his own. Wanting to let Jordan off the hook, Scotland looked at the kitchen clock. "I really need to get to bed now. We can finish this conversation another time." *When you're clear on the issues,* she thought. "Church in the morning, remember? Would you like to come with me? It's the big church a few blocks over."

"No," Jordan was quick to say, instantly wishing he hadn't been so hasty in his reply. "Maybe another time." Jordan didn't feel ready to step inside the doors of God's house. He had a long way to go before he'd feel worthy enough for that venture.

As Scotland walked Jordan to the front door, she hid her disappointment. But she also knew that she shouldn't try to push him into anything he wasn't ready for. When it came to religion and Christianity, she had allowed Jordan to set the pace he was comfortable with, and she'd continue to do so.

Attending church regularly was a huge part of Scotland's life, but she realized she had to remain patient with Jordan, especially since church had never been a part of his life. He would eventually come into his own and in his own sweet time. At least she hoped so. Having a partner with whom she could share her love of God was one of the things Scotland had continuously prayed for. Uniting with a godly man would be the answer to her fervent prayers.

Jordan surprised Scotland by lifting her up into his arms, kissing her passionately. "If we were united as one, I'd have had you down the hallway and in the bedroom long before now. We're not kids, Scotland. You know how much I want you, don't you?"

Scotland lowered her eyelids, blushing uncontrollably. "I think I do, Jordan. I want no less, but I'm sure you know as well as I do that all the conditions have to be right before that can happen for us. Whenever I give myself to a man, I need to be sure of what the future holds for us as a couple. I've made some bad mistakes before, Jordan, but none that couldn't be remedied. I made a promise then to know for sure what I'm getting myself into so as not to land in scalding hot water."

Looking thoughtful, Jordan set Scotland on her feet and then backed up to the front door. Just before letting himself out, he blew her several kisses. "I understand where you're coming from. Make no mistake about that. I'm sure we'll figure out everything in due time. Goodnight, angel. I . . ." He wanted so desperately to tell her he loved her, but he couldn't bring himself to say it. When he did tell Scotland how he truly felt about her, and he now believed he really loved her with every fiber of his being, Jordan wanted to be perfectly sure that he could give her everything she needed from him. "I hope you sleep tight, but please dream of me."

Scotland blew several kisses back to Jordan. "I don't think I'll be able to dream of anything but you. Be careful, Jordan."

Jordan's indecision about telling Scotland the truth about how he really felt about her had him pacing his bedroom floor. He kept hitting himself on his head with the palms of his hands, wishing he'd had the courage to tell her how much he loved her before he'd left her house. His feelings for her nearly had him pinned down in a strange kind of wrestling hold, and he felt as though he was about to be counted out.

Jordan dropped down on the bed. "You just have to go for it," he told himself. "You want her more than anything you've ever desired, man. The heck with all this analyzing everything to death," he shouted. "Cynthia is not coming back. And even if she does, we've already decided that there's no future for us; there never was."

Jordan looked at the telephone and then over at the clock. Another hour had already passed since he'd left Scotland. He was positive that she was already asleep. His confession could keep until the next day. "No, it can't," he yelled, feeling as though he'd already wasted too much time as it was. He grabbed the phone, and his fingers began to dance slowly over the keypad. His mind was going a mile a minute. This call to Scotland would finally liberate him. He desperately needed to be free from the prison cell he'd caged himself in years ago.

With tears running down his face, Jordan ended the call right after the second ring. He really had no right to do this to her even though he was sure of his feelings. He first needed to be darn sure about everything in his life. Gregory wasn't the only serious matter facing him, though it was something he had to quickly figure out before someone ended up getting hurt.

After sliding into bed and tossing and turning for several minutes to get comfortable, Jordan found himself laughing and crying at the same time. How could he be so indecisive? If he was so sure about his feelings for Scotland, then why couldn't he just tell her the truth? He would, he vowed in silence. Later in the day, once she came home from church. Come hell or high water, he'd tell Scotland he loved her then.

"I love you, girl. Is my inability to tell you some kind of poetic justice, or what?"

* * *

Wondering why Jordan had aborted yet another call, Scotland held the phone in her hand, looking totally perplexed. Was he all right? All she could do was wonder. Why had he bothered to wake her at this hour of the morning if he wasn't going to talk with her? Running only on fumes, Scotland decided she wasn't even going to try and figure out the method to Jordan's madness. Whatever he had to say would just have to keep until later. She had to get at least a couple of hours sleep.

CHAPTER ELEVEN

Surprising the heck of out Scotland, Jordan slipped into the red velvet–covered church pew and sat down right beside her, taking her hand in his. His warm smile caused her to glow from the inside out. She was so happy that he'd changed his mind about attending church with her, and that she hadn't tried to coerce him into coming with her. She didn't know why he had changed his mind, but it really didn't matter. All that Scotland cared about was having Jordan right there beside her, looking as content as could be.

Reverend Jesse Covington, the founder of the Ladera Heights First Tabernacle Church, hadn't begun his sermon yet, but the gospel choir was already in full swing. Marlene Covington, the preacher's wife, was the featured soloist for the early morning hour. Scotland was a member of the young adult choir, but it performed only on the third Sunday of each month.

Scotland was thrilled that Jordan hadn't missed much of the service, because she knew that he was in for a real treat. The members of the church never failed to rock the place as they gave God all the praise due Him. Since

Jordan had never attended church before, he had come to the right place to be ministered to. Scotland knew that from firsthand experience.

Reverend Jesse knew just how to speak to the soul and how to make the spirit sing with his dynamic sermons. No one ever left the Lord's house unfulfilled, not after one of his eloquent speeches. For years the Reverend and Mrs. Covington had both been mentors to Scotland. If she and Jordan ever decided to marry, Scotland planned on attending with him the Covingtons' six-week-long marriage counseling session. Their uplifting classes started newlyweds out on the right foot and had kept many of the church's veteran couples out of the divorce courts.

Jordan squeezed Scotland's fingers, bumping her gently with his shoulder. "Are you glad to see me?" he said, his tone a little above a whisper. "I'm thrilled to see you. This is a huge church. After I got in here, I didn't think I'd be able to find you among all these people."

After lightly scolding Jordan with her eyes for talking in church, Scotland put a single finger to her lips to shush him. She then signed to him how much it meant to her to have him join her for the early morning hour, telling him they could talk after the service was over. Then Scotland signed for him to open his church bulletin so he could read the program schedule.

It was rare for Reverend Jesse to run over the allotted hour. For that, Scotland was glad, because Jordan might become fidgety. She also feared that Jordan would not attend church regularly if the service was too long.

As Reverend Jesse got up to deliver his sermon, Scotland pointed toward the altar, alerting Jordan that the pastor was about to speak. His morning delivery was to be on faith. In his normal demeanor, which was always kind and loving, Reverend Jesse cheerfully greeted his parishioners and then had them turn the pages of their Bibles to Matthew 17:17-20 which he read aloud: "At the bottom of the hill, after Jesus rebuked the demon in the boy and it had left him, His disciples asked Him privately why hadn't they been able to cast out the demon. And Jesus said unto them, 'because of your little faith,' Jesus told them. 'For if you had faith even as small as a tiny mustard seed you could say to this mountain, "Move!" and it would go far away. Nothing would be impossible.'"

"In John 6:25-29," Reverend Jesse continued, "at Capernaum, after the people asked Him how He'd gotten there, Jesus told them that they wanted to be with Him because he'd fed them at the Sea of Galilee, not because they believed in Him. Jesus told them not to be so concerned about perishable things like food, that they should spend their energy seeking the eternal life that the Messiah, can provide, because God the Father has sent me for this very purpose. People then asked, what should we do to satisfy God? Jesus told them, 'This is the will of God, that you believe in the one He has sent you.'"

Reverend Jesse went on to tell his congregation that it was in this same address to the people that Jesus gave them this next passage from John 6:35-37. "I am the Bread of Life. No one coming to me will ever be hungry again. Those believing in me will never thirst. But the trouble is, as I have told you before, you haven't believed even though you have seen me. But some will come to me—those the Father has given me—and I will never, never reject them."

"What is faith?" Reverend Jesse asked, reading from Hebrews 11:1-2. "It is the confident assurance that something we want is going to happen. It is the certainty that what we hope for is waiting for us, even though we cannot see it up ahead. Men of God in days of old were famous for their faith. By faith—by believing God—we know that the world and the stars—in fact, all things—were made at God's command; and they were all made from things that can't be seen." The minister spoke of the faith of many in the Bible, like Abel, Enoch, Noah, Abraham, and Sarah, who died without ever receiving all that God had promised.

Reverend Jesse's sermon didn't come to an end until after he'd cited many other stories to do with faith, all of which were based on the scriptures found within the Bible. First and foremost, Jesse Covington was a Bible-based teacher/preacher.

Scotland was all smiles when she introduced Jordan to Reverend and Mrs. Covington during the reception always held right after the service. The Covingtons always personally greeted each member of the congregation and all visitors who had a desire to stop by and say a few words to them before departing the church. Jordan was asked to come again, and Scotland openly received the usual warm hugs given to her by the pastor and his wife.

As Scotland and Jordan were making their way to where her father and uncle were standing, right outside the chapel doors, Jordan got the strangest look on his face. Scotland quickly looked in the direction of his gaze. It was then that she spotted Jordan's parents. Dressed to the nines, Regina and James La Cour looked happy and well rested.

In dire need of a security blanket, Jordan groped for Scotland's hand, wondering why his parents were attending this particular church. It wasn't the one they'd told him they had joined recently, if he recalled correctly. Like always, when in the presence of his father, Jordan began to sweat profusely. He looked at Scotland and shrugged. "I don't know why they're here. They couldn't have known I'd be here, because I didn't know myself until early this morning. What should I do?"

"Go over there and speak to them, Jordan. They've seen you already. It looks as if you've missed your golden opportunity. Your parents are walking this way."

Regina and James came up to Jordan and Scotland, smiling at the younger couple as they greeted them pleasantly. Scotland returned the pleasantries, but Jordan just stood there looking as if a couple of ghosts of the past had rudely invaded his present.

Regina reached up and tenderly caressed Jordan's cheek. "It's so nice seeing you, Jordan, especially here at church." She then looked at Scotland. "We're so glad we decided to visit your church today. We're sure you're the reason Jordan is also here. We thank you for whatever influence you've had on our son in seeking out God."

Shaking her head from side to side, Scotland threw her hands up. "Jordan is here by choice, Mr. and Mrs. La Cour. He came here today of his own free will." Scotland knew she'd sparked Jordan's religious curiosity in many ways, but she couldn't take credit for his presence at church, especially since he'd turned down her invite to attend the morning service.

Regina smiled knowingly. "Maybe so, but we're sure you've had something to do with it. We've repeatedly tried to get him to visit our church, but to no avail. God is good."

James extended his hand to Jordan, telling him he was glad to see him in the house of the Lord. "You look good, son. I've never seen you all spiffed up like this."

Several seconds passed before Jordan responded to James's gesture. "Thank you." Jordan hated that his voice quivered so badly. "Uh, it's nice to see you both, too, but we really have to be going. Scotland and I have plans for the rest of the day."

Scotland hid her dismay over Jordan's blatant lie. They hadn't made any plans that she knew anything about. But then again, maybe Jordan had made plans for them and hadn't yet had the opportunity to share with her. Scotland decided to give him the benefit of the doubt.

"We were hoping we could all get a bite to eat at a nearby restaurant, son," Regina said with regret. "Sorry you're busy. You still plan to have that dinner with us, don't you? We've been waiting to hear back from you. We left our dates and times of availability on your answering machine a couple of days ago."

Although Scotland thought he should be, Jordan didn't look the least bit ashamed of himself for not returning their call. It wasn't as if he didn't intend to keep his promise of joining his parents for dinner, because he did. He just hadn't gotten around to getting back to them.

"What about dinner on Thursday? I can come to your place after work. That is, if Scotland is free. I'd like her to come with me." With her was the only way he'd go to their place for dinner. He still needed Scotland as his anchor when it came to his family.

Regina looked to Scotland for her response, hoping it would be a positive one.

Scotland resented that Jordan had put her in the middle like that, and she fumed inwardly. Then she remembered his deep fear of being alone with his mom and dad. "I really can't commit right here on the spot, not without checking my schedule. I'll do that later today . . . and then I'll let Jordan know if I can make it or not. I hope that's okay."

Though disappointed, Regina smiled with understanding. "That'll be fine, Scotland."

Jordan placed his hand beneath Scotland's elbow. "We have to be on our way now. You'll hear from me no later than tomorrow evening. Good-bye, Mom and Dad."

Where had she heard that line before? Scotland mused. She fought the urge to roll her eyes at Jordan's weak response. It seemed as if he became a child all over again every time he was in the presence of his parents. It was a sad sight for her to witness.

Scotland's heart went out to Jordan, yet she knew he had to get a grip on his fears before they started to consume him again. She didn't want to see him go backwards, not with all the strides he'd made. Jordan had to develop a backbone if he was to deal with his family.

Scotland gave both her dad and uncle a loving hug. She then stood back to let all the men greet each other. She wasn't surprised when her father and uncle hugged Jordan, affectionately patting him on the back.

"Jordan, we're so glad you visited our church today," Scott said, having no idea that Jordan hadn't ever been inside a chapel. "What did you think of the service?"

Fighting off a sudden wave of nervousness, Jordan cleared his throat. "It was great. I really enjoyed it. I guess Scotland has told you that I have never been involved in any type of Christian-based ministry, but I'm trying to find my way. This is all new to me. I just pray that everyone will be patient with me. Learning all about the Lord is more than a notion."

A look of deep admiration for Jordan settled in Scott's eyes. "No, my daughter hasn't mentioned a thing to me. But that's not so unusual. Scotty can be very private when she has a mind to. I admire your candor. My advice to you, Jordan, is to take things slow. It'll come. Whatever you need, God will provide. Faith is the key, just as Reverend Jesse preached to us this morning."

Brian extended his hand to Jordan, shaking it briefly.

"I admire you, too, son. Just remember that we all had to start somewhere. If you ever have any questions or need help on your journey to fulfillment, feel free to call on me. I gave you my business card at the party. Please use it. You can also get my home number from my little niece here," Brian remarked, bringing Scotland to him for a quick hug.

Scotland was so proud of the way her father and uncle had handled Jordan's revelation. Neither man was the judgmental type. If Jordan needed their help, she knew they'd be there for him. "Thanks, you two," she said, smiling broadly. "By the way, where's Bri? I just realized I haven't seen her yet." The family often sat together in church, but when one of them was running a little late, they always took seats in the back of the sanctuary. Scotland had been a tad tardy.

"Bri and Nate are visiting another church this morning. Then they plan to take a drive up the coast, toward Santa Barbara. You know how those two lovebirds like to get away and be alone," Brian offered, grinning. "They can't wait to get married, and I can barely wait, too."

Scotland laughed heartily. "Yeah, I do know all about those two. They can't see anyone else in the room when they're together. Dad and Uncle Brian, Jordan and I are going to move on. I couldn't leave without saying hello. Do you all have plans for the rest of the day?"

"Brian has a date with his ladylove, and I'm going to catch up on some work, young lady. You all get on with your day," Scott said. "Call me later this evening if you have time."

Before departing, Scotland hugged her father and uncle, telling them she'd talk to them later. Jordan, Scott, and Brian then exchanged pleasant farewells.

*   *   *

The restaurant Jordan had chosen for lunch with Scotland was charming and very cozy. That he had actually made plans for them made Scotland feel much better about what he'd told his parents earlier. She was relieved that he hadn't lied to them.

As the couple went through the serving line, Scotland marveled at the bountiful brunch buffet. There were plenty of choices for those wanting breakfast or lunch. She was as hungry as a bear, so she wasted no time in filling her plate. Salad was the course she always had first when dining out. After choosing the dressing for her greens, she went back to the booth that the hostess had assigned them, leaving Jordan behind to finish making his choices.

Jordan wasn't far behind Scotland, who waited for him to return to the table before starting. When Jordan lifted his fork before the blessing, Scotland just bowed her head in prayer, knowing it was something he'd have to get used to doing. She would do her best to guide him if he asked her to, but she certainly wasn't going to change her devout habits and ways. Praying was a large part of her everyday life. Giving thanks to God was essential to her.

Feeling like a real heel, Jordan laid down his fork when Scotland was finished blessing the meal. "I hope I didn't embarrass you by digging in prematurely. I'm sorry."

Scotland hated to see Jordan looking so down. "You don't have to go there, Jordan. I understand it all. Believe me when I say that. Like my dad said, these things will come to you in due time. Please stop berating yourself over what you're just not used to doing."

Nervous as a cat on a hot tin roof, Jordan slid closer to Scotland. He was ready to get everything out in the open. He couldn't hold it in any longer. It was now time for him to put up or shut up. He was bursting with all the information he held within. Jordan struggled to tell Scotland he loved her, finally deciding to sign his love for her. He thought it was actually a brilliant idea since that was how they'd come together in the first place. If he hadn't taken her class, they wouldn't have ever met.

Taking his time, making sure he got it right, Jordan enthusiastically used sign language to make his point. The love shining brightly in his eyes was just another indication that he was for real. In line with what Scotland had taught him about body language being a part of signing, he leaned toward her and kissed her breathless.

Ecstatic couldn't begin to describe Scotland's feelings about Jordan's heartfelt confession. She had felt his love all along, but she'd had to patiently wait for him to reveal it to her. Her eyes were filled with tears . . . but her love for him was there in plain view. The way he had signed his feelings for her had as great an impact on her as spoken words would have. He loved her. He'd finally confessed it. The very thing she'd hoped and prayed for had come true. *Thank you, God,* she silently prayed. *Thank you.*

Throwing her arms around his neck, Scotland kissed Jordan back in the same fervent way he'd shown his love and affection toward her. It didn't matter that they were in public. This was their special moment, and she didn't mind if the entire world witnessed their loving feelings for each other. A confession of love was the ultimate in any relationship. Should she confess her love for him, too? Holding her sentiments back didn't make any sense, but she somehow felt that Jordan's fears would only intensify if she told him she loved him.

Throwing caution to the wind, Scotland leaned her forehead against Jordan's. "I love you, too, Jordan." She looked deeply into his eyes. "Please don't let my love for you frighten you in any way. We've crossed over yet another bridge, but we still can take things slow. I don't want us to rush into anything. What we have is to be cherished and savored until we decide we want to go to another level. Are you with me on that?"

Just as she'd done to him in church, Jordan shushed Scotland with a finger to the center of his lips. Now wasn't the time for talking or analyzing their relationship. That she loved him, too, was more than he could've dared to hope for, though he'd felt her love for some time now. Jordan was actually stunned to hear someone confess love for him. During his childhood, his mother had stopped telling him she loved him—and his father had never said he loved him. But that was all in the past, he mused. This was here and now. Scotland loved him, and he loved her.

As thoughts of Cynthia swept into his mind, Jordan became aware that he was going to once again have a hard time sharing that chapter of his past with Scotland. Like always, he felt the timing was so wrong. Was there ever a right time for a man to tell one woman about another woman who was once in his life? He wasn't sure about a lot of things, but he was sure that in the midst of confessing his love to Scotland, he shouldn't bring up another woman. This was a time for celebration.

His mind made up, Jordan put the topic of Cynthia on the back burner, again promising himself to tell Scotland everything before the week was out. Even then might be too soon, he mused.

After raising his orange juice glass, Jordan picked up Scotland's glass of water and handed it to her so that they could make a toast. As they clinked the rims together, their smiles shone brightly. They then confessed to being madly in love with each other, barely able to contain their euphoria. Scotland and Jordan had realized with each other all their loftiest hopes and dreams.

Scotland felt that she'd finally found the kind of joy and love that Brianna had discovered with Nathan. It was only now that she realized she had envied them greatly, though she had always believed otherwise. In a silent prayer, Scotland asked God for forgiveness.

Jordan laughed nervously. "Wow! Did you ever imagine this for us, Scotland? How did we ever get from there to where we are now?"

Scotland didn't dare tell Jordan she'd known from the start that they were destined for love. She sure couldn't tell him she'd decided on him as her husband the moment she'd first laid eyes upon him. She'd reveal that bit of information to him only after the nuptials.

Scotland looked at Jordan, her love for him clear as a bell. "Destiny has a way of finding people and bringing them together, whether it be for a season or for an entire lifetime."

Jordan tilted his head to one side, looking at Scotland with deep curiosity. "What are you shooting for? A season or a lifetime?"

Jordan's question caught Scotland off guard, causing her eyes to darn near blink uncontrollably. *What a question,* she mused. She really didn't know how to answer without sounding like an idiot.

Can't you see forever in my eyes, Jordan? I'm not sure a lifetime is even long enough for me to be with you. I want every second of every minute and every minute of ever hour with you. But how do I tell you all these things without scaring the dickens out of you?

Scotland folded her hands and placed them in her lap. "I don't think I'm prepared to answer that question, Jordan," she said, instead of voicing her very desire. "In fact, I don't believe either of us is ready for it." There were times when a little white lie was easier than the truth, but her answer wasn't altogether an untruth.

Just because she knew the true answer to his question didn't mean she was ready to reveal it. A lifetime was exactly what Scotland was after.

Jordan nodded, though he didn't agree. "Yeah, maybe you're right. I keep forgetting we don't have to rush it. Please continue to remind me of that. I don't want to scare you away."

Scotland had a hard time fighting her impulse to laugh out loud at that one. He had to be kidding. The idea that she was scared was ludicrous. Then she wondered if it was possible that they were equally afraid of what was happening to them? She hadn't given that possibility a moment of contemplation, believing that she was fearless, especially when it came to loving Jordan.

Scotland smiled sweetly, snickering under her breath. "I promise to remind you of that if you promise to remind me every single day that you love me. Fair enough?"

"More than fair. I love you, Scotland. Let's kiss on it."

With a lot more to chew on than just her meal, Scotland quickly finished her salad and then excused herself from the table. As she made her way back to the buffet line, butterflies roved her stomach like they owned it, making her feel slightly ill. A lot had transpired between her and Jordan in the last twenty minutes or so, but she felt that it had only been a preview of things to come. His confession of love had come as quite a surprise, but she also felt a little confused. His lapse into silence had her worried.

For whatever the reason, Scotland sensed that Jordan had held something back from her. This wasn't the first time she'd felt that way. She'd gotten the impression several times now that he had some unfinished business pending. She wasn't sure if she was right or not, but it seemed that way to her.

What could Jordan be holding back from her? Were there other troublesome things in his past that he hadn't yet shared with her? Perhaps it was another woman. An uneasy feeling tugged at her stomach. Just the thought of another woman in his life caused the butterflies to rile her insides up again. As she thought about it, she realized they hadn't ever discussed their past relationships. She'd had only one affair, a very unhappy one, lasting about three months, but she had to wonder if he could say the same. Scotland was now quite curious about what other momentous incidents Jordan may have left out of his life story.

Just the thought of Jordan hiding something important from her made Scotland lose her appetite. Worry always did that to her. She should be basking in the joy of his confession of love, but instead, she now had a new concern, one that put her on edge. To keep from giving Jordan any hint that something might be wrong if she returned empty-handed, Scotland filled a plate with fresh fruit. There was no way she could get away with not eating anything else. Jordan would call her on that.

After taking her seat, Scotland began to slowly eat the fruit she'd gotten. The butterflies in her stomach kept her from really enjoying it, but she was not going to waste it, and she didn't want to arouse Jordan's suspicion. On what should be one of the happiest days of her life, she was feeling miserable, both physically and emotionally.

Right away Jordan had noticed the drastic change in Scotland's demeanor. He had to wonder if her altered mood had anything to do with him. He couldn't remember saying or doing anything offensive, other than eating before prayer. But that wouldn't make her withdraw like she had. Jordan decided to let it go.

He took a sip of water. "Regarding your response to my parents about dinner, do you really have to look at your schedule, or were you just buying time, Scotland?"

Scotland shot Jordan a scathing glance, wishing he

hadn't mentioned the dinner. "I'm not going to dinner with you, Jordan. I won't allow you to use me as a buffer. If you're going to mend fences with your parents, you need to do it on you own. You won't make any headway with me around. I hope you understand that."

Pouting wasn't something Jordan normally indulged in, but he resorted to exactly that. Unable to understand why Scotland wouldn't want to help him out in this situation, he looked at her with open defiance. Paradise had gone farther south than he would've ever expected. In fact, it looked as if their entire relationship was on its way south. What had happened to all the euphoria they'd experienced only minutes ago?

"I thought you understood my problems with my parents, Scotland."

"Understanding them doesn't mean I have to get in the middle. I'm here for you, Jordan, supporting you as much as I can. But there are some things only you can attend to. The state of your relationship with your parents is solely up to you. You have to get used to the idea of dealing with this problem on your own."

Jordan shook his head in dismay. "I guess I had it figured all wrong. I thought you were going to help me get through this difficult time in my life. Sorry if I was mistaken."

Frustrated with the way things were quickly going from bad to worse, Scotland exhaled a shaky gust of breath. Jordan *was* badly mistaken if he thought she could fix the problems he had with his family. It wasn't her job to repair their relationship. Jordan needed to tackle his problems and get off the fence.

Scotland wrung her hands together in anguish. "Jordan, I'm going to say a couple of more things; then I'm done with this subject matter for good. If you can't settle all the scores of the past, I don't believe your future or ours will be very promising. If you don't rid yourself of the excess baggage, you'll eventually drop it down hard on our relationship." Scotland shrugged. "I'm sorry, but that's how I see it."

"Has all this been brought on by my confession of love? Your attitude changed right after I told you I loved you. It seems that I'm not the only one who's filled with fear. What exactly are you afraid of, Scotland? I won't know if you don't tell me."

Riddled with indignation and feeling as though she were about to lose control, Scotland checked herself before she said something to Jordan she'd regret. What was going on between her and Jordan wasn't right. Not only that, they'd just gotten out of church, and now they were fighting like two heathens. Maybe she *was* fearful. It wasn't as if she didn't have anything to fear. Everyday life was scary, and so was love. If Jordan loving her back was the issue, she'd deal with it, but she had to first make sure that that was the problem.

Scotland really believed that the only thing going on with her was a plain case of nerves.

Scotland looked over at Jordan and smiled weakly. "I'd like to go home now. I don't want to fight with you, Jordan. It doesn't seem right, nor does it make me feel very good. Things were going so well for us, and now this. If I'm fearful of something, I'll eventually figure it out."

The possibility that Jordan was hiding something from her was more than likely at the root of Scotland's fears. If a person's eyes were truly windows into the soul, then what she'd often seen in Jordan's was a well-kept secret. The thought was a daunting one.

Wishing things hadn't gone so badly, Jordan decided not to let their verbal skirmish go any further. Looking down at Scotland's plate, he noticed that she had barely touched her food, and it dawned on him how upset she was. He could have kicked himself for fighting with her like that, knowing he'd been dead wrong. "Is that all you're going to eat?"

Looking ashamed, Scotland nodded. "I'm afraid I've lost my appetite. I don't mind paying for my meal, though. I know its not good to be wasteful, but I can't eat another bite."

Jordan smiled sympathetically, wishing he could put the sunshine back into her eyes. "I invited you to lunch, so I'm paying. Are you sure you really want to go home? I promise not to fight with you again. I hope we can hang out a little longer. I'd like us to take a quiet drive down to one of the local beaches. Are you up for that?"

Wishing that she could resist Jordan's charm, Scotland closed her eyes for a moment. He was so persuasive when he wanted to be. Casting his spell on her was so easy to do. As if she no longer had a mind of her own, Scotland leaned into Jordan, kissing him gently on the lips. "A little while longer it is, Jordan. But no fighting," she said, kissing him once again.

The day was sunny and bright, yet the air was chilly. Despite the wintry chill, stretches of beach were swarming with people, who appeared to be having a great time. Rarely were California beaches devoid of humans. All year-round the coastline was a favorite spot for both local residents and tourists to visit. The wildlife was abundant, too. Sea gulls swooped down over the sand and surf, looking for a tidbit or two to snack on.

Listening to inspirational music as they drove down the coastline, with Jordan at the wheel, brought a sense of peace to Scotland's soul. Only a few words had passed between them since they'd gotten back into the SUV, yet serenity engulfed them. It was as if they'd never had words. Later Jordan planned to take Scotland back to the church where she'd left her own vehicle.

With a full workweek ahead of them, they had decided to make an early evening of it.

Jordan considered himself very lucky when a car a couple of feet ahead suddenly pulled out of a parking space and into traffic. He quickly wheeled the SUV into the parking space, which was only a short distance from the sand. He couldn't have asked for a better spot.

Jordan had a walk on the beach in mind, but in looking at Scotland's church attire, he wasn't sure it was one of his better ideas. How did he expect her to walk in the sand in heels? It was certainly too cold to go barefooted, as they'd done during the camping trip. Jordan didn't care how silly he might look walking on the beach in a designer suit.

Then he thought of the spare clothes he always kept in the back of the SUV, a pair or two of warm sweats he used when jogging. He also carried around an extra pair of sneakers. The thought of Scotland wearing his sneakers caused him to howl. They would be way too big for her. She had small, dainty feet; he wore a size twelve. His sneakers would swallow her feet whole.

Scotland eyed Jordan with curiosity. "What's so funny?"

"Imagining you wearing my sneakers. I thought we could take a walk on the beach, that is, until I looked at what you're wearing. I keep some clothes and shoes in the back of my ride, but my big shoes will never work for you."

Scotland laughed. "They will if we stuff them in the front and back with a towel or something. I used to tramp around in my dad's shoes as a child. To keep me from breaking my neck, he'd always fill them with one thing or another. Make sense?"

"Not a bit of sense." Jordan chuckled. "But if you're willing to give it a try, I know I have a lot of towels in the back. I keep them in here for when I go to the self-service car wash."

Jordan jumped out of the car and then ran around to the passenger side to open Scotland's door. Holding hands, they made their way to the back of the SUV, where he pulled out several bags. As he dumped the contents of one bag onto the lowered hatch door, a pair of women's sneakers and women's jogging clothes fell out. Jordan looked as if he'd been stabbed in the gut. The sight of Cynthia's tennis shoes and clothes lying there made him nauseous.

Where? How? When? Then it all came back to Jordan. He had taken Cynthia's things over to her parents' home, but they'd refused to see him. Thinking it disrespectful to just leave her belongings on the doorstep, he'd put them back in the SUV, where they'd been ever since.

Wondering if this was her worst fear come true, Scotland felt as if she were about to start hyperventilating. The desire to crumple to the ground and cry her eyeballs out was strong. How to keep it all together was her biggest concern, yet she knew she had to do just that. She then put on her best false bravado, picking up the sneakers in the process. "I bet my feet fit in these shoes a lot better than in yours. They look to be just about my size."

After lining the women's sneakers with paper towels, Scotland put them on. "They do fit, Jordan," she said cheerfully, as if nothing was amiss. Thinking they were Jordan's mother's shoes, though she knew better, helped Scotland to pull off her act. She didn't change her clothes, but she did put on Jordan's hooded jacket.

As they walked down the beach, Jordan agonized over what had come to pass, staring at Scotland but not really seeing her. He wished he could find a deep hole in the sand to bury himself in. Things were really way out of control now. He had to tell Scotland about

Cynthia as soon as possible. He couldn't play this game of charades much longer.

Jordan figured that the woman he loved was going to end up hating him if he didn't find a way to come clean with her. It seemed like such a simple thing to do, but telling her everything would probably be the hardest thing he'd ever done. How could he explain that Cynthia's fate was a total mystery?

God forbid that Scotland should think he'd had something to do with her disappearance. His last thought hit him like a bolt of lightning. That Scotland might think he had done something to Cynthia was the real issue, the real reason why he hadn't been able to tell her the truth. What Scotland thought of him mattered the most.

Cynthia's parents had certainly thought him capable of foul play, even though the police contended that none was involved. Although he hadn't bought into the police's theory for a second, he had nothing to do with Cynthia's fate. Still, her parents had accused him of killing their daughter and then disposing of her body as if she were a pile of trash.

The visit to the Raymonds' home that night several months ago had haunted Jordan ever since. The horrified look on her parents' faces when he'd told them of Cynthia's disappearance had been replayed in his nightmares every single night. Being branded a cold-blooded murderer by Mr. Raymond had been the most soul-shattering part of all. It would kill Jordan if Scotland were to even hint that she thought he could possibly be involved in what had happened in the Caribbean.

Stopping dead in his tracks, Jordan pulled Scotland into his arms, holding her tighter than he'd ever held her before. Her warmth seeped into his flesh, making him wish he never had to let her go. *There's nothing to fear but fear itself,* he told himself, remembering Scotland's words that one night a short time ago. She'd told him so many wise things, but she'd never told him how to release all his pent-up frustration. Yes, she had, he corrected himself. She had introduced him to prayer and had taught him all about the power praying would bring to him.

Holding Scotland at arm's length, Jordan looked deeply into her eyes. Hoping to find the answer as to how she really felt about him now, Jordan studied her closely. "Do you still love me, Scotland? Have your feelings changed for me within the last hour or so?"

Scotland's feelings had changed for Jordan, but not for the worse, as Jordan now believed. Her love for him had deepened tenfold, if that was even possible. Whatever Jordan was hiding from her, Scotland was sure they could get through it. She still believed he was her soul mate. She'd never be a fool for anyone, and she didn't think Jordan thought that she would. The man she loved was in deep pain. And until she found out the reasons for all his agony, she wasn't going to desert him. Scotland sensed that Jordan needed her now more than ever before.

Scotland's fingers tenderly stroked Jordan's face. "Nothing has changed, Jordan. I love you still. I only ask that you trust me with all your heart and soul. I realize there's something going on with you, but my feelings won't change because of it. I do love you, Jordan."

CHAPTER TWELVE

"Want to go to the park and help me fly my new kite?"

After wiping the sleep from her eyes, Scotland looked at the clock. "It's five-thirty in the morning, Jordan. Not to mention that we both have to be at work this morning."

"So what. We'll make it to work on time. I promise. Will you meet me at the park?"

Scotland's infectious laughter filtered through the phone, thrilling Jordan, making him happy he'd called her. He'd been awake half the night, planning all the wonderful things he wanted to do with her. Jordan hadn't forgotten the stuff Scotland had told him about no-cost fun.

Sitting up in bed, Scotland fluffed a pillow and then put it behind her back. "I love the idea, Jordan." She paused a moment. "I have a lot of sick time on the books, and it's early enough to get a replacement. Why don't we just make a day of it?"

Jordan laughed heartily. "I thought you told me it was a sin to tell a lie, but I love your plan. A month alone with just you and me sounds even better, but we'll take this errant behavior of ours one day at a time. Make sure you sound real sick when you call in. See you at the park."

Feeling as high as the kite he planned to fly, Jordan hung up the phone. The smile on his face was huge as he ran into the bathroom and turned on the shower. "Spending the entire day and evening with Scotland is a direct order from the love doctor, Dr. Feelgood," Jordan shouted, installing his body under the steaming hot water.

Standing at the bathroom sink, Scotland surveyed her face in the mirror. She hated the puffiness around her eyes, a direct result of lack of sleep and of the numerous tears she'd shed the previous night. Today was a new day—and if Jordan wasn't going to let their first little love spat bother him, neither would she. That he'd called this morning and wanted to see her said that he was already over it. She wasn't going to fool herself into thinking all their issues were resolved, but she wasn't going to let it spoil their day. This day belonged to them.

"Happy days are here again," she sang out, jumping into the shower.

Watching Scotland running toward him, her arms outstretched, Jordan felt he was the luckiest guy in the world. He lightly fingered the black velvet box before putting it back in his pants pocket. The strange feeling in the pit of his stomach was just another indication of how much Scotland meant to him. His stomach had been doing flip-flops since the day he'd met her. Even though he'd done his best to dispel his feelings for her, he was so glad it hadn't worked. Running away from her had proved useless. Now he didn't ever want to be without her.

Scotland leaped into Jordan's arms, kissing him tenderly. With their mouths locked together in a sweet kiss, he swung her around and around. Dizzy, they fell to the ground, their laughter ringing out over the park.

Once their euphoria died down a bit, Jordan spread out the blanket he'd brought along. He then unwrapped the kite and removed the ball of string from the packaging. Grinning from ear to ear, Jordan held up the kite for Scotland to see. "Do you like it?"

Scotland took the kite from Jordan's hand and closely examined it. "A dove. How unique. It's beautiful. I thought you'd go for something more manly, like an eagle or a hawk."

Jordan removed the kite from Scotland's grasp and laid it on the ground. He then took her hand. "The white dove reminded me of you, pure and innocent. I looked at other kites, manly ones, as you so delicately put it, but I kept coming back to the dove. I was sold on it, all because I likened it to your pureness of heart."

The way Scotland looked at Jordan should've reassured him about her feelings for him. He made her heart soar sky high; he made her believe that heaven was well within her reach. "You sure know how to win me over." Scotland gave Jordan a very passionate kiss, to which he responded with much fervor.

After gently pushing Scotland back on the blanket, Jordan lay down alongside her, kissing and caressing her with infinite tenderness. He couldn't think of a better way to start a glorious day. Lifting his head, he looked down at her. "This is a beautiful day, Scotland. Think we can make it even more beautiful? I think we can."

Scotland giggled, reaching up to caress his clean-shaven face with her fingertips. "I know we can. Let's get this kite up in the air so we can get this wonderful day going. I'm so excited. I haven't flown a kite since I was around seven or eight."

"Okay, but one more thing first." Jordan reached into his pants pocket and removed the black velvet box, presenting it to Scotland with a smile. "I couldn't resist. I hope you like it."

As butterflies danced a jig in her stomach, Scotland took a deep breath. Before opening the box, she fingered the soft velvet for several seconds. Her heart leaped into her mouth at the lovely sight before her. Tears sprang to her eyes. The dainty pearl earrings were exquisite. "Jordan," she cried, "I love them. They're so beautiful. Thank you so much." Her thank-you was quickly followed up with a passionate kiss of gratitude and love.

Jordan pressed a sensuous kiss onto her forehead. "You're welcome, angel. I'm glad you like them. I wanted to get a matching necklace, but there were way too many choices. We can go to the mall later so you can pick out the one you like best. Sound like a plan?"

"It certainly does. By the way, Jordan, when did you do all this shopping?"

"Since we made an early evening of it yesterday, I ran to the mall to pick up something I needed. Several pairs of dress socks to be exact. The stores were only a couple of hours from closing. After getting the socks, I went into this novelty shop, which is where I purchased the kite. On my way out, I passed by a jewelry store window. That's when the earrings caught my eye. The rest is history."

Scotland chuckled. "You really got busy, didn't you? I go to the mall for one thing, but unlike you, I come out with everything but what I went there for." She kissed him lightly on the mouth. "Thanks for thinking of me while you were shopping. I really feel special."

Jordan hugged her tightly. "I want you to feel special every day, because you are very special to me. And you deserve special treatment." Jordan looked pensive for a few seconds. "Can you trust me to do the right thing?"

Scotland looked puzzled. "Yeah, I think so. But what specifically are you talking about?"

"I need you to trust me to tell you everything there is to tell, but I don't want you to expect it all at once. I've got years and years of poisonous gases pent up inside me, better known as frustration. If I release it all at once, I might blow up the universe. I promise you that you'll know everything there is to know about me in due time. Can you live with that, Scotland?"

Scotland's answer was a simple one, a sweet kiss to Jordan's lips. "Let's get this kite in the air before the entire day is gone."

Jordan carefully spread out the kite on the blanket. He then tied the string to the end of the kite, making sure it was very secure. Rising to his feet, he reached a hand down to help Scotland up.

The morning was rather windy, perfect weather conditions for flying a kite. Jordan hadn't flown one in a long time, but he hadn't forgotten how to make one soar. With Scotland holding on to his waist from behind, Jordan slowly unwound the string. It was just a matter of minutes before he let it rip.

As the white dove flew higher and higher, Scotland couldn't contain her animated laughter. When Jordan handed her the ball of string, she was reluctant to take it. After placing her hand on the ball, he covered it with his own. At his prompting, they both took off running across the park, with the dove soaring smoothly overhead.

* * *

It wasn't quite eight o'clock when Scotland and Jordan reached her place, each of them very pleased with how the day had gone so far. Guessing that they would spend the rest of the morning at her house, Jordan had brought along a fresh change of clothes.

While Jordan showered in the guest bathroom, Scotland finished dressing in the master bathroom. Their thoughts of each other were nothing less than torrid.

Dressed in relaxed clothing—denim jeans and a white, oversized sweater—Scotland busied herself in the kitchen, preparing a wholesome breakfast. When she saw her reflection in the stainless steel on the refrigerator, she couldn't help smiling. The pearl earrings were made just for her, she mused, hoping Jordan would notice she'd put them on to show off for him.

Scotland pulled from the fridge a package of turkey sausage, four eggs, a carton of low-fat milk, and a tub of margarine. She put the sausages in a plastic container and placed them in the microwave. Before whipping up the eggs for scrambling, she poured into the bowl a small amount of milk. Wishing she had a few more pairs of hands, turned on a low flame under a skillet after plopping in a generous amount of margarine.

Inhaling the delicious scents in the air, Jordan entered the kitchen. Sauntering up behind Scotland, he put his arms around her waist, nuzzling her face with his. "What smells so darn good, angel?"

Laughing, Scotland booted him out of the way with her rear end. "Unless you're here to help me out, go sit at the table and read the morning paper or something. I don't plan on slaving over a hot stove all day. This isn't the Stone Age, you know."

Jordan playfully swatted her on the behind. A cutesy retort was resting on his tongue, but then he noticed that Scotland was wearing the earrings. He grew very quiet, staring at her ears, wishing he'd purchased diamonds instead of pearls. "Hey, gorgeous girl, you make those pearls look like a million and one bucks. The earrings are a perfect complement to your delicate beauty. Thanks for modeling them for me. I guess you really like them."

Scotland smiled flirtatiously at Jordan. "I love them, Jordan."

Jordan kissed her and then moved her aside. "Got an extra apron around here? As slow as you're moving around in here, I think you need some professional help," Jordan joked. "Otherwise, we're both going to starve."

Reaching into one of the utility drawers, Scotland pulled out a checkered apron and then tossed it to Jordan. "Try this one on for size, Mr. Man. Then you can take care of making the oatmeal and toast. I hope that's not too hard a task for a professional chef like yourself."

Jordan put the apron on and tied the strings. "For some strange reason, being a smart mouth becomes you," Jordan shot back, throwing a dishtowel at Scotland's head.

Scotland ducked, causing the towel to overshoot its mark by a wide margin. She retaliated, and a playful battle ensued, with Jordan eventually winning hands down. Once he was declared the winner, the couple went back to working on breakfast.

While Jordan smiled into Scotland's eyes, he swiped a sausage from her plate. "Your part in this breakfast is good, girl. How's the oatmeal?"

Scotland pretended to stick her finger down her throat. "Ugh. It's too watery," she lied, laughing at the big frown on his face.

"You're lying, right?"

Laughing, Scotland shrugged. "Your guess is as good as mine, since you haven't even tasted it yet. Dissing your own cooking, Jordan?"

Just to show Scotland how much he believed in his own cooking skills, Jordan took a heaping spoonful of oatmeal and put it into his mouth. "Hmm, this is delicious, angel," he crooned, then scooted his chair closer to Scotland's. "But not as delicious as your lips. Can I have just a wee bitty taste of heaven right here on earth?"

Wetting her lips in a provocative way, Scotland leaned into Jordan. "I don't do wee bits of anything. All or nothing, Jordan."

The kiss Jordan wooed Scotland with was off the chart. As far as she was concerned, his kisses were getting better and better, making her want them more and more. Other parts of her body also reacted with wild abandon, causing her to take hold of the reins. Scotland kissed Jordan one more time before backing slightly away, a sort of cooling-off period.

Scotland sat there with a silly smile on her face, trying to catch her breath, though she felt anything but silly. She felt like a real woman, a natural one. Jordan had caused the core of her womanhood to respond, making her feel desirable but so physically needy. The way he looked at her let her know he felt the same way. Jordan's eyes were fastened on Scotland's lips, as if he didn't have the strength to pull them away.

How long could they keep on playing with fire? She had to wonder. Getting burned by Jordan was something Scotland was absolutely looking forward to, but only after they tied the proverbial knot. If that was ever going to happen was anyone's guess. All Jordan had to do was pop the question. *How soon?* That would be her only response. She was sure of it.

* * *

After recovering from their fiery moments of passion, Scotland and Jordan hurried through cleaning the kitchen and then took a seat on the sofa in the family room. While the couple looked at her old photo albums, Ray Charles's *Genius Loves Company* CD strummed the air softly and sweetly. "Here We Go Again," featuring Norah Jones, was now playing; it happened to be one of Scotland's favorite cuts on the album.

The nude pictures of Scotland as a baby made Jordan laugh uncontrollably. This was probably as close as he was going to get to seeing her without clothes, that is, unless their futures were forever entwined, he thought. She was so cute as a baby, but he preferred her all grown up. The adult curves rounding out Scotland's slender body were a sheer turn-on for Jordan.

Jordan enjoyed the picture of Scotland looking very fresh and wholesome in her cheerleading outfit. Her senior prom picture was softly seductive, but he hurried past it, since her prom date was in it, too. The photos of her and Brianna in different stages of their lives were endearing, with the two of them hugging each other in some and clowning in others.

As hard as Jordan tried to keep his mind on the photographs, he could not control its sensuous wanderings. Their time in the kitchen still had him smoking. When the song "Fever" came on, with Natalie Cole accompanying Ray, Jordan knew exactly what the lyrics meant. Scotland was definitely his flame. Unfortunately, there was only one way to douse such a scorcher. Yes, he thought, listening closely to the lyrics, it would most assuredly be a very lovely way to burn.

All these romantically charged songs were doing nothing to lessen the burning heat in the room. Seeking to liven things up yet calm them down at the same time, Scotland popped *Confessions*, Usher's award-winning CD, into the CD player. Skipping over the number one cut, she put on the number two song, "Yeah," featuring Lil Jon and Ludacris.

The funky beat made Scotland want to dance right out of her shoes, even though she didn't have any on. It was still early in the day, but there was never an appointed time to listen to greatness. If the rhythm in the music moved the spirit, it was always right on time, any time of the day or night. Good music with great lyrics was good for the soul.

As if she were suddenly alone in the room, Scotland closed her eyes, moving her hips and feet in perfect harmony with the music to "Yeah." The up-tempo song could bring the dead back to life. For sure, it made those alive want to party hearty. When the song ended, Scotland ran over to the stereo and hit the REPEAT button. Before taking center stage again, she pulled Jordan up out of his seat, all but dragging him across the tile floor.

"Come on, Jordan. Don't just stand there. You know this music has you going, too."

"True, true, but I can't keep up with you. You amaze me. I didn't know church girls had so much rhythm in their hips. Baby, you are working it better than Destiny's Child."

Scotland laughed heartily, swaying her hips even more just to make a point. "Only behind closed doors, Jordan, but you haven't seen the half of my hip-swinging abilities, sweetie. I got an A+ in belly and hula dancing. And I only dance this way for the man I love. You feeling me?"

Jordan swiped at the nonexistent sweat on his brow. "Right in here, angel," he said, patting his hand up and down in the area of his heart. "You got my heart working overtime."

For several minutes Jordan tried to keep up with

Scotland's expert dance moves, but when he saw that it was useless and that he risked making a fool of himself, he decided to just let his inhibitions fly free. As his feet started to rove the floor, he did whatever move he recalled seeing on the music video channels on television. He'd never be a great dancer like Scotland, but this wasn't a competition, either. This was all about having good, clean fun.

Like Scotland had said, what they did behind closed doors was for their eyes only. They could be themselves with each other. He could be totally out of rhythm and act like a downright clown—and no one would be the wiser.

Jordan didn't kiss and tell, and he was sure Scotland didn't, either. *Secrets and Silence* . . .

Worn out from their activities, with the day not even half over yet, Scotland and Jordan went to his place, where they both stretched out on the floor in his upstairs game room and dozed off. Scotland woke before Jordan, but she didn't want to disturb him. Just watching him sleep brought her great pleasure. She didn't know what the rest of the day would bring, nor did she care. Just being with him was always enough for her. Regardless of the outcome of their relationship, Jordan was in her heart to stay.

Stirring only minutes later, Jordan looked up at the woman looking down upon him. Pulling her head down, he nestled it upon his chest, his fingers stroking the length of her hair. "How long have you been ogling me, girl? You were out cold the last time I checked on you."

Scotland lifted her head and smiled lovingly at Jordan. "Just for a few minutes, boy. You looked so peaceful. If you were dreaming, was it pleasant?"

"No dreams, none at all, Scotland. My sleep was totally sound. If I had been dreaming, it would've been of kissing you without cessation."

Scotland turned on her side, looking directly into Jordan's eyes. "Are you sharing your kisses with anyone else?" Not knowing what in the world prompted that pointed question, Scotland wished she'd bitten off her tongue instead of asking it. Getting serious wasn't what they needed right now. Keeping their conversations light and airy was the best approach.

"No one but you, angel. Even in my dreams, it's always you I'm kissing. I'm almost afraid to ask you why you asked me that—"

"Then please don't ask, because I don't have the answer. I'm sorry for being so silly."

Jordan studied Scotland closely, wondering what was really floating around in the back of her pretty little head. He halfway understood why she might doubt him, but he didn't want her to, not for a second. "I don't think it was silly of you. You had to be thinking about it for the question to roll off your tongue as easily as it did. Are you feeling insecure? If so, no need for you to feel that way. I'm committed to you, to us."

Glad she hadn't blown it, Scotland sighed with relief. "I can't tell you how much it means to me to hear you say that. I'm committed, too, Jordan. Let's get back into the lighter mood. I don't want to spoil a minute of this day. What about looking at your photo albums? I'd like to see some old pictures of you. I bet you were an absolute cutie."

No sooner had the words left Scotland's mouth, when she recalled not seeing a single photo of Jordan at his parents' place. If they didn't have any pictures of him on display, what made her think he had any to show off? *So much for keeping it light and uncomplicated,* she mused, hoping she could keep her foot out of her mouth for the remainder of the day.

Jordan sat upright. "If you promise not to laugh, I'll show you what few photos I do have. My head wasn't big enough to match my humongous ears in my earlier years. I'm glad everything finally caught up." He quickly got to his feet. "You want to come downstairs with me, or should I just bring the photo album up here?"

Scotland was surprised by Jordan's response, having thought that there might not be any early pictures of him, but she couldn't have been more relieved, either. She was sure she'd opened up a can of worms that Jordan would rather keep the lid on. *Thank God for small favors*, Scotland cried inwardly.

Scotland then quickly pondered Jordan's question. Even with all the plush carpet in the game room, the floor was very hard compared to the leather recliners in his den. Scotland had sat in one of the recliners before and knew they were comfortable. Since the album was downstairs, she made the decision to go on down with Jordan. Besides that, she was really thirsty. A cold drink would hit the spot.

Before Scotland and Jordan sat down to look through his photo collection, he prepared several beef bologna sandwiches and filled a bowl with mini pretzel twists and potato chips. Scotland chose an ice-cold Sprite, and Jordan had his usual white grape juice over ice.

Settled comfortably in a leather recliner, with Jordan seated at her feet, his arm resting on her knee, Scotland laughed in delight. "You are adorable, just like I thought. Oh, Jordan, you look so sweet. Hmm, hmm," she moaned, kissing his little face through the protective covering. "How old were you here?"

Jordan hunched his shoulders. "Probably around two. The pictures aren't marked with a date so I'm really not sure. I'm lucky to have them. I took the photo album with me without asking when I left my parents' home at eighteen."

"I can't believe they let you keep them, Jordan. They're so valuable and precious."

Looking rather sad, Jordan nodded. "I think I'm the only one who thought so. There wouldn't have been any pictures after the eighth grade had it not been for my teachers. There was no money available for me to buy school photos, so my last few teachers always made a deal with the photographer, since the photos would be trashed, anyway. After the first teacher made the deal, I asked the others if they could try for me, too. So that's why I have all these little treasures."

Suddenly, Jordan began to wail, his tears falling everywhere, surprising the heck out of Scotland. His anguished cries sounded like those of a terribly broken man. Other than her father and uncle, who broke down during their wives' funerals, Scotland had never heard another grown man bawl like a newborn. Jordan was very distressed.

All Scotland could do was tenderly massage Jordan's head, which he'd lowered to her knees. Afraid to utter a word, fearing she might say the wrong thing, Scotland bowed her head and pressed it against Jordan's. Her heart was breaking for him. She could only guess that the old pictures had caused his emotional outburst.

Still crying his heart out, gasping for breath and hic-cupping, Jordan suddenly reached up and pulled Scotland down to the floor beside him. He then cradled her tightly in his arms, rocking himself and her back and forth. Although he felt horrible for weeping, he wasn't embarrassed by it. This was by far the best spiritual cleansing Jordan had had to date.

Jordan lifted his head and then began to laugh, once again surprising Scotland to no end. At first she thought he was going into hysterics, but the look of utter relief on his face told her otherwise. Jordan had just engaged in one of the healthiest forms of release, crying himself blue.

Jordan kissed the top of Scotland's head. "Sorry if I scared you, angel, but I really had no control over what happened. I just know that I feel so much better because of it. Whew, talk about letting it all hang out. I guess I did that, huh?"

Scotland ran her fingers through his hair. "Yeah, you did. It seems to have done you a world of good. I'm happy about that, Jordan. As I've said before, there's no shame in crying. It's all about releasing our emotions in a healthy way, which not everyone can do."

Jordan bobbed his head up and down. "There are a lot of things about growing up that I'm beginning to come to terms with. Little by little, it's all coming to a head. I see that as a good thing, Scotland. Though it can be draining, it looks like release equals relief. Do you ever have unexpected emotional outbursts like that?"

Scotland traced the outline of Jordan's lips with her fingers. "Many times, more often than you can imagine. Some of us women are very weepy by nature. One minute we're smiling and laughing. Then we totally lose control of ourselves."

"I heard that! Now how about us losing ourselves in a little maniacal shopping at the mall? But before we do that, I need to get serious another minute or two. Getting baptized has been on my mind a lot lately. What do you think of the idea?"

Although she knew much preparation had to come first, Scotland was pleased by Jordan's announcement. "I think it's a great idea. There are a couple of Bible passages you should read. Also many churches provide baptismal preparation classes, if you're interested in going that route."

"What passages are you referring to?"

"Acts 2:38 is one of them. 'Then Peter said unto them, Repent, and be baptized every one of you in the name of Jesus Christ for the remission of sins, and ye shall receive the gift of the Holy Ghost.' Acts 19:4 is another one, which is very similar to the one I just mentioned. 'Then said Paul, John verily baptized with the baptism of repentance, saying unto the people, that they should believe on him which should come after him, that is, on Christ Jesus.'"

Jordan twisted his mouth to the side. "How do you recite scripture so easily?"

"Lots of intense studying and memorizing, Jordan. And there's nothing easy about it. There are quite a few passages of scripture on baptism. You can find all the different references in the study guide by looking up the word baptism. You already know you can call on me if you need help."

"I *do* know that, Scotland. Thanks. If you weren't already baptized, I think it would be neat for us to do it together. That would be an awesome and powerful experience."

Scotland turned down the corners of her mouth in a thoughtful gesture. "I was baptized as a child, but I could always recommit myself as an adult. In fact, I have thought about it. When you're ready to be baptized, we can then consider doing it together. I'd really like for us to do that."

"Super! Glad I brought up the idea. Now let's get our shop on, girl. We have to purchase a necklace to go with your beautiful earrings."

Jordan and Scotland browsed the jewelry cases at several fine jewelers inside the mall. She was more than satisfied with just the earrings, but she didn't want to disappoint him by objecting to the additional gift. A matching set seemed very important to Jordan.

A dainty gold and pearl omega-style choker caught Scotland's eye just as she and Jordan walked up to the showcase window of the fourth jewelry store they visited. As Scotland stared at the necklace, she tried to imagine what it might look like around her neck. "That one's a real stunner, Jordan. Let's go inside and take a closer look at it."

Jordan started laughing, nodding his head up and down. "Yep, that's the one, angel! I got stuck on it, too, when I first spotted it. But then the clerk showed me several other pendants, confusing the heck out of me. That's when I decided you should pick it out. This is the same store where I bought the earrings." Taking her by the hand, he guided her into the store.

The same clerk that had waited on Jordan before wasted no time in making her way over to the couple. "Hi," she said cheerfully, extending her hand to Jordan. "I see you decided to come back. I figured you would." The clerk then smiled at Scotland, firmly shaking her hand. "My name is Joanna," she said, pointing at her name tag.

"Mine's Scotland, and he's Jordan. Nice to meet you, Joanna."

Joanna nodded and smiled. "What can I show you two today?" Looking over at Jordan, Joanna snapped her fingers. "Pearl necklaces, right? You already purchased the earrings." She then looked at Scotland's ears. "I see that you're wearing them. They're beautiful on you."

Scotland smiled at the clerk. "Thank you."

"Great memory," Jordan said. "We'd like to see the pearl necklace in the showcase window." Jordan stepped outside with Joanna and then pointed out what held their interest.

Scotland waited for Jordan and Joanna to come back

inside with the choker. Although she planned on looking at a few other pearl pieces, she was pretty sure the one in the window was the grand prize. She loved how the choker was intricately threaded through numerous dainty pearls, with one much larger pearl set in the very center of the omega.

Smiling and extremely satisfied with the jewelry purchase, Scotland and Jordan slowly made their way to the mall's food court, where they planned to share a vanilla milk shake and one of Mrs. Fields' large chocolate chip cookies. When something caught their fancy as they passed by the clothing stores, Scotland and Jordan stopped to take a look. Neither of them wanted to rush or to act as if they were on a schedule. This was to be a totally carefree day.

Jordan stopped dead in his tracks to ogle a window mannequin wearing a hot pink, sheer, low-cut top, which didn't leave much at all to the imagination. He then pointed out the wispy piece of material to Scotland. "That's kind of hot, don't you think?"

Scotland turned up her nose, looking at Jordan in disbelief. "Sleazy hot! I wouldn't be caught dead in that blouse. The color is so garish. I love pink, but not that bold shade."

Jordan's eyes had a little devilish glint. "I'm glad I didn't see it the last time I was in here. I would've had the clerk wrap it up for you in a hurry so you could model it for me. Babe, you would've been the talk of all of L.A.," he joked with heavy sarcasm.

Looking down her nose at Jordan, Scotland rolled her eyes. "For someone who's always calling me "church girl," you couldn't have possibly thought I'd wear something so ridiculous. Let's get real, okay?" Scotland laughed at the silly face Jordan pulled to mock her haughtiness; then she playfully swatted him on the behind. "I think we'd better get that milk shake before we both lose it right here in the mall." Standing on her tiptoes, she kissed his cheek. "Thanks again for the beautiful necklace and earrings, but please consult with me first if you ever decide to buy me clothing."

All the way home in Jordan's car, Scotland formulated a plan of action for the great idea she'd thought of as they'd enjoyed themselves at the food court. Since they'd made up their minds to go back to her place, executing her plan would be easy.

Once Scotland had turned on the music, had lit several candles, and had gotten Jordan settled in her family room, she ran down the hall to her bedroom. Special lighting and soul-stirring music figured heavily in her plan. It was just another no-cost way of having lots of fun. Instead of being thought of as a cheap date, Scotland preferred to have her suitors think of her as a creatively original one.

Looking quite pleased, Scotland strutted back into the family room a few minutes later, making sure her entry was a grand one. As she whirled and twirled her way over to Jordan, stopping every few steps to strike a seductive pose, she looked fetchingly naughty, smiling all the while.

Wearing an after-five, curve-hugging, arrest-me red dress bedecked with tier after tier of soft ruffles, complemented by her stunning pearl choker and earrings, Scotland looked like a woman with a purpose, a woman ready for a heck of a night out on the town. The glittery red heels she wore were quite an attractive accent.

Stunned by how gorgeous and sexy Scotland looked, Jordan sat up in his chair, unable to take his eyes off her. At a loss for words, all he could do was stare at the delicately beautiful woman who'd successfully transformed herself into a red-hot siren.

Jordan was astounded by how innovative and full of surprises Scotland was. "You look absolutely gorgeous! Are we going somewhere I don't know about?"

"I'm here to present to Jordan La Cour his very own private fashion show, featuring one of America's top runway models." She leaned over and kissed him gently on the mouth. "That would be me, big boy, Scotland Kennedy!"

Scotland, flirtatiously winking her eye at Jordan, whirled herself around the room, sashaying here and there, all in tune to the song playing on the CD. Executing a few of the latest dances steps added a dash of flair to her performance. Her smile was dazzling as she did her very best to make her show the most intriguing form of entertainment Jordan had ever experienced. A few minutes later she disappeared on the promise of returning to Jordan real soon.

Looking forward to whatever was to come next, Jordan made himself very comfortable. No one had ever given him a private fashion show, and he planned to enjoy every second of it. He wondered if the little pink top at the mall had sparked the modeling idea in Scotland. Perhaps this was her way of showing him what classy fashions were all about. Jordan didn't know why she had decided to model for him, but he loved the very idea of it.

As Scotland made yet another dramatic entrance into the room, Jordan had a hard time staying in his seat. When she removed the knitted cover-up she wore, her black one-piece bathing suit—which was sheer at the low-cut bustline, had a deep plunging back, and was cut high at the thighs—was fully exposed. Jordan thought the enticing swimwear was a real scorcher.

With his tongue hanging halfway out of his mouth,

Jordan was practically panting. Although he wasn't sure he'd want other men to see her in the beguiling swimwear, Jordan found himself wishing summer was already here.

For the next hour or so Scotland entertained Jordan in premier fashion. Wearing an array of fashionable clothing, from low-rider jeans and boots to formal wear and high heels, she had fun showing the man she was crazy about a completely different side of her personality.

Jordan was not the least bit disappointed in anything Scotland threw his way. If this was how she liked to have fun, he was all for it. Her flirtatious ways were as innocent as they were provocative. Jordan couldn't help wondering what Scotland would be like on her wedding night. If she continued to make him feel as good as she had the entire day and evening, Jordan thought that he might like to stick around and find out.

Dropping down in his lap, Scotland kissed Jordan passionately. "What did you think?"

"Do you really have to ask? Look deep into my eyes, angel. The answer is there."

CHAPTER THIRTEEN

A loud gasp escaped Jordan's lips, followed by gurgling sounds. He then became totally disoriented, feeling as if he were unraveling at the seams. Although he held on to the phone, he had no idea what was being said. Making sense of anything was hard for him since his brain felt completely numb. Yet Jordan had no doubt that his eyes were playing awful tricks on him. He finally found his voice and ended the phone call.

Cynthia Raymond just couldn't be standing inside his office, right in front of his desk. As she came closer to him, Jordan cringed in his seat, frightened by what must surely be a ghost. Then, several seconds later, he reached his shaky hand out to her just to make sure she wasn't a figment of his overworked mind.

As Cynthia's fingertips brushed against Jordan's, he nearly fainted. This really wasn't one of his nightmares. He was wide-awake, seated at his desk. And Cynthia was right there before him in the flesh. She wasn't dead, as he'd feared all these months. Cynthia was very much alive and well, looking like she'd just stepped from the pages of a fashion magazine. This fabulous-looking woman still had more fashion sense than all the top models combined.

"Hello, Jordan," Cynthia breathed in her sultriest voice. "You look like you've seen a ghost. But you haven't. I'm really here in the flesh, handsome. I hope you're happy to see me."

Looking totally confused, Jordan shook his head from side to side, wishing he were fast asleep and having one of his nightmares. Seeing Cynthia alive and well made him ecstatic, but he was still having a hard time believing his own eyes and ears. This just wasn't happening.

Was Cynthia really there, or was he just hallucinating? She'd been on Jordan's mind constantly during the last several days, as he tried his very best to figure out the gentlest way to break the news about her to his ladylove. Had he run out of time in telling Scotland?

Jordan finally got up the nerve to stand up and walk to the front of his desk. After placing his hand on Cynthia's shoulder, he moaned loudly. "You *are* here. Thank God," he cried, his eyes filling with tears. Pulling her close to him, he hugged her, squeezing her tightly. "Oh, God, thank you, God," he cried repeatedly. "Your being alive is a huge miracle."

Cynthia pushed Jordan's hair back with a flattened palm. "It's okay, Jordan," she soothed. "I'm back here with you. Everything is okay. We can pick up right where we left off."

Cynthia's last comments instantly sobered Jordan. There was no picking up where they left off. Needing to put some space between them, so he could breathe a little easier, he moved slightly away from her. "What in the world happened to you, Cynthia? Where have you been all this time? Please have a seat. I want to hear about everything that happened to you."

After Cynthia closed Jordan's office door to ensure

their privacy, she stood by the chair beside Jordan's desk, waiting for him to be seated. As she took her seat, she looked down at the floor before looking back at him. "This could take a while, Jordan. What about discussing everything over dinner tonight? We can go to Cho Ming's, our favorite Chinese restaurant."

Jordan's nervousness began to take over again. *Dinner*, he mused. He couldn't have dinner with Cynthia. He had a signing class tonight, and he'd planned to have dinner with Scotland . . . and then to spend the rest of the evening explaining to her everything about his past with Cynthia. Talk about getting derailed. His train had completely jumped the track, and the wreckage was bound to be messy.

Jordan wondered how in heaven's name he'd be able to turn down Cynthia's invitation. That would be so insensitive of him, yet he had no desire to chat with her about all this devastation over a meal. What was happening was already sickening enough. Jordan slumped forward in his chair, looking at Cynthia in utter disbelief. "You can't possibly expect me to wait until tonight to hear what happened to you. I need to know right now, not later. Please, Cynthia, talk to me about what happened after the last time I saw you in the Caribbean."

Appearing disturbed, Cynthia looked over at Jordan, but she failed to make direct eye contact with him. "Okay, Jordan. This is how it all went down. But I have to warn you; I don't know everything that occurred. I suffered with amnesia, so some of the events are still very fuzzy for me. Please bear with me as I attempt to do a recap."

Jordan's mind stayed stuck on the word "amnesia." Although it explained a few things, he was eager to learn more about her disappearance. How she'd developed amnesia was of great interest to him.

Cynthia crossed her shapely legs. "As you probably

remember, I left the ship to do some shopping. I recall taking a taxicab to the downtown fashion center I'd heard about from a couple of the other passengers. I clearly remember whipping in and out of many shops. Later, I had lunch at a sidewalk café. I've had repeated recollections of feeling dizzy after enjoying a fruity alcoholic beverage. Beyond that, everything is very sketchy at best. Certain things just started coming back to me a couple of weeks ago. But only in bits and pieces."

Jordan thought Cynthia's story was extremely strange even though he hadn't heard it all. He was having a hard time believing the information she'd already shared with him. "Your passport and purse. Didn't you have them with you?" Jordan knew that she had to show her passport to get back on board the ship. It would've identified her.

Cynthia shook her head in the negative. "Can't recall, but I'm sure I must've had them on me. The police think I could've been mugged. They also believe I was probably drugged beforehand. I heard it is a common occurrence in the shopping district. Foreign tourists are muggers' main targets. My drink was probably laced with some kind of drug, which could help explain the amnesia." Cynthia shrugged. "It's all one big mystery, Jordan."

Jordan stroked his chin. "Sounds like it. Where were you staying all this time?"

"At first I was in a hospital. Then I was moved to what seemed like a convent, which was run mostly by Catholic nuns. That's where I stayed until I returned home a few days ago."

"Did you just suddenly remember where home was?" Jordan asked, looking incredulous.

Tears welled in Cynthia's eyes. "You sound and act as if you don't believe me, Jordan. But why wouldn't you think I was telling the truth? I'd never lie about something as serious as this. You have to know that. In fact, you know me better than most. You have to believe me."

The last thing Jordan wanted was to have a hysterical woman on his hands. Cynthia looked like she was ready to break down. He didn't want to upset her any more than she already appeared. "Cynthia, I didn't say that I don't believe you. I'm just trying to gather all the information I can. I've been worried sick about you for months now. I'm just glad you're finally home, safe and sound. Forgive me if I'm coming off as insensitive. I don't mean to give that impression."

Cynthia got up from her seat, walked over to Jordan, and dropped down in his lap. Laying her head on his shoulder, she began to sob. "I'm sorry for causing everyone so much trouble. I wish I'd never gone on the trip. Freebies aren't always what they're cracked up to be. Winning that trip turned out to be the worst thing that ever happened to me."

Having Cynthia on his lap made Jordan extremely uncomfortable. He couldn't worry about hurting her feelings. He had to get her back into her own seat. If someone were to walk in, things could become very awkward. After all, he was on the job. After easing Cynthia to her feet, he remained standing so she wouldn't have the opportunity to plop back down on his lap.

Once Jordan got Cynthia to take her original seat, he stood over her. "I really appreciate all that you've shared with me thus far. I hate to end this, but I have a meeting in just a few minutes. Can we get together and discuss this some other time? This evening is really not good for me. I have a couple of important things I have to tend to."

Cynthia looked as if she was about to start crying again. "I can't believe this, Jordan. I just got back home, and I'm shocked to hear that you can't find any time to spend with me. I've been through a lot, and I really hoped you'd be there for me. I've always tried to be there for you. I'm so disappointed. Our relationship obviously doesn't mean as much to you as I thought."

Oh, boy, Jordan mused. For all that Cynthia claimed not to remember, she certainly hadn't forgotten how to give a person a guilt trip. Well, it wasn't going to work with him, not this evening. He had his own set of problems. He was glad to see her, and greatly relieved to know she was okay, but he couldn't give in to her demands. Until he talked with Scotland about all this, he had to make himself unavailable.

Against Cynthia's will, Jordan ushered her to the door. "I'm sorry, Cynthia, but it has to be this way for now. Is it okay if I call you tomorrow? Are your numbers still the same?"

"My cell has been changed. My parents gave up my apartment since they didn't know if I was ever coming home, so I don't have that number, either. I'm living with my family until I get back on my feet. You can call me there."

Jordan knew that wasn't a good idea at all. Her parents probably still hated him. The last thing they'd want would be for him to call Cynthia at their home. "Let me have your new cell number. I'll reach you that way. I promise to contact you soon."

Writing down the number, Cynthia gave Jordan a defiant look. "You said tomorrow."

"Okay, Cynthia, tomorrow it is. I have to get to my meeting now." He kissed her on the cheek. "Please be careful and have a good evening. I *will* call."

The minute Cynthia cleared the doorway, Jordan fell down on his knees. This situation would have been impossible if he hadn't already started to get to know the Lord. Tears fell from his eyes as he prayed for a solution to his dilemma, one that would keep everyone from getting hurt.

As for picking up where they'd left off, Jordan had to wonder if Cynthia had forgotten they'd agreed to only be friends long before the cruise. The intimacy between them had come to a screeching halt several months before they'd sailed off into the sunset together.

How much Cynthia remembered or didn't remember about their relationship could pose an enormous problem for Jordan. If she claimed not to remember that they were just friends, he could be in for an even rougher time of it. Getting to Scotland with his story was now a must. He had to give it to her straight and then hope and pray for the best. Losing her over his past was the worst-case scenario. Jordan wouldn't have a good life without Scotland in it.

Although everything between Scotland and Jordan wasn't all roses and rainbows, they still had a hard time keeping their feelings of love hidden during the signing class. Scotland blushed every time she looked at him, and he couldn't seem to wipe away the silly grin on his face that appeared whenever they made eye contact. He couldn't wait until the class was over so he could take her in his arms and begin to make everything right. His burdens were heavy ones, and they needed to be laid to rest.

Jordan realized things were probably going to get worse for him after his confessions about Cynthia, but that didn't stop him from praying that Scotland would understand. But as far as he was concerned, his demons would no longer get the upper hand on him. God willing, he would best them each time evil went on the attack against him. He hadn't been praying all that long—and never had he prayed like he had over the past several days, especially during the last few hours. Jordan had practically worn his knees out by hitting the floor so much. Turning one's life over to Christ was a difficult task, but he was determined. Knowing exactly what he had to do once the class was over, Jordan turned his attention back to Scotland.

Smiling brightly at her students, Scotland was very proud of how far she'd brought her class. With her competent instruction, her students were practically signing like professionals. They had learned many different techniques to use in a multitude of situations, such as asking questions and making small talk, signing for home and office, asking directions and getting around, and communicating with medical professionals. Everyone had gotten a big kick out out of the lessons on deaf etiquette. One of the cardinal rules of etiquette was never initiate conversation with a deaf person about their hearing loss, since it sent the message that the deaf were not whole and capable.

One of the most important things Scotland had taught her class was how to use the relay service, known as TTYs or TTDs, which were a combination of a Tele-Type machine and a telephone. Common terms were abbreviated when using this service. She'd informed her students that thanks to the American Disabilities Act, TTYs and other devices for the disabled were now found in hospitals, police stations, airports, and many other large public venues. Many deaf people received TTYs from the Department of Vocational Rehabilitation; they were provided at no cost in some states.

Jordan thought it was best if they dined first before he told Scotland what had transpired in the Caribbean with Cynthia. He didn't want her to lose her appetite again, like she had after church a couple of weeks ago. That had been a tough day for her all the way around. Although things had gotten better between them, they both knew that their relationship was going to get worse before all was said and done.

After their meal in a neighborhood restaurant, Jordan hurriedly paid the check so they could make it to Scotland's house before it was too late to spend an hour or two just talking. Jordan didn't expect Scotland to be the least bit thrilled about what he had to say, but he hoped for understanding.

Fiddling nervously with his car keys, trying carefully to put his thoughts into words, Jordan sat down on the sofa in Scotland's family room. She had been watching his every movement, which had unnerved him even more. The expression on her face let him know that she felt there was something seriously wrong. Finally, his fidgeting ceased, and he settled back against a sofa cushion.

Sighing heavily, Jordan took Scotland's hand in his. "I know you can see that I have something important to discuss with you. This is hard for me, Scotland, but there are several things I need to tell you, issues I've wanted to share with you for weeks now. I've told you a lot about my past, but I've left out a lot of significant stuff—"

"I've already figured that much out, Jordan," Scotland interjected. "You don't have to be nervous about telling me anything. I know that nothing you can say will change how I feel about you. We can get through whatever it is together. It can't be all that bad."

"Maybe you'd better hear what I have to say before making that kind of determination. You may never want to see me again after I'm through here. I won't blame you, though, but I pray that it won't come to that."

Scotland looked terrified. "Jordan, you're scaring me. Please get this over with."

"About my past, Scotland, there's another woman that I haven't told you about."

Feeling as though she could barely breathe, Scotland gasped for air. Her worse nightmare had finally come to pay her a face-to-face visit. Jordan *was* involved with someone else. Her suspicions had been right on the money. The shoes she'd worn on the beach had belonged to Jordan's well-kept secret. That she'd dared to put them on her own feet had been insane, but she hadn't been able to think of a more suitable alternative at the time.

Jordan was very specific in giving Scotland the details of when he'd first met Cynthia, how and where he'd met her, and how long it was until their relationship had gone from platonic to intimate. He told her all of what had happened between them before the cruise and during. He made it very clear that the intimacy between him and Cynthia had stopped long before the trip, and that he'd gone along with Cynthia to the Caribbean as just a friend. Although they had shared the same cabin, Jordan mentioned that the beds had been pulled apart to make singles.

Jordan ran his hand through his hair, frustrated to no end. "Our deicision to be just friends was mutual, though I'm the one who initiated it. She asked me to go on the cruise with her to help celebrate her birthday. Neither of us had gotten involved with anyone else, so I agreed to go with her, but with the understanding that I was going only as a friend. We weren't intimate at all. Then, before the cruise was over, Cynthia just suddenly up and disappeared. It may've happened while she was shopping downtown on the local economy."

Scotland was clearly startled. "Disappeared! She's missing?"

Jordan put his head in his hands. "She was. That is,

until recently. She showed up at my office today, after not being heard from all this time. Amnesia, it seems."

Unable to sit still for another second, Scotland rose from the sofa and began pacing the floor. The weight of the situation was more than she could bear. How she was going to hold up through all this was terribly troubling for her. He was right. She shouldn't have said anything about how she'd handle herself until she'd learned whether Jordan's feelings for her had changed since Cynthia had come back to him. How could things not change between them?

With her heart trembling something fierce, Scotland turned to look at Jordan. "Are you in love with Cynthia, Jordan? Do you plan to renew your relationship with her?"

Jordan got to his feet and rushed over to where Scotland stood. She looked so defeated and unsure of their relationship. Her demeanor made him feel really ill. He took her in his arms, stroking her back tenderly. "Never was there any love between us." He shook his head. "Don't get me wrong. I'm not in any way discounting the relationship I once had with Cynthia. I hate to admit this, but ours was not much more than a casual affair. Both of us were pretty darn needy when we got together. However, we were close friends. We cared about each other, as friends often do. Cynthia and I just didn't have the ingredients for a forever. I don't know how else to explain how it was for her and me without coming off as uncaring."

Scotland allowed herself to release the tears burning in her eyes. She felt weak with relief that Jordan wasn't in love with Cynthia, but that revelation wouldn't exactly solve all their problems. It almost seemed as if he was completely out of reach for her. Jordan was torn, no doubt. He had confessed to loving her, knowing he had unfinished business with another woman. Their relationship couldn't be any more complicated. "Why did you decide to become just friends with Cynthia, Jordan?"

Jordan directed Scotland back to the sofa, where they both took a seat. "I wanted more than what little we had, something deeper and more meaningful, something other than just a casual fling. I made the decision to stop being intimate with Cynthia when I first became highly curious about the spiritual side of life. I need you to understand all this."

Scotland's cheeks became stained with the color of anger. "What exactly do you need me to understand, Jordan? That you lied to me? Should I understand that for weeks now you've been keeping deep, dark secrets from me? Or perhaps I should try and grasp the concept that you knew about all this when you made me fall in love with you? Talk about secrets and silence!"

Jordan's eyes stretched in disbelief. "Made you love me, Scotland? What do you mean?"

No, that's not a true statement, Scotland mused, aware that she'd just made a false accusation against Jordan. She had fallen in love with Jordan the very moment he'd walked through her classroom door, with no coercion on his part. She couldn't forget that he'd actually run away from her to keep himself from developing any sort of romantic feelings for her. Her love for Jordan had been ordained by her higher power, she reminded herself, vowing not to lose sight of what destiny had mandated.

Scotland slapped her palm down on her thigh. "I think I made myself clear, Jordan," she said, despite the truth of the matter. Giving Jordan a measly inch might prove her undoing, she feared. Her love for him was more powerful than any anger and disappointment she could ever feel. "This situation is all so confusing. How am I supposed to make heads or tails of it when you obviously haven't been able to?"

Anguished beyond understanding, praying silently for God's mercy to intervene on his behalf, Jordan wrung his hands together. Scotland was right. He couldn't make heads or tails of most of what had happened with him and Cynthia. But he was darn certain of one thing.

He loved Scotland with all his heart and soul. And, with every ounce of strength he had, he was going to fight to keep her love. She wouldn't have confessed to being madly in love with him if she weren't. He knew that he'd have to hold on to the blessing of her love with all his might. Jordan believed Scotland's love was his only saving grace.

Jordan knelt down in front of Scotland, wishing he wasn't responsible for the pain in her eyes. *Just don't step on my heart. It's breakable,* he recalled her telling him. "I can't begin to imagine how you must be feeling, but I know how awful I'd feel if I were to hear something like this from you. I think I should go now and give you time to think about where you want us to go from here, if anywhere. I love you, and I hope your feelings for me will help you weather this unexpected storm. We've come so far in our relationship. I'm convinced that we're so much better together than we'd ever be apart. Please stay in love with me, Scotland. Please."

Although Scotland didn't want Jordan to leave and interpreted his departure as running away from his problems, she knew it was probably for the best. It was hard for her to think everything through in his presence. She had a lot of information to digest. Being all by herself, with nothing but her thoughts, would be scary, but in essence, she was really never alone.

God was always with Scotland, and she knew that. He would show her the way.

Jordan got up off his knees. Before turning to leave, he kissed Scotland on the forehead, though her lips were the target of his desire. "I really hope we can work through this together. I can't imagine being without you day in and day out. Can I call you in the morning, Scotland, before you leave for work?"

Scotland merely nodded, wishing she could muster up the courage to ask him to stay. She figured that Jordan needed to leave her side more than she wanted him to go. Giving him his space at a time like this would help him come to terms with everything. He wouldn't figure out if he wanted to be with Cynthia if she didn't give him a time-out. If she were honest with herself, she could use the time, too. Jordan had given her quite a lot to think about.

Scott and Brian had come running to Scotland's home right after she'd called them both. Holding his daughter in his arms, Scott allowed Scotland to cry herself out. He'd never seen her this distraught about anything, not since the death of her mother. But back then, she'd really been too young to understand all the anguish she'd felt.

Hating to see his niece so upset, Brian looked on from one of the family room chairs as his brother whispered soothing words to Scotland. All the Kennedys' problems became a family affair. If one of them was in trouble, they all rallied around to offer support.

Brian was thinking of Jordan, too, and what he must be going through. Those two kids loved each other dearly, he mused. He was sure of that. Just being in their presence was like sitting under a dazzling light. The glow from their love had a way of brightening everything in its path. He and his wife, Solange, had had a special glow about them also.

Brian was glad that Brianna wasn't around to experience Scotland's heartbreak, but she was expected to show up at any minute now. Seeing her cousin like this would tear Brianna up inside since they were so close. He knew how terribly upset his daughter would be if she and Nathan were to go through something like this.

The woeful story Scotland had shared with the two brothers was a devastating one, yet Brian didn't view the rupture in her relationship with Jordan as irreparable. He believed the young couple could eventually work it out. He planned on helping Scotland and Jordan get through the worst of it.

Knowing a little about Jordan's fragile state of affairs with his parents, Brian was certain that Jordan would also need someone to talk to. He vowed to do whatever it took to help out his niece and the man she loved. Sudden thoughts of how wonderful his life had once been with his beautiful Solange brought tears to Brian's eyes.

Scott dabbed at Scotland's eyes with a tissue. "Feeling better now?"

Sniffling, Scotland nodded. "A little bit." She looked back and forth between her father and uncle. "Do you think I'm making too much of this? I didn't get the impression that Jordan was lying to me. Quite the contrary. I believe he was being very sincere, but why did he wait so long? Keeping secrets signals a lack of trust. Jordan just didn't trust me enough to hand me the truth. If we don't have trust between us, we won't make it very far together."

Scott put his arm back around Scotland's shoulder. "This may not be about Jordan trusting you, Scotty. Perhaps he didn't trust himself to get everything across to you effectively. According to what you've told us, Jordan hasn't pulled any punches about how fearful he is. I don't think you're making too much of this, but I think your pain is making you a bit irrational."

Moving toward the edge of his seat, Brian cleared his oat. "I think your Dad's right, Scotty. You have to give yourself a couple of days to let this all sink in. The timing isn't right for you to start making any decisions about your relationship with Jordan. If you don't mind, Scotty, I'd like to talk with Jordan. He's going to need someone, too. Is that okay with you?"

Scotland was opposed to the idea. Since she didn't know why she felt that way, she decided not to protest. Besides, Jordan really didn't have anyone he trusted enough to talk to about his feelings. Scotland instantly pushed away the painful thought that Jordan had Cynthia to confide in. "It's okay, Uncle Brian, but please don't tell Jordan how upset I am. I don't want him to know how much he's hurt me. It might make him think he has power over me. I won't surrender my power to anyone."

Scott took his daughter by the arms and shook her lightly. "Get a grip on reality, Scotty. This isn't about power, either. You and Jordan are not involved in a power struggle. The man made a mistake, and you've been taught to forgive all human errors. If you keep blowing this out of proportion, the giant balloon you're creating is going to burst in your face."

Scotland looked at her father in utter disbelief. "Are you saying I should just ignore all the lies Jordan's told me? Am I supposed to just carry on like before, as though nothing has happened, Dad? Whose side are you on, anyway?"

Scott appeared downright frustrated. "I'm not saying that at all. First things first, Scotty. I don't see where Jordan has lied to you. Did you ever ask him if he had another woman in his life? As for sides, I'm not taking any. I've always stood for what's right—and you know that."

Feeling like screaming at the top of her lungs, Scotland picked up an accent sofa pillow and tossed it on the floor instead. Although she'd wondered if there was someone else in Jordan's life, she hadn't bothered to ask. "Should I not count the things Jordan omitted as lies? I don't care how you look at it, lying by omission is no different than uttering lies."

Brian came over to the sofa and seated himself on the other side of Scotland. "Scotty, I understand what you're saying, and I think I know how you feel, but you're talking out of anger. Okay, so you feel duped and dumped on. In your opinion, Jordan is a liar and a cheater. The question you should be asking yourself is what you're going to do about it. You have to make up your mind whether you're going to try and work things out with Jordan or kick his behind to the curb. None of us can make that decision for you."

Scotland stifled her laughter. Leave it up to her Uncle Brian to tell it like he saw it. Brian wasn't one for pulling punches, but neither were any members of the Kennedy family. "Those are hard questions, Uncle Brian, but I know they have to be answered. What needs to be kicked to the curb first is my pride. I can admit that my dignity has been severely wounded. What I don't want Jordan to think is that I'm a soft touch. I can't make that kind of mistake again. Been there, done that."

Scotland lost herself in thoughts of Stephen McGregor, the seemingly charming man she'd dated in her early twenties. How many times had she knowingly let Stephen get away with his lies and willful deceptions? Too many times for Scotland to ever be proud of herself.

In comparing Jordan to Stephen, Scotland realized there was no comparison. Jordan was a totally different man than Stephen had been. Jordan had tried to be honest and upfront with her from the beginning. But, with Stephen, the lies had started immediately after their first date.

Scotland and Stephen's troubled relationship had lasted less than three months. He had viewed her as a soft touch, until she'd broken things off with him. Despite his many attempts to win her back, Scotland had remained adamant in her decision to have nothing to do with Stephen.

Although Scotland's pride was badly hurt, she knew that she couldn't let her bad experiences of the past influence her present, the very same concept she'd been preaching to Jordan. "Forgive but never forget, lest you should repeat the same mistakes" had been her motto ever since she'd freed herself from the stranglehold Stephen had once had on her.

Looking worried and concerned, Brianna suddenly popped into the room, with Nathan bringing up the rear. Everyone in the Kennedy family knew where each member kept their spare keys, but they would never enter each other's houses without their loved ones knowing it, not unless an emergency situation arose that warranted it. This was an emergency in everyone's opinion.

Bracing himself for the emotional storm that was sure to come, since his daughter was quite the drama queen, Brian moved back to his chair to allow Brianna to sit down next to Scotland. Upon seeing the tears in Scotland's eyes, Brianna immediately embraced her cousin, tenderly stroking Scotland's hair. Brianna soothed Scotland with her gentle whispers.

Then Brianna's hands started to move at a rapid pace, as she fired numerous questions at Scotland. The three men in the room could only shake their heads in disbelief. It was often hard for them to keep up with Scotland and Brianna's conversations. Even though Nathan was a highly trained signer/interpreter, he also had a hard time interpreting all the movements of Scotland and Brianna's speedy hands and their animated body language.

Scott, Brian, and Nathan were glad that neither of the two women talked as fast as they signed. Both Scotland and Brianna had the tendency to talk while signing, but neither of them was speaking aloud in this instance. However, their flowing tears spoke volumes.

Brianna gave Scotland another warm hug. "It's going to be okay, Scotty. You can't forget that Jordan is your soul mate. You've been saying that since day one. Life and love have their ups and downs. This is just one of those down periods you're going through. How's Jordan?"

Scotland folded her hands and put them up to her mouth for a brief moment. "I can honestly say that I haven't been thinking about how Jordan's feeling. He seemed pretty broken up when he left here over an hour or so ago. He doesn't want our relationship to end."

Brianna narrowed her eyes. "You're not thinking it should end, are you?"

Scotland shrugged. "I don't have a clue what I think. My brain feels numb at the moment. I know Jordan and I'll talk again. When that'll happen, I don't know. We both should take some time to figure out where we want to go from here. Jordan doesn't have just one full plate, he has several."

"How's that, Scotty?" Brianna asked.

"Well, there's the strained relationship with his parents. Jordan is scared to death to be alone with his mom and dad, more so his dad. Then there's Gregory. He's not sure how much farther he wants to take that relationship. I think I added an extra plate with that one by asking him what he wanted the end result to be for him and Gregory. Jordan thought I was talking about him adopting the young boy, so that probably added to the pressure he was already under. Now he has Cynthia's sudden return to deal with."

"Wow! That is a lot of heavy stuff," Brianna signed. "I feel for him."

Brian's ears had perked up at the mention of Gregory and adoption. "Is the young man available for adoption, Scotty?" Brian asked, remembering the things he'd learned about Gregory.

"I'm sure he is, Uncle Brian," Scotland responded. "There's no natural family around for him to rely on. He's in foster care right now . . . and has been in the system for a while. But he's none too happy with the family he's been recently placed with. Why do you ask?"

Brian shrugged. "More out of curiosity than anything. As everyone here knows, Carolina and I have been discussing marriage. Because of my age and her inability to conceive, we've talked of possibly adopting a child. Neither one of us wants a small baby to care for because of our careers. We want a child who is more independent but still needs the guidance of loving parents. Since Gregory is hearing impaired, I'm wondering if he won't fare better in a family that has already raised a deaf child."

"You and Carolina would consider adopting Gregory, Uncle Brian?" Scotland asked. Her eyes quickly filled with love and admiration for her father's overly generous brother.

"I don't know that for certain," Brian said with a nonchalant shrug. "But it sure gives me plenty to think about. I'm not opposed to presenting the idea of adopting Gregory to Carolina. Of course, we'd have to get to know him first. Compatibility is an important issue. Jordan also has to be considered here. If he's thinking of adopting the boy, we won't dare interfere with that."

Brianna was beside herself with joy. "A little brother for me to spoil and pamper would be so great. Since I'm about to leave the nest, the timing couldn't be better. This is so exciting! Oh, Dad, you're so special. For you to even consider doing something as wonderful as that shows what an extraordinary man you really are. I love you, Dad."

Brian chuckled, accepting a huge hug and a big kiss from his daughter. "Don't go getting ahead of yourself, Bri. Nothing is etched in stone. We haven't even met Gregory yet."

Scott and Nathan laughed at Brianna's excitement. Things were never dull with Brianna around to liven them up. It appeared that what had once been a pity party was now an animated exchange of love and great ideas. Scotland was smiling brightly, too.

Before everyone had taken their leave, they had convinced Scotland to see Jordan and talk with him again to decide if things could be worked out between them. Scotland had agreed, but she wasn't sure there was much hope for them. If Jordan felt obligated to go back to Cynthia, Scotland knew where that would leave her. Out in the cold, on the outside looking in.

CHAPTER FOURTEEN

As Jordan drove toward his parents' place for dinner, he devised a plan of action to help him deal with all that had gone wrong in his life. He came to the conclusion that taking on one issue at a time was the best approach.

Jordan felt completely plowed under, but he was doing his very best to dig himself out as quickly as possible. It hadn't been all that long ago that everything seemed to be going his way. Then, all of a sudden, nothing was going right for him. He had come to recognize that there were just some things he had no control over. But it was definitely within his power not to give up, which was something he had no intention of doing.

Right after work Jordan had spent some quality time with Gregory at the Culver City Boys and Girls Club, an outing that had been prearranged for him by a couple of his associates. Jordan and Gregory had had a great time shooting pool and playing checkers and dominoes. It had been Jordan's intent to let Gregory best him at the board games, only to find out that he had totally underestimated the boy's skill level. No matter how hard he tried to win a game or two, Jordan wasn't able to beat the preteen. Gregory was very good at both dominoes and checkers, and he also boasted about his chess skills, a game Jordan knew next to nothing about.

Jordan had tried phoning Scotland a few times within the past few days, but he had not made contact with her. He didn't want to believe that she refused to return his calls out of anger, but he couldn't imagine any other reason for her not to respond to his messages. He had caused Scotland a great deal of pain. . . . and for that, Jordan was deeply sorry.

Once Jordan found a decent parking space near his parents' place, he turned off the engine but remained seated in his SUV. Lowering his forehead onto the steering wheel, he began to pray. Jordan wanted the meeting with his parents to go smoothly. He hadn't bothered to tell his parents that Scotland wasn't coming to dinner, because he hadn't wanted to raise any red flags. Telling them the truth would've been the right thing to do, but he couldn't seem to do much of anything right over these past few days.

Regina opened the door for Jordan, welcoming him with a warm hug. She then stepped back and took a good look at her adult son. Jordan had grown into a fine young man; she couldn't take much credit for that. Fending for himself couldn't have been easy on him, especially during his preteen years. But he'd actually fared very well, making something of himself in the process. Regina was extremely proud of her only child.

She squeezed Jordan's hand. "Thank you so much for coming to have dinner with us. Dad is waiting for us in the living room. He was happy when he learned you were coming."

It suddenly dawned on Regina that Jordan's girlfriend wasn't with him. Although he hadn't said Scotland would be accompanying him to dinner, Regina had still assumed so. "Scotland couldn't make it, Jordan?"

Jordan shook his head in the negative. "Sorry, Mom, but she'd already scheduled something for this evening," Jordan lied. Feeling guilty about being dishonest, Jordan shook his head again. "No, what I just said isn't true. She didn't come because she thought I should have this time alone with you and Dad."

Regina looped her arm through Jordan's. "Oh, I see. That was very thoughtful of her. Maybe she'll come another time. Well, we'd better get in there to your dad. James is probably very anxious by now. He never did like to be kept waiting, you know."

Jordan *did* know that about James. However, his father never minded keeping others waiting for him. James had always kept Regina waiting for him, hardly ever coming home from work on time. Jordan remembered his mother staying up all hours of the night waiting for her husband to come home to his family. There had been numerous times when James hadn't shown up until the next evening. Her anguish from waiting for her husband was probably what had driven Regina out into the streets with him, pulling her away from her child, away from the very one who'd needed her the most. Then came the day when James lost his job. He'd been fired for drinking and smoking marijuana at work.

Refusing to dwell on those painful days, Jordan followed his mother into the living room. Upon entering the room, he abruptly halted. Seated on the sofa, James was wearing his pajamas and an oxygen mask; a big green oxygen tank stood close by. Stunned by what he saw, Jordan looked to his mother for answers. "What happened since we last saw each other at church, Mom?"

Regina once again took Jordan by the hand. "A minor setback, son, but James is recovering nicely. Only a mini-stroke occurred this time. With him breathing so erratically, he needs oxygen from time to time."

"Hello, son." With a half-smile twisted on his lips, James patted the sofa cushion next to him, urging Jordan to sit. "Thank God you're here, Jordan. Sorry about my appearance, but it can't be helped."

James voice was weak but only slightly slurred, Jordan noted. He looked thinner than he had just a few days ago. The slight growth of hair on his face wasn't an unusual sight for Jordan, since James rarely groomed himself back when he was into self-medicating.

Jordan carefully dropped down on the sofa next to his father. "I'm sorry you're still having a rough time of it. When's your next doctor's appointment?"

James shifted his weight a little, making himself more comfortable. "Not until next week. Wednesday, I think. Your mother takes care of all that. I just follow wherever she leads me."

Jordan thought that that was an interesting statement coming from his father, since James had always been the leader and Regina his most loyal follower. Some things had a way of coming full circle, Jordan mused, just like they had with him and Cynthia. Jordan could only pray that he and Scotland wouldn't follow suit in a negative way.

Jordan slung his arm along the back of the sofa. "How are you feeling now, Dad?"

"A little weak, son. Been suffering with a constant headache for days now. Other than that, I'm fine. Do you think you could give your old man a hug? He could sure use one."

Caught off guard by the unbelievable request, Jordan just stared at his father. *A hug,* Jordan mused, remembering all the times he'd wished James would pick him up and give him a bear hug. The affection between father and son during Jordan's last visit to his parents' place had been the first ever of its kind. As if afraid that James might break, Jordan took great care in embracing his father.

As James's arms came around his son in a fairly tight clasp, Jordan fought back his tears. He had often dreamed of moments like this and had constantly conjured up the image of them embracing each other; it felt every bit as good as he had anticipated. His father's hug was an awesome experience for Jordan.

As far as Jordan was concerned, the warm, loving embrace ended too soon. That one single hug had carried so much power that it was hard for Jordan to withstand the impact it had had on him. Upon looking at his father, he saw that the hug had affected him, too. James's eyes had welled up also. That his father was actually capable of feeling astonished Jordan.

Close to tears herself, Regina looked on, wishing things had always been this way for her family. It wasn't hard for her to admit how badly she'd neglected Jordan, how she and James had left their young child to fend for himself. She had been a terrible mother, and James a horrific father. The hard part for her was figuring out how she could make it up to Jordan. Her regrets ran deep, but Regina knew she had no power to change the past. However, she had the power to impact the present in a positive way. Jordan would soon come to know that his mother loved him in every way possible.

Regina got to her feet. "You two chat. I'll call you once I have the food on the table."

Jordan leapt to his feet. "I'll come and help you in the kitchen, Mom. Then I'll come back and help Dad to the table."

Regina placed a stiff hand on Jordan's shoulder. "You stay right here with your dad, Jordan. I've got the kitchen duties covered."

Regina smiled knowingly. She'd seen right through

Jordan's ploy. He didn't want to be alone with his father, but facing James on his own was exactly what he needed to do. Only then would his fear of being alone with his father dissipate, Regina knew.

Acquiescing, Jordan sat back down next to James. He was sure James's feelings would've gotten hurt had he insisted on going with his mother. And he remembered that his desire to overcome all the issues he had with his parents was his sole reason for being there.

James placed his shaking hand on Jordan's knee. "I know you'd rather be with your mother, son. That's the way it's always been. I was jealous of the relationship you two had. I'd get angry when you preferred her to me, so I did everything I could to keep you two apart. I'm sure you were already aware of that. How can I make things up to you, Jordan? Or is it too late?"

There wasn't any way that James could make things up to him, Jordan mused. The past was irrevocable. *But it was never too late for forgiveness.* Scotland had taught him that—and so much more. Jordan knew that he was capable of forgiveness, but he didn't think forgetting was possible. The scars etched upon his heart couldn't be eradicated. They made him stronger.

Jordan dropped his arm around James's shoulder. "I was aware of what you were doing, Dad, but not until I was much older did I understand it. I wanted you to love me as much as Mom did, but it was your attention that I needed the most. There comes a time when boys need their dads more than their moms. I always felt ignored, as if I didn't exist for you. I don't feel that we can ever make up for past mistakes, but I do believe we should learn from them."

Jordan felt an immediate sense of relief. He was proud of himself for confronting his father about the past. He was also proud of the fact that he'd gotten his point across without displaying anger. His demons hadn't won out this time. Jordan didn't want to be angry with his parents. He only wanted to love them and receive their love in return. *One step at a time,* he reminded himself.

James remained silent as Jordan continued. "No, Dad, it's not too late. I don't ever want it to be too late for us as a family. Scotland taught me a lot about family loyalty, as well as family values. But then there's this thing called *trust.* I hear it has to be earned. I've been told that trust is extremely fragile. Scotland taught me that, too. I hope you understand what I'm trying to say. I'm not so good with words."

James nodded, wincing as if it hurt him just to move his head a fraction of an inch. "I sure do, Jordan. I understand perfectly. You keep mentioning Scotland. Where is she?"

Jordan's expression was whimsical. "Where is she? Good question, Dad. Wish I had an answer for you. I'm afraid I'm having double girl trouble. I don't know much about young woman, Dad. I guess I should be calling them young women. Sometimes I get the feeling they're all one and the same. Scotland has the incredible wisdom of a much older woman, but there are times when she has the vulnerability of a little girl. She wears both hats very well. I'm hopelessly intrigued with both sides. Say, Dad, how'd you manage all these years to hold on to a great woman like Mom?"

James looked thoughtful. Then he smiled broadly. "You know something, son, I ask myself that question every single day. The only answer I've been able to come up with lately is that God sent me an angel. I'm sure He knew I'd mistreat her, but He sent her to me, anyway. After years of abusing and misusing my angel, I finally decided to read the operating instructions God provided me. The Bible is a blueprint for us to closely follow, though we rarely do. God knows everything, Jordan, yet He doesn't have the arrogance of a know-it-all like me."

Tears streamed from Regina's eyes. She'd heard every bit of the conversation between the two men she loved dearly. Jordan didn't know anything about women because she hadn't taught him a thing about the fairer sex. When she could've been teaching her son to love and treasure women, to protect them at all cost, and above all else, to respect them, she was too busy running around behind her husband, a party animal. James had been her priority back then.

Regina was aware that she wouldn't have made a very good teacher for Jordan, not on the subject of women. Men treated women the way women treated themselves, Regina knew. James hadn't valued her back then because she hadn't placed any value on herself. If nothing else, though, she should've been a role model for her son. Still, Jordan had managed to find a soul mate. She loved the fact that Scotland was her own woman, and young and adventurous. Jordan's girl was everything Regina wished she could've been at that age.

Regina was aware that she hadn't been there when Jordan had needed her the most, but she was here now. If her only son would give her another chance, she would show him that she could be a supermom. But Regina suspected that her son wasn't looking for a supermom. He just wanted a mom, period. The one he used to love and adore.

After wiping away her tears, Regina stepped quietly into the room. The look of love was in her eyes as she faced her husband and son. "Dinner is on the table," she sang out, reveling in the delicious sound of those few spoken words. Her family was going to break bread together, finally. The La Cour family would finally sit down to a meal at the same table, in the same house, all at the same time. Only God could've made this possible.

Regina retrieved James's wheelchair from the hallway. She then pushed it over to the sofa, where Jordan used extreme caution in helping his father get into it. The sight of the shiny silver wheelchair had alarmed Jordan. It had also served as a reality check for him, since he hadn't known before now that his father required the use of one.

Jordan wheeled James to the head of the table. Regina and Jordan sat down next to each other. Then James blessed the food, trying hard not to slur his words. The food smelled as good as it looked, and Jordan remembered the scents he loved most as a child. The aroma of Regina's baked apples drizzled with cinnamon and brown sugar had been his favorite. That was when she still sought to please her son and make him feel loved.

Although it wasn't his childhood home, Jordan no longer felt like a stranger in his parents' house, which had always been a very unfamiliar place to him. Now it had a cozy warmth, and he liked how the space embraced him, as if he was an old friend.

The pot roast with white potatoes and baby carrots that Regina had prepared was James's favorite dish. The rich brown gravy was thick and flavorful, just the way he liked it. Jordan watched his father's right hand shake as he attempted to feed himself. The stroke had done more damage to James's motor skills than Jordan's mother had led him to believe. He made a mental note to later discuss with his mother James's prognosis.

Jordan swallowed the food in his mouth and then laid down his fork. "Mom and Dad, how did you two come to know God?"

James and Regina exchanged knowing glances. The slight nod from James to Regina seemed to signal the okay for her to answer the question.

Regina took a small sip of water. "It was when your father hit rock bottom, Jordan. Had he not found God when he did, he would've died out there on the cold streets of L.A. The constant use of drugs and alcohol was killing him. Although we don't belong to the church we visited over the weekend, it was Reverend Jesse Covington who set your dad on the right path. On a cold wintry night, he introduced your father to God."

Jordan thought his mother's answer was strange. For a woman who always used "we" instead of "I," she had spoken only of his father in this instance. "Since you were out there on the streets, too, wasn't it your rock bottom also?"

"My rock bottom was leaving my home and my child to follow after your father in the first place. I couldn't possibly sink any lower than that, Jordan."

"But you were taking drugs and drinking, too, Mom."

"I wasn't doing a lot of it, but no one ever knew that, not even your father. I played the role that I had to. I was out there for the sole purpose of looking after James, to see that no harm came to him. Had I not been there, he would more than likely be dead now."

"But what about me, Mom? Why weren't you concerned with the harm that might come to me when I was left alone? Anything could've happened to me in that house all by myself."

"But it didn't, Jordan." Regina formed a steeple with her hands and blew a shaky gust of air into it. "I relied on others, neighbors and friends, to look out for you. You just didn't know it, son. I made some very wrong choices, yet I thought I was doing the right thing at the time. I really can't explain it—not in a way that will make any sense to you—because it still doesn't make a lot of sense to me. I stayed out there on those streets to keep your father alive."

Closing her eyes, Regina laid her head on Jordan's shoulder. "Today is the only day that's ours to keep, son. Yesterday is gone. Tomorrow is not promised. Time marches on."

Jordan gently placed his hand on the side of Regina's face. Her soft skin felt good beneath his fingers, causing him to recall the numerous times he'd stroked her face as a small child. Fighting off his emotions was hard, but he managed to stay in control. He didn't want to have an emotional outburst like he'd had with Scotland, especially not in front of them.

Jordan then lifted Regina's head upward, kissing her lightly on the cheek. "That was really deep, Mom. If only that could sink into my brain and never be forgotten. I need you both to know that I'm struggling with a lot of things. Our relationship is definitely one of the problems on my list. But I'm growing in the spirit as I speak. Prayer is what I need most."

Prayer and Scotland, he mused unhappily. Jordan was highly aware that he desperately needed in his life both positive entities. He would love to be able to discuss his relationship woes with his parents, but since they'd handled their own so badly, he didn't know what meaningful advice they could offer him.

Still, he resolved to give his parents a shot at it just to see what might come of it. It was obvious to him that they'd changed. Maybe they could now give him what they hadn't been able to provide when he'd needed them the most. Admitting that he desperately needed James and Regina was an important step.

Jordan suddenly realized that his desperate need for his parents' love was only natural. After all, without James and Regina, he wouldn't exist. Neither would he have met the love of his life, his angel of mercy,

Scotland Kennedy. Just as it wasn't too late for him and his parents to make amends, it was not too late for him and Scotland.

Jordan took a long gulp of water, pondering the things he wanted to say to his mother and father. He decided that he should reveal it all. As Jordan told Regina and James everything about him and Cynthia, he was able to see more clearly all the things that had been wrong with their relationship, yet he also saw the one common denominator that had brought him and Cynthia together in the first place.

Loneliness.

A range of emotions assaulted Jordan as he delved into the details of what little he knew about Cynthia's disappearance. Talking about how terribly he'd been treated by her parents and the names they'd called him caused him the most pain, until he got to the part of how his heart was breaking over Scotland's response to his long silence about Cynthia. Tears fell from Jordan's eyes as he explained to his parents that he might've lost the only woman he'd ever truly loved, his one and only soul mate.

As if she were attempting to soothe a young child, Regina embraced her son, bringing Jordan's head to her chest, then rocking him back and forth in her arms. She found it hard to believe that she was actually holding her son against her. She was truly amazed that he allowed her to shower him with love and affection. Other than establishing a personal relationship with God, nothing in Regina's life had felt so right in a very long time.

After wiping his eyes with a paper napkin Regina had handed him, Jordan lifted his head. "I'm trying hard not to believe it's over between us, but I don't know what else to think, especially when I can't get Scotland to return my calls. I've really messed up big time with her. What's so bad about this is that I knew all along that what I was doing was wrong. I was aware of my deception, but I couldn't seem to stop myself. Fear is the root cause of it all."

"Jordan, dear, don't be so hard on yourself," Regina said soothingly. "You did the only thing you knew how to do at the time. We can't do better until we know better. Fear has a way of getting a tight hold on us. My entire life has been driven by fear. Don't let yours be."

"Both of our lives were fear driven. Until we met up with the Lord, Jordan, we were scared of our own shadows. Our demons had a death grip on us," James said softly. "There is peace in the valley, son. The Lord can provide you with a peace that passes all understanding. All you have to do is ask Him."

Jordan looked directly at his father, the man who'd once been the biggest demon in his life. "I know exactly what you mean about demons. They're hard to shake off. Fear has dragged me down every time. It was only a short time ago that I realized why I hadn't told Scotland everything about me right after I decided I wanted us to have a romantic involvement."

"What's your reason for not telling her, son?" Regina asked, looking curious.

"I was so scared that she might think I was directly involved in whatever happened to Cynthia. Her seeing me in that kind of darkness would've destroyed me." Jordan looked at his mother and then fixed his gaze on his father. "Why wasn't the Lord a part of our household when I was growing up? Why didn't we ever go to church or to Bible study?"

Since Jordan was looking right at him, James had no choice but to respond, though he thought Regina was the one who could answer the question the best. So as not to be too hasty, James took a moment to reflect. After a couple of seconds of pondering, he knew there was only one way to answer Jordan truthfully.

James stroked his chin. "Getting high on drugs and alcohol was more important to me than being uplifted to heights unknown by the Holy Spirit. Partying under the influence was the only thing I was interested in. Unlike you, I was taken to Sunday school and church. So was your mother. I believe we're back in the church because of our upbringing. We strayed far, far away from the Lord, Jordan, but we found our way back. We also failed you in that area. And there are no excuses to be made. Your mother and I have discussed over and over again how sorry we are for not bringing you up in the church. I think I speak for both of us in sincerely apologizing to you. Son, be grateful that you've found your way into God's house without us. There are plenty of folks who'll never find their way back, as well as those who've never been there period."

Satisfied with his father's answer, Jordan nodded. "I appreciate the honesty. Since we can't change the past, I'd like to get back to my situation with Scotland. I don't know if you can help me out here, but there's nowhere else for me to go. I need some advice on how to right the wrong I've done. I can't go on like this, Mom and Dad."

James rubbed his hand across his forehead. "I think you know exactly what you need to do, Jordan. You just mentioned appreciating honesty. I'm sure Scotland does, too."

Regina nodded her head. "Dad's right, Jordan. Go to Scotland and tell her the truth about the things Cynthia's parents said to you. Tell her you feared what she might think of you. She deserves complete honesty from you. The longer you wait, the harder it'll be. I know it's a tired old cliché, but I'm going to say it, anyway. The truth will set you free."

Jordan shook his head. "It's that plain and simple, isn't it?"

Regina smiled at Jordan. "It really is, son."

"Thanks, guys, for the advice. I'll take everything you've said under serious consideration."

During the drive home, Jordan thought about what Regina had said about staying out in the streets with James to keep him safe. True or not, it was a sad commentary. It seemed to him that a loving mother would protect her child first and foremost, even if it meant forsaking all others in the process. Jordan regretted that all his grandparents had died before he was born. Thinking about what he'd heard today, about how his parents were raised in the church and all, he couldn't help but believe that his grandparents would've protected him.

Jordan had to admit to himself that he'd done well despite Regina and James's absence. It was true that he hadn't run into any real difficulties. Being left alone was his biggest issue. He had hated being abandoned so frequently. But he'd beaten the odds.

The things Jordan had begun to remember during the visit with his parents, like the delicious scent of baked apples with cinnamon, made him wonder if life had really been all that bad. Had he simply blocked out the good times?

Maybe he should try to remember all the things that he had forced himself to forget, Jordan told himself. Although he'd vowed not to revisit the past, he thought it might help him piece his entire life together, only this time he thought he could do it with more objectivity.

* * *

As Jordan had done on so many occasions since Scotland had come into his life, he stared at the clock and the phone. His desire to talk with Scotland was nearly killing him. That she hadn't returned any of his calls certainly wasn't a confidence booster. His heart was yelling at him to pick up the phone, while his head was telling him he'd be a total fool to do so. She had said he could call her before going to work the next day, and he'd done so, but she hadn't answered one of his calls. That was three days ago. What was he supposed to think?

Jordan's heart finally won out over his head. His fingers trembled as he dialed her number, but he had made up his mind not to hang up. Resorting to cowardice wasn't going to help him overcome his fears—or get back the girl of his dreams. If Scotland rejected him, Jordan knew he'd be heartsick, but he had to risk it. She had once told him that life was all about taking risks.

Jordan licked his dry lips when Scotland's sweet, sleepy voice came over the line, causing him to gasp with relief. Her voice still did such amazing things to him. At that moment he felt as though she were lying down right next to him. Closing his eyes, he laid his head back on the pillow, stretching his legs out fully on the bed. If this were a dream, he didn't want to wake up. "I smiled as I awakened this morning, all because I dreamed of you last night. Did you dream of me, Scotland?"

With tears filling up her eyes, Scotland's hand closed over her heart. That Jordan hadn't given up on her was a good sign. If he hadn't kept trying to reach her, she would've had her answer as to where his heart lay. "Every night since the last time I saw you. I'm sorry I've been so darn stubborn about calling you back. If my family knew I'd reneged on a promise to them, they'd have my head. I need you desperately, Jordan. When can we talk?"

"Is five minutes from now too soon, Scotland?"

"Make it twenty, Jordan, and we have a date. I need to take a quick shower."

Jordan started to protest but thought better of it. Letting Scotland control the tempo of this meeting was in his best interest. Being too pushy wasn't going to help when it came time for him to plead his case. "See you in twenty, angel."

"You know where the spare key is, Jordan. I haven't moved it."

Immediately after hanging up the phone, Scotland moaned and groaned, wishing she had given herself more time to get ready. What woman did she know of who could shower, dress, and put on make-up in twenty minutes? Absolutely none, not a one!

Laughing out loud, she scooted out of bed and grabbed her robe. As she danced her way into the bathroom, Scotland thought that she might vie for mention in *The Guinness Book of World Records* for the quickest shower ever taken by a woman. Perhaps she should time herself.

Timing is everything, she thought.

Singing at the top of his lungs, Jordan rushed through his shower, hardly able to wait to have Scotland right by his side. This was his chance to make everything right, once and for all. "You can't flub it this time, man. Knowing that a lifetime with Scotland is what you really want, you have to go for it, the whole kit and caboodle. This is it! The real moment of truth."

As Jordan stepped out of the shower, thoughts of Cynthia knocked him right off the cloud he'd been floating high upon. How was he going to break the news about Scotland to her, especially after she'd voiced her desire to pick up right where they'd left off? That wasn't possible, not when he was so madly in love with Scotland Kennedy.

CHAPTER FIFTEEN

Jordan threw his arms around Scotland as she opened the front door. She looked darn good for having had a short time to prepare for company. Only about twenty minutes had passed since he'd called her, yet Scotland looked fabulous.

Scotland couldn't take her eyes off Jordan as she directed him toward the kitchen, where she had a fresh pot of coffee brewing. She thought the kitchen was a more neutral setting for them to talk in. In the family room the opportunity existed for them to practically sit on top of each other. A little distance might be good in this instance.

Jordan thought he'd go stark raving mad while waiting for Scotland to pour two cups of coffee. She seemed to be taking her own sweet time, which had him wondering if it was some sort of torture tactic she was using on him. If so, Scotland sure knew how to make a brother sweat.

As though Scotland had read Jordan's thoughts, she looked at him over her shoulder. "I'll be right there. I thought a couple of slices of toast would be nice to go with the coffee."

Biting down on his lower lip was all Jordan could do to keep from screaming out loud. Toast was the last thing he was interested in. Scotland was driving him to distraction by allowing him too much time to think, too much time to second-guess himself.

Thinking wasn't good for him right now, especially when it was about Cynthia and how unfair it was that he did not tell her that he had moved on with his life, that he was in love with the most intriguing woman in the world. *Please Scotland, get over here now.*

Scotland was busy with her own thoughts. Reciting in her head the words to Usher's song "Confessions," she kept fidgeting around the kitchen. Now that Jordan was here, she was suddenly afraid of what he might have to say. There hade been no indication during their brief phone conversation that he intended to end what they'd built between them.

Stop it, she screamed inwardly. *Just stop it.* Shaking off her fears, she smoothed back her hair. She then put the coffee and toast on a tray and carried it over to the table. Smiling with confidence—though she didn't feel as if she had a single ounce left—she set the tray down.

Remembering the jelly and margarine for the toast, Scotland scurried back across the room to the refrigerator, all but taking Jordan's self-assurance with her. With his patience nearly gone, Jordan could only sigh. Scotland rushed back and finally took a seat.

Though Scotland kept the conversation light, Jordan was pleased that they'd finally begun to converse. He felt his self-confidence slowly returning, but he wasn't sure how long it would last. There were so many little trigger points that could send him into the next orbit. If he was going to get out what he'd come there to say, he had to quiet her and say it. Otherwise, this day would turn out to be just another disaster.

Jordan tenderly put his hand over Scotland's mouth, hoping it wouldn't upset her. "I know you're nervous, baby. So am I. You are so busy rambling on, angel, it's keeping us from talking about all the things standing in the way of our happiness. Can we do that? Please."

Astounded by his gentle but abrupt way of hushing her, Scotland could only shrug. If she hadn't been in love with Jordan, she would be contemplating which planet he'd landed on right about now. Putting his hand over her mouth was tantamount to slapping her face. To convey her dismay, Scotland gave Jordan a hard, evil stare.

Ignoring the glare in Scotland's eyes, Jordan sucked in a deep breath and quickly blew it out. "I love you, Scotland. That's a sure thing. I know you've been upset with all the things I recently told you about my past. . . . and so you should be. As I said before, I don't have any excuses for not coming clean with you. Especially after we decided to take our relationship to another level—"

"Perhaps your feelings for the other woman are responsible for that. Is that possible, Jordan?" Scotland instantly felt bad for cutting Jordan off, but she couldn't wait another minute to speak her mind. If he had come there to feed her a bunch of mumbo jumbo, he'd better reassess his motives. Scotland wasn't dealing with any kind of nonsense.

Exhaling, Jordan ran his fingers through his hair. "Scotland, I thought we were clear about my feelings. I guess not. At any rate, are you going to allow me to finish what I have to say? Or do you want to go on?"

Scotland knew that her fears had started to get the best of her, but she didn't know how to stop them from taking over in what might very well be the final act of their relationship. She was supposed to be fearless—she had told Jordan that on numerous occasions—so how could she act otherwise? She was the woman who didn't fear anything she had no control over. Well, she thought, she had no control over Jordan's feelings or the outcome of their relationship.

If that were true, then why could she smell all over herself the foul odor of fear? "Please go on, Jordan," Scotland finally responded, her tone rather curt and unyielding.

The urge to pull Scotland to him and kiss away the fear he saw in her eyes was darn near overpowering to Jordan. He couldn't do that just yet, not if he was going to say his piece. "Look, this is what I propose. I think it'll solve all our problems. I need you to be comfortable with my past if we're to have a future. You've been telling me that I'd have to do that with myself from day one. I've tried to do that. I propose that I go see Cynthia and take care of our unfinished business so you and I can move forward. How does that suit you?"

The light immediately went out in Scotland's eyes. Suddenly nothing but darkness existed in her world. She hated to admit it, but she'd been trying too hard to win Jordan's heart. It was now obvious to her that his heart was not available. That he was putting Cynthia's feelings before hers was a strong indication of whom Jordan really cared about the most. Despite all that Jordan had said about how he'd ended his intimate relationship with Cynthia, he was still involved with her in a very deep way. She still had a strong hold on him.

Knowing what she had to do, Scotland took Jordan's hand, wishing there was another way to handle this. Her heart was broken, but it would heal in time. If she kept up this charade, she'd never get on with her life. There came a time when a person had to know exactly when to throw in the towel. The time had come for Scotland to wave the white flag of defeat.

Blinking back her tears, Scotland ran her fingers through Jordan's hair. "You're very special to me, Jordan. And if I've somehow failed to reveal that to you, I'm really sorry. . . ."

Scotland's voice had begun to break so she thought it best to take a moment to regroup. The intense way in which Jordan was looking at her had also unnerved her.

The look in Jordan's eyes was soft and vulnerable, making it hard for Scotland to keep from breaking down. He, too, was in so much pain, and there wasn't a thing she could do to ease his emotional anguish. If only she could take on the brunt of his hurt.

Looking into Jordan's eyes, Scotland smiled weakly. "I've always been told this: when you really care about someone who is struggling with their true feelings for you, you have to set them free. As much as I hate to say this, I'm letting go of the desire to have you want me the same way I want you. You're still preoccupied with the woman in your past. Whether your preoccupation stems from guilt over her disappearance or from love for her, I don't know. I just know that you're really not as available to me as you think, nor are you free to love again, period."

Jordan wondered how he could tell Scotland she was so wrong about him not being able to love her, but so right about his obsession over his part in Cynthia's disappearance. Until he brought that chapter of his life to a close, he didn't see how he could ever have a happy future with Scotland.

Jordan loved Scotland exactly the way she needed him to, with all his heart and soul. Still, he wanted to make sure Cynthia was okay before he reminded her that they were just friends. That's what friends did for each other. Scotland would do no less for her best friend, yet she was making this so hard for him. Jordan didn't understand her motivation.

Jordan wrung his hands together. "Scotland, I don't know what I can say—"

Scotland hushed him the way she always did, by putting two of her fingers to his lips. "You don't have to say anything, Jordan. Inviting you over here is about what I have to say. Things between us have been great, and we've developed a wonderful relationship. The problem is I want to be everything to you. I want all your love, every ounce of it. Since I know that's not possible right now, I'm backing off. I love you so much, and I don't want to spoil what we've had by reacting to the rejection I'm starting to feel. I don't want to live in the pain."

Jordan couldn't figure out where Scotland was coming from. It seemed to him as if she had suddenly wigged out. "I'm not rejecting you, Scotland. Rejection has nothing to do with it."

Scotland blinked hard. "You're only responsible for your intent, not my perception of your intentions. I just happen to view it differently. And I can see it only through my eyes. So I'm saying good-bye before things get awkward between us. I don't want that to happen. I only want you when you're ready to be wanted, ready to be loved . . . and to give love back without reservation. You may never love me the way I need you to, and that's okay, but I'm not willing to risk blowing what we've built. I fear that I may come to resent you for not being able to love me as much as I love you. That may very well happen if I stick around."

"But what about our future, Scotland? Are you willing to throw that away all because I need to take a little time away from you, from us, to settle my past? I don't see why we can't continue on just the way we are. Why is that not possible? I desperately need to know why it has to end here, Scotland." The desperation in Jordan's voice frightened him. Asking her to marry him now was out of the question. With this unexpected exchange, his confidence had up and flown the coop.

It was very hard for Scotland to explain how deeply her feelings ran for Jordan. She wanted him in the biblical sense, wanted to know him as intimately as possible, the way a man and woman deeply in love come to know each other. In his present state of mind, it just wasn't going to happen. She couldn't force herself on him, nor did she want to. Being his girlfriend was simply not enough, not when she burned so hot for him every second of every day.

Scotland wanted to be Jordan's wife; she would not settle for anything less than the title of Mrs.

Bravely fighting off her tears, Scotland got up from her chair and reached for Jordan's hand. "Let me walk you to the door now. I don't know how much longer I can hold up emotionally. Please let me lose my dignity in private. It's all I have to hold on to right now."

Jordan got to his feet and pulled her into his arms. "Let me go on record by saying I don't want this to happen, Scotland. Since I have to do what I need to, I really have no right to object." He held her away from him and looked into her eyes. "You're special to me, too, lady, very special. We met in silence, and now it looks like we're going to be sentenced to silence once again. I don't want to spend the rest of my life missing you, craving the sound of your voice, dying for a glimpse of your smile. Please don't allow that to happen, Scotland. I love you; I'll love you until the day I die. I just don't know what else I can do to convince you of that."

Jordan's mouth sought out Scotland's, kissing her like a man kissed the woman he loved, heatedly, passionately. If he never had the chance to taste her lips again—though he'd much rather she come to her senses—Jordan wanted Scotland to forever remember the taste of his hungry kiss upon her sweet lips and the thundering beat of his heart when he held her close.

Although Jordan thought it might be selfish of him, he hoped Scotland would think of him every single day for the rest of her life. Jordan already knew that it would be that way for him. Scotland Kennedy was simply unforgettable.

Scotland waited until she heard the door catch, and then she moved into the living room and sat down. Screaming as though she were being physically assaulted, she punched away at the sofa pillows. For the next several minutes she took out her frustrations on the plump, inanimate objects. She actually felt like she wanted to die. . . . and that scared her something awful. Nothing had ever made her feel like she just wanted to curl up in a ball and stop breathing. Not even the painful death of her mother.

In spite of all the signals she'd gotten from Jordan about his fears of getting into another relationship, she had had the nerve to totally ignore each and every one of them. There were so many signs that he was unready for anything more than friendship, but she'd completely dismissed them, selfishly continuing on in her quest to win his heart. Scotland knew she had no one but herself to blame for the situation she was now in, yet she held Jordan partly accountable for her broken heart. They'd both failed at destiny.

The reasons why Jordan wanted to see Cynthia and settle things with her completely eluded Scotland. If it was over between them like he'd said, why was he so worried about what Cynthia thought of his involvement with someone else? It shouldn't matter to her.

In all her grief, Scotland wasn't able to see that

Jordan cared about Cynthia in a way that had nothing to do with romantic love. She couldn't grasp that he was doing the right thing by finding out if she was really okay just because she was his friend, one who'd been missing for months. Jordan was a great guy, but Scotland wasn't able to acknowledge that now.

It never crossed Scotland's mind that Jordan would probably show her the same kind of respect under the same or similar circumstances. Giving Jordan credit for being sensitive to another human being's feelings just wasn't something Scotland could wrap her mind around at the moment.

Scotland's reality, true or not, was that Jordan had left her to be with Cynthia; that was all she got out of their conversation. Nothing else made any sense to her.

Although Cynthia had moved into her new apartment only a couple of days ago, it appeared to Jordan as if she was already completely settled in. Everything was neat as a pin. Just like her fashion sense, Cynthia had great taste in furnishings.

As Jordan impatiently waited in the living room for Cynthia to reappear, a beautiful conch shell on the mantelpiece caught his eye. The seashell reminded him of Scotland's magnificent collection, along with how much she loved shells. Jordan smiled when he thought of how her eyes had glowed when she'd told him the history behind each of her shells.

Jordan couldn't help wondering if this was what it was going to be like without Scotland in his life. Was everything he saw or did going to somehow remind him of her? Jordan could easily see that happening, especially since his happiest memories were of her. But he wasn't giving up. Once he got everything settled with Cynthia, he was going back for the woman he loved. By hook or by crook, Jordan was going to get Scotland back.

The large conch shell seemed to beckon Jordan, so he walked over to the mantel to take a closer look. Just as he'd seen Scotland do, he picked up the shell and placed the opening against his ear. She'd told him that you could hear the roaring of the ocean if you listened closely enough. Although he really didn't hear a thing coming from inside the shell, Jordan was intrigued by its size and shape.

As he attempted to put the shell back in its place on the mantel, it slipped from his hands and shattered on the marble floor surrounding the fireplace. Horrified by what he'd done, Jordan froze.

Then he spotted a folded paper, which was a little dog-eared. He knelt down and picked it up. When he glimpsed his name printed on the fold of the paper, he was stunned. Upon recognizing the writing as Cynthia's, he opened up what turned out to be a letter and began to peruse it. Several different expressions crossed his face as he read the entire letter.

Rage suddenly filled Jordan to the brim. This was downright coldhearted and mean-spirited. How could Cynthia do something so cruel? He knew there were a lot of evil people in the world, but he hadn't counted her among them. Since Cynthia knew how hurt he'd been over the years, Jordan viewed her actions as criminal.

Jordan started to clean up the pieces of broken shell, but then he thought better of it. Let Cynthia clean up her own ugly messes. Just as he was about to go and search for her, Cynthia suddenly sashayed into the room.

A horrified expression crossed Cynthia's face as she looked down at the smashed shell. Then she spotted in Jordan's hand the letter she had tucked inside the conch. She looked Jordan in the eye and shook her head. "It's not what you think, Jordan. It's . . . not," she stammered.

"And exactly what am I thinking, Cynthia?" Jordan murmured between clenched teeth.

"The letter was written as part of an experimental writing assignment. None of what's in it is true. I never would've sent it to you, Jordan. Never!"

Jordan bent down and picked up the letter, waving it in the air. "That much is obvious. But I happen to believe that every single word written in it is true. How could you allow your family and me to go through that torture, letting us believe you were missing or possibly dead? Why, Cynthia? Amnesia my foot! Talk about cruel intentions—"

"Jordan," Cynthia shouted, "just stop it! What you're saying is not true."

"Neither is a word of anything you've said since you first came into my office. What happened to the filthy rich islander you ran off with, Cynthia? Did you decide that he wasn't man enough for you? Or did he dump you? Which one is it, girl? 'Cause according to what you wrote in this letter, you'd finally found your soul mate. Soul mate, indeed," Jordan spat out with undisguised sarcasm. "It seems to me that you don't have a soul."

Cynthia crossed the room and attempted to take Jordan by the hand, but he pulled away from her. "Will you please sit down and listen to what I have to say, Jordan. Of all the people I know, I'd thought you'd be the most understanding."

Jordan fought hard to contain his anger. Just shaking her hard would be too kind. Cynthia had such nerve. "That is ludicrous. Friends or lovers, this shouldn't have happened. Do you know that your father accused me of being a cold-blooded murderer? Your parents actually accused me outright of being responsible for your disappearance."

Cynthia shook her head from side to side. "My parents knew—" Cynthia bit down on her lower lip, knowing she'd made a terrible slip of the tongue.

Jordan's eyes narrowed to tiny slits. "What were you going to say? Never mind that question. Let me guess. Your parents knew you weren't missing. Didn't they? And don't you dare lie to me one more time, Cyn. Sin, not Cyn, is more like it," he said nastily.

Jordan had thought of Cynthia's personalized license plate, which read CYN-FUL.

How appropriate.

Anger couldn't begin to describe what he felt. Here he'd ruined his relationship with Scotland out of genuine concern for Cynthia. Out of his guilt over her disappearance, he'd felt such torment. What Cynthia had done to him was unconscionable. It had also been an extremely dangerous venture. She could've easily been killed pulling such a crazy stunt, running off with a perfect stranger in a foreign country. She had left him on board a cruise ship while she'd foolishly run off with some rich guy to seek out paradise. It appeared to Jordan that all Cynthia had found was hell on earth. Jordan believed that Cynthia was now trying to steal his joy out from under him because she hadn't been successful at finding her own.

Cynthia once again approached Jordan, trying to take his hand, and he again backed away from her. Her gesture was repulsive to him. She had dishonored him in a very painful way. All the respect he'd had for her was gone. What he found so hard to believe was that her parents had gone along with her deceptive behavior. "By the way, how can your parents live with themselves knowing the accusations they made against me were totally false? How did you get them to lie for you like that? They had seemed liked decent people to me."

Cynthia sucked her teeth and rolled her eyes up to

the ceiling. "You're assuming they knew. You finished my sentence. I never said that they knew. None of it happened the way you're saying it did. Jordan, I don't know how you can take that letter so seriously. I was only experimenting with a story line. You know I've been thinking of writing a book. It's something I've always dreamed of doing."

Jordan laughed with cynicism. "Yeah, I do know about that. But this letter isn't fiction, lady. This is a deadly weapon you've used to practice deception. Your friends even warned you about all the professional pickup artists on the islands. Did you think you made a great catch, only to find out that you were the one who was caught up in a crazy scheme? I wonder if your rich suitor ever mentioned a green card?"

Jordan had heard and read about the lengths foreigners would go to get into the United States. Marrying an American citizen to gain the right to live in America was a very common practice. Jordan didn't know for sure, yet he sensed that Cynthia had gotten scammed but good.

Cynthia began to sob. After dropping down on the sofa, she picked up a pillow and buried her face in it. Her sobbing grew louder and louder, making Jordan wish he could just up and walk out on her.

As much as Jordan tried to remain impervious to Cynthia's anguished cries, he couldn't squelch his empathy. He knew exactly how it felt to have someone inflict undue pain upon him. He didn't want to be guilty of doing the same to Cynthia. He had already said many cruel things to her. Though he'd meant them at the time, he wasn't pleased with his retaliatory behavior. And it seemed to him that someone had already done Cynthia in.

Quickly crossing the room, Jordan knelt down in front of Cynthia, moving the pillow away from her face. "I hate to see you hurting like this, Cynthia, but it seems that you've brought all this on yourself. I don't like what you've done. In fact, I hate it. I'll eventually forgive you; I have no choice but to do so, but right now I'm seething with anger. I pray that you'll find the strength to own up to what you've done, as well as atone for it. I've got to go in a few minutes, but I need to tell you what I came here to say."

Jordan paused for a moment, hoping Cynthia was strong enough to withstand the truth. He knew she wasn't in love with him, and that she might not even care to preserve their friendship, but he still wanted to make a clean break of it. And he didn't want to see her hurt needlessly. "Since I last saw you, I've fallen in love with the most magnificent woman I've ever met. I pray that I haven't blown my future with her in trying to do the right thing by you. Much to her dismay, I left her side to come here because I was very concerned about you, only to learn that you're not the least bit concerned about anyone but yourself. Still, I want you to know that I hope to marry Scotland Kennedy, the girl I'm truly crazy about."

Jordan lifted Cynthia's head so that he could look directly into her eyes. "I came here solely to settle things between us and to stop you from thinking we could ever pick up where we left off. We had agreed on a platonic friendship long before the cruise. And now that I know you aren't suffering from amnesia, I know you remember everything that happened with us. I'll ask you no more questions, so that you don't have to tell me more lies. As your friend, Cynthia, can you please wish me luck in getting Scotland to marry me? Please wish us well."

Cynthia felt sick inside. It was hard for her to look Jordan in the eye. He was right about the letter; she had written it to him the night before she'd left the ship, never to return. She hadn't told him of her plan because she knew Jordan would try to talk her out of it. She hadn't meant for things to go this far, but they had. Cynthia had purposely left all her belongings on the ship to lead Jordan and the local authorities astray. Taking them all would've been impossible, anyway.

As for her parents' part in the deception, Cynthia had asked them only to feign pain and sorrow when Jordan came to see them. She had no idea they'd accuse him of murdering her. She truly understood how much that had to have hurt him.

In putting together her grandiose plan, Cynthia had expected to return to the States a happily married woman. She had also figured that Jordan would forgive her and then give her his blessings once he saw how happy she was with her new husband.

Rafael Tortola, her suitor, had promised her the world, but he hadn't delivered on a single thing.

Rafael's agenda wasn't clear to Cynthia for quite a long time. He'd wined her and dined her, and then he'd kicked her out of his lavish place, which turned out not even to be his. Rafael had simply found another victim to latch on to, a very rich American woman.

He had been nothing more than an overpriced gigolo. Once Cynthia had opened her eyes and figured it all out, she realized that she'd been the one financing the entire charade. But it was too late for her to save herself from his clever machinations. All her credit cards were over the limit, and she'd even had her parents wire her thousands of dollars from her life savings, which had dwindled to only a few hundred dollars.

Cynthia wouldn't reveal any of these details to Jordan, at least not now. She couldn't bring herself to come clean with him. She was too embarrassed by the fact that she'd been taken for a hard ride to nowhere by a handsome, charming, slick devil. So she decided to let Jordan go on thinking whatever he wanted. She had come back with high hopes of resurrecting their intimate relationship, but if she was honest with herself, she knew that he wouldn't go for it. Jordan had been completely out of reach for her for a very long time.

When Jordan had instituted a moratorium on the intimacy in their relationship, Cynthia had tried for months to lure him back into her bed, but nothing had worked. In searching for his authentic self and a more spiritual way of life, Jordan had completely changed on her. No longer was he the fun, anything goes kind of guy, and Cynthia quickly grew bored with him.

Cynthia put her arms around Jordan's neck and hugged him tightly. "Good luck, my friend. If you need me to help you win her back, let me know. Good-bye, Jordan."

Jordan figured he was going to need help in winning back Scotland, but he wasn't about to accept any from Cynthia. God was the only being Jordan was going to solicit help from.

His anger lessening, Jordan kissed Cynthia on the forehead. "Thanks, but no thanks for the offer of help. I wish you the best of everything. If you ever decide to repent, look me up. Maybe I can teach you all the things Scotland taught me about God. One thing is for sure: You need Jesus, honey. God bless you, Cynthia."

Jordan and Cynthia shared a good laugh over his words of wisdom. And then, without uttering another word, Jordan strode toward the door.

Jordan sat down on the side of his bed and picked up the phone. When he heard the dial tone, he punched in the number to his voice mail and went through the prompts. Upon hearing Scotland's voice, his heart rate quickened, and his eyes filled with tears. Jordan made himself comfortable on the bed while he intently listened to her message, which turned out to be quite a lengthy one.

Scotland had called Jordan to explain to him about her uncle's desire to meet Gregory. She also mentioned that Brian and his fiancée might consider adopting Gregory if they were all compatible. According to the message, Brian wanted to talk to Jordan about his intentions regarding the boy before arranging a meeting with him. Scotland then left her Uncle Brian's home phone number, asking Jordan to call him as soon as possible.

As long and as detailed as Scotland's message was, she never once said anything about their relationship. Jordan was hurt by it, yet he understood. He was thrilled about the possibility of Gregory being adopted into the Kennedy family, especially since he didn't think he was quite ready to take on such a great responsibility. Jordan thought Gregory would fit nicely into the Kennedy clan. Everyone already knew how to sign, so communication wouldn't be a problem. He couldn't think of a better match for the youngster, but he also knew that lots of prayer was needed to make it happen. Jordan thought it was too late for him to call Brian, but he planned to do so first thing in the morning.

The early morning had found Jordan tired and severely disillusioned, but a long talk with Scotland's Uncle Brian lifted his spirits considerably. Brian had left him feeling very optimistic about Gregory's future, though Jordan knew there was a lot of red tape to cut through. Brian had told him that Carolina was so excited about the possibility of adopting Gregory that she was going to enroll in Scotland's next signing class.

Brian had already taught her a little about signing, since Carolina had a strong desire to communicate more effectively with Brianna, her future stepdaughter.

Jordan had told Brian to arrange the meeting with the boy through Gregory's caseworker. Jordan had a gut feeling that Gregory wouldn't be living with the Turners much longer. He had recently been contacted by Gregory's social worker—and she'd given him a strong indication that the young boy might be moved yet again. The timing couldn't be better if Brian and Carolina decided to adopt Gregory.

During the lengthy conversation, Brian talked to Jordan about Scotland. Jordan gave Brian his side of the story and was very honest with him about everything, even the details of his very last encounter with Cynthia. Brian advised Jordan not to give up on Scotland, reassuring him that his niece's feelings for him had not changed one iota. The last thing Brian told Jordan was to call Scotland as soon as possible.

As soon as he hung up from Brian, Jordan dialed her number, hoping she'd pick up. He had caught on to the caller ID thing, so he knew she'd know who was calling.

When Scotland's sweet voice came on the line, relief washed over Jordan. "Good morning, Scotland. How are you?"

"Hey, Jordan. I'm fine. How about you?"

Jordan was happy she sounded so pleasant. That was a good sign. "I received your message about calling your uncle, and I wanted you to know that I did so."

"How'd the conversation go?"

"Actually, it went great. I'm so happy that he and his fiancée are interested in meeting Gregory and getting to know him. I hope it all works out for everyone involved."

"So, does that mean you've decided not to adopt Gregory yourself?"

"I hadn't decided one way or the other. But once I heard about your uncle's interest in adopting him, I realized I wasn't ready for such a major undertaking. I'm just beginning to work things out with my own parents. I had that very first dinner with them, and we plan to eat together at least once a week. My dad is not doing too well, so I really need to be there for him and my mom. My parents aren't getting any younger."

"I'm sorry to hear about your dad. The last time I saw him he looked well. I understand you need and want to be with your family. That's only natural, Jordan. I'm so happy for you."

"Thanks. Dad had another stroke since you saw him, a mini one. I'm sorry I didn't tell you about it the last time we saw each other. So much other stuff was going on at that time. Well, I called to tell you I got your message, but I also want to know if you'd still consider getting baptized together. How about it, Scotland? As friends, of course."

Scotland winced at the word "friends." We had been so much more than friends, but I certainly blew that, Scotland mused sadly. "When would you do it, Jordan?"

"As soon as possible, but I have to take the baptism preparation classes first. Can you contact Reverend Covington so I can sign up for the classes?"

"Yeah, I'd be happy to do that, Jordan. I'll give Reverend Jesse a call this afternoon and see when he can put you on his class roster. Then I'll let you know."

"Great. Thanks. But, Scotland, you haven't said if you're going to get baptized with me."

"I promised you, so, yes. As your friend, I'll rededicate my life to Christ at the same time you do. Once all the details are worked out, we'll talk again."

"Scotland, before you go, I need to know if we can keep our friendship intact. We seem to enjoy each other so much." He chuckled lightly. "I miss the free fun." *I miss you desperately.*

"Jordan, we've both said and done some things that aren't very Christianlike. I've been much more unruly than you. As far as I'm concerned, we parted in good standing. I couldn't bear it if we chose not to remain friends. I miss the no-cost fun, too. Now I have something to ask of you. It's about Gregory. You have a couple of minutes more?"

"Sure, Scotland. Let's hear it."

"Uncle Brian thinks it might be better if you and I are present when he and Carolina meet Gregory for the first time. He's interested in having the meeting in a family setting, like a dinner or something, with Brianna and Nate present as well. Is that something you'd agree to?"

"I'm all for it. It's a super idea. Do you have any idea when he wants to do it?"

"He talked about this weekend, but I told him I'd get back to him after I asked you. He would've asked you himself, but under the circumstances, he thought I should be the one to ask so you'd know I was okay with it, too. Good-bye, Jordan, for now. You'll hear from me soon."

"I'm glad we're seeing eye to eye on the issue of friendship and also on what's best for Gregory. Later, Scotland. Have a great day."

Jordan wanted to shout out to the world about how relieved he felt about how the entire conversation with Scotland had gone. Remaining friends with her was a fantastic start. He also hoped it would keep the door open for them to stay in love. He wasn't going to push for anything more than that right now. If they were meant to be, they'd learn that in due time.

CHAPTER SIXTEEN

The Kennedy family decided on an informal barbecue dinner for Brian and Carolina's first meeting with
Gregory. The festivities were held at Brian's home.
Scott agreed to pitch in and help his brother grill all the
family favorites, including steaks, ribs, chicken, and hot
dogs and links. Baked beans, roasted corn on the cob,
and homemade potato salad were also on the menu.
Chocolate cake and apple pie were the chosen desserts.
It wasn't summertime, but the Kennedy clan didn't
need a special season to hold a family cookout.

In Brian's spacious galley-style kitchen, which was
loaded with all the modern appliances known to mankind, Scotland and Brianna were busy mixing the ingredients for the potato salad. Carolina did her part by
seasoning the steaks and boneless chicken, while the
two brothers and Nathan fired up the brick barbecue
pit out on the back patio.

Feeling extremely nervous about seeing Jordan in a
social setting for the first time since their disagreement
about Cynthia, Scotland kept a close eye on the clock.
Jordan was expected to show up with Gregory within

the hour. She missed him. When he'd come to the last few signing classes, he'd always left at the end without uttering more than a somber good-bye. Now the class was over . . . and so was their romantic relationship. Though she tried hard not to think of him, Scotland failed on a daily basis. They had come so close to a forever paradise, but things hadn't gone the way she'd hoped.

Whether Jordan and Cynthia had picked up where they'd left off, Scotland didn't know.

Brianna looked over at Scotland, wondering why she was so quiet. "Hey, what's on your mind over there, Scotty? You seem a little spacey to me. You thinking about *the* man?"

Scotland nodded, wishing that Brianna couldn't always see right through her. "That's all I seem to do lately. Jordan is constantly in my thoughts and my prayers. I'm really nervous about seeing him, especially since I've been such a brat about everything. He must think I'm the most selfish person he's ever known, which is really not true."

Brianna shot Scotland a concerned look. "Well, since you couldn't bring yourself to call him and tell him you were wrong to react the way you did, what else would you expect?"

"Nothing more than what I've been getting from him, which is nothing. However, he did ask if we could remain friends when he called about Uncle Brian. We've talked a couple of times since then, but only about the schedule for the baptism classes and to plan this little outing for everyone to meet Gregory. Jordan has yet to say a single word about us, other than remaining friends. I see that as a start."

"A start to what, Scotty?" Carolina asked Scotland.

Scotland shrugged, looking perplexed. "I don't know, Auntie." Scotland had begun calling Carolina "Auntie" after she and her uncle expressed their desire to get married. Although they weren't officially engaged, there was definitely going to be two weddings in the Kennedy family. Scotland had hoped there'd be three ceremonies.

"Yes you do know, Scotland," Brianna chimed in, her hands animated. "You want Jordan back, but you've been letting your pride stand in the way. That's so unlike you. What's really holding you back?"

Scotland sighed hard. "I've asked myself that question at least a hundred times. I guess I've been waiting for him to tell me the outcome of his meeting with Cynthia, but he hasn't breathed a word about it. I've wanted to ask him about it, but I think that's where my pride comes in. If he doesn't offer to tell me, I won't dare ask him."

"Pride always goes before a fall, Scotty," Carolina warned. "You should think long and hard about that. Don't let your pride keep you from what you want most, a life with Jordan."

Scotland removed the tea towel from her shoulder and slapped it against the granite counter. "Can we please change the subject? This is supposed to be a fun day, not a time for you guys to throw me a pity party. Somebody please turn on some slamming music."

"I'd be happy to," Nathan said, walking into the kitchen. "What about a little Usher?"

Scotland groaned. "Anything but a CD about confessions. Let's get some Destiny's Child going on in here. I could definitely use a soldier or someone wonderful to leave me breathless. The CD is in my car, Nathan, and the keys are out on the hall counter."

"Okay. See you guys in a few." Nathan kissed Brianna before leaving the kitchen.

"Speaking of breathless," Brianna signed, "Nathan sure knows how to take my breath away. As for you, Scotland, we all know there's only one man who can do that for you, dear cousin. He can also be your very own private soldier. If only you'd let him, I'm sure Jordan would still love to take your breath away, Scotty. I'm with Carolina on the pride thing. You certainly need to kick yours to the curb."

Minutes later Nathan popped back into the room, with Jordan right behind him. Following closely behind Jordan was Gregory, who was grinning from ear to ear.

Scotland rushed over to Gregory and took him into her warm embrace. Then her hands immediately went to work, introducing the young boy to everyone in the room. She then turned to face Jordan. With her insides trembling something fierce, she hoped her voice wouldn't reveal how nervous she felt. "Hey, how's it going, Jordan? Nice to see you."

Chuckling, Jordan threw up both his hands. "What's up, girl? Don't I get a big hug, too? It *has* been a while since we last saw each other, you know."

Scotland looked hesitant, but that didn't stop Jordan from pulling her to him and hugging her. Relieved that the ice was now slightly broken, Jordan smiled. "Now that's what I'm talking about!" Jordan then greeted the other women in a cheerful manner.

Scotland gave a huge sigh of relief when Nathan took Jordan and Gregory outside to greet Scott and Brian. Seeing Jordan again had completely unnerved her, and his loving hug had made her heart race. Memories came flooding back.

Scotland ran a shaky hand across her forehead. "Oh, gosh, guys, please tell me my nervousness wasn't too obvious. My cheeks feel like they're on fire."

Brianna cracked up at the panicked expression on Scotland's face. "A red flag couldn't have made it any more obvious. Get a grip, cousin. Jordan's just a flesh and blood man."

Scotland laughed nervously. "Yeah, and you don't

think I already know that! A hot-blooded male is more like it. Jordan is just as hot as he's ever been. His touch is still sizzling."

Brianna and Carolina couldn't help laughing over how unglued Scotland appeared. Each of them gave her a hug to help calm her down before she had to see Jordan again. Seeing him was much harder than she'd expected, but Scotland was also thrilled that he had made it there.

When everyone was seated at the table in the formal dining room, Brian, the man of the house and host for the event, asked the Lord to bless the food and all the hands that had prepared it. Once the blessing was over, animated chatter began, much of it a mixture of sign language and body language.

During the course of the meal, Scotland and Jordan's eyes soulfully connected from time to time. She'd always be the one to disengage first. With all the sweet intimacy they'd once shared, it was hard for her to sit across from him and not indulge in reminiscing.

Scotland's eyes were so revealing. They could not keep secrets, at least not where her feelings for Jordan were concerned. If Jordan were to read the messages in her eyes, he'd know how much Scotland still loved him. She didn't want that to happen. Until Jordan saw fit, if ever, to bring up the topic of their relationship, for her, it would remain taboo. Scotland still believed wholeheartedly that the eyes were windows to the soul.

Once everyone had their fill of the delicious food, the entire group moved into the large downstairs game room, where they indulged in playing a few board games, chatting, and relaxing.

Scotland sat down in a leather wingback chair from where she could easily observe the interaction between

Gregory, her Uncle Brian, Brianna, and Carolina. She could see by Brianna's expressions that she was genuinely thrilled to have Gregory around. She would be a wonderful sister for Gregory in Scotland's estimation. Brianna had more love and compassion in her heart than anyone could ever imagine.

Carolina and Nathan appeared to enjoy Gregory as well. Carolina had a tendency to touch the person she was communicating with, especially those she had taken a liking to. Gregory was no exception. Every now and then Carolina's hand would go up to the boy's face or come to rest on his arm.

Gregory looked as if he was on a cloud. He loved all the attention paid him by the adults. Although he seemed to be very comfortable with everyone, Scotland noticed how often he looked over at Jordan for reassurance.

Much to Scotland's surprise and pleasure, Jordan suddenly came over, seating himself on the floor at her feet. Having Jordan so near unnerved Scotland once again, but she'd rather have him near her than anywhere else.

Scotland looked down at Jordan. "It looks like it's going very well for Gregory. What do you think, Jordan?"

Jordan rubbed his hands together. "I couldn't be more pleased. This could be a miracle in the making. I can easily see how well Gregory would fit into this family. Brian knows about his criminal history, but he's still willing to give him a shot. That in itself is amazing."

Scotland nodded. "Yeah, I think so, too. Most people would completely shun the idea of adopting a kid with a criminal history, no matter how petty the crimes. It takes courage to even consider what Uncle Brian may be willing to undertake."

"Brianna amazes me, too," Jordan remarked. "Her willingness to share her father with a stranger is almost unbelievable. I don't know that I could be that generous of heart."

"Bri *is* pretty darn amazing. She's so genuine. Gregory couldn't handpick a better sister for himself. That is, if everything works out. I happen to believe it will, knowing my uncle as well as I do. If he and Gregory decide on each other, Uncle Brian will move heaven and earth to try and make it happen."

"What about Carolina, Scotland? Do you think she'll be okay with everything? She'll be a newlywed and a mother figure at the same time, which might be challenging for her."

Scotland laced her fingers together, contemplating Jordan's question. "If Carolina wasn't okay with this, she would've let everyone know it by now. She's not a bit shy about voicing her opinions. She'll be okay with it. Most definitely."

Jordan pursed his lips. "That's certainly good to know." He looked closely at Scotland, wanting desperately to touch her, but not daring to do so. "And how are you really doing, Miss Kennedy?"

Surprised by Jordan's pointed but benign question, Scotland was momentarily at a loss for words. After a few seconds of dead silence, she hunched her shoulders. "I'm good. Staying busy. With Brianna's upcoming nuptials, I imagine I'll be even busier. I'm the maid of honor, of course!"

Jordan laughed. "I can't imagine anyone else for that position. You two are really close. You're more like sisters than cousins."

The mention of Brianna's plans to marry made Jordan want to broach the topic of his and Scotland's relationship, but he quickly decided against it. This wasn't their time. Today was all about Gregory and his future.

As if Scotland had read Jordan's mind, she suggested

that they rejoin the others. The laughter and joy coming from the other side of the room were infectious. Scotland wanted to take part in the fun and games. She loved getting together with her family; she thought they were all very special people. The day had been perfect thus far, and Scotland was very optimistic that the rest of it would go well.

For the remainder of the afternoon, and well into the evening, the Kennedy clan and their guests had a real blast. They played several board games and enjoyed a lively karaoke session. By the time the day had come to a close, everyone was completely sold on the idea of making Gregory the newest member of the family.

The entire process of becoming a foster parent with the intent to adopt would be a lengthy one, but the hardest part was out of the way. All parties concerned wanted to forge ahead. Gregory seemed as happy with the Kennedys as they were with him. Everyone was eager to spend more time with the boy so they could all really get to know each other.

Gregory didn't know all of the details of what was being considered. No one wanted to give him false hopes by giving out too much information too soon, since nothing had been worked out officially. However, he did know that he'd be spending a lot of time with the Kennedy family. That pleased the young boy to no end. Regardless of what happened during the legal process, Gregory had finally found himself a family for life.

Before bidding him farewell, Scotland gave Jordan all the details related to registering for Reverend Covington's upcoming baptism session. They engaged in a little small talk but neither one brought up the subject of their relationship, much to Scotland's dismay. The estranged couple parted on the promise of talking soon.

The First Tabernacle Church was filled to capacity. Not a seat was left vacant on the first floor or in the balcony, which was pretty much the norm. Only during the summer months, when families traveled, did attendance dip.

As usual, Reverend Jesse Covington warmly welcomed Jesus' precious flock. It gave him great pleasure to look out over his congregation and see all the souls he'd won for Christ.

"This is the day the Lord hath made. Let us be glad and rejoice in it," Rev Jesse said.

Sweet gospel music rocked the rafters as shouts of "amen" and "thank you, Lord" crackled in the air. The choir was swaying from side to side, in tune with the heart-pounding music of the spirit, which never failed to compel some church folk to rise to their feet.

Standing knee-deep in water, with Scotland holding tightly onto his hand, Jordan prepared himself to be baptized, He viewed this holy event as the most amazing time in his life. His parents were seated in the front row, and Jordan could not help but feel the power of their love. Gregory was seated in the same row as Scotland's family members, which made Jordan want to shout for joy.

Glancing over at Scotland, Jordan recognized her as his greatest joy. Over the past few weeks they'd once again grown very close, but the passion between them hadn't been reignited. Sharing the baptism classes with her had been awesome. It had been a last-minute decision on her part to retake the course. Having Scotland there in the classroom had bolstered Jordan's confidence, making him feel as though he could accomplish anything he desired. Their special friendship had blossomed into the kind that lasted an entire lifetime.

Jordan was also extremely proud that he'd completed the signing course, receiving a B+ as his final grade. He had no doubt that Scotland had graded him fairly. He knew he had earned that B+ with his hard work and determination.

If Jordan had his way, this Sabbath day would end in a roaring blaze of glory.

Smiling broadly, Jordan gave a slight nod of his head to Reverend Clay Robinson, the head pastor of the youth ministry. Reverend Robinson, who stood to his right, reached into his pocket and handed Jordan something that no one could see.

Squeezing Scotland's hand gently, Jordan turned to face her, looking deeply into her sparkling eyes. "I'm about to be baptized for the first time in my life, and I'm so grateful that you've decided to recommit your life to Christ right alongside me. I want to thank you for that. I also have something I want to ask you."

Scotland felt breathless, sure that her heart would either stop beating in the next second or just beat itself right out of her chest. The pounding of her heart roared in her ears like a hungry lion. She tried to figure out what the pastor had given Jordan, but she found that she couldn't think straight.

Scotland took a few deep breaths. "You have my undivided attention, Jordan, along with the attention of the entire congregation," she whispered, looking around at all the eyes on them.

With his tears spilling over, Jordan produced a one-carat princess-cut diamond ring, holding it in a way that only Scotland and the pastors could see it. "As we commit our lives to God, I'd love for us to commit to each other for life, for forever. Will you marry me, Scotland?"

Scotland's mouth fell wide open as she stared at Jordan with deep, abiding love shining in her moist eyes. Then her shoulders suddenly began to shake from the heavy weight of the emotionally charged moment. She had always expected to marry Jordan, had always recognized him as her soul mate, but when things changed so drastically between them as a couple, Scotland had nearly given up on the idea of forever with him.

Even though she had finally come to see Jordan's relationship with Cynthia for exactly what it was, Jordan hadn't tried to be anything more than a best friend to her. Now he was suddenly asking her to be his wife. *What the heck are you waiting for? Answer him!* said a voice echoing inside Scotland's head, jump-starting her heart.

"Yes, Jordan," she cried. "Yes!" Scotland would've jumped up and down had she not been standing in water. "I'll marry you today, tomorrow, next week, whenever you'll have me."

Taking Scotland in his arms, Jordan hugged her tenderly, showering her face with quick kisses. The few kisses they shared were shy, innocent, and butterfly soft. Since they were in church, standing in front of the entire congregation, Jordan knew the passionate kisses would have to wait until they were alone. He had his answer; the woman he loved so completely had finally returned to him.

They sealed their promise to wed with a much longer, sweeter kiss.

As Revered Covington and Reverend Robinson recited the rites of baptism, Scotland and Jordan, hand-in-hand, were immersed in the baptismal pool together.

Minutes later, when the two were presented to the congregation as new and newly committed believers in Christ Jesus, the Lord and Master, hearty hallelujahs rang out amongst the excited parishioners. There wasn't a dry eye in the house of the Lord.

Just as Jordan had hoped and prayed, the day would definitely end in a blaze of glory.

I can do all things through Him who strengthens me, he thought, quoting Philippians 4:13.

The congregation gave a standing ovation to Scotland and Jordan as they left the pulpit, holding each other's hands. Once the service had ended, Scotland and Jordan walked up the aisle as a newly betrothed couple. It was almost as if it was their wedding day, as all the parishioners clapped and cheered as they left the sanctuary. The only thing missing was a shower of birdseed or confetti on the church steps.

As Scotland and Jordan reached the dressing area located in the rear of the church, Jordan took her in his arms and kissed her the way he'd wanted to earlier, fervently. He then held her at arm's length. "I love you. Thank you for making me the happiest man alive."

Still unable to believe that Jordan had asked her to marry him, Scotland pinched herself hard on the arm, letting out a muffled yelp at the stinging pain. Happier than she could've ever imagined, she threw her arms around Jordan's neck, kissing him passionately. "I love you, too, Jordan. I can't wait until the day when we become as one. We can then begin our forever."

The couple then split up to change clothes so that they could join their families. Scotland was sure that a family celebration had been planned, just as she was sure that her entire family knew that Jordan had intended to pop the question during the baptism.

As Scotland changed into her street clothes, she smiled brightly, remembering why she'd chosen to wear white on this day of recommitting her life to Christ. *Purity*, she thought, *in mind and in body and in spirit.* She had once again completely surrendered her life to God. "Thank you, God, for this incredible blessing. As your loving children, may Jordan and I always adhere to your holy word, collectively and individually, in mind, body, and spirit, worshiping only you, the Divine Creator, our Lord and Master."

Outside, on the church steps, Scotland and Jordan met up with their families. James was as proud of his son as any father could ever be. Regina, Brianna, and Carolina were openly weeping with joy, ecstatic over the engagement. Brian and Gregory seemed so happy as they looked on in admiration of the two people they both loved dearly. Nathan was thrilled that Scotland and Jordan had found what he and Brianna had. Scotland took a moment to remind Brianna of the crow dinner.

Scott was at a loss for words, but his heart was filled with joy over all the miracles that God had seen fit to perform on this beautiful day of the Lord. His beautiful daughter was to marry the man of her dreams, just as he'd married the woman of his. Victoria would be so happy to see their only child so happy and madly in love.

As Scotland rushed toward her father, Scott opened his arms wide to receive her. At the same time, Jordan gathered his mother and father into his warm embrace. After Scott hugged his daughter, he pulled his future son-in-law into the circle, offering his sincere congratulations. Seconds later all the others joined the newly engaged couple, making the family circle complete.

Jordan stepped up to Scotland and brought her into his arms. At the prompting of the cheering families, he kissed her tenderly. "Now that all the secrets and silence are a thing of the past, and you've agreed to marry me, can we have a very short engagement?"

Scotland glowed all over. "How short?"

Jordan smiled impishly. "How does next week sound?"

Scotland wrinkled her nose. "Too soon. What about the week after?"

"That sounds super! Shall we tell everyone our plans? We can say it together."

Beaming all over, Scotland and Jordan turned and faced their family members. "We're getting married in two weeks. Everyone is invited!"

Dear Readers:

I sincerely hope that you enjoyed reading *Secrets & Silence* from cover to cover. I'm very interested in hearing your comments and thoughts on the inspirational love story of Scotland Kennedy and Jordan La Cour, who share a deep spiritual connection.

I love hearing from my readers, and I do appreciate the time you take out of your busy schedules to write. Please enclose a self-addressed, stamped envelope with all your correspondence and mail to: Linda Hudson-Smith, 16516 El Camino Real, Box 174, Houston, TX 77062. You can also e-mail your comments to *LHS4-romance@yahoo.com*. Please also visit my Web site and sign my guest book at *www.lindahudsonsmith.com*.

Linda Hudson-Smith

ABOUT THE AUTHOR

Born in Canonsburg, Pennsylvania, and raised in the town of Washington, D.C., Linda Hudson-Smith has traveled the world as an enthusiastic witness to other cultures and lifestyles. Her husband's military career gave her the opportunity to live in Japan, Germany, and many cities across the United States. Linda's extensive travel experience helps her craft stories set in a variety of beautiful and romantic locations.

It was after illness forced her to leave a marketing and public relations career that she turned to writing. *Ice Under Fire* (2000), her debut Arabesque novel, has received rave reviews. Voted Best New Author by the Black Writer's Alliance, Linda received the prestigious 2000 Gold Pen Award, and *Romance in Color* chose her as Rising Star for the month of January 2000. She has also won two *Shades of Romance Magazine* awards in the categories of Multicultural New Romance Author of the Year and Multicultural New Fiction Author of the Year 2001. Linda was also nominated as the Best New Romance Author at the 2001 Romance Slam Jam. Her novel covers have been featured in such major publications as *Publishers Weekly, USA Today,* and *Essence* magazine. More recently, Linda was named the Best New Christian Fiction author of 2003 by *Shades of Romance Magazine.* Her romance novel *Fearless Hearts* won the AALAS Open Book Award in the romance category at the African-American Literary Awards Show held in New York in September 2004.

Linda is a member of Romance Writers of America

and the Black Writers Alliance. Though novel writing remains her first love, she is currently cultivating her screenwriting skills. She has also been contracted to pen several other novels for BET Books.

Dedicated to inspiring readers to overcome adversity against all odds, Linda has served as the national spokesperson for the Lupus Foundation of America for the past four years. In making lupus awareness one of her top priorities, she travels around the country delivering inspirational messages of hope. Her Lupus Awareness Campaign was a major part of her ten-day book tour to Germany in February 2002, where she visited numerous U.S. military bases. She is also a supporter of the NAACP and the American Cancer Society. She enjoys poetry, entertaining, traveling, and attending sports events. The mother of two adult sons, Linda shares her life with her husband, Rudy, in League City, Texas.

Put a Little Romance in Your Life With
Bettye Griffin